Praise for Sarah Morgan's

How to Keep a Secret

"Emotional, riveting and uplifting. If you've got a sister, you've got to read this book!"

—Susan Mallery, #1 *New York Times* bestselling author

"Jane Green meets Sophie Kinsella. Heartwarming, emotional, funny and real—I adored this book!"

—Jill Shalvis, *New York Times* bestselling author

Praise for Sarah Morgan's Acclaimed Series

From Manhattan with Love

"Snappy dialogue, well-developed characters mix with sweet romantic tension."

—*Publishers Weekly* on *Sleepless in Manhattan*

"Morgan's novel delivers the classic sweep-you-off-your-feet romantic experience."

—*Publishers Weekly* on *Sunset in Central Park*

"Sweet, sexy and funny."

—*Library Journal* on *Holiday in the Hamptons*

"An amazing, unforgettable second chance romance."
—*RT Book Reviews* on *Holiday in the Hamptons* (Top Pick)

"The perfect must-read on a cold winter's night."
—*RT Book Reviews* on *Moonlight Over Manhattan* (Top Pick)

The O'Neil Brothers

"Uplifting, sexy and warm, Sarah Morgan's O'Neil Brothers series is perfection."

—Jill Shalvis, *New York Times* bestselling author

"This touching Christmas tale will draw tears of sorrow and joy, remaining a reader favorite for years to come."
—*Publishers Weekly* on *Sleigh Bells in the Snow* (starred review)

SARAH MORGAN

the *Christmas* sisters

HQN™

Recycling programs
for this product may
not exist in your area.

ISBN-13: 978-1-335-94647-8

The Christmas Sisters

Copyright © 2018 by Sarah Morgan

This edition published by arrangement with Harlequin Books S.A.

For questions and comments about the quality of this book, please contact us
at CustomerService@Harlequin.com.

HQNBooks.com

Printed in U.S.A.

To the wonderful Lisa Milton, with love and thanks.

Life is so constructed that an event does not, cannot, will not, match the expectation.

CHARLOTTE BRONTË

1

Suzanne

There are good anniversaries, and bad anniversaries. This was a bad one and Suzanne chose to mark the moment with a nightmare.

As usual, she was buried, her body immobile and trapped under a weight as heavy as concrete. There was snow in her mouth, in her nose, in her ears. The force and pressure of it crushed her. How deep was she? Which way was up? Would anyone be looking for her?

She tried to scream, but there was nothing, nothing…

"Suzanne…"

Someone was calling her name. She couldn't respond. Couldn't move. Couldn't breathe. Her chest was being squeezed.

"Suzanne!"

She heard the voice through darkness and panic.

"You're dreaming."

She felt something touch her shoulder, and the movement catapulted her out of her frozen tomb and back to reality. She sat up, her hand to her throat, gulping in air.

"It's all right," the voice said. "Everything is all right."

"I had…a dream. The dream." And it was so real she expected to find herself surrounded by ice crystals, not crumpled bedding.

"I know." The voice belonged to Stewart, and his hand was on her back, rubbing gently. "You were screaming."

And now she noticed that his face was white and lines of anxiety bracketed his mouth.

They had a routine for this but hadn't had to use it in a while.

"It was so vivid. I was *there*."

Stewart flicked on the light. A soft glow spread across the bedroom, illuminating dark corners and pushing aside the last wisps of the nightmare. "You're safe. Look around you."

Suzanne looked, her imagination still trapped under the weight of snow.

But there was no snow. No avalanche. Just her warm, cozy bedroom in Glensay Lodge, where the remains of a fire danced in the hearth and the darkness of the endless winter night shone black through a gap in the curtains. She'd made the curtains herself from a sumptuous tartan fabric she'd found on her first visit to Scotland. Stewart's mother had claimed it was their clan tartan, but all Suzanne cared about was that those curtains kept the cold out on chilly nights and made the room cozy. She'd also made the quilt that was draped across the bottom of the bed.

On the table near the window was a bottle of single malt whiskey from the local distillery, and next to it sat Stewart's empty glass.

There was her favorite chair, the cushions plumped and soft. Her book, a novel that hadn't really caught her attention, lay open next to her knitting. A new order of wool had arrived the day before and she'd been thrilled by the colors. Deep purples and blues lay against softer hues of heather and rich cream, ready to brighten the palette of white and gray that lay beyond her windows. The wool reminded her of the wild Scottish heather that grew in the glen in early and late summer. Thinking of it cheered her. When the weather warmed, she liked to walk early in the morning and see the heather as the sun burned through the mist.

And there was Stewart. Stewart, with his kind eyes and infinite patience. Stewart, who had been by her side for more than three decades.

She was in the Scottish Highlands, tens of thousands of miles from the icy flanks of Mount Rainier. Still, the dream hung over her like a chilling fog, infecting her thoughts.

"I haven't had that dream in over a year." Her forehead was damp with sweat and her nightdress clung to her. She took the glass of water that Stewart offered.

Her throat was parched and the water soothed and cooled, but her hand was shaking so much she sloshed some of it over the duvet. "How can a person still have nightmares after twenty-five years?" She wanted to forget, but her body wouldn't let her.

Stewart took the glass from her and put it on the nightstand. Then he took her in his arms. "It's almost Christmas, and this is always a stressful time of year."

She leaned her head on his shoulder, comforted by human warmth. Not snow and ice, but flesh and blood.

Alive.

"I love this time of year because the girls are home." She

slid her arm round his waist, wishing she could stop shaking. "Last year I didn't have the dream once."

"It was probably that call from Hannah that triggered it."

"It was a good phone call. She's coming home for the holidays. That's the *best* news. Not something to trigger a nightmare." But enough to trigger thoughts and memories.

She suspected poor Hannah would be having her own thoughts and memories.

Stewart was right that this time of year was never easy.

"It's been a couple of years since Hannah, Beth and Posy were here together."

"And I'm excited." Anticipation lifted her mood. "It will be all the more special because Hannah couldn't make it last year."

"Which increases the expectation." Stewart sounded tired. "Don't put pressure on her, Suzanne. It's tough on her, and you end up hurt."

"I won't be hurt." They both knew it was a lie. Every time Hannah distanced herself from her family, it hurt. "I want her to be happy, that's all."

"The only person who can make Hannah happy is Hannah."

"That doesn't stop me wanting to help. I'm her mother." She caught his eye. "I *am* her mother."

"I know. And if you want my opinion, she's damn lucky to have you."

Lucky? There had been nothing lucky about the girls' early life. At the beginning Suzanne had been terrified that Hannah's life would be ruined by the events of her childhood, but then she'd realized she had a responsibility not to let that happen.

She'd done everything she could to compensate and influence the future. She wanted nothing but good for her daughters and the burden of it was huge. It weighed her down, and there were days when it almost crushed her. And she'd made him carry the burden, too.

Survivor's guilt.

"I worry I haven't done enough. Or that I haven't done it right."

"I'm sure every parent thinks that from time to time."

Suzanne slid her legs out of bed, relieved to be able to stand up. Walk. Breathe. Watch the sun rise. She rolled her shoulders and discovered they ached. She'd turned fifty-eight the summer before and right now she felt every one of those years. Was the pain real or a memory? "The dream was bad. I was back there."

Suffocating in an airless, snowy tomb.

Stewart stood up, too. "It will fade." He reached for his robe. "I'm not going to ask if you want to talk about it, because you never do."

And this time was no different.

She couldn't stop the nightmares, but she could prevent the darkness from creeping into her waking hours. It was her way of taking back control. "You should go back to sleep."

"We both know there's no going back to sleep after you have one of your dreams. And we have to be up in an hour anyway." His hair was standing on end and his eyes were rimmed with fatigue. "We have a group of twenty arriving at the Adventure Centre this morning. It's going to be busy. I might as well make an early start."

"Are they experienced?"

"No. School party on an outdoor adventure week."

Anxiety washed over her. Her instinct was to beg him not to go, but that would have meant giving in to fear. It also would have meant asking Stewart to give up doing something he loved and she wouldn't do that. "Be careful."

"I always am." Stewart kissed her and walked to the door. "Coffee?"

"Please." The thought of staying in bed held no appeal. "I'll take a quick shower and then start planning."

"Planning what?"

"Only a man would ask that. You think Christmas happens by itself?" She belted her robe, knowing from experience that activity was the best way to drive the shadows from her head. "It's only a few weeks away. I want to do all the preparation beforehand so I can spend as much time as possible with our grandchildren. I thought I'd buy a few extra games in case the weather is bad. I don't want them to be bored. They have so much to do in Manhattan."

"If they're bored, they can help with the animals. They can feed the chickens with Posy, or round up the sheep. They can ride Socks."

Socks was Posy's pony. Now eighteen, he was enjoying a well-earned, hay-filled retirement in the fields that surrounded the lodge.

"Beth gets nervous when they ride."

Stewart shook his head. "A lot of things make Beth nervous. She is overprotective, we both know that. Kids don't break that easily."

"As if you weren't the most protective father ever. Particularly with her."

He gave a sheepish grin. "Posy was like a little ball. She bounced. Beth was a delicate little thing."

"She's always been a daddy's girl. And if she is an overprotective mother, then we both know why."

"I didn't say I didn't understand, but you've got to let kids have some fun. Explore. Make mistakes. Live life."

"Easier said than done." Suzanne knew she was overprotective, too. "I'll talk to Beth. Try to persuade her to let the girls ride. And if the weather is bad, they can help in the kitchen. We can do some baking."

"Here's a radical idea…" Stewart picked up his empty whiskey glass from the night before. "Instead of planning everything and driving yourself crazy with stress, why don't you keep it relaxed this year? Stop trying so hard."

Suzanne's mouth dropped open. "You think food magically appears? You think Santa really does deliver gifts already wrapped?"

But the comment was so typical of him, it made her laugh. To an outsider they probably seemed ridiculously traditional, but her life was exactly the way she wanted it to be.

"I'll have you know that the key to relaxation is planning. I want it to be special." The fact that it was the only time the three girls were together increased the pressure for it to be perfect. She walked to the window, pulled back the curtains and leaned her forehead against the cool glass. From the window of her bedroom she had a view right down the glen. The snow was luminous, reflecting the muted glow of the moon and sending flickers of light across the still surface of the loch. Framing the loch was snow-dusted forest and behind that the mountains rose, dominating everything with their deadly beauty.

Even knowing the danger waiting in those snowy peaks, she was still drawn to them. She could never live anywhere that didn't have mountains, but she no longer did any winter climbing. She and Stewart took low-level hikes in the winter, and longer, more ambitious hikes in the spring and summer when the weather warmed and the snow receded.

"Was it selfish of us to move here? Should we have lived in a city?"

"No. And you need to stop thinking like that." His voice was rough. "It's the dream. You know it's the dream."

She did know. She loved living here, in this land of mist and mountains, of lochs and legend.

"I worry about Hannah." She turned. "About what being here does to her."

"I'm more worried about what her being here does to you. Maybe I'm being haunted by the ghosts of Christmas past." He put the empty glass down and rubbed his fingers across his forehead. "You need to let her be, Suzy. You can't fix everything, although I know you'll never give up trying." The light softened the hard angles of his face, making him seem younger.

His job kept him fit and lean and there were days when he barely looked fifty let alone sixty. The only clue as to his age was the touch of silver in his hair, the same silver that would have shown in hers if she hadn't chosen to avail herself of a little artificial help.

They'd fallen in love when they'd worked together as mountain guides, when life had seemed like one big adventure. All they'd cared about back then was the next climb. The next summit. They'd been together ever since and, for the most part, their life had a comfortable rhythm. A rhythm that was rocked at this time of year.

The past never went away, she thought. It faded, and sometimes it was little more than a shadow, but it was always there.

"I'm going to make the lodge as welcoming as possible. Hannah works so hard."

"So do you. Your life isn't all about the kids, Suzanne. You run a successful business and this is one of your busiest times of the year in the café."

The source of her anxiety shifted. "And now you've reminded me that I still have forty stockings to knit to raise funds for the local mountain rescue team. Thank you for stressing me."

Stewart grinned and scooped up his clothes from the chair

where he'd left them the night before. "Now, *that's* something I'd like to see. The rest of the guys wearing stockings. I'll be taking a photo of that and posting it on the team Facebook page."

Suzanne pulled a face. "They're not for wearing, you idiot, they're for stuffing with presents. We sell them for a good profit. And before you mock, I should point out that the profit from last year's Christmas stockings bought the team a new avalanche transceiver and contributed to that fancy stretcher you use."

"I know."

"Then why—"

"I like teasing you. I like the way you look when you're mad. Your mouth pouts and you have these cute little frown lines and— Ow!" He ducked as she crossed the room and flung a pillow at him. "Did you really just do that? How old are you?"

"Old enough to have developed perfect aim."

He threw the pillow back on the bed, tossed his clothes back on the chair and tumbled her underneath him.

She landed with a gasp on the mattress.

"Stewart!"

"What?"

"We have things to do."

"We do indeed." He lowered his head and the last thing she saw before he kissed her were his blue eyes laughing into hers.

By the time they got out of bed for the second time, the first fingers of weak sunlight were poking through the curtains.

"And now I'm late." Stewart dived into the bathroom. "I blame you."

"And it's my fault because…?"

But he was already in the shower, humming tunelessly as the water splashed around him.

Suzanne lay for a moment, her brain fuzzy and contented, the dream all but forgotten.

She knew she ought to make a start on those stockings.

Knitting was the perfect form of relaxation, although it had taken her years to discover it.

She hadn't knitted a thing until she was in her thirties.

To begin with it had been her way of showing her love for the girls. She'd clothe them and wrap them in warmth. When she'd picked up her needles and yarn, she hadn't just been knitting a sweater; she'd been knitting together her fractured, damaged family, taking separate threads and turning them into something whole.

Stewart came out of the shower, rubbing his hair with a towel. "Did you want me to sort out a Christmas tree on the way home?"

"Posy said she'd do it. I thought we'd wait a few more days. I don't want the needles falling off before Christmas. How many trees should we have this year? I thought one for the living room, one for the entryway, one in the TV room. Maybe one for Hannah's room."

"Are you sure you don't want one for the boot room? How about the downstairs bathroom?"

She studied him. "There are still plenty more pillows on this bed that I can fling."

But he'd distracted her from her nightmare. She knew that had been his intention, and she loved him for it.

"All I'm saying is that maybe you should leave a few in the forest." He threw the wet towel over the back of the chair and then caught her eye and put the towel in the bathroom instead. "Every year you half kill yourself turning this place into a cross between a winter wonderland and Santa's workshop." He dressed quickly, pulling on the layers that were necessary for his job. "You have big expectations, Suzanne. Not easy to live up to that."

"It's true that things can be a little stressful when the girls are together—"

"They're women, not girls, and 'a little stressful' is an understatement."

"Maybe this year will be different." Suzanne stripped the sheets off the bed. "Beth and Jason are happy. I can't wait to have the grandchildren here. I'm going to hang stockings above the fire and bake plenty of treats. And Hannah won't need to do a thing, because I plan on getting everything done before she arrives so I can spend time with her. I want to catch up on her news." She held the sheets to her chest. "If only she would meet someone special, she'd—"

"She'd what? Eat him for breakfast?" Stewart shook his head. "I beg you do *not* mention that to her. Hannah's relationships are her business. And I don't think she's that interested."

"Don't say that." She refused to believe it might be true. Hannah needed a close relationship. She needed her own family. A protective circle. Everyone needed that.

Suzanne had craved it. At the age of six, she'd dreamed about it. Her early years had been spent with a mother too drunk to be aware of her existence. Later, when her mother's internal organs had given up fighting the relentless abuse, Suzanne had been placed in foster care. Every story she'd written at school involved her being part of a loving family. In her dreams she had parents and siblings. By the time she was ten, she was resigned to the fact that it was never going to happen for her.

Eventually she'd ended up in residential care, and that was where she'd met Cheryl. She'd become the sister Suzanne had longed for, and she'd poured all the surplus love she had into their friendship. They'd been so close people had assumed they were related.

Cheryl's love filled all the gaps and holes in Suzanne's soul, like glue bonding together broken fragments. She stopped feeling lost and alone. She no longer wished for someone to adopt her because then she'd have to leave the care home and that would mean leaving Cheryl.

They'd shared a bedroom. They'd shared clothes and laughter. They'd shared hopes and dreams.

The memory was vivid and the need to hear Cheryl's infectious laugh so strong that Suzanne almost reached for the phone.

It had been twenty-five years since they'd spoken, and yet the urge to talk to her had never gone away.

The part of her that missed her friend had never healed.

"Suzanne? What are you thinking?" Stewart's voice dragged her back to the present.

He'd thought Cheryl was a bad influence.

The irony was that Suzanne never would have met Stewart if it hadn't been for Cheryl. She wouldn't have been a mountain guide if it hadn't been for Cheryl.

"I was thinking about Hannah."

"If you mention her love life, I guarantee she will be on the first flight out of here and we will not have a happy Christmas."

"I won't say a word. I'll ask Beth for an update. I'm glad they're both living in New York. It's good for Hannah to have her sister close by. And Beth is settled and happy and loves being a mother. Maybe spending time with her will be an inspiration for Hannah."

Soon, the three sisters would be together again and Suzanne knew that this year Christmas was going to be perfect.

She was sure of it.

2

Beth

M otherhood was killing her.

Beth was trying in vain to extract her children from their favorite toy store when the call came. For a moment she felt guilty, as if she'd been caught doing something she shouldn't.

She'd promised Jason *no more toys*, but she wasn't good at saying no to the girls. Jason continually underestimated the persistence of children. No one could chip holes in a person's resolve like a determined child. *Please, Mommy, pleeeease—*

She found it particularly difficult because she badly wanted to be a good mother and had a more than sneaking suspicion that she wasn't. There was, she'd discovered, an annoying gulf between intention and reality.

She grabbed her phone and coaxed Ruby away from yet

another oversize fire truck, this one with flashing lights and blaring horns that was no doubt the brainchild of a young single man with no children.

The number wasn't one she recognized, but she answered anyway, reluctant to pass up what might be an opportunity for adult conversation. Since having children, her world had shrunk, and Beth felt she'd shrunk with it.

These days she was willing to befriend anyone who didn't want to talk to her about problems with eating, sleeping or behavior. The week before, she'd found herself prolonging a conversation with someone trying to sell her car insurance even though she didn't have a car. Eventually they'd hung up on her, which had to be a first in the history of cold calling.

"Hi there." Her phone was sticky and she tried not to think about the provenance of the substance stuck to her phone. Melly's favorite treat? When Beth had been pregnant, she'd resolved never to give her kids sugar, but that, like so many other resolutions, had evaporated in the fierce heat of reality.

"I want the fire truck, Mommy!"

As usual, the children ignored the fact she was on the phone and carried on talking to her. There were no breaks from motherhood. No commercial breaks, no bathroom breaks and certainly no phone breaks.

Her needs were right at the bottom of the pile.

Beth had always known she wanted children. What she hadn't known was how much of herself she'd have to give up.

She turned away slightly so she could hear what the person on the other end was saying.

"Beth McBride?" The voice was crisp and businesslike. A woman with a purpose, ticking this call off her to-do list.

Once upon a time Beth had been that woman. She'd luxuriated in the glamour and glitter of Manhattan. Energized by the frantic pulse of the city, she'd thrived. It had been like trying on a dress and discovering it fitted perfectly. You never wanted to take it off. You wanted to buy two in case you damaged one and somehow tarnished the perfect look.

And then one day you woke up and discovered the dress was no longer yours. You missed it. You saw other people wearing it and wanted to tear it from their bodies.

"This is Beth McBride speaking."

McBride.

No one had called her that in years. These days she was Bethany Butler.

"Beth, it's Kelly Porter from KP Recruiting."

Beth would have dropped the phone had it not been for the sticky goo welding it to her palm.

Before having children, Beth had worked in public relations for a number of beauty companies. She'd started at the bottom but had rapidly worked her way up, and Kelly had found her at least two of her roles.

"Hi, Kelly. Good to hear from you." Beth smoothed her hair and stood a little straighter, even though it wasn't a video call.

She was Beth McBride, someone who took calls from recruitment agencies.

"I have something you might be interested in."

Beth was interested in anything that didn't squeak, leak or leave marks on the floor, but for the life of her she couldn't understand why Kelly would be calling her.

She and Jason had talked about her going back to work at some point when the children were older. Now that Ruby was in preschool, it was time to have that discussion again, but Beth usually found herself too exhausted to put together a case.

And then there was the part of her that felt guilty for wanting to leave the girls.

"I'm listening."

"I understand you've had a career break." Kelly's tone suggested she classified such a thing in the same group of unfortunate life events as typhoid and yellow fever.

"I've taken time out to focus on my family."

Beth extracted the princess outfit from Melly's hand with a shake of her head. Melly already had a closetful of princess outfits. Jason would go insane if she bought another one, especially this close to Christmas.

"Have you heard of Glow PR?" Kelly ignored the reference to family. "The team is young, dynamic and making a name for themselves. They're looking for someone with your profile."

What exactly was her profile?

She was a wife, a mother, a cook, a cabdriver, a cleaner, a play leader and a personal assistant. She could clean spaghetti sauce off the walls and recite all of Ruby's picture books without lifting them from the shelf.

On the wall next to her was a mirror surrounded by enough pink and glitter to satisfy the most demanding wannabe princess. The mirror might look like something out of a child's fairy tale, but there was nothing fairy tale about the reflection staring back at Beth.

She had dark hair, and her few early attempts to dye it a lighter shade had convinced her that some people were meant to be brunette. Right now she had perfectly coordinated dark patches under her eyes, as if nature was determined to emphasize how tired she was.

Beth had once thought she knew everything there was to know about beauty and how to achieve a certain look, but she knew now that the best beauty product wasn't a face cream or an eye balm—it was an undisturbed night's sleep, and unfortunately that didn't come in jars.

"Mommy—" Ruby tugged at her coat "—can I play with your phone?"

Whatever Beth had, Ruby wanted.

She shook her head and pointed to the fire truck, hoping to distract her younger daughter.

Ruby wanted to be a firefighter, but Beth thought she'd be better suited to being in sales. She was only four years old but could talk a person into submission within minutes.

"Ms. McBride?"

"I'm here." The words came out of her mouth, pushing aside the words she'd intended to say. *I'm a stay-at-home mom now. Thanks for calling, but I'm not interested.*

She *was* interested.

"The company is headquartered right here on Sixth Avenue, but they have a diverse network and a bicoastal presence."

A bicoastal presence.

Bethany's imagination flew first-class to the West Coast. Today, a toy store. Tomorrow, Beverly Hills. Hollywood. *Champagne.* A world of long lunches, business meetings where people actually listened to what she was saying, glamorous parties and being able to use the bathroom without company.

"Mommy? *I want the fire truck.*"

Beth's brain was still luxuriating in Beverly Hills. "Tell me more."

"They're growing fast and they're ready to expand their team. They'd like to talk to you."

"Me?" She bit her tongue. She shouldn't have said that. She should be projecting confidence, but confidence had turned out to be a nonrenewable resource. Her children had stripped hers away, one sticky finger at a time.

"You have the experience," Kelly said, "the media contacts and the creativity."

Had, Beth thought.

"It's been a while since I was in the business." Seven years to be exact.

"Corinna Ladbrooke asked for you specifically."

"Corinna?" Hearing her old boss's name stirred up a tangle of feelings. "She's moved company?"

"She's the one behind Glow. Let me know when you have an opening. I can arrange for you to meet everyone."

Corinna wanted her? They'd worked together closely, but Beth had heard nothing from her since she'd left to have children.

Corinna wasn't interested in children. She didn't have them herself, didn't want them, and if any of her staff were foolish enough to stray into the realms of motherhood, Corinna chose to ignore it.

Ruby started to whine and Beth stooped to pick her up with one arm, automatically checking that her daughter was still holding Bugsy. Nothing parted Ruby from her favorite soft toy and Beth was careful not to lose it.

Would she worry less about the children if she had a job?

She was too anxious—she knew that. She was terrified of something bad happening to them.

"Kelly, I'm going to need to call you back when I've taken a look at my schedule." It sounded more impressive than it was. These days her "schedule" included ferrying the girls to ballet class, art class and Mandarin immersion.

"Do it soon." The phone went dead and Beth stood for a moment, her head still in fantasy land and her arm in the dead zone. How was it that children seemed to increase in weight the longer you held them? She put Ruby down.

"Time to go home."

"Fire truck!" Ruby's wail was more piercing than any siren. "You promised."

Melly was rifling through the dress-up clothes. "If I can't be a princess, I want to be a superhero."

I want to be a superhero, too, Beth thought.

A good mother would have refused and proffered a clear explanation for her decision. The children would then have left the store feeling chastened and with a greater understanding of the value of money and the concept of delayed gratification, as well as behavior and reward.

Beth wasn't that mother. She caved and bought both the fire truck and another dress-up outfit.

Loaded down with two happy children, an armful of parcels and a nagging feeling of maternal failure, Beth stepped out of the store onto the street.

To see Manhattan in December was to see it at its wintry best. The dazzle of lights in the store windows and the crisp bite of the winter air mingled together to create an atmosphere that drew people from around the globe. The sidewalks were crowded, the population of Midtown swollen by visitors unable to resist the appeal of Fifth Avenue in the festive season.

Beth loved Manhattan. After she'd graduated, she'd worked for a PR company in London. When they'd transferred her to their New York office, she'd felt as if she'd made it, as if simply being in Manhattan conferred a certain status. When she'd first arrived, she'd been torn between euphoria and terror. She'd walk briskly down streets with familiar names— *Fifth Avenue, Forty-second Street, Broadway*—trying to look as if she belonged. It was fortunate she'd been living and working in London prior to the move, otherwise the contrast between the noise levels of New York City and her home in the remote Scottish Highlands would have blown both her mind and her eardrums.

Every day she'd walk down Fifth Avenue on her way to work feeling as if she was on a film set. The excitement of it had more than compensated for any homesickness she might have felt. So what if all she could afford was a tiny room where she could touch both walls without leaving her bed? She was in New York, the most exciting city on earth.

Through marriage and two children, that feeling hadn't left her.

Their apartment was bigger now and they had more disposable income, but other than that, nothing much had changed.

Holding tightly to Ruby's hand, Beth called Jason to tell him about Kelly, but his assistant told her he was in a meeting.

Only then did she remember he had a major pitch that day and a busy week ahead. Would he be able to make time to take care of the children if she went to meet Corinna and the team?

"Mommy—" Ruby hung on her hand, the pressure making Beth's shoulder ache "—I'm tired."

Me, too, Beth thought. "If you walk faster, we'll soon be home. Hold Bugsy tight. We don't want to drop him here. And don't walk too close to the road."

She saw accidents everywhere. It didn't help that Ruby was a fearlessly adventurous child with no apparent sense of self-preservation or caution. Melly was virtually glued to Beth's side, but Ruby wanted to explore the world from every angle.

It was exhausting.

Beth wanted to work for Glow PR. She wanted to walk along Fifth Avenue without needing to be alert to potential disaster. She wasn't the first mother to want both work and family. There had to be a way to make it happen.

Jason's mother lived nearby, and Beth was hoping that if she found a job, Alison might be prepared to help out with childcare. Melly and Ruby adored Jason's mother. Beth adored her, too. Alison defied all the mother-in-law clichés. Instead of resenting Beth as the woman who stole her only son, she welcomed her like the daughter she'd never had.

Beth was sure Alison would be delighted to help, which left the small problem of finding a job.

Did she have what it took to impress Corinna after seven years out of the game?

She felt woefully unequipped to return to the corporate world. She wasn't sure she was capable of conducting an adult conversation, let alone dazzling people with creative ideas.

Maybe she should call her sister. Hannah would understand the lure of a career. She worked as a management consultant and seemed to spend most of her life flying first-class round the globe being paid an exorbitant amount to fix corporations unable to fix themselves.

They were due to meet up the following night, and Beth had been meaning to call and confirm.

Hannah answered in her usual crisp, no-nonsense tone.

"Is this an emergency, Beth? I'm boarding. I'll call you when I land if there's time before my meeting."

How are you, Beth? Good to hear from you. How are Ruby and Melly?

Beth had always wanted to be close to her sister and wasn't sure whose fault it was that they weren't. It had got worse lately. Regular dinners had become less regular. Was it her fault for only having the children to talk about? Did her own sister find her boring?

"Don't worry." Beth tightened her grip on wriggling, writhing Ruby. It was like trying to hold hands with a fish, but she didn't dare let go or Ruby would end up under the wheels of a cab. "We can talk tomorrow over dinner. It's not urgent."

"I was going to call you about that— No champagne, thank you, I'm working. Sparkling water will be fine—" Hannah broke off to speak to the stewardess and Beth tried to suppress the stab of envy.

She wanted to be in a position to turn down champagne.

No, thanks, I need to keep a clear head for my meeting where I will say something important that people want to hear.

"You're canceling on me again?"

"I have a job, Beth."

"I know." She didn't need reminding. And here she was, a stay-at-home mom with a growing complex that was fed and nurtured by her more successful sister. She tried not to think about the lamb marinating in her fridge or the extravagant dessert she'd planned. Hannah ate at all the best restaurants. Was she really going to be impressed by her sister's attempts at Christmas pavlova? Whisked egg whites were hardly going to change the world, were they? And was Beth really so desperate that she needed the approval? "Where are you off to this time?"

"San Francisco. It was a last-minute thing. I was going to text you right after I finished this email."

It was always a last-minute thing with Hannah. "When are you back?"

"Late Friday, and then I'm off to Frankfurt on Sunday night. Can we reschedule?"

"This *is* a reschedule," Beth said. "In fact, it's a reschedule of a reschedule of a reschedule."

The rustle of papers suggested Hannah was doing something else at the same time as talking to Beth. "We'll fix another date. You know I'd love to see you."

Beth didn't know.

What she knew was that she was the one who put all the effort into the relationship. She often wondered whether Hannah would bother to get in touch if Beth were to give up trying. But she would never give up. Even though Hannah frequently drove her crazy and hurt her feelings, Beth knew how precious it was to have family. She intended to hang on to hers even if it meant leaving fingernail imprints on Hannah's flesh. "Have I offended you in some way? You always have some excuse not to see us."

There was a pause. "I have a meeting, Beth. Don't take it personally."

Beth had a horrible feeling it was as personal as it could get.

Like Corinna, Hannah didn't do children, but this was more than that. Beth was starting to think her sister didn't like Ruby and Melly, and the thought was like a stab through the heart.

"I'm not overreacting. You've pulled away." Corinna had been her boss—there was no obligation on her to like Beth's children, but Hannah was their *aunt*, for goodness' sake.

"We're both busy. It's difficult to find a time."

"We live in the same city and we *never* see each other. I have no idea what's going on in your life! Are you happy? Are you seeing someone?" She knew her mother would ask her, so she considered it her duty to be an up-to-date source of information. Also, she was a romantic. And then there was the fact that if Hannah had a partner they might see more of each other. The four of them could go out to dinner.

But apparently it wasn't to be.

"This is Manhattan. It's crowded. I see a lot of people."

Beth gave up trying to extract information. "Ruby and Melly miss you. You're the only family that lives close by. They love it when you visit." She decided to test a theory. "Come over next weekend."

"You mean to the apartment?"

Beth was sure she hadn't imagined the note of panic in her sister's voice. "Yes. Come for lunch. Or dinner. Stay the whole day and a night."

There was a brief pause. "I'm going to be working right through. Probably best if you and I just grab dinner in the city one evening."

A restaurant. In the city. A child-free evening.

Beth scooped Ruby up with one arm, feeling a wave of love and protectiveness.

These were her children, her kids, *her life*. They were the most important thing in her world. Surely her sister should care about them for that reason if nothing else?

The irony was that because Hannah rarely saw them, the girls saw her as a figure of glamour and wonder.

Last time Hannah had visited, Ruby had tried to crawl onto her lap for a hug and Hannah had frozen. Beth had half expected her to yell *Get it off me!* In the end she'd removed a bemused Ruby and distracted her, but she'd been hurt and upset by the incident. She'd remained in a state of tension until her sister had left.

Jason had reminded her that Hannah was Hannah and that she was never going to change.

"Fine. We'll grab dinner sometime. You work too hard."

"You're starting to sound like Suzanne."

"You mean Mom." Beth unpeeled Ruby's fingers from her earring. "Why can't you ever call her Mom?"

"I prefer Suzanne." Hannah's tone cooled. "I'm sorry I'm canceling, but we'll have plenty of time to catch up over Christmas."

"Christmas?" Beth was so shocked she almost dropped Ruby. "You're going home for Christmas?"

"If by 'home' you mean Scotland, then yes—" Hannah's voice was muffled as she said something else to the stewardess—*I'll have the smoked salmon and the beef*—

Beth might have wondered why her sister was ordering smoked salmon and beef when they both knew she'd take two mouthfuls and leave the rest, but she was too preoccupied by the revelation that her sister would be home for Christmas. "You didn't make it last year."

"I had a lot going on." Hannah paused. "And you know what Christmas is like in our house. It's the only time we all get together and the place is a pressure cooker of expectation. Suzanne fussing and needing everything to be perfect and Posy blaming me when it isn't…"

It was so unusual for Hannah to reveal what she was thinking that Beth was taken aback. Before she could think of an appropriate response, Hannah had changed the subject.

"Is there anything in particular the girls would like for Christmas?"

The girls. The children. Hannah always lumped them together, and in doing so, she somehow dehumanized them.

Beth knew her sister would delegate gift buying to her assistant. It would be something generous that the girls would forget to play with after a week and Beth would be left with the feeling that her sister was compensating.

She thought about the fire engine currently smacking against her leg as she walked and knew she wasn't exactly in a position to criticize anyone for overcompensating. "Don't buy anything that squeaks or emits sirens in the middle of the night. And spend the same amount on both of them."

She kept a mental tally and watched herself constantly to check she wasn't showing a preference, that she wasn't admonishing one more than the other, or showing more interest in one than the other.

Her children were never going to feel their parents had a favorite.

"I am the last person you need to say that to."

In that brief moment, she and her sister connected. That single invisible thread from the past bound them together.

Beth wanted to grab that connection and reel her sister in, but the blare of horns and the general street noise made it the wrong place to have a deeply personal conversation. And then there were the listening ears of the girls, who missed nothing.

"Hannah, maybe we could—"

"What are they into at the moment?" With that single question, Hannah chopped the connection and floated back to that safe place where no one could reach her.

Beth felt a pang of loss. "Melly wants to be a ballerina or a princess, and Ruby wants to be a firefighter."

"A princess?"

Beth heard judgment in her sister's tone. "I buy her gender-neutral toys and tell her she could be an engineer and apply to NASA, but right now she just wants to live in a castle with a prince, preferably while dressed as the Sugar Plum Fairy." She didn't bother adding, "Wait until you have children and then you'll know what I'm talking about."

No matter how much their mother longed for Hannah to fall in love and settle down, anyone vaguely grounded in reality could see that was *not* going to happen.

3

Hannah

*P*regnant.

Hannah closed her eyes and tried to control the panic.

There was still a chance she might *not* be pregnant. True, she was five days late, but there were other things that could cause that. Stress, for example. She was definitely stressed.

She dropped her phone back into her bag, feeling guilty about Beth.

She hadn't forgotten dinner. She'd canceled because she knew she couldn't handle an evening in the child-centered chaos of her sister's apartment.

Was she crazy going home for Christmas this year? Last year she'd lost her nerve at the last minute and pretended she was working. She'd switched off her phone and spent the time in her apartment numbing her feelings with several bottles of good wine and a reading marathon. By the time she'd closed the final book, the festive season had been over.

This year that wasn't an option.

She dreaded the forced togetherness of Christmas and the pressure that came with it.

Her family thought she was a career woman, with no time for relationships.

That was going to make for an interesting conversation if she was pregnant.

She should do a test. Find out one way or another. But then she'd know, and right now she'd rather cling to the vague hope that her perfectly organized life wasn't about to become complicated.

"Everything all right, Hannah?"

Hannah opened her eyes. Adam was standing in the aisle of the first-class cabin, stowing his overnight bag.

"Everything is fine." Hannah already had her bag safely tucked away and her laptop by her seat. She lived with a sense that things were about to go horribly wrong, and did what she could to prevent it by planning and controlling every last detail of her life.

"Are you sure? That conversation sounded tense." He sat down next to her. He was tall and rangy, his long legs filling the abundant space in front of his seat. "Problems?"

Normally when she was traveling, Hannah preferred to keep herself to herself. If such a thing as a Do Not Disturb sign existed for passengers, she would have been wearing it.

Today, however, she was traveling with Adam. Adam was her colleague and, for the past few months, her lover.

Turned out he might also be the father of her child, which she knew would be as much of a shock to him as to her.

"I was talking to Beth."

Guilt pricked like holly. Beth was right that she hadn't seen her nieces for a while. The girls were adorable, but being with them made Hannah feel inept and inadequate. She found it impossible to read fairy stories where everyone lived happily ever after. She couldn't bring herself to perpetrate that lie. There was no Santa. There was no tooth fairy. Love couldn't be guaranteed.

She'd tried explaining that to Beth once, but her sister had thought she was being ridiculous.

Maybe life doesn't always end happily, Hannah, but I'd rather protect my kids from that reality when they're young if that's all right with you!

Hannah thought it was healthier if one's expectations of life were grounded in reality. If you didn't expect much, you didn't have as far to fall when you finally realized that no amount of planning could stop bad things happening.

A few years before, after an unexpected snowstorm, Hannah had been forced to stay the night at Beth's apartment. In the middle of the night, Ruby had crawled into her bed. Hannah had felt the tickle of soft curls against her skin and the solid warmth of the child through the brushed cotton of her pajamas as she'd snuggled close for reassurance. It had reminded her so much of that one terrible night when Posy had climbed into her bed that the memories had almost suffocated her.

The fact that her sister didn't understand simply made her feel more isolated.

She'd left before breakfast, choosing to battle snowdrifts and bad weather to escape the memories. She'd been careful never to put herself in that position again. Until now.

She ran her fingers around the neck of her sweater, even though it wasn't tight.

Christmas was going to be hard, but even she couldn't find a way to evade it for a second year. The McBride family always gathered at Christmas. It was tradition. She'd resigned herself to the fact that it was something she was going to have to live through, like a bad bout of the flu. But now she had this added complication.

"She was upset that you canceled?" Adam watched her, concerned, and she looked away quickly. He noticed things. Small things that other people missed. It was one of the attributes that made him good at his job. It was also part of the unsettling attraction she'd felt since his first day at the company. Hannah had been completely unprepared for the startling chemistry between them. She was so good at controlling her feelings it had come as a nasty shock to discover they were capable of rebellion.

"I've hurt her."

He removed his phone from his pocket and handed his jacket to the steward. "Why don't you tell her the truth? Tell her you find it hard being around the kids."

Oh the irony.

If I'm pregnant, I'm going to have to find a way to be around kids.

It still surprised her that she'd talked to him about her family, but Adam was remarkably easy to talk to.

She hadn't told him everything, of course, but more than she'd shared with anyone else.

"It's…complicated." She noticed that a couple across the aisle from her were traveling with a baby. They hadn't even taken off but already the baby was fussy and restless. Hannah hoped it wasn't going to cry for the whole flight. Listening to a child cry made her stomach hurt.

"Introduce me to her, and I'll do it."

"What?" She turned back to Adam, confused.

"I want to meet your sister."

"Why?"

"Because that's what people do in our position."

"Our position?"

"I'm in love with you." He said it easily, as if love wasn't the most profoundly terrifying thing that could happen to a person. "Or are we going to ignore that?"

"We're going to ignore it." At least for now. She had the same control over her feelings as she did over her schedule. She'd learned to hold them back. If there was one thing she hated in life, it was emotional chaos.

"I should be offended that you're treating my heartfelt declaration of love so lightly."

"You were drunk, Kirkman."

"Not true. I was in full control of my faculties."

"As I recall, you'd consumed several glasses of bourbon."

"It's true that I may have needed a little liquid support to give me courage—" he shrugged "—but saying *I love you* is a big deal to a guy who has been single for as long as I have."

She hadn't allowed herself to believe that he was serious.

For Hannah, love was an emotional form of Russian roulette. It was a game she didn't play.

Her emotional safety was the most important thing in the world to her.

She didn't even want to think about how complicated it would be if there was a baby in the mix.

"You're worried I'm going to strip you of your assets?" He leaned closer. "We'll sign a prenup, but I should warn you that in the event of an irrevocable breakdown of our marriage I want possession of your books. Given time and medication, I can probably learn to live without you, but I can't learn to live without your library. Do you know what a turn-on it is knowing that you have a first edition of *Great Expectations* on your shelves?"

She could barely concentrate on what he was saying. *She should do a test.* "We won't be needing a prenup."

"I agree. A love like ours is going to last forever. You could say I have Great Expectations." He winked at her, but this time she didn't smile.

Love was fickle and unreliable, and definitely not something you could control. If someone's feelings weren't right, then you couldn't force it. She preferred to build her life on a more secure footing.

He rejected the offer of champagne from the steward and asked for bourbon instead, raising an eyebrow when Hannah refused, too.

"Since when do you refuse champagne?"

Since I might be pregnant. "I need a clear head to finish this presentation."

"You can handle this presentation with your eyes closed. I don't understand why you're stressed. What happened to the woman who danced barefoot in the office around an empty pizza box?"

She slid off her heels. "Can we forget that happened?"

"No. I have photographic evidence, in case you ever tried to deny it. And I intend to show it to your sister to prove how misunderstood you are." He dug out his phone and scrolled through the photos. "Here. This is my favorite."

She barely recognized herself. Her hair had fallen out of the neat style she favored for work and she was barefoot and laughing. What really stood out was the expression on her face. Had she really revealed that much?

"Give me that!" She tried to snatch the phone from him, but he held it out of reach.

"I will never forget that night."

"Because I took my shoes off and danced?"

"I was thinking more of the pizza. It was good pizza. There were other nights, and other pizzas, but that was the best. I think it was the olives." Smiling, he leaned forward and kissed her. "I love it when you laugh. You are always so serious in the office."

"I'm a serious person."

Adam eased away. "Who told you that?"

"My father."

You're so damn serious, Hannah. Lift your head out of a book for five minutes and have some fun.

Even now there were days when she felt guilty for picking up a book, unable to shake the feeling that there was something more valuable she should be doing with her time.

"I've got news for your father—he's wrong."

Adam had gradually chipped away at her defenses, and he'd done it so subtly she hadn't even realized she needed to defend herself.

Her work often demanded that she work late, and there had been nothing notable about that until the first time Adam had strolled into her office carrying a pizza box.

She'd raised her eyebrows.

I don't eat pizza.

There's a first time for everything, McBride.

Somehow they'd ended up sprawled on the office floor eating pizza out of the box long after everyone else had gone home.

Hannah had never eaten pizza out of a box before she'd met Adam.

Hannah had never kicked off her shoes or sprawled on the office floor.

She wasn't sure she'd even known how to relax before he'd arrived in the company, but those late-night work sessions had fast become the favorite part of her day. She looked forward to being overloaded just so that she could have an excuse to stay after everyone else had left.

They'd worked, they'd shared food and they'd talked.

There was something about being in the nighttime stillness of the office cocooned by the glitter of the city outside that made it easy to say things she never would have said in other circumstances.

One night he'd confessed that his aunt had insisted he learn ballroom dancing because she thought it was an essential life skill.

He'd insisted on teaching Hannah.

Everyone should be able to dance the tango, McBride.

I don't dance, Kirkman.

But somehow, with him, she'd danced barefoot around the empty pizza boxes.

It was ridiculous, but she'd ended up laughing so hard she couldn't breathe.

And that was how intimacy happened, she thought, watching as he took a mouthful of his drink. Not in a giant leap, but step by gentle step, each movement forward as stealthy as the incoming tide. One minute you were standing alone on dry land and the next minute you were in over your head and drowning.

Light wings of panic fluttered across her skin. If she could have fastened those wings to her back, she would have flown away. For some people, fear was a dark alley at night or a growling dog with sharp teeth. For her, it was intimacy.

Maybe he *thought* he loved her, but she knew that whatever she had to offer, it wouldn't be enough.

A crash and a curse dragged her out of her thoughts and she saw a woman trying to wrestle her case into the overhead bin.

Adam stood up to help, using his superior height to wedge it into place.

Hannah saw the woman's eyes linger on his profile and then slide to his shoulders. A faint smile acknowledged this prime specimen of manhood, and then she turned and registered Hannah's presence. Her smile went from interested to resigned. Hannah could almost see her thinking *all the good ones are taken.*

"When are you going to tell Beth about us?" Adam sat down again. "Not that I mind being your dirty little secret, but it would be a lot easier if you told them. I could come to dinner with you. I'm great with kids."

Hannah hoped he would still feel that way if it turned out she was pregnant.

He stretched out his legs again. "We've been virtually living together for the past six months. You can't hide me forever."

Six months? "I'm not hiding you."

Prior to Adam, her longest relationship had been two months. Eight weeks. It was a time frame that suited her. Hannah preferred to focus her efforts on things she excelled at. Relationships fell outside that category.

With Adam, it had been different.

The connection had been so powerful she hadn't known how to handle it. At first their only interaction had been at work. She couldn't recall who had made the first move.

The first time they'd had sex had been in his apartment. They hadn't made it as far as the bedroom. The second time had been at hers, and that time they'd made it as far as the floor of her living room. She'd assumed that urgency would fade, but some days they didn't even pause for conversation. It was as if everything they held back in public during their working day demanded to be released the moment they were in private. Twice in the past week they'd made love standing up in the entryway with the lights still on. Part of her had wondered why sex with Adam always felt desperate. Maybe because in her head she believed it was going to end soon.

Everything ended, Hannah knew that, and yet here they were, six months later.

She shifted in her seat.

If she was pregnant, she'd know, surely? Weren't women usually sick?

She didn't feel sick.

As the plane's engines screamed ready for takeoff, Adam finished his drink. "If you're going home to your family this Christmas, I should be there."

"To cause trouble?"

"To protect you." This time he wasn't smiling. "I hate seeing you like this. I want my Hannah back."

My Hannah.

Her family, she knew, wouldn't recognize the Hannah that Adam knew. She barely recognized that woman, either.

"I don't need you to come with me, but it's kind of you to offer." She could just imagine Suzanne's reaction if she showed up with Adam. She would have booked the church and bought a hat before Hannah had even unpacked.

Above their heads the seat belt light went out and Adam made himself more comfortable. "If Christmas is stressful, why go?"

"I don't want to disappoint Suzanne." And that feeling that she was falling short, not delivering, brought back uncomfortable memories.

"Suzanne? You don't call her mom?"

"She isn't my mother. My mother is dead."

She saw the shock in his eyes and wondered what had possessed her to blurt out that fact in these stark, impersonal surroundings. She never talked about her real parents, but there was something about Adam that unraveled the part of her she usually kept tightly wound.

"I didn't know." He spoke quietly. "I'm sorry to hear it."

"It was a long time ago. I was eight."

"Dammit, Hannah. That's a difficult age to lose a parent.

Why haven't you told me this before?" He held out his hand, palm upward, and she hesitated for a moment and then slid her hand into his. His fingers closed over hers, strong and protective, and she could feel the ropes of intimacy tightening around her.

I love you, Hannah.

"It's not the kind of thing that comes up in general conversation. We lost both our parents. They died in the same accident."

"Car?"

"Avalanche. They were climbers."

He raised an eyebrow. "So you weren't always a city girl?"

She had a feeling she'd always been a city girl.

"So who is Suzanne?" His tone was neutral, as if he'd recognized her need not to be smothered with sympathy.

"Suzanne and Stewart adopted us. Suzanne is American. Stewart is Scottish. After the…accident…we moved back to Scotland to be close to Stewart's family." Her heart was thumping. "Can we work now?"

He hesitated. "Sure." He retrieved his laptop and opened it. "Unless you want to finish that game of chess we were playing?"

"I captured your knight."

"I remember." His smile was almost boyish. "I can still take your king. Give me a chance to try. You won the last two games we played and my confidence has taken a severe blow."

His confidence had always seemed to her to be indestructible.

"I think we should finish the proposal."

"You're afraid you're going to lose." He leaned forward and kissed her on the mouth. "I looked at your presentation. It's brilliant. We're going to win this business."

Relaxing slightly, she leaned across to scan the spreadsheet on his screen. "You need to change that." She tapped one of the numbers. "Didn't you get my email?"

"The one you sent at 3:00 a.m? Yes, I picked it up this morning on our way to the airport, but we're not all as lightning fast as you." He altered the number. "You have a hell of a brain, McBride, but why weren't you sleeping?"

"I like work." More specifically, she loved numbers. Loved data and computer code. Numbers were reliable and behaved the way she wanted them to. Numbers didn't wrap themselves round your heart and squeeze until the blood stopped flowing. "I wanted to finish this project."

"You couldn't have done that in the eighteen-hour day you put in?"

"I had things on my mind." And not just the fact that her period was late.

She'd been thinking about the two voice mail messages that had been sitting on her phone for a month.

She'd had similar calls before over the years, particularly at this time of year as the anniversary of the accident approached. This time she didn't recognize the name. She'd learned not to respond, but still the message sat like a leaden weight in the pit of her stomach, reminding her of things she didn't want to think about.

She'd almost asked Beth if she'd had a call, too, but then she would have had to talk about it and she didn't want to.

It was something she and Suzanne had in common. They both preferred to ignore the past.

Adam saved the file they were working on. "Suzanne and Stewart were relatives?"

"Friends of my parents. They adopted the three of us." Which only served to intensify her guilt that she couldn't be the person they wanted her to be.

"And that's why you feel you have to be there at Christmas. Because you owe them." It was a statement of fact, not a question, and she didn't argue with him.

She did owe them, and she knew she could never repay the debt. "That's part of it."

"Take me with you."

"My family live in Scotland, in the remote Highlands. I can't imagine you dealing with dodgy Wi-Fi and an intermittent phone signal." She eyed his polished loafers. "You'd hate it."

"I would not hate it. For a start, I'm a lover of single malt. Do your folks happen to live near a distillery?"

Hannah sighed. "In fact, they do, but—"

"Well, there you go. I'm already sold. Also, I appreciate beautiful scenery. A few romantic walks in a misty glen would be a perfect way to unwind."

"A misty glen? You've been watching too much *Braveheart*. At this time of year the glen is usually buried under a foot of snow, and if there's mist, you're going to be lost and die of hypothermia."

He gave an exaggerated shudder. "I knew there was a reason I chose to live in Manhattan. Seriously though, think about it. If I was there with you, we could work on the presentation. Believe it or not, I can live without the internet. No internet might turn out to be the greatest Christmas gift of all."

It was one thing to tell Adam about her family. Quite another to introduce them.

Champagne corks would pop.

Hannah would be swept along by an uncontrollable tide of expectation.

"You're going to the Caribbean and that, believe me, is going to be a thousand times better than Christmas in the Scottish Highlands. It's likely we'll be snowed in." The thought of it made her hyperventilate. Trapped. Unable to breathe. Buried.

She heard Suzanne's voice, thick with tears. *They're gone, Hannah. They're dead.*

Maybe she should have invented a business trip to some far-flung corner of the globe to get herself out of it for another year. If she visited a client in Sydney, she could be on a plane for almost all of the festive season.

Last year she'd chickened out at the last minute and she knew Posy hadn't believed her limp excuse.

Who the hell decides they need to revamp their company on Christmas Eve, Hannah?

Even Santa leaves his corporate evaluation until the New Year.

There had been a time when Posy had worshipped Hannah and followed her round like a shadow. She'd crawled into her bed and refused to be dislodged. She'd held her hand. She'd sat on her lap. She'd clung like a burr, all softness and vulnerability.

Hannah felt the tightness in her chest increase as she thought about it.

To say that they'd grown apart would be an understatement, and Hannah knew the whole thing was her fault.

Her relationship with her youngest sister was yet another piece of evidence to support her belief that she'd be a terrible mother.

So what was she going to do if she was pregnant?

4

Posy

In a remote valley in the Scottish Highlands, Posy McBride stood at the base of an avalanche field buffeted by an icy wind. It froze exposed skin and crept through gaps in clothing. The air smelled sharply of winter and each breath emerged as a cloud of vapor.

Snow the size of boulders lay strewn across an area that attracted climbers from all over the world. This area of the Highlands was known for its steep cliffs, challenging routes and its tendency to avalanche in the winter months.

The dog waiting next to her was tense with anticipation and excitement.

"Away find!" Posy gave the command and the dog bounded onto the debris field, weaving to and fro, nose to the snow.

Other members of the mountain rescue team had formed a probe line and were searching with slow, methodical purpose.

"She's a champ," Posy muttered, striding to catch up as Bonnie struggled over the huge boulders of snow, a smudge of gold in a sea of white as she searched for human scent.

Rory, the training officer for the team, walked up to her, a radio in his hand. "Phil fell over a few times. His scent will be all over the snow. That's going to confuse her."

"It's not going to confuse her. She's trained in air scent and trailing." Posy didn't take her eyes off Bonnie. "See? She's showing interest in that spot right there. She's a natural."

"Phil would have put human scent on the surface."

At that moment Bonnie started barking. Then she flew across the snow back to Posy.

"Show me!" Posy followed her back to the place that had caught her attention.

Rory followed at a slower pace, cursing as he stumbled. "I bet Luke a tenner she wouldn't find him."

"And for that lack of faith you're going to have to pay up." Posy reached Bonnie, who was now playing tug-of-war with a sweater. "You're Wonder Dog. Good girl, good girl." This, fortunately, was a training exercise, but still she made a big fuss of the dog, giving Bonnie her favorite squeaky toy as a reward. Then she grinned down at the man lying half-buried in the snow. "Hello there. How are you feeling today?"

He returned the smile, even though she knew he must be freezing and uncomfortable. Snow clung to his jacket, his jaw and his eyelashes. "I'm not sure. I might need mouth-to-mouth resuscitation."

"You should be so lucky." Posy stroked Bonnie's soft fur. Working with the dog thrilled her and she was in awe of the animal's skills. They could do so much more than a human.

"You are the best search and rescue dog who ever roamed the planet."

Their "victim" cleared his throat. "Excuse me—I'm still in this hole. Aren't you at least going to pull me out? Is this how you treat someone caught in an avalanche?"

"Don't be a wimp. You can haul yourself out."

"Wimp?" He struggled upright, wincing as snow slid inside the neck of his jacket. "Hell of a date, Posy McBride. When you said you wanted my body, this wasn't what I imagined."

"No?"

"No." He removed a lump of snow from his neck. "You said, 'I want your body on Saturday,' and I was good with that. I like a woman who knows what she wants. I thought to myself, dinner and then a movie. Or maybe a cozy evening in the Glensay Inn followed by a romantic stroll. Setting the scene before we get naked together." He levered himself out of the snowy hole and she laughed.

"You look like the Abominable Snowman."

"Your concern warms me, which is good because I may have hypothermia."

Her smile widened. "You think?"

"That's generally what happens when a person lies buried by snow for a couple of hours waiting for a dog to find him." He brushed thick layers of snow from his sleeve. "I have snow in places I didn't even know snow could reach. Any chance of a wee warming dram?"

"Somehow that phrase doesn't sound right spoken in a New York accent."

"I'll use whatever accent you prefer as long as you pour me whiskey."

"Alcohol and hypothermia aren't a good combination."

She enjoyed their banter, probably more than she should. Luke's arrival at Glensay had calmed the restlessness inside her that always seemed to be present these days. It was as if he'd brought part of the outside world with him, quenching some of her thirst for adventure.

Bonnie was bounding in happy circles, tail wagging.

"You're lucky she is a superstar, or you would have been lying there for a lot longer."

"I'm supposed to feel grateful that I'm cold and wet?"

"If this was a real avalanche, you'd be falling at her furry paws and pledging lifelong love and allegiance."

He stamped the snow from his boots. "If this was a real avalanche, I would have been wearing a transceiver and carrying a shovel and probe."

"That assumes you would have been climbing or skiing with people who knew what to do with a transceiver, a shovel and a probe."

"Do people volunteer to do this more than once?"

"Yes. We have a team of 'dogsbodies' who volunteer during our training exercises."

"And they're still alive?"

"Mostly. We don't often do avalanche training. Sometimes you just get to lie in a soaking wet grassy hole on the side of the mountain."

"Stop or I'll never recover from the searing disappointment that comes from knowing I missed that experience." He had the lean, athletic build of a climber and the rugged looks of a man who spent his life exposed to the elements.

The strength of the attraction had come as a surprise to her.

She was wary of relationships. In a small community like the one she lived in, you couldn't walk away when a romance ended. There was a strong likelihood you were going to see the person every day. It had happened to her, and she wasn't in a hurry to repeat the experience.

Rory called out to them. "Everything okay over there?"

Posy turned her head. "I think the victim has hypothermia."

"Victim?" Luke arched an eyebrow. "Less of the 'victim,' thank you. It's not how I see myself." He bent to stroke Bonnie. "You're the only girl for me. If I really had been buried in that avalanche and you rescued me, I'd have to marry you."

"Mr. and Mrs. Golden Retriever. I predict many years of happiness." Before Posy could dodge, Luke stuffed a handful of snow down the neck of her jacket.

Ice trickled over her skin and she gasped. "That's immature."

"But satisfying. And now you're cold, too, which levels the playing field. We should warm each other. Hot shower. Log fire. Bottle of red wine."

It would be easy enough to do because technically they lived under the same roof.

On their land was a barn, complete with hayloft. Her parents had cleverly converted it into two properties. Posy lived in the loft, which had sloping ceilings and views of the stars. The barn was offered as a rental. It was half a mile from Glensay Lodge, where her parents lived, and bordered by pine and birch woodland. A short walk led you to the deep loch, spring fed and stocked with brown trout.

Its isolation wasn't for everyone, and in the summer the occupants were mostly couples seeking a romantic week in the wild Highlands. It was perfect for cycling, bird-watching, hiking and loch swimming, but the biggest draw was its proximity to big mountains. In the winter the barn was often booked by climbers.

Short rentals meant more work for Posy. With frequent changeovers, she was always cleaning, changing beds and doing laundry, so she'd been thrilled when Luke Whittaker had booked it for four months with an option to extend.

He was a climber and writer. He needed peace and quiet

to finish a book, and a base that would allow him to climb. The barn offered opportunities for both.

Occasionally, when she'd arrived home late after a training session, Posy had seen his lights burning, so she already knew Luke Whittaker was a night owl.

She also knew he was good with animals. Like now, for instance, when he was sending Bonnie into ecstasy with a stomach rub.

He glanced up at her. "I'm assuming Bonnie passed the test?"

"She did. She picked up your scent right away."

He straightened. "Are you telling me I smell?"

"Be grateful that you do. It's how she finds you. She is trained to look for human scent. If you're panicking and sweating, you give off a stronger smell."

"I was buried in snow. I can assure you not a drop of sweat emerged from my frozen pores."

"That's where you're wrong. She sensed your fear." She enjoyed teasing him. "And she could probably feel the vibrations in the snow where you were shivering. But seriously, thanks. It was a good thing you did and we're all grateful."

"She seems like a pretty good rescue dog to me."

"Fetch is her favorite game, which helps. You need a dog who has a strong drive to retrieve. And also scenting is her superpower."

They picked their way over the lumps of snow, back down the track to where Posy had parked her car. A fresh layer of soft powder dusted the surface of the snow and the freezing air numbed her cheeks.

"Have you rescued many stranded climbers and hikers?"

"Yes. And sometimes I'll get called by the police to help search for a missing person. A couple of weeks ago Bonnie found an elderly guy with dementia who had gone walkabout. His family were beside themselves—apparently he'd managed to unlock the front door and wander. They were relieved when we found him."

"Wait—" He stopped walking. "I thought a trailing dog is a different type of rescue dog."

"More often than not it is. Dogs either air scent, where they follow any human scent, or they follow the trail of a specific scent. It's rare for a dog to be trained to do both."

"And she is?"

"What can I say? She's a superstar."

They carried on walking. "The man you found was all right?"

"He was pretty cold. Bonnie found him sheltering behind a hedge. Spent a few nights in the hospital, but doing okay now. Bonnie and I went to visit him."

"Is there anything she can't do?"

"She doesn't love helicopter rides—" Posy pulled a face "—and we get a few of those."

Bonnie jumped into the back of the car and wagged her tail expectantly while Posy changed her boots and removed the outer layers of her clothing.

She stuck out her hand. "Have a great day."

Luke stared at her hand. "I give you my whole body, and all you give me in return is your hand? The least you could do is invite me to join you for a mug of hot chocolate in that cozy café you run with your mother."

"Can't. Today I'm staff, not a customer." She slid into the driver's seat. "But I'll bring you home a slab of chocolate cake."

"Dinner, then. I'll take you to the Glensay Inn. Roaring log fire, local ale, good food and great company."

And all the gossip you could handle.

"I've lived here for most of my life, Luke. You don't have

to sell the charms of my own village to me. And tonight, I'm busy."

"You, Posy McBride, are always busy. When you're not out tracking down lost souls with your dog or guiding someone up an ice wall, you're working in the café, tending the sheep or collecting eggs from your hens. Which, by the way, taste like nothing I've ever eaten before."

"Everything tastes better here. It's the air. I have to go." She knew her mother would be overwhelmed. "It's our busy period and Mom is handling it on her own because Vicky is feeling under the weather."

He stood, legs spread, hands on hips. "You're good to your mom."

It seemed like a strange thing to say. "She's my mother. Why wouldn't I be?"

"Have you always been close?"

Posy's earliest memory was being rocked to sleep by Suzanne. She remembered the warmth, the tightness of her arms, the feeling of comfort and security. "Yes."

"And you're going to take over the café from her one day?"

"That's the plan."

He studied her thoughtfully. "And you're okay with that? You've never been tempted to travel? Do something different?"

It was as if he'd pressed down on a tender wound.

Should she admit that, yes, she'd been tempted? Should she admit it was something she thought about a lot at night and then dismissed during the day when she worked alongside her mother, who had been there for her through thick and thin? How could she ever explain the aching sense of responsibility she felt? It was an anchor, keeping her trapped in the same place. She was grateful for that anchor, but sometimes she wanted to tear it loose and set sail. There were big, beautiful mountains out there just waiting for her. A whole world of adventure.

During the day, she smiled at customers, cooked and made a perfect cappuccino, but at night in the privacy of her loft, she studied difficult peaks, ice and rock walls, planned routes, watched endless videos on the internet, until she felt as if she'd climbed those challenging faces herself.

"This is my home. My family is here and my job is here. Goodbye, Luke, and thanks for today." *Thanks for stirring up thoughts I didn't want to have.* "Rick will give you a ride back to Glensay Lodge." She started the engine. "Don't you have words to write?"

"Yes, but generally I need thawed hands for that."

"I put fresh logs in the barn this morning before I left for the training session. I presume you know how to light a fire?" It wasn't a serious question. Luke Whittaker had written a book on wilderness survival, and even had she not had that volume on her bookcase, she would have known he was the sort of man who could survive in the harshest of conditions, the sort of man who could produce a spark from two sticks before you could say *flame.*

"You could come and light my fire for me."

"That is the cheesiest line I've ever heard. I hope you're better at lighting fires than you are at picking up women or you're about to suffer from a nasty case of frostbite."

She put her foot to the floor and the last thing she saw before she drove away was the smile on his face.

Winter days in the Scottish Highlands were often gray and gloomy, but today was a perfect blue-sky day. The landscape was shrouded in white, smooth and undisturbed, like icing on a Christmas cake. The surface caught the sun and sparkled like a million crystals.

Why would she even think of leaving this beautiful place,

filled with people who loved and cared about her? Being here wasn't a sacrifice, it was a choice. She'd been four years old when Suzanne and Stewart had packed up their lives and moved from their home in Washington State to Scotland to be close to Stewart's family.

Unlike her sisters, Posy had no memory of it.

She drove past the Parish Church and waved to Celia Monroe, who was emerging from an appointment with the doctor.

On impulse, she screeched to a halt outside the small library and grabbed the bag from the back seat.

This was a job she'd been putting off for weeks.

"I'm going to be told off like a six-year-old," she confessed, and Bonnie wagged her tail in sympathy.

Bracing herself, Posy strode into the library. It had been threatened with closure many times, but the locals had defended it as fiercely as a clan defending their lands.

The woman behind the desk clucked her disapproval. "You have a nerve showing up here, Posy McBride. Your books are more than a month overdue."

Posy leaned across and kissed her. "I was stuck up a mountain, saving lives, Mrs. Dannon."

"Oh, go on with you. You were the same with your homework. Always late, and always an excuse." Eugenia Dannon had been her English teacher at school and she'd despaired of Posy, who had spent her days gazing out of the window at the mountains.

"I probably owe you a lot of money in fines."

The woman waved her away. "If I fined you every time your books were late, you'd be bankrupt."

"I love you, Mrs. Dannon, and I know that deep down you love me."

"Aye, more fool me. Now run along and help your mother."

Run along? Did people actually still say that kind of thing?

Posy grinned. In Glensay they did, even when you were almost thirty.

"Next time you're in the café, I'll give you an extra-large slice of chocolate brownie." She was halfway to the door when Mrs. Dannon's voice stopped her.

"Did you read any of the books?"

"Every one of them. Cover to cover." Grinning, she jogged out of the library.

She hadn't read the books, and Mrs. Dannon knew it. Posy was willing to bet that half the people from the village who used the library didn't read the books. But taking books out meant that Eugenia Dannon kept her job, and since her husband had died two years before, she needed both the money and the companionship the library offered. Everyone in the village had suddenly developed a serious reading habit.

When the officials looked at the statistics, they probably marveled at how well-read the people who lived in Glensay were.

Posy knew for a fact that Ted Morton used the complete works of Shakespeare to stop his kitchen door blowing shut on windy days.

Still smiling, she popped into the small store next to the library. Glensay had one general store that sold all the essentials.

"Hi, Posy." The girl behind the counter smiled at her. "Your lodger was in here yesterday. He bought a packet of razors and deodorant."

"Right." Posy grabbed toothpaste and soap and dumped them on the counter. She'd often wondered if Amy and her mother kept a list of what people bought, and used it for profiling. "Maybe he's going to help me shear the sheep."

"Really?"

"No, not really. I was joking." She'd been at school with

Amy and the other girl hadn't got her jokes then, either. Obviously she didn't have a future in comedy. "Ignore me."

"Personally, I like a man with stubble." Amy rang up Posy's purchases. "He's sexy. You're lucky having him living with you."

"He's not living *with* me, Amy. He's in a different part of the building. Separate properties. There's a floor and a door between us." It seemed important to clarify that, given Amy's tendency to draw interesting conclusions and then broadcast them widely.

"Still—it could be romantic."

It could be, but if it was, then Amy wasn't going to find out about it.

Trying to work out a way of keeping her private life private, Posy stuffed the toothpaste and soap into her pockets. "Thanks, Amy. Have a good one."

She paused outside the door to read the noticeboards. They provided a fascinating snapshot into the life of the village. Pets lost and found, a tractor for sale, minutes of two local meetings and a plea for new members of the village choir. Posy loved to sing. She might have joined the choir had people not told her that her voice sounded like a cat being tortured. Her family encouraged her to find other ways to express her happiness, so these days she sang in the bath and sang to her dog, who often howled in perfect harmony.

Seeing a minibus approaching from the distance, Posy hurried back to her car.

The older members of the community who couldn't get to the village store by other means used the minibus service. Posy tried to avoid its arrival whenever possible because greeting everyone took half a day.

Five minutes later she hurtled through the door into the welcoming warmth of Café Craft. She ripped off her coat as she half ran to the counter where her mother was deep in conversation with two women from the village. Christmas music played softly from the speakers and the fairy lights that she and her father had secured around the windows shone like tiny stars. The exposed brickwork of the walls was partially covered in paintings by local artists. Posy rotated them regularly. This month she had selected those with winter themes.

As well as art, they sold pottery made locally, knitwear produced exclusively for them, locally made heather honey and a variety of crafts hand selected by her mother, who had a keen eye for what would sell.

"Sorry I'm late."

"Not a problem." Her mother's cheeks were flushed from the heat of the kitchen and she looked at least a decade younger than her fifty-eight years. "How did it go?"

"Brilliant. Bonnie was a champ."

Posy was about to provide details but stopped herself. She knew her mother wouldn't want details. There was an unspoken agreement in their family that anything to do with snow and avalanches weren't to be mentioned.

She knew from her father that her mother had experienced another one of her nightmares a few nights before.

She wished she could help wipe out those nightmares, but she had no idea how. She didn't really understand how someone could still have bad dreams twenty-five years after an event, no matter how terrible it had been.

She darted into the small office, wincing as she saw the growing stack of paper on the small desk. Paperwork, Posy thought, was the waste of a life. Someone needed to sort through it, or they'd miss something important, but it wasn't going to be her.

She ripped off her outer layers until she exposed the blue

T-shirt emblazoned with the Café Craft logo. Then she swapped weatherproof trousers for jeans and her trainers.

If she was going to be on her feet all day, there was no way she was wearing heels.

She slipped a clean apron over her head, tied it around her waist and emerged into the cinnamon-scented warmth of the café.

Her mother had an almost-magical ability to create a welcoming, cozy atmosphere wherever she went. In Café Craft you felt as if you were cocooned and protected, not only from the icy Highland winds, but from the icy winds of life. Reality was forced to wait outside the door until you were ready to let it in.

"Let me just finish this order and you can tell me all about Bonnie. Two cappuccinos and a chocolate brownie to share—" Suzanne turned to the machine, a look of determination on her face, and Posy nudged her aside.

"I've got this."

"Could you deal with the paperwork later if it's quiet?"

Posy hunted desperately for excuses. "You're better at it than I am."

"Which is why I think you should do it," Suzanne said. "This place will be yours one day and you need to know everything there is to know about running it."

Oh joy and bliss.

A lifetime of paperwork stretched ahead of her.

"Plenty of time for that. You won't be retiring for ages." *Please don't retire.* "I took a slab of your fruitcake to the team this morning. They almost bit off my hand to get to it. You'd think those guys never eat."

Pushing the thought of running the café to the back of her head, she ground the beans, tamped the coffee and timed the pour. The aroma of fresh coffee wafted upward and she had to fight the impulse to drink the first cup herself. There was nothing, she decided, nothing in the world better than good coffee when you'd been out in the cold and the snow.

She heated the milk and created a leaf pattern on the surface of the coffee that satisfied her artistic instincts.

"Take a seat, Jean," she called out. "I'll bring these to your table."

The café was already filling up. There was a comforting hum of conversation, a feeling of camaraderie and inclusiveness. In the summer the place was always packed with tourists eager to soak up the whole "Scottish experience," which they generally assumed to be tartan and shortbread. If they'd returned in the winter months, they would have experienced the true Scottish experience. This was a community that supported all its members through the harsh winter months. Everyone knew each other and looked out for each other.

As the last village in the valley, Glensay was sometimes cut off in the winter. For decades the Glensay Inn had been the only place to eat out, and it had been Stewart's parents who had come up with the idea for a café. Suzanne had eventually taken over the business, and she was the one who had expanded the space and added crafts. As well as a place to sell the pieces she and her friends knitted, it was somewhere for the locals to meet on cold winter days.

Suzanne had created a place that people wrote about when they arrived home. As a result they had visitors from all over the globe. But the beating heart of Café Craft were the locals.

Three evenings a week Suzanne opened up for different groups, as a way to combat the dark nights. Monday was Book Group, Wednesday was Art Club and Friday was Knitting Club.

Posy wondered how she was going to keep that part going when she eventually took over. Despite her frequent trips to the library, she never had time to read, the only thing she'd ever painted was the henhouse and she couldn't knit.

She'd be qualified to run an Outdoors Club, but there wouldn't be much point in holding that indoors.

Posy glanced at her mother, noticing the blue sweater for the first time. The wool had a hint of silver that sparkled under the lights. "That's pretty. New?"

"Finished it last night. I should probably be wearing one of our shirts, but I figured as I'm the boss, I can wear what I like."

"It looks good on you."

"I'm knitting a few to sell in the café. I had another box of yarn delivered yesterday. I can't wait to get started, but I have those Christmas stockings to knit first. Anytime you'd like me to teach you—"

"No, thanks. I'm scared of needles, and that includes knitting needles."

All but two tables were occupied, and Posy knew that by the time they closed at five, her legs would be aching more than they did when she went ice climbing.

She put the cups on a tray and added a slice of perfect gooey brownie, so deliciously chocolaty that it probably should have come with a health warning. Posy had to employ every last morsel of willpower to carry it to the table and not eat it herself.

"Here you go, ladies."

Jean took one of the coffees. "You were out training with the team this morning?"

"Yes. We've had people from the Canadian mountain rescue team giving us avalanche training." Posy tucked the empty tray under her arm. "The whole community will be pleased to hear that we didn't disgrace ourselves."

"I hear your long-term tenant volunteered to be a body."

"He did, and Bonnie had no trouble finding him." Posy didn't bother asking where she'd heard it. Jean was married to the leader of the mountain rescue team, but even if she hadn't been, the gossip still would have spread. It was the reason Posy was reluctant to have a relationship with anyone locally. She'd done that once, and it had been a disaster. She and Callum were back on speaking terms now, but for years they'd done nothing but glare whenever they'd passed each other, which in a village the size of Glensay was often.

"I wouldn't have had a hard time finding him, either. There are some folks I'd happily leave under the snow, but that man isn't one of them. I'd dig him out with my bare hands." Moira gave a laugh and Posy smiled as she cleared plates from an unoccupied table nearby.

"Moira Dodds, that is the dirtiest laugh I have ever heard. Shame on you."

Moira sliced into the brownie. "All your girls will be home for Christmas this year, Suzanne?"

"That's right." Suzanne wrote a label for the St. Clement's cake she'd baked that morning. "It's great Hannah is able to make it."

Great that her sister had found time in her busy life to finally remember she had a family.

Posy realized she was grinding her teeth and made a conscious effort to relax her jaw. If she ground her teeth every time she thought of her sister, she'd be reduced to chewing her Christmas lunch with her gums.

Jean beamed at Posy. "I bet you can't wait to see your big sister again."

Posy beamed back, although it took some effort.

She knew that by the end of it she'd want to drive her sister to the airport early.

Beth would come bearing gifts and goodwill. She'd willingly help with everything and anything.

Hannah would bring emotional turmoil.

Memories of Christmas past grew in Posy's mind.

There had been the year Hannah had barely left her room except to eat a Christmas lunch that other people had prepared. And the year she'd spent most of the time in the café, not helping as Beth had done, but availing herself of the free Wi-Fi, which was unreliable in the lodge.

Posy didn't really understand what it was her sister did. The conversations she'd overheard might as well have been conducted in a foreign language. She knew nothing about strategy, economics or five-year plans, but evidently her sister did and people were prepared to pay a great deal for her expertise.

Posy found Hannah a little intimidating, but the root of the problem was that her sister hurt her feelings. Posy was naturally affectionate and Hannah was distant with her.

Jean and Moira went back to their coffee and chat, and Posy strode into the small kitchen and started making up lunch items with Duncan, their chef.

"Today is curried parsnip and winter vegetable." Duncan pointed to the board and she nodded.

"Got it." Every day in the café they offered two soups, and they changed daily so that regular visitors didn't end up eating the same thing.

Posy loved chopping vegetables. There was nothing like attacking something with a sharp knife to let off aggression.

Damn Hannah, she thought as she slaughtered a helpless onion. This year she wasn't going to let herself be upset. She wasn't going to be sensitive.

The parsnips suffered the same fate as the onion, as did the potatoes.

Duncan glanced across at her. "Promise me if I ever annoy you, you'll tell me before you reach for the knife."

"You have my word on it." She'd been Duncan's babysitter when she was a teenager, so seeing him working in the kitchen always made her feel old.

Her life was slipping through her fingers. At this rate she'd still be here when she was ninety, taking the minibus to the store.

With a sigh, she dropped the vegetables into the pot.

She would rather have been climbing a rock face than cooking, but her work as a mountain guide was sporadic, and working in the café brought in an income, as well as helping her mother. It was a family business, and family was everything to Posy. It was a warm blanket on a cold day, a safety net when you fell, a chorus of support when you attempted something hard.

The vegetables and spices were simmering when Suzanne walked into the kitchen.

"I've written today's specials on the board." She gave the soups a stir. "You should have brought Luke to the café for a bowl of hot soup, poor man."

"There's nothing 'poor' about him." Posy rinsed tomatoes. "He has a log burner, a stocked freezer and the facility to heat up his own bowl of soup if that's what he wants." And apart from that, her feelings about him were complicated.

Still, Luke's presence here was temporary, so if something did happen, at least she didn't have to worry that she'd be bumping into him for the rest of her life.

Posy chopped herbs and sliced tomatoes while her mother helped Duncan with the leek and ham pies.

Suzanne rolled out pastry. "You and Luke seem to be getting along fine."

Posy threw herbs on the tomato salad. She knew what her mother was asking, and the one thing she had in common with Hannah was that she wasn't prepared to discuss her love life with her mother. "He's paying us good money to rent the barn. I make sure I stay on good terms with him."

And yes, she liked him.

Take this morning. How many men would volunteer to lie buried in snow while patiently waiting for a dog to find them? And he loved mountains, which made him interesting as far as she was concerned.

Right now, he was writing a book on the great climbs of North America.

Posy had never climbed in North America.

Once, when she'd been doing her weekly clean and bedding change in the barn, Luke had come back early and she'd asked him to tell her about Mount Rainier.

"Why do you want to know?"

She wasn't ready to tell him that. "It's going in your book?"

"Rainier? Yes." He opened his laptop and hit a couple of keys.

An image appeared on the screen of a white snowcapped mountain.

She'd seen the same, or similar, before of course, but somehow the fact that it came from his own photo collection made it more real.

She stepped closer, studying the heavily glaciated faces of the mountain. She had so many questions, but she knew he wouldn't be able to answer any of them. "You've climbed it?" Her voice didn't sound like her own.

"Many times."

"And it's a volcano. Dormant, though."

"We call it episodically active." He saw her surprised glance. "I worked for the US Geological Survey after I graduated. Lived just outside Seattle. I could see Rainier from my bedroom window."

She'd almost confided in him then, but something stopped

her. She didn't want to risk him raising it with Suzanne. "Which route did you climb?"

"I've climbed all of them, at different times of the year. In the summer you have wildflower meadows. In the winter you find yourself waist deep in snow. You've never climbed in the US?"

"No. Scotland, and the Alps."

"You should come to the US."

One day, she thought, although she wasn't sure she was ready for Mount Rainier. Maybe she never would be. Going there would upset her mother.

Posy thought back to that conversation as she made large bowls of salad.

"Hannah emailed me last night," Suzanne said. "She sent a list of the foods she is avoiding at the moment."

Posy focused on the salad. If she rolled her eyes, there was every chance they'd be stuck in her skull never to emerge again.

"Right. Well, you'd better forward that email to me so I can adjust my list. What was it she asked for last time? Quail eggs? I found that deli in Edinburgh that did mail order." And used half the Christmas budget in the process. "If I'd thought about it, I would have explored the possibility of keeping quails."

"I read somewhere they get easily stressed."

"And that's *before* they meet Hannah." Posy caught her mother's eye and swiftly changed the subject. "Talking of our feathered friends, Martha has stopped laying."

"It's December." Suzanne trimmed the pastry with a knife. "Not enough light."

"I'm using artificial light. I don't think it's that." Maybe Martha knew Hannah was coming home. Maybe she didn't see the point of laying whole eggs when Hannah ate only the egg white. "I need to give Gareth a call. With a houseful of people, we're going to need eggs. Normal eggs," she added. *Normal eggs for normal people.*

Her mother wiped her hands. "I wish you and Hannah were closer."

"Me, too." That part wasn't a lie. "But she lives so far away."

That, of course, was only part of the problem.

If her sister had been a laptop, Posy would have run antivirus software because there were times when she was convinced Hannah had been taken over by malware.

Posy considered herself to be tough and hated the fact that her feelings could still be hurt.

Fortunately, she wouldn't have to handle Hannah alone. Beth, Jason and the girls would be there, too.

Posy and Beth were still close.

There was no drama in Beth's life.

5

Beth

Beth had settled the girls in bed and was clearing toys out of the bath when Jason arrived home. This was her favorite time of day, when the chaos was almost behind her and the prospect of a calm evening stretched ahead. Sometimes she poured herself a glass of wine and allowed herself to read a few pages of a magazine before she started on dinner.

Tonight, she was too excited to contemplate reading anything, but she knew she had to at least let Jason take his coat off before she told him her news.

As she scooped up wet towels, Beth could hear him talking on the phone.

"We nailed it. They loved the ideas. I'm going to talk to Steve in the morning and get those figures sent over. The

London office is closed now, but I'll call first thing tomorrow. I'll be in the office at six."

Beth turned off the light. Six would mean a 5:00 a.m.
alarm call, which also meant that if the girls disturbed her in
the night, which Ruby did with frustrating frequency, Beth
would be woken again predawn by her husband.

Trying not to think about her sister flying first-class with
her own cubicle and champagne on tap, Beth dealt with the
towels and then walked to the living room, where Jason was
ending the call.

Soft light bathed the room in a warm glow. She'd cleared
away all traces of the toys, tutus and tiaras that had been
strewn around the room a few hours earlier. The glossy fashion magazines that were her indulgence were neatly stacked
on the table. A vase of lilies added an illusion of elegance only
slightly marred by the two Lego bricks peeping out from
under the sofa.

Beth loved flowers. She loved their fragility, their femi-
ninity. She loved the way they transformed a room and lifted
her mood. She associated them with happiness, and she associated them with Jason.

At the beginning of their relationship, he'd bought her
flowers every week. Once they'd had the girls and money was
tighter, it had happened less often, and the occasions when
he'd splurged and brought home a bunch of blooms had been
all the more special.

For this brief moment in time the apartment seemed like a
child-free zone, an adult-only space, where the conversation of
the occupants might revolve round current affairs, travel and
Manhattan restaurant experiences rather than debates about
whether the next game should be "ballerina" or "firefighter."
A tidy apartment gave Beth the fleeting sense that she was in
control, even when she knew she wasn't. When it came to the

kids' mess, there were many days when she felt as if she was bailing water out of a sinking boat.

Jason ended the call and smiled at her, his face transforming from serious to sexy.

Today he wore a bespoke suit with a black shirt open at the neck. She noticed absently that his hair needed a cut.

They joked together that as Creative Director of the agency his appreciation for design started with himself. *This is a creative business, honey, and before I pitch for a brand, I have to pitch myself.*

They'd met when Jason had been working on an ad campaign for one of the beauty brands she'd also worked on.

Jason's star had continued to climb, whereas hers had fallen to earth so hard she was still stepping over the broken fragments.

For a moment she saw the businessman rather than her husband.

This, she thought, was how the people at work saw him. They didn't see him sprawled with the Sunday papers and a severe case of bedhead. They saw the dynamic creative director of a top Manhattan multimedia agency.

Jason had done well. His boss liked him and he was due another promotion and a fat salary increase.

Beth would have forfeited the extra money to have him home more. It wasn't only that she would have loved more family time, it was that somewhere along the way she'd lost the feeling they were a partnership, but she was about to address that.

She'd thought all afternoon about the best way to handle the conversation but in the end decided to be straight.

Jason pulled her toward him and kissed her. "How was your day?"

Beth wrapped her arms round his neck. She liked the fact that Jason was only a few inches taller than she was. They fitted perfectly.

"Hannah has canceled tomorrow. Business trip."

"Does that mean I don't have to rush home from work for an early dinner?" He let go of her and took off his jacket. "What's wrong? Has she upset you? This is Hannah, remember? Her canceling is not exactly a surprise, is it?"

It wasn't a surprise, but that didn't mean she wasn't disappointed.

She was about to tell him how she felt when there was a chorus of girlish screams followed by the muted thunder of bare feet as the girls pounded out of their bedroom.

"Daddy, Daddy." They were so excited it was hard to be annoyed, even though she knew she'd have to settle them again and that meant another hour at least before she could have the conversation she was desperate to have.

"Whoa." Jason caught Ruby and swung her up high until she squealed. "How's my girl?"

"Mommy bought me a new fire engine."

"She did? Another one? So I guess that means you have a whole fleet now." His gaze snagged Beth's and she felt herself blush.

Ruby squeezed him tightly. "I want to be a firefighter."

"You will be a *fantastic* firefighter. No fire will dare to burn with you nearby."

"Will you play with me? Can I save you from a burning building?"

"Not now because you're supposed to be asleep. Maybe tomorrow."

Melly pressed close to his leg, more reserved than her sister. He set Ruby down and scooped her up. "How's my other girl?"

Melly laid her head on his shoulder. "Ruby is always telling me what to do."

Jason laughed. "She has great leadership qualities, don't you, Ruby? And so do you."

"I don't like shouting."

"Leadership has nothing to do with shouting, honey." He stroked her hair. "One day you are going to have a very important job and *everyone* is going to listen to you. You won't need to shout."

Beth loved the fact that he never favored one child over the other. She loved the way he was with the girls, even though she knew he got the good parts. If parenting was a meal, then Jason came straight in at dessert, bypassing all other courses including vegetables. He skipped the tantrums, the food fights and the relentless arguments. He also escaped the unique brand of loneliness that came from being at home with young children. Not that she was *alone*, of course. With two young children, she was rarely alone, but that didn't stop her feeling lonely. She'd discovered it was an impossible concept to explain to people who weren't in the same situation.

"If you want to put them back to bed, I'll finish off dinner."

"Daddy, will you read us a story?"

"Yes." Jason caught Beth's eye. "Why are you looking at me like that? What have I done?"

"I've already read them two stories and settled them down. They need sleep." Also, Beth had been with them all day and she was ready to sit down with a glass of wine. She felt brain dead, which made no sense because these days her brain didn't get much of a workout.

Jason frowned. "One story won't hurt, surely? I haven't seen them all day."

Three pairs of eyes watched her hopefully. She knew she should say no.

"They need routine, Jason."

"I know, but just this once." He leaned across and kissed

her, which basically meant she no longer had any say in it, then held out his arms to the girls and carried them back to bed.

Ruby's voice carried from the bedroom. "Daddy, can I sleep with my new fire engine?"

Beth walked to the kitchen and checked the casserole.

She stirred, adjusted the seasoning, breathing in the cinnamon and spice scent of the warming winter dish. It was one of her mother's recipes and it reminded her of home.

She loved this time of year. She found the lead-up to the holiday season almost as seductive as the holiday itself. She loved gazing into brightly lit store windows, enjoyed ice-skating in Central Park and their annual trip to the Christmas tree lighting at the Rockefeller Center. The previous year they'd taken the girls to see the New York City Ballet perform *The Nutcracker*. For once, Ruby had stopped wriggling, hypnotized by the dancers whirling round the stage. Melly had been enchanted, utterly lost in the world of Sugar Plum Fairies and glistening snowflakes, all her princess fantasies coming true to Tchaikovsky's romantic score.

Even Jason, who had previously declared he'd rather stand in Times Square buck naked than go to the ballet, had admitted the evening had been magical. What he was really saying, of course, was that watching the faces of his children had been magical.

I love these moments, he'd said as they'd walked along snow-dusted streets to a small bistro with fogged windows and fairy lights that had been bathed in so much festive atmosphere Ruby asked if Santa would be arriving soon.

Beth loved those moments, too, but the difference was that Jason *only* had those moments.

He had the bathed, excited, scrubbed, fantasy version of parenthood.

She had the reality.

Was it wrong of her to want more?

By the time Jason joined her, she had laid the table and warmed the plates.

"They're growing up fast." He'd taken a quick shower and changed out of his suit. Dressed in jeans and a black sweater, he looked younger. Less the ambitious creative, and more the man she'd married. "Something smells good. What are we having?"

"Lamb. I was going to cook it for Hannah tomorrow, but since she isn't coming—" She shrugged and picked up one of the plates.

"Hannah's loss is my gain."

Beth spooned rice onto a plate, added a generous portion of casserole and passed it to him. She didn't want to think about Hannah.

"How was your day? How was the pitch?" She held on to her own news, wanting to pick exactly the right moment.

"It was good." He waited for her to serve herself and then picked up his fork. "Sam called me into his office today."

Sam was Jason's boss. "What did he want?"

"Conrad Bennett is leaving."

"Leaving?" Beth toyed with her food. It wasn't that she wasn't interested in his office gossip, but all she could think about was the phone call she'd had earlier. "But he's Chief Creative Director. Why would he leave?"

"He's setting up his own agency, and you know what that means—"

"He's taking you with him?"

"No. Better than that." Jason picked up his wine and raised the glass in a toast. "I'm being offered his job."

Beth gave a squeal. "You got a promotion?" She ignored the little voice in her head shouting out that this conversation was supposed to be about her career, not Jason's.

"In the last year I've brought in more clients than any other member of the agency."

She wondered what the promotion would mean for her and felt guilty for being selfish. "Chief Creative Director. I'm proud of you." And she was. Was it wrong that she was also a teeny bit jealous?

There was a gleam of excitement in his eyes. "Yes. It's the best Christmas gift. And talking of Christmas gifts, tell me what you'd like and it's yours. New dress? Coat? Sexy boots? Think about it and write a letter to Santa."

I'd like to go back to work.

She'd counted on Jason adapting his schedule to finish work early a couple of days a week. She'd counted on him being there for the girls. It was as if he had mapped out his future and forgotten her.

"It was a shock, although a good shock, obviously—" he dug his fork in the rice "—but it got me thinking about you. About us, and our future."

The vague feeling of resentment floated away, leaving warmth in its place.

"I've been thinking about us, too." She took a mouthful of wine. "There's something I need to say to you, and I'd like you to hear me out before you speak. We talked about it a while ago, but not recently." Nerves fluttered in her stomach. She had no idea what his reaction was going to be.

"Stop." Jason reached out and covered her hand with his. "I know what you're about to say."

"You do?"

"Yes. It didn't seem worth mentioning again when the girls were little and such a handful, but they're older now and you have more time on your hands."

It hadn't occurred to her that this might be easy. "You've been thinking about it, too?"

"It's perfect timing for our family." He went back to his food. "This is delicious, by the way. You're a great cook, Beth. In fact, you're great at pretty much everything."

Did he realize exactly what it would entail? "If we did this, I'd be under a lot more pressure. I thought perhaps your mother might help out. And you'd have to help more. You wouldn't mind?"

"We're a team, Beth. And of course my mother will help. Try keeping her away. She'll be as excited as I am." He helped himself to more rice. "The timing of these things is never perfect, but this is about as perfect as it gets. We should go for it."

She felt a rush of elation.

She should have talked to him sooner. She should have mentioned how lonely she was, and how she'd felt her skills and confidence slowly draining away. She was touched that he'd noticed she needed more. "How would this fit with your promotion?"

"Sam knows the score. I'm a father. Sometimes I need to be there for my family. I can juggle work and home. I've been doing it for years. It's one of the reasons I wouldn't leave the company. It has a great culture."

Was *juggling* the right word? She knew that for her to work, too, they were going to need to display more juggling skills than a circus performer.

"It's going to be a big change for us as a family, but I know we can make this work. I'm excited."

"Me, too. I love you, baby."

"I love you, too." Tears stung her eyes. She was so very lucky to be married to him. "Do you think the girls will be okay with it? I feel guilty." She was desperate for reassurance that she wasn't a bad mother. "I'm worried they'll think they're not enough."

"It will be great for the girls. So they'll have a little less of you…" He reached for his wine and shrugged. "Quality, not quantity, right?"

Beth shifted in her seat.

Did the girls have quality?

There were days when she felt the best she achieved was to hold it all together, but right now she was feeling too euphoric to indulge in a session of maternal self-flagellation.

Jason stood up and cleared the plates, and she followed him into the kitchen and fetched dessert.

Was it too late to call Kelly back tonight?

"I need to arrange a time to go and meet them. Is there a day this week that you could work from home?"

He piled the plates onto the countertop above the dishwasher. "Meet who?"

"The team." Beth carried dessert to the table. Instead of the frothy, extravagant offering she'd planned for Hannah, she'd baked plums in rum and brown sugar. Normally she was careful with dessert, but she'd managed to convince herself this was fruit.

"You want to see someone before you're even pregnant?" Jason sat down again. "Is that usual?"

Beth stared at him. "What?"

Jason spooned plums into the deep-sided white bowls that had been a gift from his mother the previous Christmas. "I guess it never hurts to have a doctor check you out. You do look pretty tired. Maybe you're anemic. But if you're seeing someone, I want to come with you. I want to be there for you." He pushed the plums toward her. "Aren't you having any? Or are you already off alcohol?"

Beth felt as if she'd stepped off a cliff. Her stomach swooped and her head spun. "Pregnant? What are you talking about?"

Jason froze, the spoon in his hand suspended in midair. "Having another baby. What were *you* talking about?"

"Work." Her throat was dry. The situation should have been comical, but she'd never felt less like laughing. Another *baby*? The thought of it made her heart pound with panic.

There was a long, loaded silence. *"Work?"*

Beth sat down hard on the chair. "Yes. That's what I wanted to talk to you about. That's what I thought I *was* talking to you about."

The spoon clattered back into the serving dish, spattering juice and rum. Neither noticed. "I thought you were talking about growing our family. Having more kids."

"Jason, the *last* thing I want is more kids. How could you even think that would be a good idea?" She was almost hyperventilating and Jason looked as stunned as she felt, although for different reasons apparently.

"But we adore the girls." He sounded bemused.

"Of course we do. I'm not saying I don't love the children. I'm saying I can't handle more."

"Don't underestimate yourself. You're incredible. I mean, look at this—" He waved his hand in the general direction of the table and the kitchen. "You've been with them all day and you still manage to produce this. You're a superstar."

"Let me rephrase, Jason—I don't *want* to handle more. At least, not more parenting. I want to go back to work. I want more from life than domestic grind."

The warmth in his eyes was replaced by hurt. "I didn't realize the girls and I came under the heading of 'domestic grind.'"

How had this conversation gone downhill so fast?

It was like watching a spool of thread unravel, knowing there was nothing she could do to stop it.

"It's tough being at home with kids all the time, Jason."

"I know you work hard." His jaw was set. Rigid. The way it always was when they had difficult conversations. "We both work hard."

"This isn't a competition. It's not about agreeing who works hardest. The difference is that you're doing what you love, while I'm losing every skill I ever had."

He stood up so suddenly the chair crashed to the floor.

Beth was on her feet in an instant. "You'll wake the girls and it will take ages to settle them again."

"And that would be bad, wouldn't it," he said, "because you've had enough of them for one day?"

The injustice of his words stung. She knew she wasn't doing a good job of explaining how she felt, but she also knew he wasn't really listening. He was thinking about his own feelings, not hers. "I love the girls, and you know it."

"We talked about having three kids. Maybe even four."

"That was before we had any. I didn't realize how much of me they'd consume."

"Consume? You make them sound like monsters."

"No! I—" How could she make him understand? No matter how many different ways she phrased it, he didn't seem to hear her. Or maybe he didn't want to hear her. He didn't want his world overturned. "I love being with them, but I've been with them every day for the past seven years, and now I'm ready for something more. I can't just be an adjunct to everyone else in the family."

Jason lifted the chair and sat down again. "You said it was what you wanted."

"When I was first pregnant, yes." She thought about Melly's first steps and the first time Ruby had smiled at her. "I wouldn't have missed it for anything. I know I'm lucky to have been able to be at home in the early years, but things change."

"Family has always been the number one priority for you." He rubbed his fingers over his forehead. "You were so young when you lost your own parents—"

"I don't want to talk about that."

"I know. No one in your family talks about it, but it's relevant, Beth!"

"Something that happened twenty-five years ago has no relevance to my life today." She tried not to think about the message she'd deleted from her phone. Had Hannah had the same phone call? She could have asked, but there was no way she'd broach that topic with her sister. Neither Hannah nor Suzanne liked to talk about the accident and Beth understood that.

She'd taken a look at news clippings from that time and had felt as if she was living the trauma firsthand.

There had been a particularly distressing one of Suzanne being hounded by the press.

It had disturbed Beth so badly she'd never looked at it again.

No doubt Hannah had her own memories about that time, but when it came to removing things from her past that she didn't like, Hannah was like a surgeon with a scalpel. She cut it out and sutured the wound.

Beth buried it and put up with the occasional ache, but she'd been younger than Hannah.

"I'm boring, Jason. I'm a boring person. Last time I saw my sister she was talking about flying here, there and everywhere—what did I contribute to the conversation?"

"Wait… This is because of Hannah? What has she been saying to you?"

"Nothing." Beth sat down again. "This has nothing to do with Hannah."

"If she's made you feel inferior, then—"

"She hasn't made me feel inferior. I manage that all by myself."

"You want Hannah's life?" A muscle flickered in his cheek. "You want her child-free, commitment-free life? A life, by the way, which you've previously said looks cold and lonely."

"I do not want her life." Although it was true that there were parts of Hannah's life she'd like—the first-class flights and the interaction with adults, the fact that she was respected by her peers and could come and go without once thinking about babysitters.

But she didn't envy the isolation of Hannah's life.

Hannah had closed herself off. She didn't want intimate connections.

She hadn't always been that way, of course.

Once, she, Beth and Posy had been close. They'd been so close that their mother hadn't bothered to invite friends over for them because the three of them occupied each other.

It was so long ago Beth could hardly remember those days. Occasionally her mind drifted there and along with the thoughts came memories of warmth and laughter, of games played, of inconsequential fights and making up. Childhood.

She felt a stab of guilt that she'd snapped at her sister earlier.

As soon as Hannah was back from her trip, Beth would call and make amends. She'd buy a gift for their mother from both of them. She'd meet in a restaurant, or wherever Hannah preferred to meet. Beth didn't want to lose what little connection she had with her sister. Family counted.

But now wasn't the time to be worrying about her sister. She had worries enough of her own.

"I was an only child," Jason said. "And I never wanted that for our kids."

"Which was why we had Ruby."

She'd always known how badly Jason wanted children. The moment Melly started sleeping through the night, he'd raised the idea of having another one. He'd been determined that Melly was going to have someone to play with, and turn to later in life.

Having experienced ups and downs with Hannah, Beth

wasn't sure that a sibling came with a guarantee of support and friendship, but she also wanted more than one child, so she'd tried to put aside the memory of her traumatic birth—first deliveries were often the worst, weren't they?—and by the time Melly was three, she'd been pregnant again.

Ruby had been delivered eight weeks early as a medical emergency, and the flurry of drama and high anxiety had convinced Beth that two was enough. Given that Jason hadn't raised the topic of having more, she assumed he'd agreed.

She wasn't good at having babies, and it wasn't exactly something you could perfect with practice. The mere thought of going through it again filled her with dread.

"I can feel my confidence draining away, Jason. If I don't go back to work soon, I'll be unemployable."

Maybe she already was. She wondered how hard it would be to morph back into work mode. Could she project confidence if she didn't feel it? What if she wasn't even offered the job? Was she emotionally robust enough to take rejection? "I want this and it's a good time to do it. Melly is in first grade now and Ruby is in preschool three mornings a week."

"But you take them and pick them up. You do activities with them. Who would do that?"

They'd reached the "juggling" part. "I thought maybe you could leave early a couple of days a week and I thought Alison might help."

"I'm sure my mother would help, but I have a job. It makes no economic sense for me to give that up so that you can go back to work."

"I'm not asking you to give it up. Maybe compromise a little. This isn't about economics, it's about my sanity. I've lost *me*, Jason. I have no idea who I am anymore. And I'm lonely."

"You're always complaining you never have five minutes to yourself. That you can't even use the bathroom without Melly banging on the door or Ruby getting into trouble. You have the girls. How can you possibly be lonely?"

She felt a rush of despair followed by another emotion she didn't recognize.

"I want to meet them, Jason. I want to find out more about the job."

"Who is 'them'? You haven't given me the details."

She took a deep breath. "Corinna has set up her own company."

"Corinna?" The word exploded out of him. "This is the same Corinna who made your life a misery when you worked for her before?"

"She didn't make my life a misery."

"No? You were sick with stress. She fired three of the staff in the six months before you left."

"It was a busy time in the company. We were all under pressure."

"And Corinna was the source of that pressure. She used to call you up and scream at you at 3:00 a.m. There wasn't a single moment of your day that she respected as private. If you're looking for sisterhood, and women supporting other women, you're not going to find it in any company she's a part of. She's not going to cut you any slack because you have kids, Beth."

"I wouldn't want her to."

He studied her for a moment. "Fine. Go and meet them. Talk to Corinna. Let me know when and I'll cover the childcare."

She relaxed slightly. "You'd do that?"

"Yes. When you remember what Corinna is like, you'll probably decide you'd rather be at home with the girls."

He thought she wasn't going to get the job.

Even her own husband thought she no longer had anything to offer.

What did that say about him?

And what did it say about her?

It said that she had to get the job, no matter what, if only to prove that she could.

6

Suzanne

"Can you hang those lights a little higher?" Suzanne narrowed her eyes. "They're too low."

Stewart took another step up the ladder and raised the rope of stars. "Here?"

"Too high." The man was so patient, she thought. So patient.

He sighed. "Suzy—"

Maybe not so patient.

"A fraction lower." She watched as he lowered them. "Perfect. Don't you love them?"

"Fairy lights are right at the top of my Christmas list. If Santa doesn't bring at least ten sets, I'm going to break down and cry like a baby."

"Sarcasm is unattractive. On the other hand, now I know

what you want, I'll make sure Santa returns the perfect gift he bought you and buys fairy lights instead."

"Don't!" He gave her a look of wild-eyed panic. "I know you're capable of it."

"Are you going to hang those fairy lights without complaining?"

He secured the fairy lights with exaggerated care. "Have pity. I'm a man. I can't get excited about fairy lights, whatever shape they are. They come under the same heading as throw cushions. In other words, something that serves no purpose."

"You think?" Suzanne flicked the switch and the stars gleamed white. "They look good. Let's hang another set over the hearth." Creating comfort was at the heart of everything she did, from cooking good food in the café to knitting sweaters. It was as if part of her was determined to erase the cold and loneliness she'd felt in her early childhood. She'd had no one to nurture her, so she'd learned to nurture herself. She'd been afraid of the dark, but night-lights hadn't been allowed, so now she made up for it. Warm lights, soft cushions, *family*—everything she'd never had, she had now in abundance.

"Another set?" Stewart climbed back down the ladder. "How many do you have?"

"Ten. I bought them for the café, and these were left over. On the other hand, maybe candles would be better on the hearth." Suzanne folded a throw over the base of the bed and carefully added cushions. "Do *not* say anything."

Stewart looked at the cushions. "My lips are sealed, but only because I'm shallow and care about my Christmas gift."

"I asked Posy to fetch some extra logs for the basket so we can light a fire when she arrives. I don't want Hannah to be cold."

"She lives in New York. Do you have any idea how cold New York is in the winter?"

"There's a difference between Manhattan and the Scottish Highlands."

"That's why we live in the Highlands."

Suzanne straightened a lamp and surveyed the room. The curtains were the same deep green as the moss that clung to the side of the mountain in the summer. The fabric was rich and velvety and fell in a pool to the polished oak floor. They were heavy enough to keep out the cold wind that sneaked through cracks and rattled the windows in the winter months. The position of Glensay Lodge, idyllic in the summer, was exposed in the winter. For that reason, Suzanne made sure there was warmth in the furnishings. She'd made everything herself, from the curtains to the soft throw draped across the base of the bed.

She'd longed for a home of her own, and there was never a day when she wasn't grateful for it.

Stewart took it for granted, but that was because he'd always had it. She knew he was equally content sleeping on a snowy ledge, thousands of feet up a mountain.

Thanks to Cheryl, she'd experienced that, too.

The first time her friend had dragged her climbing still stuck in her mind. Would she have done it without Cheryl? Probably not. To her surprise, she'd enjoyed the crunch of snow under her boots and the icy slap of the wind against her face. It was true that she hadn't shared Cheryl's single-minded passion for it, but she'd enjoyed the physical challenge and the beauty of watching the sun rise above snowcapped mountains. Most of all she'd enjoyed the friendship and the teamwork that came with climbing.

"This is all I want from life." Cheryl lay on her back in her sleeping bag staring up at the stars. In the still of the night they could hear the glacier creak and groan. *"Not a mansion in the Hollywood Hills,*

or a swanky apartment on *Fifth Avenue*. Who wants to be trapped between four walls when you can have this? It's the best."

Suzanne was cold and wished Cheryl hadn't insisted on sleeping outside the tent. "Don't you want a family one day?"

"I suppose so." Cheryl shrugged. "I've never thought about it."

Suzanne thought about it all the time. "You can't raise a family in a sleeping bag. You'll need a home."

"No, I won't. I'll travel around. Buy a van. We can all sleep in the back, or camp out."

It sounded exhausting and insecure to Suzanne. Before she'd met Cheryl, she'd been moved between so many different foster homes it had made her dizzy. Living out of a van didn't sound any different, except perhaps colder in the winter months. "Is that fair on them?"

"Kids get used to whatever life they're living. That's their normal."

Suzanne hadn't got used to hers. "What if they're not happy doing that?"

"They will be. I'll teach them that you don't need possessions to enjoy life."

Suzanne frowned. "It's not about possessions, it's about security."

"You mean predictability."

Did she mean that? Suzanne didn't think so. "Security isn't the same as predictability. It would be nice to go out for the day and know that the things you love will be waiting for you when you get home."

"If you get attached to things, it just hurts more when you lose them. Better to let all that go. I won't need paintings for my wall because I'm going to be looking at views like this."

"How is that practical? You're going to need to make a living somehow. You still need to eat."

"I've thought about that." Cheryl sat up suddenly, as if she couldn't possibly make an important announcement while lying flat. "I'm going to be a mountain guide. That way I can do what I love and be paid for it. How cool is that?"

It was the first Suzanne had heard of that plan. "Getting the training and qualifications will cost you a fortune."

"I'll find a way." As usual, Cheryl dismissed the practicalities as nothing more than an inconvenience. "How about you? You'll go to college and study law or something. You'll have a house with a neat yard, a handsome husband, two point four polite children and a well-behaved dog."

The laughter in her voice stopped Suzanne admitting that she would have been happy with all that, except perhaps the law part. But what would her life look like without Cheryl in it? Their friendship was the most important thing in her world. "I'm going to be a mountain guide, too."

"You're kidding." Cheryl turned to look at her. "I thought you only did all this because I do it."

"I love it, too." Although until that moment she hadn't considered being a mountain guide. But why not? She had to do something with her life. "We could do the training together. Get our qualifications together."

"I'd love that." Cheryl hugged her. "We're going to be friends forever. Promise me we'll be friends forever."

"I promise."

Suzanne glanced around the room again. "I'm not sure about the rug. Do you think we should give her the sheepskin from our bedroom?"

"What I think," Stewart said, "is that you should stop." He put the lights down and held out his arms to her. "Come here."

"Why?"

"Do I need an excuse to hug my wife?" He lowered his head and kissed her and she forgot about Hannah. She was eighteen again, and in love with a man who wanted all the same things she did.

"Where do you want these?" Footsteps and the sound of Posy's voice interrupted them.

She was carrying logs under one arm and used her other hand to shield her eyes. "Whoa. Sorry. If I'd known you were occupied, I would have sung loudly to announce my arrival."

Stewart stopped kissing Suzanne. "Don't sing. I beg you don't sing."

Posy pulled a face. "Maybe the two of you should get a room. I'm way too young to witness this."

Suzanne eased out of Stewart's arms. "Put them in the basket by the fire. Thank you, honey." She watched as Posy dropped the logs into the basket. Two of her three daughters were settled and happy and she was grateful for that. Both Beth and Posy had found the life they wanted.

Posy straightened and glanced round the room. "It's pretty, Mom. I almost want to move in myself. This turret bedroom is great. I bet we could rent it out on Airbnb and make a fortune." She noticed the Christmas tree in the corner. "What's Eric doing in here?"

"Eric?" Stewart adjusted the lights. "I can just about handle you naming the chickens, the sheep and the pigs, but since when have we started naming trees?"

"Trees are living things. At least, that one is. Meet Eric, the eco tree. He comes complete with roots. I repotted and nurtured him this year and look how he's grown and flourished. Usually I put him in the barn when we have guests over Christmas."

Suzanne added a couple of books to the nightstand. Hannah had always loved books. "Will Luke want a tree? He doesn't strike me as the kind of man who needs to be surrounded by glittery trappings."

"Everyone has to have a tree at Christmas." Posy unwrapped a nut bar and took a bite.

"Which is why Hannah should have one, too. Don't drop crumbs in here. I just cleaned." Suzanne eyed her youngest daughter, thinking once again how like Stewart she was, always on the go. It occasionally surprised her when she remembered Posy wasn't his child.

But she might as well have been. Stewart was the only father she remembered.

"I was up at five and I haven't had breakfast." Posy took another large bite, catching the crumbs in her palm. "Hannah won't remember to water him. Eric will die. And I bet she won't even come to his funeral."

Suzanne knew she was supposed to smile but couldn't quite manage it.

Her stomach was in a knot. It had been two years since Hannah was home. Would it be difficult?

"I hope she doesn't miss Manhattan. It's wonderful during the holidays." She walked to the window and stared at the jagged profile of the mountains in the distance. Already they'd had more snow than usual for the time of year. How would Hannah react? Would she get cabin fever? Would log fires and home baking be enough to keep her here, or would she be wishing she'd made an excuse as she had the year before?

Behind her back, Posy exchanged worried glances with her father. "You've never been to New York at Christmas."

"Beth has told me all about it." Suzanne turned. "She takes the girls skating in Central Park."

Stewart cleared up the empty boxes. "That patch of ground in front of the henhouse often freezes over. It would work as a skating rink."

"You'd have to pick up the chicken poo first." Posy stuffed the empty wrapper into her pocket. "You think I should buy skates for Martha? She could be the world's first skating chicken. Oh, and great news. She laid this morning! I've been over there this morning giving her love and attention. Why is the desk from the study up here?"

"Because Hannah may need to work. If something important comes up, I don't want her to feel she has to leave."

"She's not the leader of the free world. I'm sure she can be spared for a few days without the economy plunging." Posy smiled. "Relax. And now I have to go."

"You're working this afternoon?"

Posy exchanged looks with her father. "I'm taking Luke ice climbing."

Suzanne felt the blood drain out of her face. The tips of her fingers tingled. "Have you checked the forecast? Leave a note of your route. Let us know what time you'll be back."

"I will leave my intended route with Dad, but you know what it's like at this time of year—things change as we go along. Please don't worry. I'm good at what I do. It's the reason they pay me."

"There's not enough money in the world to make it worth you taking a risk."

Posy crossed the room and hugged her. "We'll be fine. Luke doesn't know the area, but when it comes to ice climbing, the man has serious skills. Not that I intend to tell him that, because his ego is doing just fine without the boost." She walked to the door and Suzanne called out to her.

"Thanks for the logs, sweetheart."

"You're welcome. Now go and put your feet up and have a cup of tea. Ho ho ho, away I a-go." Posy left the room and they heard her feet clattering on the stairs and her voice calling for Bonnie.

Suzanne sank onto the edge of the bed. "Did you know she was going ice climbing?"

"Yes."

"But you didn't mention it to me."

"I didn't want to worry you. Neither did she."

"I'm officially worried. How could I not be?"

She felt like this every time Posy went into the mountains. She couldn't concentrate until she knew she was safely home.

Stewart sat down next to her. "Posy is a skilled climber and she's careful."

"She's too much like her mother."

"Be thankful she isn't like her father." Stewart stood up. "Then we'd really be in trouble."

Suzanne didn't argue with that. She'd tried hard to like Rob because of Cheryl, but it hadn't been easy and Stewart had actively disliked the man.

If Cheryl hadn't met Rob, would she be alive now?

It was a ridiculous way to think, because without Rob there would be no Hannah, Beth and Posy.

"This whole thing with Hannah—" She took his hand. "I'm overcompensating, aren't I?"

"Yes, but I understand."

She knew he did. She also knew that the loss hadn't only been hers. Stewart had lost the life they'd planned together, the future they'd mapped out so carefully.

And then she felt guilty, because no matter how many compromises or changes they'd had to make, they'd lived and they had a beautiful family.

"Hannah guards herself. Shuts everyone out. And I can't blame her. No child should have to live through what she lived through."

"They all lived through it, Suzy, not just Hannah."

"I know, but Posy was so little she barely remembers it. Beth remembers it, but her reaction was what you'd expect it to be. Hannah was older. It was different. More complicated. And some of that was down to her relationship with Rob." It made her heart ache to think of it. "All I want is for us to be a normal family. But we're not, are we? We never have been. There is so much damage." And not just to her family. She took a deep breath. "It would have been twenty-five years this week."

It had been a day much like this one, she remembered. Changeable weather. The mountains playing a game of hide-and-seek behind the clouds.

And then the accident.

Five people had gone up the mountain and only one had walked away.

It was one anniversary she wouldn't be celebrating.

7

Posy

The Glensay Inn was a traditional Highland coaching inn with stone floors, rustic wooden tables and a beamed ceiling. A log fire crackled and danced in the hearth and hurricane lamps hung either side of the bar. In the summer people spilled out into the garden, but on a freezing winter's night like tonight the place was crowded, the atmosphere thickened with the smell of whiskey and locally brewed beer. A stranger venturing inside out of the cold would find warmth not only by the fire, but also in the welcome.

Posy and Luke fought their way to an empty table close to the fire.

It took about five minutes to cross the room because she knew almost everyone there and they all had something to share with her about her dad, her mom, the mountain rescue team and the weather forecast.

When they finally reached the table, a roar of laughter had them both glancing toward the bar.

"Someone is having a good time." Luke unzipped his jacket and hung it over the back of his chair.

"I hope you weren't expecting somewhere private." She unwound her scarf and waved at Geoff, the landlord, who raised his hand in return. Ignoring the throng of people trying to get his attention, he walked across with two bottles of beer.

"This will get you both started."

"Thanks, Geoff. You're my hero. How is your knee?" Posy kissed him on the cheek and Geoff flushed to the roots of his hair.

"Playing up, but that's the cold weather. I shouldn't complain, but I do it anyway because this place gives me a captive audience. I hear she took you ice climbing, Luke."

"She did." Luke settled himself by the fire. "We climbed three long pitches of continuous ice and my muscles are screaming. And watching the way she smacked her ax into that ice—well, let's just say I'm going to be careful not to upset her."

Geoff put the bottles on the table. "If you want a mountain guide, you can't do better than our Posy."

Our Posy. As if she was somehow the property of the local community, like the books in the library.

"Thanks for the vote of confidence, Geoff."

"She knows her way round these hills like I know my way round a beer barrel. There were folks who didn't take her seriously when she first joined the team." He rested his hands on the back of Posy's chair, settling in to tell his story. "Back then it was mostly six-foot men, and there was Posy, this wee wisp of a thing with her hair in bunches."

"I never wore my hair in bunches." Posy shrugged out of her coat, showering snow onto the floor. "And the 'wee wisp' would love to be able to get to her beer, if you'll excuse me."

Geoff stepped to one side and let her sit down. "She's the best mountain guide in these parts."

"Hey! Can we get some service around here?" A man at the bar bellowed and Geoff's benevolent expression was replaced by a scowl.

"You'll have to excuse Callum. Why did you ever date him, Posy?"

"Lapse in judgment." And she wasn't ever going to be allowed to forget it.

That, she thought, was the major downside of living in a small community. You could never escape your mistakes, and Callum was most definitely her biggest one.

As Geoff walked away from them, she saw Luke glance toward the bar, where Callum was holding forth, and then back to her.

"You dated that guy?"

"What can I say? I was twenty-two. I didn't know any better. We broke up after six months." Thinking about it was embarrassing. Talking about it, more so.

His brows rose. "It lasted six months?"

"Half of that was me trying to work out how to break it off without having to move to a different part of the country."

"I can imagine relationships can get a little awkward in a community of this size."

"You have no idea. Callum was the first and only time I dated anyone from the village."

"Who do you date now?"

"Mostly I seduce the people who rent the barn, and when I'm done with them, I drop their bodies in the loch. *Slàinte!*" She tapped her bottle against his, unwilling to admit how barren her love life was. "To a great day in the mountains. You're not a bad climber, Luke Whittaker."

"Thank you. You're not bad yourself for a wee wisp of a thing."

She paused with the beer bottle halfway to her mouth and narrowed her eyes. "Are you going to give me problems?"

"Maybe."

"Thanks for the warning." She drank, and the beer was cool and delicious. All in all, she was in a good mood. Climbing did that for her. She'd inherited that love from her parents.

The focus required was almost like meditation. Out there in the mountains there was no anxiety or stress beyond the danger of the ice. There was only the thwack of her ax, the smack of the spike at the front of her boots, the flexing of muscle. Just her and the challenge. The rock. The mountain.

And, today, the man sitting in front of her.

In the center of the table a candle flickered in the jar, sending a glow of soft light across Luke's features.

He reached for his beer. "The ice climbing here is incredible. More challenging than I expected."

"I'm glad you didn't fall and die."

"Good to know you care, Wisp." He lifted the bottle and drank.

"We need you to pay rent on the barn, that's all it is. And don't call me Wisp."

They ordered food and chatted as they waited for it to arrive. He talked about the climbs he'd done in Yosemite, the Cascades and the Tetons. She listened and then pounded him with questions, thirsty for more information. What routes had he taken? How did the climbing differ from the Alps?

The conversation left her revved up and excited.

"You're a good climber." Luke finished his beer. "I'm surprised you haven't been tempted to spread your wings and try some of these climbs yourself."

She'd been tempted.

"No wings. Just my boots and my ice ax." And a big, heavy anchor holding her in place.

He put the bottle down. "You'd like to leave, wouldn't you?"

"I don't know what you're talking about."

"I saw your expression when we talked about it the other day. And I've been watching you."

She felt as if she'd been caught naked. "Are you some sort of stalker?"

"No."

"Then you're interested in human behavior."

He smiled. "I'm interested in *you*, Posy McBride." His confession made her heart beat faster.

Was he flirting? What did it say about her that she didn't even know?

"I'm not that interesting."

"I disagree. And I'm intrigued as to what makes a woman with your gifts stay in one place her whole life."

"You make it sound as if I've never left the village. You should know I've often ventured beyond the Scottish border." She fiddled with the bottle in her hand. "I'm happy."

"But that doesn't stop you wondering what it would be like to climb in other places. And live somewhere the local population doesn't know everything about you."

"They don't know everything. That's ridiculous."

Geoff arrived at that moment and put plates of food in front of them. "I swapped your carrots for peas, Posy, because I know you hate carrots."

Great!

"Thanks." She waited for Geoff to walk away and shrugged. "So he knows I don't like carrots. That doesn't prove anything."

Luke leaned across and stole one of her chips. "It's not wrong to question the life you're living, Posy. It's understandable that someone like you would want to explore the world."

"I don't know why you're eating my chips when you have a bowl of your own." She picked up her fork but immediately put it down again. "It would devastate Mom if I left. And anyway, I'm going to take over the café one day."

She owed Suzanne and Stewart everything.

They'd sacrificed their own plans for the future, their dreams, to take in three orphaned children.

Without them, what life would she have had? Not this one, that was for sure.

Luke tucked into his food. "Maybe you should talk to her about it."

Mom, I've been thinking of leaving Glensay.

Mom, I'd like to spend some time climbing in North America.

Mom, I don't want to take over the café.

"I don't think so."

She stared miserably at her plate, feeling trapped.

Luke reached across and closed his hand over hers. "I didn't mean to upset you."

"I'm not used to talking about it, that's all. By the way, the fact that you held my hand will be all around the village by morning." But she left her hand in his. She wasn't sure why, given that there would be a price to pay in terms of teasing, except that it felt right.

He turned her hand over. "Your hands are pretty smooth for a climber." He ran his thumbs over the tips of her fingers.

"I don't climb as much as you do. Also, I have a secret weapon."

"You avoid washing up and lounging in hot tubs?"

"That, too, but also I use a honey moisturizer that we sell at the café. It's good. You?"

"Grapeseed oil. And I rely on athletic tape." He let go of her hand and sat back.

She felt a pang of regret. "You're worried about gossip?"

He smiled. "I was thinking about you. You're the one who has to carry on living here after I've left."

It was a reminder that he'd be moving on and she'd be staying here, doing the things she always did. Talking to the same people she always talked to. Climbing the same mountains she always climbed. Running the café.

She reached for her beer and took a mouthful.

The years stretched ahead of her and she caught a glimpse of her future, which looked the same as her present. No surprises. No adventure. The only change would be the patterns she created on top of her cappuccinos. Her life was depressingly predictable.

And whose fault was that?

She put the bottle down. "I feel I ought to warn you that I'm about to kiss you."

His expression didn't change. "Interesting. But if handholding will create gossip, what will kissing do?"

"We're about to find out. It's my civic duty to give the community something new to talk about."

There was a pause. "And you're all right with that?"

"I'm going to learn not to care. This is a good place to start." She stood up, took his face in her hands and pressed her mouth to his before she could change her mind.

At first the kiss was slow and gentle. She controlled it, he responded, and although his mouth was warm and undeniably skilled, he was also careful and restrained as if he was holding back. And then something shifted.

She'd intended the kiss to be fun. A statement perhaps, or

possibly an experiment. She hadn't anticipated that he might play an active part in that experiment.

He slid his hand behind her head, keeping their mouths fused as the kiss turned hotter and more urgent. She felt the skill of his mouth, the slide of his tongue, and lost all sense of time and place. It was insanely erotic, her response to him shockingly raw and primal. To anybody watching, nothing had changed, but for her everything had changed. Her heart hammered against her chest. Pleasure exploded inside her and her body was saturated with need. She lowered her hands to his shoulders, no longer confident that her limbs could hold her.

When he eventually withdrew his mouth from hers, she couldn't work out why he would end something that felt so good.

His gaze held hers, his eyes sleepy and dark with desire.

Her heart was pounding. The loud hum of background noise faded to nothing. It was only as she floated back to earth that she heard the catcalls.

Why, oh why, had she chosen to do something so personal in a public place?

Having to stop almost killed her. She wasn't sure she would have done it if he hadn't eased away.

She stared into his eyes. "You...kissed me."

"I did. My memory is a little hazy right now, but I seem to remember you started it."

Her gaze dropped to his mouth. "You have hidden talents."

He stood up. "Pick up your coat, Posy McBride."

"Why? Where are we going?"

"Home, so that I can demonstrate more of my talents without getting arrested." He threw a handful of notes down on the table and she blinked.

"What are you doing?"

"I'm paying for our meal." He clamped his hand over her

wrist and propelled her to the door, dealing with the inevitable comments with a sure smile and a few well-chosen words that made it clear he didn't give a damn about how many suggestive comments were thrown at him.

Posy stumbled through the door and into the cold. "I think you just overpaid."

"Do I look as if I care?"

"You look as if you're in a hurry."

He tugged her toward him and gave her a quick, scalding kiss on the mouth. "You're right, I am. Which is the quickest way home?"

She was breathless and as desperate as he was. "I might know a shortcut."

Posy knew her family considered her to be bold and adventurous, and in some ways that was true, but she'd never done anything reckless with relationships.

That, she thought, was about to change.

This was one adventure she could have right here at home.

8

Hannah

"I bought gifts for your nieces, Miss McBride." Angie had been told to call her Hannah but was too intimidated to risk it.

Seeing her boss on the phone, she put the bags on the floor of the glass corner office and slunk to the door.

Not that Hannah McBride had ever been rude or aggressive. Far from it. It was more that she was machinelike in her interactions. In a big meeting the day before, Hannah had done a complex calculation in her head while the others in the room were still hunting for calculators and scribbling on notepads. She was so smart she made Angie feel humble. What must it be like to have a brain like that?

The floor-to-ceiling glass that made up two sides of Hannah McBride's corner office offered an enviable view of Manhattan.

Hannah sat with her back to it.

It seemed to Angie that Hannah had turned her back on a lot of things.

There had been rumors about her and Adam Kirkman, but Angie couldn't imagine it. She was sure that any man getting too close to Hannah McBride would risk frostbite.

"Angie?" Hannah interrupted her call. "Would you wait a moment, please?"

Hannah saw her assistant freeze and felt a flash of guilt. She knew people found her unapproachable because it had been raised at her last performance review. Fortunately for her, she shone in other aspects of her work. Her outstanding financial contribution, together with the respect of her clients, meant that her job was unlikely to be at risk.

Still, as a naturally competitive person, the feedback niggled and she knew it was something she needed to address. It wasn't that she was a bully, far from it. It was more that she approached people management in the same way she approached everything else—with an analytical style. She cared very much about the growth and development of her staff, but she wasn't good at engaging on a personal level.

Adam, she knew, was more touchy-feely.

What was she supposed to do? Hug the staff every morning?

She returned briefly to her call. "I need those numbers by close of business." She put her phone on the desk and smiled at Angie. "Thank you for buying the girls' gifts."

"You're welcome, Miss McBride—I mean Hannah. It must be hard for you trying to choose the right gift when you don't have kids. I hope they're pleased."

When you don't have kids—

Seven days late, Hannah thought.

She still hadn't plucked up the courage to do the test and get a definitive answer. If she carried on like this, she'd have confirmation that she was pregnant when she was pushing in the delivery suite.

Oh God—

"You have a child, don't you, Angie?"

Angie's face brightened. "Yes, Miss Mc—Hannah. I have a little girl."

Was she an accident?

Did you want to get pregnant or did you freak out and panic?

"I guess—well, life must have changed when you had her."

"That's an understatement." Angie crossed the room and picked up the two empty mugs from Hannah's desk. "They say you don't know worry until you have kids, and they're right. Take the past couple of weeks—she's been ill and we've been back to that emergency room three times. Terrifying. The one word you never want to hear as a mother is *meningitis*. Fortunately, it wasn't that, but we all had some sleepless nights. She's home now but still taking meds. She's been a little fractious, which isn't easy to handle. She's awake most of the night coughing, so I'm awake, too, worrying, you know?"

No, she didn't know. And the fact that she didn't *want* to know was the reason she didn't have children. That depth of searing anxiety and raw emotion was something she could happily live without.

For a brief moment she remembered Posy clinging to her, a sodden heap of inconsolable grief and confusion.

Where's Mommy? Want Mommy. When will Mommy be home?

Emotions smashed through the wall she'd built, cascading over all her defenses and flooding every part of her. She pushed back, trying to cage those feelings and control them, the way she always did.

Angie peered at her. "Are you all right?"

"I'll be fine." Her mouth was dry and her hands were shaking. "And I hope your little girl is better soon."

"Thank you. I sometimes think that being a parent is the hardest thing in the world."

It was exactly what she didn't need to hear.

Hannah felt terror grip her throat. Her body felt tingly and a wave of dizziness smashed into her. The walls of her office seemed to be closing in and she couldn't see Angie properly. There were spots in front of her eyes.

Panic attack, she thought. She was having a panic attack, right here at her desk, when she was due in an important client meeting in a matter of minutes. Worse was the terror that her colleagues might discover that Hannah McBride wasn't exactly the woman she presented to the world.

Angie looked alarmed. "I'm going to fetch you a glass of water."

Hannah forced herself to slow her breathing.

"Hannah? Oh, hi, Angie," Adam's voice cut through the clouds of panic. "How's little Emma? Better?"

"Yes, thank you. Miss Mc—Hannah isn't feeling too good. I'm going to fetch her some water. Will you stay with her a minute?"

Hannah's pulse rate revved up to dangerous levels. She didn't need Adam to stay with her. She needed to use the few minutes she had before the meeting to compose herself.

She saw Angie smile at him the way all women smiled at Adam, even the married ones, and then melt out of the room.

Adam closed the door to her office. "Hannah? You're not well?"

She gripped the edge of her chair. She needed to respond, but she couldn't breathe.

She forced words through her constricted airways. "Need a minute—start without me."

"Apart from *I love you*, three little words I have never in my life heard you say before are *start without me.*" Adam strode across to her. "What happened?"

"Nothing. Busy."

He walked round her desk, spun her chair so that she was facing him and dropped to his haunches in front of her. "You're shaking."

Her fingers were tingling. Her chest hurt.

Through a fog, she felt him take her hands in his.

"You're going to be fine, honey. Breathe slowly. That's it." He held her hands tightly and gently stroked her wrists with his thumbs. "This isn't like you."

It was like her, but of course he'd never seen this side of her. He saw Work Hannah, and Barefoot-Eating-Pizza-from-the-Box Hannah. He'd never met Panic-Attack Hannah.

Slowly, gradually, the terrifying panic loosened its grip, leaving her weak and exposed, and with a whole new problem.

She'd believed she could talk her way out of anything, but she had no idea how to talk her way out of this.

Her fingers were freezing and even the firm pressure of his hands did nothing to warm them.

She registered the slow stroke of his thumbs on her skin and the reassuring pressure of his fingers.

Could a panic attack hurt a baby?

She needed to do the test so that she knew what she was dealing with.

"Not feeling well. A bug—it's going around." She knew that what she had wasn't contagious, but she didn't intend to share that fact.

"Something upset you. Was it Angie?" He cupped her cheek and she leaned into his hand, allowing herself that single moment of intimacy.

She knew with a terrifying clarity that once she did the test there would be no hiding the result from him. She wouldn't be able to take time to think about it. He always saw through her.

She stood up carefully, testing the strength in her legs. "We have a meeting to get to."

Adam rose to his feet, too. "A meeting you're in no shape to attend. I'm going to tell them you won't be joining us."

"No." She grabbed her phone. Her legs felt like jelly, and not up to the task of supporting her. "I can do this."

"We're friends, Hannah. You can trust me. You can lean on me."

She'd already done too much leaning. And too much laughing, talking and dancing.

Too much of everything.

She glanced at the door. "This isn't appropriate."

"You've been working too hard. Forget Scotland for Christmas. Come to the Caribbean with me. We'll swim in the ocean and make love on a beach."

She needed some distance from Adam so that she could work out what to do, so she said the first thing that came into her head. "I have to go to Scotland tomorrow."

He frowned. "I thought you were flying on Christmas Eve."

"My sister is ill."

"Since when?" His confusion turned to concern. "Why didn't you say so right away? No wonder you're stressed. What's wrong with her?"

Hannah floundered. "They're not sure. That's why I need to be there."

"Of course. No wonder you were looking panicked. I know you're not that close to your sister, but you must be worried." He was all brisk efficiency. "How can I help? Would you rather go tonight? Should I send someone round to your apartment to pack you a case? Book you a flight?"

Hannah almost whimpered aloud. Now she was going to

have to either admit to the lie or go home to Scotland early. "Tomorrow is fine. I'm sorry. I know we have the presentation to finalize, but I'll work from there."

"Don't worry about it." He drew in a long breath. "Let me know which flight you book and I'll take you to the airport."

"I'll take a cab." Maybe going back to Scotland wasn't a bad idea. At least she'd have room to think there. She scooped up her jacket from the back of the chair. "We should get to this meeting."

His face was inscrutable. "I love you, Hannah."

There was a thickening in her throat and a pressure in her chest.

This wasn't a path she'd wanted to take. Love, marriage and kids—that life wasn't for her. Love made you vulnerable, and she'd been determined never to be vulnerable again.

Except that now she might be pregnant.

The first thing she was going to do when she arrived home was buy a test.

9

Beth

Across town Beth was also walking into a meeting. Like her sister, Beth was relying on her acting skills to get her through.

She'd already texted Jason twice to check that the girls were okay. Part of her wanted to leave him to it, but maternal instinct—or was it anxiety?—forced her to interfere.

She'd promised the girls that if they behaved well she'd do crafting with them later. Normally the thought of all that glitter, glue and paint spread around her kitchen was enough to squash all her "good mommy" intentions, but she'd been desperate enough to promise anything.

Trying to focus her mind on the job, she walked into the elevator and smoothed her skirt.

I am a competent professional.

Although I am an expert at cutting up children's food, that is not my only skill.

The offices of Glow PR were on the thirtieth floor of a high-rise in Midtown and the huge expanse of glass behind the elegant curve of the reception desk offered breath-stealing views over Manhattan.

Beth had forgotten what it was like to see the city from up above.

Sometimes, when you were down there among the crush of people, the beauty was invisible, but up here it was laid out before you like a buffet of opportunity and hope.

"How may I help you?" The receptionist smiled, her lips a perfect curve of shiny red.

Beth resisted the urge to check that she didn't have sticky fingerprints on her new dress.

"I'm Bethany Butler. I have an appointment with Corinna."

The receptionist checked her computer screen. "I have a Beth McBride."

"That's me." Even when she'd married Jason, Corinna had continued to introduce her as Beth McBride, refusing to accept that Beth's circumstances had changed.

The receptionist's expression suggested it was time Beth figured out her own name. "Take a seat. She'll be right with you."

Too nervous to sit, Beth walked to the window and stared at the view.

She hoped Jason had managed to find Ruby's gloves before he left the apartment. She'd left him a note. Would he read it?

He'd probably be too busy trying to get them out of the door on time. She should have texted him.

She heard the brisk tap of stiletto on marble and turned to see Corinna striding toward her.

"Admiring our view? The whole world is right there at

your feet. It's been a while, Beth." She leaned in and Beth was engulfed in a cloud of expensive perfume. It brought back so many memories. Laughter, teamwork, stress, late nights, hard work, exhaustion, more stress, elation, glamour, success and more free samples than she'd known what to do with.

Over the last seven years the only outlet for her creativity had been finger painting.

"I'm excited to be here." She could feel the energy seeping into her, as if someone had plugged her into a power source.

Through an internal wall of glass she could see four immaculately dressed women in a meeting and could almost feel the buzz and energy in that room. Here, people worried about something other than what they were eating for dinner and whether the children had clean clothes.

She wanted badly to join this world.

What if Jason felt as strongly about having more children as she did about going back to work? Where would that leave them?

"I've been busy since we last met." Corinna stepped back and surveyed her. "I'm loving that look, Bethany. Did you style that yourself?"

No, my seven-year-old daughter advised me.

After sixteen different outfit changes, all of which Melly had patiently observed from the bed, Beth had settled for a short black dress with her favorite over-the-knee boots. She rarely wore them because they weren't the ideal footwear for chasing after two little girls in Central Park.

"You need to wear your hair up," Melly had said. "But keep it wispy on the sides. And red lipstick."

Beth had been pleased with the result.

Melly might not achieve her ambition to be a princess, but she would make a great stylist.

"Let me give you the tour. We've only been in these offices for three weeks, so we're still making ourselves at home." Corinna led her down the light-filled corridor. The walls were covered with photographs of skinny, angry-looking models. It was obvious Corinna had been working with some major brands since Beth had last seen her.

"This is impressive."

"I always wanted my own agency. I never was any good at doing what other people told me to do." Corinna flashed her a smile devoid of warmth or humor. "We have big clients, but I want more. I'm hungry, and everyone on my team is equally hungry. Are you hungry, Beth?"

Beth knew how hungry Corinna was. She'd worked for her before.

She tried not to think about Jason's warning.

"I'm hungry." It wasn't a lie. She'd been too nervous to consume more than a cup of black coffee before leaving the apartment and her stomach was already protesting.

"We are pitching for a major cosmetics brand right now." Corinna gestured to the group of people huddled over storyboards in the glass-walled office. "They've created a range of looks that are simple to apply so even if you know nothing about makeup, you can look polished. When we win, we'll be hiring."

Beth noticed she said *when* and not *if*. Corinna never entertained the possibility that life might not go her way. Had she ever had that much confidence? "Sounds great."

"The number one quality that I look for in a team member is loyalty. I want one hundred and fifty percent."

Beth didn't even bother doing the calculation to work out how much of herself that would leave for her family.

"You know me, Corinna," she said. "I'm loyal."

She was also a wife and a mother, but she'd think about how to balance that equation later.

"I'd like to hear your ideas on this one."

Beth felt a jolt of shock. "Are you offering me a job?"

"Let's see what you have first. If I'm impressed, then you'll join us for the pitch. After that, we'll talk." Corinna opened another glass door and strode into a large office. "Sit down. I'll give you a copy of the brief—you'll have to sign a confidentiality agreement of course—and then you can take it home and put together some ideas. Write the proposal you think will wow me. Come back next week."

And there it was. The pressure. The expectation.

Beth hadn't expected things to move quite so fast. She felt as if she'd been walking on a treadmill and someone had suddenly pressed Sprint. She was in danger of falling flat on her face and it wasn't going to be pretty.

She slid into a chair, relieved to take the weight off her feet. The boots looked gorgeous, but it turned out that after five minutes' wear they were horribly uncomfortable. "I won't be here next week. I'm going home to Scotland."

"Death in the family?" Corinna's tone suggested that nothing short of death would coax a person to leave Manhattan.

"It's Christmas."

It was obvious that someone had forgotten to write that date in Corinna's schedule.

"The pitch will give you an excuse to escape from all the awful family stuff."

Beth decided this probably wasn't a good moment to admit that she loved the family stuff.

She noticed that Corinna hadn't once asked her about the children. "When is the pitch?"

"January. We need to knock this one out of the park." Corinna gave her details on the company and outlined the key marketing strategy for the new makeup range. "We have dozens of samples. Take some when you go. Your ideas are very important to me. The moment we were given the brief, I thought to myself, *Beth McBride*."

Beth was ridiculously flattered. She forgot about the stress, the pressure and the obstacles.

Corinna thought her ideas were important.

She had something to contribute.

She sat a little straighter. "I can't wait to read the brief."

"Tell me what you've been doing since we last met." Corinna's desk was made of glass and topped by neat piles of glossy magazines. *Vogue, Cosmopolitan, Elle* and *Harper's Bazaar*, sat alongside the *New Yorker*. Everywhere she looked there was the gleam of glass and the dazzle of white. The place smelled of success.

"I've been at home with the children."

Corinna's expression made her wonder if she should have lied about that.

"That's what I heard, and I was surprised. You were so good at what you did, I thought you'd be back at work before you could say *diaper*." Corinna picked up her phone, her nails gleaming under the lights as she dialed. "Annabelle? Bring us drinks."

Beth resisted the temptation to interject with *say please*. She'd been a mother for far too long. Next she'd be cutting up Corinna's food. "That's kind. I'd love a c—" She'd been about to say coffee, when a young woman, presumably the long-suffering Annabelle, entered the room carrying a bottle of champagne and two glasses. "Champagne. Delicious."

"We work hard and we play hard. Annabelle, ask Dan and Sylvia to join us."

By the time she left, Beth was floating on air, and the feeling wasn't entirely due to the quantity of champagne she'd consumed on an empty stomach.

She'd entered the building unsure of herself, but now she felt glamorous and confident. She was no longer just Ruby and

Melly's mother. She was Beth McBride, fashion and beauty PR. She was the type of woman who knew what to wear and when to wear it.

She felt as if she'd been stuck behind traffic and suddenly the road ahead had opened up. She was ready to put her foot on the gas.

She was back in the fast lane.

The excitement was dizzying, and the first thing she did when she arrived back at her apartment was to grab a note-pad and start scribbling ideas. Not only was she determined to impress Corinna, but she needed to prove to herself that she still had what it took.

By the time Jason arrived back with the girls, she was on fire. The kitchen table was piled high with samples, and paper covered in her scrawl. Her laptop was open, the screen glowing.

Ruby and Melly tumbled through the door with him, their cheeks pink from the cold.

Ruby's cheeks were also smudged with brown.

Chocolate.

Beth was too high on champagne and life to care that Jason had obviously used chocolate as a bribe.

"Hi! Did you have a great time with Daddy?"

"Melly was late to school," Ruby said, "and she cried. She said she hated Daddy and that he was doing everything wrong."

There was a flush on Jason's cheekbones. "She's exaggerating. And we weren't that late. We couldn't find Ruby's shoes or her gloves."

"She hides them." Some of Beth's euphoria faded. Wasn't he even going to ask her how her meeting went?

"I want to draw with you." Ruby clambered onto the chair and reached for Beth's neatly sorted papers.

"Don't touch those!" Beth flew across the kitchen and

scooped up Ruby before she could leave chocolaty prints. "It's Mommy's work."

Ruby turned saucerlike eyes on her. "You don't work."

That's going to change, Beth thought.

"I do. I'm putting together ideas for a new campaign."

"What's a campaign?"

"Wait—" Jason's voice sounded strange. "You took the job? Without talking to me first?"

She didn't point out that he'd accepted his promotion without talking to her first.

How did it go, Beth? Did you like them? Did they like you? Tell me about it.

She found a tissue in her purse and wiped Ruby's mouth. "Go and wash your hands and face, baby. I want to talk to Daddy."

"I'm not a baby. Can we play fire stations?"

"Maybe. We'll see. You, too, Melly." She waited until both her daughters had vanished into the bathroom before turning back to Jason. "Don't you want to know how it went?"

"I only just walked through the door. Give me a chance."

"To answer the question you didn't ask, it went well. They're pitching for a major brand in the new year and they want me to be part of that. If we win, the job is mine."

"If you win." He let out a long breath. "Do I need to remind you what Corinna is like, Beth? She is a machine, and she expects her team to display the same qualities."

"She's committed. That's why she is good at her job." She wasn't sure if she was defending Corinna or her own choices.

"She is good at her job because she doesn't have a life. And she expects the people who work for her to not have lives, either. Is that really what you want? Think about it, Beth. What happens when one of the kids is sick? Corinna isn't one of those bosses who is going to smile sweetly and hurry you out of the door. She's never acknowledged your kids exist! She didn't even send a card when they were born and you were upset about that. She hurt you."

"I'd had a baby. I was hormonal. And if one of the kids is sick, maybe *you* could come home early. Why does it have to be me?" Only now did she notice that Jason looked exhausted. Was that what one morning looking after the children had done to him? "You're trying to put me off because you don't want me to do this."

He jammed his fingers into his hair. "That's not it. And if you think Corinna's changed, you're deluding yourself. If anything, she's likely to be worse now that she owns the business. Every moment you give to your family is a moment you're not giving to her and she isn't going to like that."

"You wanted her to reject me, didn't you?"

His hesitation was infinitesimal. "I'm concerned that working with her won't make you happy."

"Oh please. Why not at least be honest and admit you don't want me to work for her?"

"Do I have a choice? We hadn't agreed that you were going back to work, but it seems you've already accepted the job."

"I haven't even been *offered* the job. First I have to come up with some ideas and go to the pitch with them."

"What's her agenda?"

"What do you mean?"

"Why does she want you?" His blunt question exposed all her insecurities.

"It can't be because she thinks I'm the best person for the job? Thanks for that vote of confidence, Jason."

"That isn't—"

"Do *not* say anything else." She hadn't thought it possible for her feelings to be so badly hurt. She stalked toward the bedroom and he followed her, closing the door so that the girls wouldn't hear them.

"All I'm saying is that you've been out of the business for a while. There has to be a reason that she is chasing you so hard."

"Stop, Jason. Just stop! And don't close the door. I need to listen out for the children."

He spread his hands. "Beth, please—she is going to make you miserable."

"You don't want me to go back to work. You want another child, but you barely see the two you already have." She saw his expression change, but it was too late to pull the words back.

"I take the girls on Sunday mornings while you have time to yourself."

"And you go to the park and spend quality time. And because you don't see much of them during the week, spending time with their daddy is a treat for them. It's not the same when you have them day in, day out, when you're trying to get them out of the house in the morning and they don't want to wear what you want them to wear, or eat what you want them to eat. When you're with the kids and you have to take a call, you hand them back to me. I have to take calls with both girls tugging at me and talking to me."

"My calls are important."

"Whereas nothing I do is important? That's *exactly* why I want to go back to work."

"Do you know how many women would like to be in your position?" He didn't bother disguising the exasperation in his voice. "You have a great life, Beth."

She was so stunned that for a moment she couldn't move. "You don't know anything about my life. You're not here."

"Because I'm working day and night to earn money that *you* then spend on yet another fire engine and princess outfit." His voice hardened. "Maybe if you could say no once in a while, I wouldn't have to work so hard! I'm the one hauling myself out of bed in the dark to go earn enough money to keep us all. I'm the one playing politics day in, day out, to make sure I don't lose the job that brings in enough money to allow you to stay at home! It doesn't take a genius to see who has the easier deal here."

She was so outraged she couldn't respond.

This couldn't be happening. They couldn't be speaking to each other like this.

Her insides were boiling and she felt tears of frustration and fury sting her eyes.

"Right." Finally she found her voice. "Well, if being at home with the kids is so easy, then maybe you should try it for a while. Give yourself a break from hauling yourself out of bed to go to work, and haul yourself out of bed for the kids for a change. Take a break from playing politics, and play fire engines. Take your eye off Ruby for five seconds and see what happens." She stalked across the bedroom and grabbed her coat.

Jason watched her. "What are you doing?"

"I'm giving you the opportunity to immerse yourself in parenthood, seeing as you seem to think that's the 'easier deal.'" She dragged open a drawer so violently a lamp toppled over. She caught it before it hit the floor. She could barely see through the heat haze of anger but somehow managed to find her passport. "You can look after the girls and enjoy some quality time."

"Oh for—" He pressed his fingers to the bridge of his nose. "The last thing we need right now is drama, Beth."

"Drama?" She slammed the drawer shut. She'd never felt so angry. Never. "This isn't drama, Jason. This is me feeling strongly about something, and you not listening. The kids' schedule is written down in the kitchen." She emptied the contents of her purse into a larger bag. Her hands shook. Her heart was pounding so hard she half expected it to burst from her chest. They'd never had a fight like this. Never. "The number for the pediatrician is in the drawer, along with the dentist's number and the numbers for Melly's school. Don't forget ballet. It's half an hour earlier than it used to be. Make sure you're there in plenty of time. Melly needs to change and gets upset if she's late. And she hates the black tights, so make sure you take pink. And pack a spare pair in case of accidents."

"Wait—" His face had drained of color. "You're leaving me? And the kids?"

"I'm not leaving you. Nor am I leaving the girls. I would never, ever, leave our girls. I'm simply doing what you do every day, which is to walk out that door and leave another person with full responsibility for our family. When I am sure you really understand the impact of having another child, we can talk again."

"You can't be serious. This has got out of hand and you need to calm down."

It was the worst thing he could have said.

"I'm calm." If you didn't count the fact that she was seeing him through a red mist. "Maybe *you* need to start listening."

"What are you going to do? Walk around the corner and order a coffee somewhere until I text you an apology?"

"I'm having a week to myself to think about my life."

"A *week*? But—you haven't even packed a bag. You never travel anywhere without at least two suitcases."

"I can buy whatever I need. That's what I do, isn't it, Jason? I spend your money."

He sucked in a breath and spread his hands in a gesture of apology. "I didn't mean to say that. I didn't mean it like that."

"I think you did."

"But—where will you go?" As it sank in that she really was walking out, he seemed to deflate. He looked so bemused and shell-shocked her anger receded a little. But not enough to make her change her mind.

"I'm going home."

"You're already home. This is home, Beth. Our apartment. Manhattan. Your family. The family you don't seem too interested in right now."

She felt a stab of guilt but refused to let him manipulate her. "I'm going home to Scotland. To my parents."

His skin lost the last of its color. "You don't want to spend Christmas with us?"

"Of course I do. I don't want Christmas without the girls. You can fly out a few days before as planned. You have the tickets. If parenting is as easy as you seem to think it is, I'm sure you'll have no issues. The presents are all bought, wrapped and labeled. Remember to pack them." She grabbed her phone and called the airline. Before she could change her mind, she'd booked and paid for a ticket flying out of JFK that evening.

"But—" He muttered something under his breath "I have meetings tomorrow." There was a note of panic in his voice that she'd never heard before.

"I'm sure you'll find a way."

"Beth—"

"I need you to see that the decision to have another child is not like buying another sofa or a new vase. Quite apart from the fact that giving birth to two babies destroyed my insides and my nerves, they take commitment and compromise."

"This is insane." He ran his hand over his jaw. "Are you at least going to leave me a list of food they eat? And I don't know what clothes you'd want me to pack for them for the trip at Christmas."

"Figure it out. You have full control, although I suggest

you don't let Melly wear her best dress to the park because she'll be sad if she ruins it."

"I can't believe you're doing this."

Neither could she. "You'll be fine, Jason."

"What about my promotion?"

"You said Sam understood that you have a family. Let's test that understanding. If he wants you that badly, he'll be prepared to wait a few weeks. Don't forget to take Ruby's inhaler whenever you go out. The cold weather sometimes triggers an asthma attack. Do *not* feed them chips, no matter how much they beg you, because they need fruit, vegetables and healthy food, and whatever you do, do *not* lose Bugsy, because Ruby can't sleep without him."

She felt a moment of anxiety as she contemplated all the things that could go wrong, but her anger was too great for her to back down. And anyway, she knew exactly what would happen.

As soon as she was out of the door, he'd call his mother.

10

Posy

The sun poured through the skylights in the loft, sending shafts of light across the bed.

Posy lay naked, her skin damp and her heart pounding. "Usually I don't take a lunch break."

Luke pulled her close. "Since neither of us has eaten, this doesn't count as a lunch break."

"Good point. Are you hungry? We should grab something to eat before we go back to work."

"Is it a choice between sex and food? Because I choose sex." He shifted so she was underneath him, then lowered his mouth to hers, his kiss lingering and full of erotic promise.

She felt the weight of him, the roughness of his thigh against hers and then the slow stroke of his fingers as he explored every sensitive part of her.

She wrapped her arms round his neck, wondering how it was possible to feel this close to someone you'd known for only a couple of months. It surprised her. More than that, it shook her.

He wasn't her first lover, but in the past sex had felt more like a pleasurable workout than something special. On some level she'd always been aware that her emotions weren't deeply engaged. With Luke, she'd discovered how different sex was when the feelings shared were more than just physical. She trusted those feelings. She'd trusted them when they'd told her that Callum was all wrong for her and she trusted them now as they told her that being with Luke was right.

Since that evening in the pub, they'd spent every night together as well as every lunchtime and the occasional hour in the afternoon. She hadn't known life could be this exciting.

She'd never felt the need to protect her heart but felt a fleeting moment of anxiety, not that her heart might be hurt, but that this intimate connection, *this bliss*, might end. Emotionally, she could feel herself sliding deeper and saw no reason to stop herself.

She wound her legs round him and arched upward in blatant invitation.

"Luke Whittaker," she purred, "I think you should—" Her phone beeped, cutting off her indecent suggestion in midsentence.

"You were saying?" His voice thickened and she sighed.

"I'd better check that, in case it's something important. Can you grab it for me?"

He kissed her again and then reached across and picked up her phone. It took him a minute to focus. "It's a text from Beth."

"What does it say?"

"Nothing important." He put the phone back and shifted

over her again so that his body was intimately aligned with hers. "You have great legs. Have I already told you that?"

"No. Yes. I don't know. I can't think too well when you're doing what you're doing." She slid her hands down his back. "What did Beth want?"

"Nothing." He kissed his way down her neck to her shoulder. "Something about being worried about the weather."

Posy stilled. "The weather?"

"Yes."

"Those were her exact words? Damn." Posy wriggled out from under him and sprang from the bed, cursing as she tripped over their abandoned clothing. "I need to talk to her. Sorry. Bad timing, but this is an emergency." She ignored the part of herself that was screaming at her to get back into bed with him.

"Since when has bad weather been an emergency?" Luke raised himself up on his elbow, his hair in disarray and his eyes sleepy and sexy. "Could you be overreacting? It snows a lot in New York, although admittedly the heavy snow usually comes after Christmas."

"That text is nothing to do with the weather. It's a code." Posy scooped up her shirt and her socks. "We used it when we were teenagers and didn't want our parents to know about what we were doing. It means she's in trouble."

"Trouble?" Luke frowned and sat up. "What sort of trouble?"

"I don't know yet." Posy tugged on her socks, glanced in the mirror and recoiled. "I look as if I've been caught in a howling gale." She scraped her fingers through her hair and then gave up and scooped it up in a ponytail.

Luke leaned back against the pillows. "I think you look like someone who just had great sex. Three times. I was about to make it four times, but—"

Her phone pinged again and this time Posy grabbed it herself, trying not to think about the fourth time that wasn't going to happen now.

"She's at the airport. Not JFK, our local airport." She felt a flash of concern. "Why is she at the airport?"

"Because flying is the normal way to travel from the US?"

"She's not due home for another week. And usually she—" She broke off and stared at her phone in shock as she noticed the time. "It's half past three! How can it be half past three?"

"I don't know. I can't honestly say I was thinking about the passage of time. Seeing you naked impairs my ability to think about anything much."

"I'm going to need some fancy excuses to explain away this one. And still more excuses for going to pick up my sister." Posy leaned down and kissed him, feeling a tug of regret. "I don't know how long this is going to take. You should probably—"

He cupped her face in his hands, kissing her until she was dizzy.

The kick of desire almost had her sliding back into bed with him.

She groaned. "Can't. Mustn't. I need to—" She pulled away, then changed her mind and crushed her mouth to his again. It was a full minute before she found the willpower to step back. "I'd tell you to stay right where you are, but this might take a while." She slid out of his arms for a second time and glanced around the room. Where were her jeans? She didn't even remember Luke taking them off, but she'd ended up naked, so it must have happened at some point.

"This isn't an elaborate excuse to leave my bed?"

She found her jeans on the floor by the sofa. "It's *my* bed, so no. And I don't play those games. If I wanted you out of my bed, I'd say *get out of my bed*."

"I know. It's one of the many things I like about you. I'll go back downstairs and work, but bang on my door when you're back." He hesitated. "And if you need anything—if she's in trouble and there's some way I can help—call me."

"Thanks." Touched by the offer of support, she finished dressing, grabbed her coat and car keys, and gave him a last sorrowful look. "This was fun."

He gave a half smile. "Go. I'll keep Bonnie company. And drive carefully."

Posy picked her way down the icy steps that led from her hayloft, then sprinted to her car. Thoughts about Luke mingled with concern for her sister.

What was wrong with Beth?

Why was she home a week early?

She did the airport run in record time and spotted Beth immediately. She was standing alone outside the arrivals door, looking forlorn. There was no sign of Jason or the kids.

Posy couldn't remember a time when Beth had come home on her own.

What was going on?

She swerved into a space and leaned on her horn. Beth carried on staring into space.

Posy sprang from the car and sprinted across to her, checking quickly for airport police. They took a dim view of people abandoning their vehicles.

"Hey, Beth!" She was only a few strides away from her sister when Beth finally noticed her.

"Posy! You came."

Posy had never seen such relief in anyone's face before. "Of course I came." She glanced behind her sister. "Did they lose your bags? Where's your luggage?"

"This is it." Beth slung her medium-sized bag over her shoulder.

"But you always travel with at least two suitcases."

"Don't start. Can we go? I'm freezing." She swayed slightly and Posy decided that questions could wait until later.

Her sister was obviously tired, and also right about the air temperature. An icy wind blew in front of the terminal building, discouraging people from lingering.

She ushered Beth to the car. The airport was busy and the driver in the car behind her was revving his engine and hovering, waiting for her to vacate her space. He leaned on his horn and she resisted the temptation to make a rude gesture. "And a Merry Christmas to you, too, Mr. Scrooge. A Merry Christmas to one and all." It was supposed to be the season of goodwill, but mostly it seemed to be the season of impatience.

She slid back into the driver's seat and waited while Beth settled in next to her.

Posy turned the heating up. "Your call was a surprise. We weren't expecting you for another week."

"Thanks for coming at short notice. Were you in the middle of something?"

"As it happens, I was in bed with a tall, dark, handsome man having the best sex of my life. But I forgive you."

Beth laughed. "You're so funny."

What did it say about her life that her sister assumed she'd made a joke?

Was her life really so boring and predictable that it was impossible for her family to envisage her ever having an active sex life?

"Actually, I really was—"

"Feeding the chickens. I know. You don't have to sex up your life for me. I happen to know there are no tall, dark, handsome strangers in Glensay." Beth yawned. "I'm relieved you weren't out on a rescue. I was worried you might be. You're a great sister."

"I know. I'm the best." Maybe this wasn't the right moment to mention Luke anyway. Posy wanted Beth to do the talking. "Everything okay?"

"Never better." Beth giggled and tried in vain to fasten her seat belt.

Frowning, Posy took over. "Bethany McBride Butler, are you *drunk*?"

"No. It takes more than a few glasses of champagne to get me drunk."

"A few?" Posy fastened her own seat belt, ignoring the repeated blare of the horn from the car behind her. "How many is 'a few'?"

"I lost count. Who is going to turn down free champagne? You'd better get out of here before you become a victim of road rage. That guy behind looks as if he's about to have a heart attack."

"That's what happens when you become emotionally attached to a parking space. You didn't bring the children?"

"If I'd brought the children, would I be sitting here on my own now? You think I abandoned them in lost luggage? For once in my life, I traveled light. No kids. No bags."

Posy proceeded with caution. "You decided to come home early for Christmas?"

"That's right. And the airline upgraded me. I felt like Hannah. Do you have any idea how civilized it is?" Beth's eyes were still closed. "Movies, reclining seat, a screen between me and the rest of the world, and people asking me whether they can get me anything. That never happens. I'm the one that gets things for other people and there is never a screen between me and anybody. For the first time in seven years, I used the bathroom without someone hammering on the door wanting my attention. I got to eat chocolate without having to share it."

Posy deduced that there was more to Beth's early arrival

than a desire to spend quality time with her family. "Well, you're sharing a bathroom with Hannah this Christmas, so you can expect a lot of hammering if you're in there for too long."

Beth didn't open her eyes. "She'll cancel. She always cancels. Dinner, Hannah? *Sorry, I have to cancel.* Spend the weekend? *I'm overwhelmed with work.* Visit your nieces? *Oh wait, sorry, can't make it.*"

Posy thought about the time their mother had spent in the kitchen. "If she cancels, I'll kill her."

"Maybe it would be better if she did cancel. At least I wouldn't have to spend the whole time telling the kids to be quiet."

"Why would you do that? It's Christmas. Overexcited kids is part of the fun."

"Hannah doesn't like my girls."

Posy was startled. "What are you talking about?"

"Nothing. Ignore me. I don't suppose there is any chance I could stay with you instead of being in the lodge?"

Posy thought about Luke. "No chance at all."

"Thanks. I love you, too."

"It's nothing to do with not loving you, and everything to do with the fact that I live in the hayloft. It's not exactly a family-friendly space. There's only one bed and I'm in it."

She didn't bother adding that her bed had seen a lot of action lately.

"Hannah won't be home until the last minute, so I'll have the bathroom to myself for a while. I need my own bed," Beth said. "And I'm going to sleep in the middle of it, alone. No more getting up to Ruby in the night while Jason snores next to me. No more broken nights. No more early mornings. For the next week, it's all about me."

Posy felt a flash of alarm. Beth was starting to sound like

Hannah, and there was no way she was going to be able to handle two Hannahs over Christmas.

She pulled into the flow of traffic and headed out of the airport. The place was busy, but in a week's time it would be busier still as more people arrived home for the holidays.

She waited until they were on a straight stretch of road to continue the conversation.

"What is going on, Beth?"

Beth shook her head. "I do not have to answer that."

"You called me in the middle of the afternoon using a secret code we haven't used since we were teenagers and begged for an airport extraction without Mom knowing. The least you can do is give me an explanation."

"Can it wait? And can you slow down? I don't feel so good."

"That's what happens when you consume your body weight in champagne."

"If you're going to be judgy, I'll be forced to point out that the last time we used the secret code was on your seventeenth birthday when you drank so much you couldn't walk home and I had to sneak you past Dad."

Posy grinned. "I remember that. I'm not being judgy, but I am going to stop somewhere and pour black coffee into you. I can't let Mom and Dad see you like this. And while I do that, you can tell me what's going on." They were now a distance from the airport and the road had narrowed. Snow lay in banks at the side of the road and Posy slowed her pace. The surface was icy and she wasn't sure when it had last been gritted.

"I've left Jason—that's what's going on."

Posy managed to stop herself swerving across the road. "For a moment there I thought you said you left Jason."

"That's what I said."

"But you're drunk, so you're not yourself."

"I don't know who I am anymore. Am I Beth McBride, lipstick queen, or am I Beth Butler, wife and mother?"

Posy was starting to think this conversation was too complicated for the road conditions. "Can't you be both?"

"Apparently not. According to Jason, I'm supposed to devote my life to the sheer pleasure that is motherhood. I used to be a highflier, but I crash-landed a long time ago and no one has noticed the wreckage."

Okay, enough!

They were driving through a village and Posy checked her mirror and pulled sharply into a parking space while Beth clutched her seat for balance.

"Whatever you're doing, could you do it less violently? My stomach just traveled around my body at supersonic speed. What *are* you doing?"

"I'm stopping to pour some coffee into my drunk sister so we can have a proper conversation."

"I am not drunk. And I don't want to stop here. It looks sad and miserable." She peered out of the window. "Where are we?"

"A place where no one knows us. A place where the fact that you're drunk won't have reached Mom by breakfast."

"I want to go home. I need cheering up and this place looks depressing." Beth's voice wavered. "Can't we go to the Glensay Inn? It's tradition. Lunch in the café, dinner at the pub. I want to sit by a cozy log fire and chat about everything under the sun like we did in the old days. I want to see Geoff and everyone I know."

Posy didn't want to chat about everything under the sun. She wanted to chat about why her sister was home early, and on her own. And she didn't want to see Geoff or anyone else she knew. She hadn't been back to the Glensay Inn since she'd kissed Luke in public. She wasn't ready to deal with the fallout.

Still, she was going to have to brave the locals at some point, so it might as well be with her sister by her side.

As anticipated, she walked into the welcoming warmth of the pub to cheers and catcalls. There were at least five members of the mountain rescue team leaning on the bar, and the way they grinned at her told her that word had spread as efficiently as ever.

Maybe kissing Luke in public hadn't been such a good idea. On the other hand, it was nothing compared to what they'd been doing in private.

Thinking about it made her smile.

Beth smiled, too, although for different reasons. "I didn't expect this kind of reception. It's good to be home. You're lucky to live here, doing what you love among all these people who care about you."

And gossip about you. And wink at you. And tease you until you're ready to punch them.

"Sit down." Braving it out, Posy bundled her sister to the same table she and Luke had sat at a few nights earlier.

The smell of wood smoke mingled with the oaky notes of whiskey. Turned out it was tasting night at the inn, and the local distillery had brought bottles for the locals to try and hopefully buy.

Posy had already bought a bottle for her dad. Not the most imaginative gift, but she knew he'd like it.

"They have a Christmas tree!" Beth sank into a chair and gazed at the shimmer of lights on the tree. "I love Christmas."

It was Geoff's night off and his son, Aidan, strolled over from the bar. "Good to see you home, Beth." He bent and kissed her on the cheek. He had an unruly mop of dark hair and was famous locally for having won a haggis eating competition at the local Highland games. "How are the kids?"

Tears bloomed in Beth's eyes. "They're great. They're not

with me right now, and I'm already missing them, which makes no sense because—"

"We'll have strong coffee, please, Aidan." Posy was wishing she'd stopped at the soulless roadside café instead.

"I'd like wine," Beth said. "A *very* large glass of chilled white. Maybe a sauvignon blanc. Or do you think we should be extravagant and order champagne?"

"No champagne and no white, chilled or otherwise." Posy peeled off her coat. She couldn't remember ever seeing her sister like this before. "Coffee. Strong. Large. And something to eat."

Aidan waited. "I could bring you a menu, but there's not much point, since you already know what's on it."

"Isn't that great?" Beth gave a wavering smile. "We don't even have to look at the menu. I love the tree, by the way. Tell Geoff the only thing that's missing is mistletoe."

"Your sister seemed to do all right without it the other night." Aidan winked at Posy, who kept her expression deadpan.

"We'll have two burgers, thanks, Aidan."

"Coming right up." He looked at Beth. "And you don't eat tomato, is that right?"

"That's right. Oh, Aidan—" she stood up and flung her arms round him "—I love that you know that about me, and I love being home."

Aidan looked nervous as he patted her on the back. He had a cute lopsided smile that ensured he was never short of female company. "Right. Well, customer satisfaction is important to us, so that's great. Always good to see you, Beth." He retreated to the kitchen, no doubt to tell someone that strange things were happening to the McBride sisters.

Beth plopped back into her chair. "Don't you *love* the fact that everyone knows everything about you?"

"No. It drives me insane." Posy was starting to wish she'd

ordered something other than coffee. Would it be hypocritical for her to order a beer while she poured coffee down her sister?

"What did he mean about you doing all right without mistletoe?"

"No idea." She watched as Rory Wilson, the training officer for the team, detached himself from the others and strolled across to her. He greeted Beth warmly and then slapped Posy on the shoulder. "I hear you've discovered America."

"Very funny. I'm catching up with my long-lost sister, Rory, so I'll see you at training next week."

"I hope you have the energy to attend."

Definitely a mistake to kiss Luke in the Glensay Inn.

She didn't want gossip to spoil what they had. On the other hand, she wasn't sure exactly what they did have. Was it just sex for Luke? Or was it more than sex? Was it going somewhere, or nowhere?

"I have plenty of energy. And you can tell the guys to calm it down because I'm getting annoyed, and I'm dangerous when I'm annoyed. Also, Bonnie tends to bite people who irritate me."

"We're happy for you. It's past time you met someone." He rejoined the group at the bar and Beth focused on her.

"You met someone?"

Posy leaned forward. "Tell me about Jason. What's he done?"

"Nothing."

"You don't travel without two suitcases for no reason. There must have been *something*."

"Nothing. That's why I left."

"You don't leave a man who has done nothing wrong."

"Doing nothing can be wrong." Beth slumped in the chair. "I mean he literally does nothing with the girls. He swans in at the end of the day, undoes all my hard work settling them down, enjoys ten minutes of quality time designed to rev their excitement levels to Christmas Eve proportions and then leaves me to calm them down again."

"You've left your husband because the girls are excited to see him at the end of the day?"

"Are you being judgy again? Because if you are, I'm walking out of here right now."

Posy decided not to point out that her sister wasn't capable of walking anywhere until some of the alcohol in her system had evaporated. "I'm trying to understand, that's all. You and Jason seem perfect together. You're such a solid couple." And she was horrified. She'd thought Beth was settled and happy. She'd had no idea there was anything wrong. "Does Hannah know? Did you talk to her?"

"You really think I'd turn to Hannah for relationship advice? Her longest relationship is with her laptop. She doesn't know how it feels to be in love, let alone how it feels to have problems."

"Well, you should have called me. When did you start feeling unhappy? Did something happen?"

"We had a terrible row." Beth dropped her head into her hands. "I don't want another baby."

"Baby?"

Posy glanced nervously over her shoulder, but the noise levels were back up to normal levels and no one appeared to be paying attention.

Beth lifted her head. "I don't want it. It feels wrong." She thumped her head back down in her hands again, just as Aidan arrived with the food.

He looked confused. "If you don't want the burger, then we can—"

"She wants the burger. Thanks, Aidan." Posy grabbed the plates from him. "Don't worry, I've got this."

"My problem isn't the burger," Beth said, her voice muffled, "it's the baby."

Aidan froze and Posy felt like dropping her head into her hands alongside her sister.

"Ignore her." She waved him away and nudged Beth's arm. "Sit up. I can't talk to you while your head is in your hands and people are staring."

"I don't care if people stare."

"I do, and I have to live here after you've gone. I'm already handling enough gossip. Are you telling me you're pregnant?"

"Pregnant?" Beth lifted her head. "No, I'm not pregnant. At least, I'd better not be pregnant."

"Then what— Oh for goodness' sake." Posy pushed the coffee across the table. "Drink. The sooner you drink, the sooner you will start making sense."

Beth took a sip of coffee and then started to talk. It all slid out in a jumble of disjointed statements. *Jason wants more kids, I want to go back to work, need to have some time to myself, horrible fight, feel like a terrible mother, maybe Jason will walk out, maybe he'll kill the girls—*

"He is not going to kill the girls. He's their father! He adores them." Posy could see now how pale and tired Beth looked and it tugged at her heart. This was her sister and they'd always been close, despite the geographical distance. They didn't see each other often, but they emailed and talked on Skype. How had she not known how miserable she was?

She ignored the fact that she hadn't shared her thoughts with her sister, either.

"I meant by accident. What if he forgets to carry Ruby's inhaler?"

"Then she'll have an asthma attack, he'll have to take her to the ER and he will never forget it again. But I don't think he's going to forget."

"When it comes to the kids, I'm the one who thinks of everything."

"That doesn't mean he can't do it if he has to." She processed what she'd heard. "So Jason wants more kids, but you want to go back to work?"

"Yes. He thinks my day involves getting a manicure and lounging on the sofa with a book." Beth put the coffee down and picked up her burger. "Do you mind not mentioning any of this to Mom? I'd like to keep it between us. She's always busy at Christmas. I'm hoping she won't notice anything is wrong."

"I think she's going to notice you're here without Jason and the girls. Not to mention the small fact that you have no luggage."

"I'm planning on telling her I'm here early because I wanted to spend quality time with her and help out before the kids arrive. I know how much work we are."

That was probably true, but Posy knew their mother wasn't going to fall for that. "Why not be honest?"

Mom, I don't want to take over the business.

Hypocrite, Posy. Hypocrite.

"I don't want her to worry. She's already worried enough about Hannah. Do you want a bite of my burger?"

"Why would I want a bite of your burger? I have my own."

"Sorry, I'm not used to having food all to myself. At home I have to share everything. Breakfast cereal. Smoothies. You name it. Sharing food is so ingrained I even offered to share my smoked salmon with the guy in the seat next to me on the plane. He probably thought I was insane."

"I'm sure he thought you were generous." Posy decided to deal with the issue of their mother later. "Instead of leaving, have you tried explaining to Jason how you feel?"

"Do you really think I'd be here if there was an easier way?

He doesn't get it. That's why I left him with the girls. But if I know Jason, he'll call his mom."

"You love his mom."

"That's not the point. It will mean the kids won't starve or miss ballet, but it will also mean that nothing will have changed."

"Why do you want to go back to work?"

"Because I'm boring, have no conversation and have forgotten how to do anything except play princesses and fire stations."

"You're not boring." Posy took a mouthful of burger. "Actually, right now you *are* boring. But normally, you're not."

"Thanks."

"I'm your sister. I'm supposed to tell you the truth. So your plan was to come here alone with no luggage and decide if you want to go back to work?"

"I wanted to try on a life that isn't mine and see how it fitted. I wanted to order the salmon and the steak."

"I have no idea what you're talking about."

"Hannah flies everywhere first-class. She has this amazing job and an apartment with a view to die for."

"Which she never sees because she's always on an airplane." Posy put her half-eaten burger down. "You seriously envy Hannah?"

"She doesn't have to answer to anyone. People listen to her and pay her good money for her expertise. She can shop in Bloomingdale's without having to stop her child touching everything or running away. She never has to share anything. Yes, I envy her. Is that really such a surprise?"

Posy, who had never envied Hannah, was at a loss for words. "You want Hannah's life?"

"I'd like to have the freedom she has. Does that make sense?"

"Not a lot, but that's probably because you're drunk and I'm sober. Eat your burger."

"I came in from my job interview and he didn't even ask how it went." Beth picked the lettuce out of her burger. "We said awful things to each other, and the next thing I was grabbing a cab to the airport. What is wrong with me? Why can't I just be happy with my life, like you and Hannah?"

Posy shifted uncomfortably. "Everyone questions their life once in a while."

"You love what you do. My earliest memory is of you climbing. First it was the kitchen table, then the cabinets, and then Dad took you bouldering. Remember that?"

Vague, indistinct memories swirled around Posy's head. "I think I remember the boulder, but not Dad."

"I remember because Suzanne was there, and they had a fight." Beth stared into the fire. "I remember her saying, *Rob, you can't let a three-year-old climb that. It's dangerous.* And he laughed and put you on that rock anyway."

Posy frowned. "Our mother wasn't there?"

"Yes, but she thought Dad was some sort of climbing god. If he said something was safe, then it had to be safe. *Listen to your father*, she used to say."

It frustrated Posy that she couldn't remember her parents. All she had was photographs. "Where was Hannah?"

Beth fiddled with her drink. "They left her in the van with her book. Suzanne often stayed with her because she didn't like the fact that they left her alone. I didn't think anything of it at the time because it was our normal, but sometimes I look at my girls now and wonder how they could have done that. No way will I be leaving my kids on some lonely campsite when they're eight years old. The thought of what could have happened makes me cold. I remember Dad hauling you in front of friends and boasting about what an amazing climber you were. You were always Dad's favorite and he didn't bother hiding it."

Posy squirmed. It made her uncomfortable to hear it. "I didn't apply for that position, I can assure you."

"It was his fault, not yours. It's only when you have your own kids you realize what awful parenting it was. I'm careful to treat both girls exactly the same. I don't ever want them thinking Jason and I favor one of them over the other." Beth finished her food. "I might have to borrow pajamas from you."

"Sure." Posy dug her hand into her pocket and pulled out money. "You can choose between llamas or unicorns."

"I like my nightwear to be sexy. I should pay for this."

"I've got it." Posy pushed her way to the bar and handed Aidan the money. "Thanks."

"Is Beth okay, Posy?"

"She's fine."

Aidan glanced over her shoulder and watched Beth stagger to the door. "That's good. And by the way, I think it's sisterly of you to stick to coffee, too, because she's given up alcohol."

"What makes you think she's given up alcohol?"

"I heard her talking about the baby."

Posy closed her eyes briefly. "Aidan—"

"Yes?"

"I'm going to ask you a favor."

He grinned. "Right. Wow, Posy. I'm a little overwhelmed. You're very friendly lately."

"Not that sort of favor. Come closer." She leaned across the bar and beckoned to him.

He raised an eyebrow. "Are you about to kiss me in public?"

"No. I'm about to whisper something in your ear because I don't want everyone to hear. Which I know is probably a waste of time because keeping a secret in this village is impossible, but a girl can dream."

Aidan leaned forward. "What's the secret?"

"Beth isn't pregnant and I'd really appreciate it if you didn't mention that you heard her say the word *baby*."

"She's not pregnant?"

"Not pregnant."

"So why the coffee? Usually she likes a glass of white wine."

"Forget what she usually likes." Posy didn't want to tell him her sister had already drunk more than enough. "Thanks for the burger and the chat, Aidan."

"Anytime. And anytime you want to grab me and kiss me, that's fine, too."

"You're right. The customer service here really is outstanding." She patted him on the cheek. "Good night, Aidan."

She extracted Beth from a conversation with a group of people she didn't know and propelled her out of the pub.

Beth lurched unsteadily toward the car. "I'm looking forward to seeing Mom and Dad. Are they in?"

"No. Dad's giving some talk on mountain survival, and Mom has Knitting Club at the café. And if you want my honest opinion, it might be safer for you to see them tomorrow when you've slept off your champagne lifestyle."

"You could be right. I have a toothbrush, by the way."

"Good to know."

"First-class, they give you everything you need. Except pajamas, of course. And a new life."

"You don't need a new life." Posy bundled her sister into the car and leaned across to fasten the seat belt. "All you need to do is reshape the old one."

"Can I raid your wardrobe?"

"You always say my wardrobe is an abomination."

"It suits your lifestyle."

"Insulting someone isn't generally the best way to ask a favor." Posy started the engine. "As long as you're not expect-

ing couture, I'm sure we can kit you out. Mom will have knitted you a sweater for Christmas. You could open that early."

Beth pulled a face. "Is it the itchy, scratchy variety?"

"People pay a fortune for her sweaters, and no, I don't think
she's knitting itchy, scratchy at the moment."

"Any smiling reindeer? Delirious-looking Santas?"

"She hasn't knitted that kind of thing for at least two decades. Her knitwear is gorgeous. Last time I looked, she was
making something in a soft purple cashmere." She drove out
of the pub car park, taking care because the roads were icy.

"Remember the year she knitted us matching snowman
sweaters?"

"Yeah. Hannah put hers on the goat because she was worried it was going to be cold." Posy wondered if those early
Christmases were really as trouble free as she remembered or
whether it was simply that she hadn't been aware of the tensions when she was younger.

"It was a good year. You're right. I should probably talk to
Mom." Beth leaned her head back against the seat. "I don't
know what I want, but I do know what I *don't* want."

"Llama pajamas?"

"No." Beth stared out of the window. "I don't want another baby. But Jason does, which means we're in trouble."

11

Suzanne

Suzanne sat at the table with her friends, listening to the gentle hum of conversation and the rhythmic clack of needles.

The café was closed, but it felt as warm and lively as it did during the day. If anything, the atmosphere was more intimate, because this was a gathering of friends, not strangers.

Her fairy lights were strung around the windows and the glow of the wood burner in the corner gave the place a warm, festive feel.

Suzanne knew it wasn't the atmosphere that offered comfort, as much as the friendship.

"Those blue hats are selling well, Rhonda. I can't keep them on the shelf." She reached for another ball of yarn, checking as she did so that everyone in the group had drinks and food.

On the evenings when she ran her craft sessions, she and

Posy pushed the tables together to form one large one, a setup that allowed for chat and companionship.

"It's because the weather has turned so cold. I'll have another twenty for you by Friday."

"You're a wonder."

"It's given me something to do while the weather has been so bad," Rhonda said, "and you're the wonder, giving us somewhere to sell our goods. You've turned this place into a destination. I almost died when I walked past on Saturday and saw the coach in the car park. How many people descended on you?"

"Forty-five. They were Americans, on a tour of Scotland. I had to bring a few extra chairs in and we ran out of shortbread, but we managed." She never minded being surrounded by people. The more the merrier. "Fortunately, they called in advance."

"You're part of a tour itinerary now?"

"It seems so, which is good because they bought out the place. Cleared me out of everything tartan, spent a fortune in the café and bought a ton of secondhand books, especially those Highland romances that have a half-naked man in a kilt on the front."

"I'd love to see a man striding around bare-chested in the middle of a Highland winter." Maggie had the dirtiest laugh Suzanne had ever heard.

They'd met the first week Suzanne and Stewart had arrived at Glensay.

Before she married Stewart, Suzanne had never lived in one place for more than a few months. She'd trained as a mountain guide. She'd lived in tents and vans, and traveled.

And then everything had changed.

She had a promise to keep and three grieving children to care for.

No more roaming the mountains and sleeping in a tent or the back of a truck. No more dining on dry ramen noodles and washing her clothes in a mountain stream. She had to create a home, something she'd never done.

You don't have to change your whole life, Suzanne.

Suzanne had wanted to.

The life she'd chosen didn't fit with having kids. It might have worked for Cheryl, but it didn't work for her.

She couldn't give the girls their parents back, but she could give them consistency and stability.

There had been times when she'd wondered whether Stewart's love for her would be strong enough to withstand this new, unforeseen pressure on their relationship, but he'd handled it the same way he weathered storms on the mountains— with quiet calm.

Suzanne had readily agreed to move from Washington State to Scotland, where they would at least be close to Stewart's family. To begin with, they'd rented a small cottage a mile outside Glensay village, where Stewart's parents owned a small café.

With his skills as a climber and mountain guide, Stewart was immediately in demand and he went to work at the Glensay Adventure Centre, while Suzanne did what she could to furnish their home on a shoestring budget. While Stewart was out in the fresh air, she taught herself to cook something that wasn't dried rations and picked up bargains to make their small rental property cozy.

She'd felt out of her depth and hopelessly ill equipped to handle the challenge that lay ahead. Most people had nine months of pregnancy to prepare themselves for motherhood. She'd woken up one day and found herself responsible for three children of different ages, with no instruction manual.

A month after arriving in Scotland, Suzanne had taken

refuge from the cold in a local store, drawn in by a beautiful sweater displayed in the window.

She'd been eyeing it when the owner had approached. "The color would look perfect on you."

With three children to raise, Suzanne didn't have the money for pretty sweaters.

"It will be outside my budget."

"The sweater itself isn't for sale. I hung that there so that people could see how it looks when it's finished."

"You knitted this?" For the first time, Suzanne noticed the rainbow of wool that covered one wall of the small shop. The shop didn't sell sweaters, it sold yarn.

"You don't knit? You should learn. It's a great way to pass a Highland winter." The woman smiled. "You're Elsie McBride's daughter-in-law, aren't you? You and Stewart are raising those poor wee girls who lost their parents."

Suzanne had wondered if the woman was feeling sorry for the children, living with someone who had no clue how to knit. "I'm Suzanne."

"And I'm Margaret Cameron." She held out her hand. "My friends call me Maggie."

Suzanne had quickly become one of those friends.

Maggie had invited Suzanne to join the knitting group she held in her home every week. At first Suzanne hadn't cared much about the knitting itself. What she'd enjoyed was the conversation and companionship. The opportunity to seek advice from other women. But gradually she discovered the knitting had therapeutic properties. The first time she knitted a sweater for Posy, she'd felt a sense of achievement. It didn't matter that the hem wasn't perfectly straight or that some of the stitches were uneven. She'd made it herself. It was even more gratifying that Posy refused to take it off. She'd slept in that sweater, Suzanne remembered, until she'd worn a hole in it.

Eventually Maggie had given up selling yarn and concentrated on knitting.

After a couple of years Suzanne took over the café from Stewart's parents and added a small section where she sold hand-knitted goods made locally. They proved so popular she increased the space. Then she extended the stock to include other crafts, including locally made whiskey marmalade and heather honey. She couldn't keep up with demand, so used a portion of the profits to extend the property. Visitors to the café were almost always tempted to venture down the two steps into the shop, and visitors to the shop rarely left without sampling one of Suzanne's cakes and a frothy cappuccino.

Suzanne had lived in many places, but Glensay was her first real home.

She'd arrived with Stewart and three bewildered and sad young children at the start of a harsh Scottish winter, and the community had embraced them.

The people felt like family. She couldn't imagine ever living anywhere else.

"How is Doug's leg, Rhonda?"

"Playing up in this cold weather, but will he go and see the doctor?"

"I don't know what it is with men," Maggie said. "My Pete wouldn't go to the doctor if his leg was hanging off. You're quiet, Suzy. Are you going to tell us what's wrong? Is it Hannah?"

Despite all the stereotypes of small communities and gossip, Suzanne knew that nothing she said would leave this group of women.

They had supported each other through illness, unemployment and tragedy.

Suzanne wasn't sure how her life would have looked without them. Right from the beginning, she'd given up consulting books when she had a problem and asked her friends instead. Armed with their own experience, they'd shared ideas on dealing with temper tantrums, sleep problems, friendship issues.

They were the first people she turned to when she had a problem, and she had one now.

"For once, it's not Hannah." She reached for another ball of yarn. "Beth is home. Arrived a few hours ago. Which is lovely, of course, but we weren't expecting her until next week." And Beth wasn't given to unpredictable behavior. She rang when she said she was going to ring, never missed a birthday and was a devoted mother.

"I saw her." Rhonda stood up and stretched, rolling her shoulders to shake off the stiffness that came from sitting still. "She and Posy drove past me on the way here."

"Posy went to fetch her from the airport. She called me a little while ago to say that Beth was fine, and that they were going to the pub together to catch up."

"You must be excited to have your grandchildren home."

"The girls are still in New York with Jason. They're flying later." At least, she hoped they were.

"Maybe she wants a little time to herself, and no one is going to blame her for that." Rhonda sat down again and picked up her knitting. "With kids of that age, it's hard to find a moment to breathe."

"That's true, and I'm sure you're right. That's probably all it is." Suzanne put her knitting down on the table. She'd tried calling Stewart, but his phone had gone to voice mail, so she'd left a message asking him to check on Beth if he was home before her. "Beth is my steady one. No problems."

"That's always the way with children. Just when you think

it's safe to breathe, they do something you weren't expecting. I remember how I felt when my Alice suddenly announced she was divorcing Will."

Suzanne felt a flicker of alarm. Were Beth and Jason having problems? No, surely not. The two of them seemed so happy together. She'd never seen anything in their relationship to give her cause for concern. "I don't think it's anything like that."

"We need wine." Maggie put her knitting down and headed to the fridge, returning with a bottle of sauvignon blanc and four glasses. She put the tray down on the table. "This is Beth, not Hannah. Couldn't you just ask her? Or could Stewart talk to her? They've always been close."

"He's out giving a talk to a youth group tonight and she'll probably be in bed by the time he gets home."

"When is Hannah arriving?"

"Not for another week." Suzanne opened the wine. "She didn't come last year. I'm going to try hard not to smother."

"You should stop trying, Suzanne, and enjoy your own Christmas."

"I want to see her happy." She poured the wine into glasses and everyone took one.

"You've done everything you can. No mother could have done more."

Rhonda shook her head. "I sometimes think children are sent to worry us. My Rose has decided to give up her safe, secure, well-paid job as a doctor to retrain as a primary school teacher."

Elaine glanced up from her knitting. "She'll make an excellent teacher."

"But all that training."

"Does it matter? In the end you want them to be happy."

Was Beth happy?

Suzanne had assumed she was, but now she was wondering.

Whatever had brought her home early, Suzanne hoped it wasn't something serious.

Maybe Stewart should talk to Beth. If anyone could get to the bottom of what had brought her home early, he could.

12

Beth

Beth woke to bright winter sunshine and knew it was late. On the table next to the bed was a large glass of water, painkillers and a piece of paper covered in her sister's untidy scrawl.

She reached out and grabbed the note.

Drink the water, take the painkillers and come down to the café for breakfast. The perfect cure for a hangover is a Scottish breakfast.

The thought of anything fried made her stomach turn, but she swallowed the painkillers and sat up.

She couldn't remember the last time she'd woken naturally, without the assistance of a child.

Mommy, will you play with me?
Mommy, Melly is being mean.
Mommy, Ruby has broken my favorite doll.
I'm hungry.
Thirsty.
Need the bathroom…

The house was quiet. There was no clattering in the kitchen. No thundering of footsteps on the stairs. Fingers of sunlight poked through the slim gap in the curtains.

She glanced around her bedroom. The walls, once plastered with pictures of fashion models, were now painted over in neutral tones. Other than that, the room looked much the way it had when she was growing up. Her favorite books nestled in the bookshelf together with Betsy, the doll she'd refused to be parted from when she was young. It didn't matter that Betsy had lost one eye and half her hair, that doll had got her through the most difficult time of her life. Presumably Suzanne knew that, which was why Betsy hadn't been consigned to the attic with the other remnants of Beth's childhood.

Melly adored Betsy and the first thing she did when they arrived in Scotland was to adopt the doll.

If the children were here, they'd be in bed with her now, wrapped around her in a tangle of warmth, smiles and squabbles.

Their absence somehow made the silence louder. It should have felt blissful, but instead it felt hollow and empty, as if something was missing.

Had Jason called while she'd been asleep?

She reached for her phone and checked her messages, but there was nothing.

What did that mean?

There was a tap on the door and her mother appeared with a mug of tea.

"You slept late. You must have been exhausted."

Beth had seen her mother briefly the night before, but she'd been too tired to exchange more than a quick hug.

She stuffed the note from her sister under the pillow. "Thanks, Mom. I thought everyone was out." She noticed a stack of neatly folded clothes on the chair and silently blessed her sister.

"Your dad was hoping to see you, but he had to leave early and he didn't want to wake you. I'm leaving soon." Suzanne handed her the mug and walked to the window to draw the curtains. "It's been snowing again."

Beth curled her hands round the mug and tried to ignore her throbbing headache. All that free champagne didn't feel like so much fun this morning. "It looks pretty, but I guess it makes a lot more work around the place for you and Posy." Why hadn't Jason left her a message?

"Beth?"

"Sorry. You were saying?"

"I was surprised to see you home early, and without the girls. Is everything all right?"

"Everything is fine." She wondered when her mother was going to comment on the fact that she was wearing a pair of Posy's pyjamas.

"It's a beautiful day out there. Cold, though. What would you like to do today?"

Get rid of her pounding headache.

Figure out her life.

Talk to her sister.

"I thought I'd go over to the café and help Posy."

"That would be good. We're rushed off our feet over there, and I'm at the Christmas Market this afternoon, so she's on her own. Vicky was supposed to help, but she's gone down with flu. She can't even get out of bed. I've made chicken soup and I'm going to drop it off to her on the way to the market and check on her."

Suzanne sold crafts at a number of Christmas markets throughout the festive season.

"Should you be visiting her if she has flu?"

"She's on her own. Someone needs to keep an eye on her. And I'm never ill, you know that. I've put fresh towels in the bathroom. If you're ready in half an hour, I can drop you off on my way to Vicky's. You'll need boots. We've had a lot of snow this week. How are the girls?"

Beth didn't know, and the fact that she didn't know made her want to hyperventilate. It was the first time since Melly had been born that she had no idea what was happening with her children. Why hadn't Jason been in touch? Should she call his mom? "They're great. Excited about coming to visit you." What if Jason didn't bring them? What if he was so upset by her walking out and leaving him with the girls that he decided not to join her? On the other hand, he'd said terrible things, too. It was the things he'd said that had triggered this situation.

"Your dad and I can't wait to see them. I'm sure they've changed a lot. They always do at that age." Suzanne's gaze settled on the stack of Posy's clothes on the chair. "Where's your luggage?"

Beth's brain fused. "The airline lost it."

She didn't want to worry her mother by admitting that she and Jason had hit a rough patch.

"That's terrible." Suzanne frowned. "Can't they trace it?"

"They'll call me if they find it. I can manage. Posy lent me some things."

"Your old boots are probably lying around somewhere. Do you want me to dig them out?"

"Thanks, Mom. That would be great." Beth forced herself out of bed and snatched up her phone. "I'll use the bathroom."

"You're taking your phone into the shower with you? You girls and your phones. But it's great that you can't be away from Jason for one night without wanting to talk to him."

She was going to be struck down for lying to her mother.

Santa was going to leave a lump of coal in her stocking because she'd definitely been naughty, not nice.

She showered and pulled on Posy's clothes.

On her way downstairs she checked her phone again and found a text from her dad, which made her smile because Stewart only texted as a last resort.

Good to have you home. Looking forward to seeing you later. Dad. xx

Those two kisses brought a lump to her throat.

She wanted her dad so badly her chest ached.

She cleared her throat and pulled herself together. What was *wrong* with her? She was a grown woman, not a small child. She should have moved beyond needing her dad in times of trouble. But now she was wishing she'd set her alarm so that she could at least have grabbed a hug before he left for work.

There was still nothing from Jason.

It was the first time in their marriage that they'd disagreed about something important. And this was major. Marriage was all about compromise, but where was the compromise in this? You couldn't exactly compromise on having another baby. Either you had one or you didn't.

One of them was going to have to give up on a dream.

Could she do it? Could she have another baby to keep her marriage alive?

For the first time since Jason had raised the issue, she rested her hand on her abdomen and imagined it. Closing her eyes, she remembered those first wondrous flutters when she felt the baby moving. *Ours, Jason. Our baby. Our little family.*

Then she thought about the delivery. When other mothers described their easy labor and textbook delivery, Beth stayed silent. For her, labor was about pain, bruising, stitches and pediatricians hunched over her babies with anxious expressions on their faces.

The thought of going through it again made her pulse rate rocket, and that was before she started to think about sleepless nights and the sheer relentlessness of having young children.

How could Jason even *think* it was a good idea?

Miserable, tired and hungover, she grabbed her coat and joined her mother in the car.

"Put your seat belt on. The roads are icy." Suzanne drove carefully and Beth stretched out her legs to warm her toes under the heater. The roads were clear, but snow lay in thick layers over the fields and mountains.

"How are you, Mom?" She felt a stab of guilt. "I'm sorry I haven't called much lately. It's been crazy busy with the girls."

"You don't have to apologize." Suzanne concentrated on the road. "I remember how it was having young children. I used to make so many plans for the day, and then somehow the time would be eaten up and I wouldn't have done any of the things on my list."

"That sounds familiar." Beth suppressed a yawn. "How did you ever cope?" One minute, Suzanne's life had been a child-free zone, and the next she'd had three orphaned children to deal with.

Her mother smiled. "I had your dad. We were a team."

Thinking of her dad made Beth feel ridiculously emotional.

To distract herself, she stared out of the window as they passed familiar places.

There was the McAllisters' farm, and beyond that the mountains.

In the early days when they'd moved here, she remembered feeling traumatized. But then slowly, gradually, they'd been absorbed into the community.

She wasn't sure exactly when she'd started to treat the place as home. It had happened gradually and coincided with her thinking of Suzanne as her mother.

Had she ever really considered how hard it must have been for Suzanne? And how lucky the three of them were to have her? She and Stewart had stuck by them through thick and thin.

"How is Dad?"

"He's great. You know your dad—" Suzanne slowed as she approached a junction "—always on the go. Says yes to everything, which is why he wasn't here when you arrived home last night and was gone before you woke up. Of course, if we'd known you were coming—"

"It was a spontaneous thing."

Suzanne reached across and squeezed her hand. "We're always here for you, you know that."

"Thanks." Beth felt tears sting again and blinked them back. Apparently she'd turned into a fountain overnight. She was never drinking again.

Her mother slowed and lowered her window as they passed a couple hauling a Christmas tree to their car. "Fiona! We've moved Book Group to Tuesday."

"I heard." Fiona stepped toward the car. "Are we making food, as it's the last meeting before Christmas?"

"That's the plan."

Fiona and Suzanne talked for a minute and Beth tried to imagine a similar exchange happening in Manhattan and failed.

If the time of her yoga class changed, someone sent her a text. They didn't stop her halfway down Fifth Avenue.

She smiled as her mother waved to Fiona and pulled away. "It's good to be home."

"You don't miss the bright lights of the city? How is Jason? Job still going well?"

"Yes. He's been offered another promotion."

"Promotions usually come with longer hours and that would be tough on you with two little ones."

How was it her mother always understood?

"You had three little ones." *And we weren't even yours.* For some reason, her brain kept coming back to that. The conversation with Jason had made her think about the realities of having three children.

"And that was lucky for me."

Was it? She'd never talked to her mother in depth about that time, about the decision she'd made. Had she ever considered saying no? Had she, like Beth, ever thought *that's too much*?

Before she could decide whether or not to ask that question, Suzanne had pulled up outside the café.

"Have fun with your sister. I hope it's not too busy."

Beth hoped that, too. She wasn't sure her head could stand too much noise.

She pushed open the door of the café, relishing the sudden rush of warmth.

Posy was behind the counter, serving generous slabs of chocolate cake onto plates. Her curls bounced around her face and her cheeks were flushed from the heat.

She smiled when she saw Beth. "How are you?"

"Honestly? I feel as if one of Santa's reindeer kicked me in the head. And I keep wanting to cry."

"If you must live a champagne lifestyle, then you have to pay the price."

"Thanks for the sympathy. And for the water and pain-killers."

"You're welcome. You can make it up to me by hanging your coat up and taking this to table 2."

Beth suppressed a yawn. "Which is table 2?"

"The one by the fire. It's the table everyone wants." Posy loaded cups and a teapot onto a tray. "How's Mom?"

"Fine, I think. She wanted to know when you're going to fetch the tree."

"I'm taking Luke to the forest tomorrow. We'll get one for us and one for the barn."

Luke?

Beth delivered the tea with a smile and a greeting and then walked behind the counter and studied the coffee machine. With its flashing lights and dials, it looked like the cockpit of a jumbo jet. "Who is Luke?"

"Our current lodger. He's rented the barn for three months. Don't touch that!" Posy nudged her to one side. "I can't afford you to break the coffee machine right now."

"Thanks for that vote of confidence." Beth leaned against the counter and watched as Posy produced an espresso that would have impressed the most exacting New York barista. "I haven't heard from Jason. I'm worried."

"Worry is your middle name." Posy put the coffee next to her and greeted a couple who walked through the door bringing with them a flurry of snow and freezing air. "Cold out there today. What can I get you?"

They ordered, and Beth sipped her coffee, remembering all the hours she'd spent here as a child.

Growing up, all three girls had come here after school and done their homework on one of the tables while waiting for their mother to finish work. There was always a treat. Sometimes it was a buttery, sugary square of crumbly shortbread warm from the oven, and sometimes their mother would make them hot chocolate with whipped cream and a chocolate flake.

Suzanne had recognized the nurturing properties of a cozy environment before it had become a global trend.

When they'd finished their homework, they'd snuggle down on the beanbags in front of the bookshelves and read until she was ready to close the café.

"Hey—" Posy pushed her gently to one side "—you're in my way."

"Maybe you haven't noticed, but I'm having a personal crisis here."

"I noticed. I'm the one who picked you up from the airport, sobered you up and lent you my favorite pajamas. I'm sympathetic, but your crisis is going to have to fit round my lunch orders. You said you wanted to go back to work—you can start now." Posy handed her an apron and Beth sighed.

"What do you want me to do?"

"You can serve. And don't forget the smile and the big Scottish welcome."

"I live in Manhattan and I was born in Seattle."

"And you spent your formative years right here in Scotland, so stop pretending you're a city slicker." Posy gestured to the board. "For specials today we have two soups—leek and potato, and creamy mushroom. Served with warm rosemary and sea salt bread, or plain sourdough. For vegetarians, we have a goat cheese and red onion tartlet—served with salad—and for raging carnivores, Mom's venison and mushroom pies."

Hearing it made Beth hungry. "My favorite."

"You're serving, not eating. But if there are any left, you can have one."

"Do you ever have any left?"

"Never."

Deciding that her sister was a sadist, Beth took an order from a couple of Australian tourists and vanished to the kitchen.

For the next two hours, she was rushed off her feet. She barely had time to talk to her sister, let alone pause to check her phone.

The café was busy, and so was the gift shop area.

While Beth was serving soup into bowls, Posy sold four of Suzanne's blue sweaters with sparkles, eight hats and two pairs of fingerless gloves.

Beth yawned. "This place is insanely busy. How do you cope?"

"Normally we have Vicky, but she succumbed to the dreaded flu."

"What if the mountain rescue team gets called out?"

"Then I drop everything and you end up running this place." Posy bagged up three packets of Christmas cards painted by a local artist and added a hand-wrapped gingerbread man. "On the house." She handed it over with a dazzling smile and another family of happy customers left the café.

"You're lucky."

"Excuse me?"

"You have your life sorted. You have your cozy loft, your animals, the mountains and this café. You know what you want and you're doing it. I envy that."

Posy didn't look at her. "Seems to me you're envying everyone right now. Did it ever occur to you that we might envy you?"

Beth helped herself to shortbread. "Why are you so snappy?"

"I'm not snappy. It's just—"

"What?"

Posy shook her head. "Nothing. I think you make a lot of assumptions about people's lives, that's all."

"Correct assumptions. Hannah doesn't want a family, and you don't want to live in Manhattan."

"That last part is true."

The bell on the door clanged and a tall, dark-haired man strolled into the café. He had a brooding, slightly dangerous air to him and Beth stood up a little straighter.

"Hot man alert," she murmured. "Get his name and number. Alternatively you could hold him captive and warm yourself on him until the snow melts."

"I already know his name and number. He's my lodger." Posy nodded to the man. "Productive morning?"

"I deleted more than I wrote. Hazards of the job, but nothing a good brownie won't cure." The man unzipped his coat and Beth saw her sister smile up at him.

"One brownie coming up. Usual coffee?"

"Please."

"Anything else you need?"

"As a matter of fact, there is." He reached out and hauled Posy close, kissing her as if the world was about to end and this was their last goodbye.

It was like watching the closing scene of a romantic movie.

Beth gaped. She was stunned and, yes, maybe a little envious.

She'd thought she knew everything about Posy's life, but apparently not. This man was clearly more than her sister's lodger. And now she remembered the comment Posy had made in the car. *As it happens, I was in bed with a tall, dark, handsome man having the best sex of my life.*

Beth had assumed it was a joke.

She glanced around the café, but all she saw was benign smiles.

Beth felt as if she was the only person not in on a secret.

When Luke finally lifted his head, the look he shared with

Posy was so personal, so intimate, that Beth felt as if she'd walked into their bedroom.

When had she and Jason last looked at each other like that?

When had they last been spontaneous?

Their lives were scheduled down to the minute, and more often than not, their plans centered around the girls.

Luke finally released Posy, but it was clear to Beth that he only did so because they were in public.

She waited for her sister to introduce them, but Posy was staring dreamily into space.

No need to ask if he was a good kisser, Beth thought, and took the initiative.

"We haven't met." She stuck her hand out. "I'm Posy's sister. The middle, married sister. Beth." *The boring one with a rotting brain.* "Good to meet you."

He shook her hand, his grip firm. "Luke Whittaker. Climber, writer and all-around bad influence. Good to meet you, too." He turned back to Posy. "I'll grab a table while one is available because we all know that situation won't last long."

Luke Whittaker. Bad influence.

Beth watched as he walked to the table.

Posy tipped fresh coffee beans into the grinder, spilling a fair few. "Oops."

"Don't apologize," Beth said. "If I'd just been kissed like that, my hand wouldn't be steady, either."

"Do you mind not staring at my customers?"

"I'm only staring at one customer." Beth didn't shift her gaze. "Did he say his name was Luke Whittaker?"

"He did." Posy cleared up the beans. "You're still staring, by the way."

"The name is familiar."

"He's written a book and been on TV. He's Adventure Guy. The one who tells all those stories of survival. You know, your ship goes down in the Atlantic, how do you not get eaten by sharks, that kind of thing. Particularly useful information when you live in the Highlands of Scotland." Posy knocked a carton of milk off the counter and Beth caught it midair.

"You need to take a breath before you break something." She watched as he paused on his way to a table and exchanged a few friendly words with Mrs. Chappell, who owned a few holiday cottages in the village. "*Adventure Guy.* I've never watched that show, but…I guess that must be where I heard the name. How long has he been kissing you like that?"

"Not long enough." Posy slid a large slice of brownie onto a plate.

"Now I understand why you kept hinting about things going on in your life, too." Beth watched as he shrugged off his weatherproof jacket to reveal broad shoulders encased in a cable-knit sweater. "He looks like an advert for quality outdoor wear. Tough enough to withstand buffeting wind, sluicing rain and freezing ice."

"He's easy on the eye, that's true." Posy poured the silky milk onto the coffee, producing the pattern of a Christmas tree. She dusted it with cinnamon and carried the coffee and brownie to the table.

Beth waited until she returned. "So you weren't kidding when you said you were in bed with a tall, dark, handsome man."

"I wasn't kidding. And can I just say I'm a little offended that the mere thought of me having a sex life seems so hilarious to you."

"It was nothing to do with you, and everything to do with the fact that there aren't exactly that many sexy strangers roaming the village." Beth studied Luke. "And you left him to fetch me from the airport."

"I did. Which means you owe me in a massive way." Posy glanced at Beth. "Your eyes are shiny. Are you crying again?"

"I'm very emotional this morning."

"That's what happens when you drink ten bottles of champagne." But Posy gave her arm a squeeze. "Everything will be fine. You need to chill."

"I'm not a very chilled person."

"Then go and roll in the snow or something, but stop crying or you're going to worry Mom and Dad."

"Do you ever think about the sacrifice they made taking us in?"

Posy looked incredulous. "Not in the middle of my working day, no. What is *wrong* with you?"

"I've been thinking about some stuff, that's all."

"Well, stop thinking. It's bad for you and it makes your eyes red. Drink some strong coffee and put some makeup on, or whatever it is you do to make yourself feel normal. And stop wallowing."

"I'm not wallowing." But Beth whipped out her lip gloss and slicked it over her lips. In fact, Posy was right. She was wallowing, and she needed to stop. "It's good to know your love life is flourishing, because mine certainly isn't." At that moment her phone rang and she grabbed it, relieved. "Finally! That must be Jason. I was starting to worry. Do you mind if I take this?"

"Go." Posy gave her a gentle push. "Take it in the kitchen. I don't want your emotional make-up session putting my customers off their food."

Knowing that Duncan would be in the kitchen, Beth chose to step outside the café.

It was only as she pressed the button to answer that she realized it wasn't Jason, it was Corinna.

"Hi, Corinna." She should have been thrilled to hear from

Corinna, but all she could think was how much she wished it had been Jason.

"I want you here this afternoon. We're having a team meeting."

No small talk. No *how are you?* No *are you ready for the holidays?* No question about whether it was convenient for Beth.

Still, at least Corinna was still keen to have her on the team.

"I'm not in Manhattan, Corinna. I'm in Scotland. I decided to travel early."

There was a brief silence. "Beth, I'm asking myself if you're taking this seriously. If you really want to be involved, then I need to be sure of your loyalty and commitment."

When she'd worked for Corinna the first time round, she'd been bombarded with the same kind of emotional blackmail. It was as uncomfortable to listen to now as it had been then. "I'm committed, Corinna. I've been working hard, pulling together ideas."

"Send them across. I'll take a look."

"I'll email them later today." She'd intended to think about the campaign on the flight, but instead she'd focused on champagne and the novelty of having a chair to herself and sole charge of the remote control.

"If you can get them to me by 2:00 p.m., I can take them into the meeting. We'll send you a link and you can join us."

"I can't." Beth cringed as she said it. Was she going to blow this chance because she'd come home early? "The signal isn't strong enough where I am. I'll email you."

"I'll be waiting." Corinna's disapproval traveled across thousands of miles.

"Thanks. I'll—" But Corinna had gone, and Beth was standing with a phone in her hand and a creeping sense that nothing she did was ever going to be good enough.

The cold air seeped through her clothing and she shivered and pushed her way back into the café.

She'd forgotten how pressured and unforgiving work could be.

Posy glanced at her. "Are you getting a divorce?"

Sisters could be so blunt. "It wasn't Jason. It was my old boss Corinna, who I was hoping would also be my new boss." Divorce? There was no way she and Jason would get divorced. It was a disagreement—that was all. All marriages had them. "And if you could keep your voice down, that would be great."

"Corinna?" Posy frowned. "Corinna the evil— I'm not saying the word here because my customers are sensitive, but the word I'm thinking of rhymes with *witch*."

Beth hated to be reminded of Corinna's bad side, especially so soon after a call when it had been very much in evidence. "I have to send some ideas through to her by 2:00 p.m. her time, which means I have until 7:00 p.m. to come up with a genius idea that will knock her stilettos off her feet. Will you be okay if I go back to the house and work?"

"I'll manage." Posy glanced up as the door opened and Suzanne hurried in. "Mom. Everything okay? How is Vicky?"

"Worse. I've called Dr. Burn and asked him to check on her. I'll go back tomorrow."

"I thought you'd be on your way to the Christmas Market by now."

"I was, but I had an email from Hannah. She must have sent it last night, but I only check my emails once a day."

Beth contemplated a universe where a person checked their email only once a day. "What did she say?"

"She's arriving earlier than planned."

Posy was balancing a tray of coffee. "How much earlier?"

"Today."

"Everyone is coming home early," Posy said. "There must be something in the water."

Suzanne was frowning. "I confess your dad and I are worried. Why would she be coming home early? Beth, have you talked to her lately? Do you know if something is wrong?"

"Last time I talked to her she seemed fine. Busy. She canceled dinner." Beth felt a flash of guilt because she'd snapped at her sister. It hadn't occurred to her that everything in Hannah's life might not be perfect.

Suzanne glanced at the clock. "Her flight arrives in an hour. I'm going to call and let them know I'll be late at the market."

"I'll pick up Hannah." Posy moved swiftly to one of the tables, delivered the order with a big smile and then ripped off her apron. "You go to the Christmas Market and Beth can hold the fort here."

Beth shook her head. "I can't! I don't know how to work the coffee machine, and anyway I have to spend the afternoon working on some ideas for Corinna." She needed to compensate for not being part of that call. She needed to show Corinna she was both loyal and committed.

"Duncan knows how to work the coffee machine, and you have two kids, so I'm guessing you know how to multitask. Serving cake and coffee to happy people will stimulate your creative juices." Posy hung up her apron and grabbed her coat. "You go to the market, Mom."

"But Hannah is expecting me."

Posy smiled. "Then she's going to be pleasantly surprised to see her baby sister."

Oh God, Beth thought. How could she have possibly thought that coming home early might be relaxing? And how was she going to develop a knockout campaign while she was serving shortbread and gingerbread men?

13

Hannah

Hannah hovered in the doorway of arrivals.

People flowed past her, haste making them clumsy and careless. She was bruised by elbows and stabbed by the corners of sharp parcels. Gritting her teeth, she moved closer to the glass for protection.

She felt vulnerable and not up to the challenge of handling Suzanne. The journey home would be punctuated by a cheery stream of well-meaning chat, which would exclude all the questions Suzanne was desperate to ask.

Hannah knew there would be things she was expected to say, and she wouldn't be able to say any of them.

If she was lucky, Stewart would be home early. His steady presence seemed to calm Suzanne and Hannah had always found him easy to be around.

It crossed her mind that he might be the one to talk to about what was happening in her life.

She'd switched her phone on after the flight and found a message from Adam.

Call me. Let me know how your sister is.

What had possessed her to lie to him?

The airport was busy and she was wondering if she should call Suzanne to get an idea of how far away she was, when a familiar car swerved into a space.

Hannah picked up her two suitcases and her laptop bag and braved the howling wind, but it wasn't Suzanne who sprang out of the driver's seat, it was Posy.

Her sister wore faded jeans and hiking boots. Her outdoor jacket was a zingy shade of blue and unzipped, as if she'd been in too much of a hurry to fasten it. Everything about her screamed energy. The way she walked, the way she smiled, the way she turned her head. Even her ponytail swung with enthusiasm. She wasn't capable of strolling anywhere.

She wore no makeup, but her cheeks were pink and her hair, a rich chocolate brown, gleamed as if it had been polished. She could have appeared in an advert for multivitamins or wholesome breakfast cereal. Looking at her made Hannah feel pale and unhealthy. Did she ever look that vibrant and full of life? The answer was no, at least not without considerable help from expensive cosmetics.

"Well, if it isn't my prodigal sister." Posy stepped forward and hugged her.

The hug took Hannah by surprise.

She felt the soft brush of her sister's hair against her cheek, breathed in the smell of fresh lemons. Something fluttered in her chest, an emotion she hadn't felt in a long time.

The cold chill that had gripped her for the past couple of weeks melted under the warmth, taking with it another layer of her carefully erected defenses.

That felt so scary that she stepped back and promptly planted her soft suede boots into a slushy puddle.

Icy meltwater seeped through the inadequate fabric.

It said a lot about her need to avoid intimacy that she was willing to sacrifice an expensive pair of boots and possibly a couple of toes to frostbite.

"I was expecting Suzanne."

"She has a stall at one of the Christmas markets today. You got me instead. I think I'm the jackpot, but I could be biased."

Hannah wished she hadn't been in so much haste to pull away from the hug, which made no sense.

You couldn't reject love one minute and then want it the next.

Fortunately, her sister didn't seem to have noticed anything strange or different about Hannah.

"Be careful with the suitcases. The blue one is new."

Posy straightened, and wisps of hair slid around her flushed cheeks. "If you're going to complain, you can haul your own luggage. And there's plenty of it. You don't travel light, do you?"

"The house isn't usually that warm. I brought extra clothes."

"It's warm enough if you're working." Posy swept up the luggage and flung it into the car. "Providing you don't sit around, you won't feel the cold."

Already they were sniping at each other. That, at least, felt familiar.

No matter that she was on her way to the top of her profession, her youngest sister always made her feel inadequate, as if all the skills she had amounted to nothing. "I've been here less than two minutes, so do you think you could give me a break?" Depression settled on Hannah like a fine mist of rain, slowly seeping through her remaining layers of protection. "I'm sorry. And I'm grateful for the ride."

"You're welcome. I'm sorry, too." Posy gave a quick smile. "I'm hoping it's my massive Christmas gift that's straining the edges of your suitcase."

Hannah stepped into the car and slammed the door shut, relieved to be insulated from the chaos of the airport even though she knew all her problems were sealed in the car with her.

Expensive Christmas gifts she could manage. Handing over her credit card was the easy part, although in fact the weight of her suitcase could mostly be attributed to the books she carried with her when she traveled. Sometimes she could find room for only one or two, but for this trip she'd sacrificed clothes to make room for six of her favorites.

It was like traveling with friends. Simply knowing they were there made her feel better. Later she'd turn to them, lean on them as she always had, seeking comfort in the worlds hidden between their pages.

She watched as a couple hurried toward a taxi, juggling cases, parcels and two young children.

Home for Christmas.

Most people found the concept comforting and soothing. Hannah wasn't one of them.

Posy opened the driver's door, letting in a blast of ice-cold air. "Why the dark glasses? You're in the Highlands, not Hollywood."

It said a lot about their relationship that her sister assumed the glasses were for anonymity, rather than to conceal the fact that Hannah felt beaten.

Posy didn't know the details of her life, and whose fault

was that? Hannah had allowed misconceptions to stack up like bricks in a wall, cutting her off from other people.

"You're stressed. I'm sure the last thing you needed was to pick your sister up from the airport. I would have taken a cab, but last time I did that Suzanne was upset."

"You mean Mom." Posy leaned on her horn as someone pulled out in front of her. "And I'm not stressed. She's thrilled you're home for Christmas. I'm glad you came."

Hannah knew her sister's words were driven by her love for Suzanne. She envied her sister's ability to love so fearlessly and completely. Posy handled love the same way she would handle a difficult rock face—boldly, and without fear of falling.

For Hannah, it was a true demonstration of bravery.

It made her feel cowardly.

She leaned her head back against the seat and closed her eyes, but doing so made her think of Adam and that made her feel even more cowardly. She opened them again. "Tell me how everything is. I feel out of touch."

"An email or a phone call would help with that." Posy's hands tightened on the wheel. "Sorry. Ignore me. Too much to do, too little time—you know how it is. Update. Right. Dad's busy. The Adventure Centre is doing well. Martha stopped laying for a while, but I can't imagine you're going to lose sleep over that. Mom's business is thriving. The café is insanely busy, but that's good, too. Bonnie and I have been busy with the mountain rescue team and I've been doing a lot of ice climbing. I think that about covers it."

"Ice climbing?" Hannah shivered and pulled the edges of her coat closer together. The fabric was damp and cold. "I hope you're careful."

"Now you sound like Mom."

"How is she?"

"Not bad, considering. This is always a difficult time of year for her."

"Yes." Hannah's stomach did a strange roll. It was a difficult time of year for her, too. In the distance she could see snow-covered mountains and for a moment she wished she'd stayed in Manhattan. She could have made some excuse and hidden away in her apartment. She didn't have to put herself through this. Mountains made her conscious of her failures and frailties. As a child, she'd wondered what was missing in her that she couldn't feel the same passion for climbing her parents did. Whatever it was she'd lacked had meant she was excluded from the club that contained all the people she loved.

"She still has nightmares." Posy glanced in her mirror and checked the road. "Twenty-five years and she still has them. I don't understand that."

Hannah understood it.

Hannah had her own nightmares, although she was sure hers were different from Suzanne's.

"It's the time of year." She hoped her sister didn't intend to linger on this particular topic of conversation.

Posy drove confidently, her eyes fixed on the road. "Didn't expect to see you home this early. Something happen?"

I think I might be pregnant.

"I had a window in my schedule."

"That's a relief, because I'm not sure I could handle two sisters having a crisis simultaneously."

"Two sisters?"

"Beth is home."

"Oh." So no time to pull herself together before having to handle her nieces. On the other hand, if Beth was home early, maybe Hannah could enlist her help in tracking down a pregnancy test. "I thought they weren't arriving for a few more days."

"It was spontaneous. She didn't mention any of this to you?"

"When would she? We're both busy. Beth and I aren't exactly falling over each other every day, you know." Guilt was a constant background hum in her life, but occasionally it exploded out of control. Like now, when she was reminded just how bad she was at keeping her fingers on the pulse of her family. If there had been a change in rhythm, she wouldn't have known about it.

Posy glanced at her. "It was a simple question. No need to overreact."

She was overreacting to everything these days. It was an uncomfortable experience. "How can Beth be home early? Isn't Jason working?"

"He's not with her. Nor are the kids. She wanted some time on her own."

"She's having a crisis?"

Was that why Beth had called? Because she was in trouble?

Hannah's guilt intensified. She'd assumed the call was to confirm dinner. It hadn't occurred to her something might be wrong.

She cast her mind back to the conversation, searching for clues, but all she could remember was the fact that Adam had strolled onto the plane and she'd tried to finish the call as fast as possible to avoid the different parts of her life colliding.

"Do you know what's wrong?"

Posy hesitated. "You should probably ask her yourself."

She was the last person to advise anyone on their personal problems, and she could hardly ask for Beth's support when she'd been so bad at offering any herself.

She made a decision. "Posy, could we stop at a pharmacy?"

Posy frowned. "Are you sick? Champagne headache? I have something for that back home."

"I'm not sick."

"Then—"

"I need to buy a pregnancy test."

"You're pregnant?" Posy slammed her foot on the brake and Hannah was grateful for the seat belt.

"I don't know. That's why I need the test."

"Right." Posy stared straight ahead, her hands still gripping the wheel. "Well—let me think."

"What is there to think about?"

"A place where we can buy a pregnancy test without the whole of the village knowing. Why didn't you buy one in the airport?"

Hannah sighed. "I tried. They'd sold out."

"They don't sell pregnancy tests in Manhattan?"

Hannah turned her head and stared out of the window. "I've been putting it off. I'm probably not pregnant. I don't feel sick or anything."

"But you're late."

"Yes."

"And—you've been seeing someone?"

Hannah turned her head to look at her sister. "Did no one ever tell you the facts of life?"

"Sorry. Of course you've been seeing someone. Got a little carried away there with the whole donkey-in-a-stable, Christmas theme." Posy turned the car round and headed back in the direction they'd come from. "There's a pharmacy not far from here. Do you want me to go in for you?"

Hannah was touched by the offer. "Thanks, but I'll do it. At least that way if we bump into someone we know, it won't start a rumor you're pregnant." All the same, she felt awkward and conspicuous as she picked up the test and paid for it.

If she did this, there would be no more denial.

She'd know, and she'd have to decide what to do.

She kept her sunglasses on and felt faintly ridiculous.

As she slipped the test into her bag, she felt sick for the first time.

Posy drove back toward the village, but now the atmosphere in the car had changed. "Do you want to talk about it?"

"No."

"Okay." There was a pause. "I mean, you don't look exactly happy, so I just wanted you to know that you can always—"

"I'm fine, but thanks."

"Right."

Posy turned off the main road onto the narrow lane that led to Glensay Lodge. They bumped their way over ruts and potholes and finally pulled up in the yard.

The house was exactly as Hannah remembered it, framed by dramatic peaks and forest. Originally a Victorian hunting lodge, it had been refurbished by the family who had owned it before Suzanne and Stewart. Everything had been updated and modernized, apart from the wireless broadband and phone signal, which, because of the surrounding topography, appeared as randomly as the sun.

In summer, the slopes behind the house were a sea of purple heather, but winter had coated them with deep layers of snow. There was both a beauty and a bleakness to the landscape. Hannah knew that was part of the attraction for many people. If you wanted to escape from the modern world, this was the place to come.

She slid her sunglasses into her bag and stepped out of the car, gasping as an icy wind punched her. The cold found the cracks in her clothing and took advantage of her wet feet. The ground was frozen and she felt her boots slide. It was almost as if the place was sending a warning. *You don't belong here.*

"Let's get you inside. You're not dressed for the weather. And don't slip on the ice, just in case you are...you know..."

Posy dumped a suitcase by her feet and then paused. "What happened to your face?"

"My face?" Her sister looked so shocked Hannah almost reached for a mirror to check for herself.

"Have you been crying? Is that why you were wearing sunglasses?"

"What? No, of course not."

"Your eyes are red."

She *had* been crying, but it had been hours ago, when she'd hidden her face under the thin, scratchy airline blanket. "It was a long flight. I've been working hard. It could be allergies. And I've had a cold." She shouldn't have offered up so many explanations. One would have been enough. Four smacked of desperate. It seemed Posy thought so, too, because she studied her for a long minute.

"If you're upset—"

"I'm not."

Posy hesitated, as if she wanted to say something more. "Okay, well, let's get these cases indoors. I'll carry them. You shouldn't be lifting, just in case—and I'm sorry I can't hang around, but I need to get back to the café."

Hannah was relieved to have time to herself. The first thing she intended to do was apply layers of makeup. Just because she was falling apart on the inside, didn't mean it had to show on the outside. Camouflaging her real self was a big part of her life.

"There's soup in the fridge if you're hungry, and cake in the tin."

Hannah hadn't touched sugar for almost a year. She'd hoped her new regime might help her sleep, but it had made no difference. The only time she slept was when Adam stayed over. "I ate on the flight."

"Then take a nap, or something. You look tired."

"I don't sleep well." Why was she discussing her insomnia issues with her sister?

Posy strode to the door of the lodge, opened it and put Hannah's cases onto the floor. "Have you tried counting sheep?"

"What?"

"Sheep. You should count them. It's what people do to help them sleep."

"I wouldn't even know how."

"You could look out of the window," Posy said. "Plenty of sheep out there just waiting to be counted. You're in the turret room. Come to think of it, I should take your cases up." She carried Hannah's luggage upstairs with no apparent effort and reappeared moments later. "There are fresh logs in the basket, so light a fire if you're cold. Mom has festooned the place with lights, so try not to electrocute yourself. I'll see you later, and make sure you water Eric."

"Eric?"

But Posy had gone, already halfway to her car.

Hannah closed the front door, peeled off her soaking boots.

The slate floor was heated and for a moment she stood still, allowing the warmth to slide into her freezing limbs.

Semi-recovered, she went upstairs to the turret room.

The bedroom had a high, conical ceiling and tall windows that offered a spectacular view of the loch and the mountains beyond. Following the curve of the window was a seat, padded with a nest of soft cushions that invited the occupant to snuggle and relax.

The room was cozy, thanks to crisp white linens and the stylish use of plaids and tweeds.

Even without Posy's warning, Hannah would have known who was responsible for the tiny lights that framed the window and the hearth. Suzanne hated the dark. She hung lights in places other people wouldn't think to hang them and burned them in rooms she wasn't going to use.

Hannah glanced at her case and decided to unpack later.

Instead she walked to the window, wanting to soak up the last of the natural light before it faded for the day.

In a moment she'd take that test to the bathroom and find out once and for all, but for now she wanted to savor this one last moment of not knowing.

Kneeling on the window seat, she stared out across the valley.

The sky was a rose-tinted pink, the sun low in the sky.

This place shouldn't trigger memories for her, and yet it did. It was the mountains, she decided. Their jagged edges glinted under the fading sun, just as they had that day when she'd stood in the window and watched and waited.

These weren't even the same mountains. Nothing bad had happened to her here, but still the ghosts of possibility haunted the fringes of her imagination.

Turning away, Hannah set up her laptop on the small table near the fire.

Alongside the lamp, there were several new notepads and fresh pens, no doubt courtesy of Suzanne, who thought of everything.

For once, the internet connected immediately and she checked her emails, more from force of habit than any desire to work. Concentration proved elusive and she couldn't work up any enthusiasm for the hundred emails that had landed in her inbox during her flight. Only self-discipline and force of habit made her deal with them and she worked through them methodically, responding to some and forwarding others to the appropriate member of her team.

One email she ignored.

It was from Adam, sent half an hour earlier, and the subject line simply said Call me!

She closed her laptop and stood up, noticing the Christmas tree for the first time.

Eric.

She gave a half smile, because only Posy would name a tree.

But she knew Suzanne would be the one responsible for putting the tree in her room.

Every year was the same. Suzanne filled the house with a surplus of good cheer, as if lights, decorations and a cheery attitude could somehow compensate for what was missing. In Hannah's case, what was missing were her parents.

They'd gone climbing four days before Christmas and never come back.

And Hannah hadn't even had a chance to say goodbye.

14

Suzanne

There had been weather warnings, but that wasn't unusual. This was Mount Rainier, the highest mountain in the Cascade Range of the Pacific Northwest and quick-changing weather was a fact of life.

They began their climb at the White River trailhead, hiking through thick forest to a soundtrack of crashing water as the glacier-fed river thundered down the mountain. They'd roped up and safely traversed the Winthrop Glacier and the previous night they'd camped at the Curtis Ridge.

Now Suzanne stood on the snow and watched the dawn light cast a reddish glow over the jagged, snowcapped mountains that loomed ahead. "That storm dumped thirty inches overnight."

"Hello, deep snowpack, how much do I love you?" Rob

slapped her on the shoulders as he trudged past her. "It's going to be the best damn climb we've done in a while. I tell you, I'm psyched."

"Me, too." Cheryl joined them. "And it had better be a great climb because this little trip is costing us a ton of money in babysitting."

"I told you we should have brought the kids," Rob said, and Cheryl laughed.

"Apart from the fact they don't issue climbing permits to three-year-olds, you don't think Posy is a little young to climb Rainier in the winter?"

"Got to start somewhere and that girl has got what it takes. Climbs everything. Last week I found her up on the roof. Can you believe that? I yelled to her, *Get the hell off that roof, Posy.* Do you know what she said? *Why?*" He bellowed with laughter. "The apple doesn't fall far from the tree. I'm taking her bouldering again next weekend."

Suzanne imagined a delicate, beaming Posy clinging to a rock. She expected Cheryl to protest that her barely out of toddlerhood child wouldn't be climbing anytime soon, but her friend was still laughing.

Since Cheryl had fallen in love with Rob, she'd shared not only his home, but also his cavalier attitude to risk.

Suzanne thought about the conversation she'd had with Stewart the night before she'd left for this trip.

"I don't like you climbing with those two, Suzanne."

Suzanne had her equipment spread over the floor, and the top of her backpack was open. "Cheryl is my best friend. We've climbed together since we were fifteen."

"But now she's married to Rob."

He said nothing more. He didn't need to.

Suzanne knew Rob was a weak link. Hot tempered, impetuous, fiercely competitive. To be competitive with oneself on a mountain was one thing, but to be competitive with another climber? Rob's attitude was a constant source of tension between her and Cheryl.

You don't like him, Suz. I know you don't like him.

That's not true—

But it was true.

What were the rules when your best friend married a man you disliked?

"They won't take risks. They have three kids."

Stewart grunted. "Since when has that made a difference? Rob is selfish and ego driven and always has been."

But so were many climbers, Suzanne thought. It was that single-minded passion that drove them to push themselves to almost inhuman lengths.

It was also true that your choice of climbing partner could make the difference between life and death. It wasn't only about choosing someone who could make the summit, it was about how a person would react and cope in an emergency. One weak team member could expose the whole team to danger.

"We do it, too," she said. "We all want that first ascent. The most difficult route."

Stewart watched as she laid out her gear for the climb. "I love you. Watch that snowpack. I wish you weren't climbing Liberty Ridge."

"It's the best climb on the mountain."

"Leave camp early," he warned, "be careful on the Carbon Glacier, and when you crest the ridge, climb on the west side."

"I know this, Stewart."

"You're climbing steep ice with a heavy pack."

"I know that, too." She pushed down her own feeling of unease. The route they'd chosen wasn't particularly extreme, but Stewart was right that it was steep and exposed and this was a winter climb. "I've climbed it many times before. And guided the route."

"You haven't climbed it with Rob. You know how many crevasse falls there have been between the cap and the summit."

She knew. The crevasses on Rainier were big. It was the most glaciated peak in the continental US. "I'm careful, Stewart."

"I wish the same could be said for your climbing companions." He cupped her face and kissed her. "If Rob doesn't listen to you, I'm going to drop him into a crevasse myself. And I won't be pulling him out."

"David and Lindsey will be with us, too."

She didn't know the other pair well, but she liked what she knew. David was remarkably civilized given that he was a friend of Rob's.

She eased away from Stewart. "I wish you were coming." That wasn't entirely honest. Rob and Stewart didn't like each other and climbing a technically difficult winter route with someone you didn't like caused tension. Tension didn't lead to happy climbing. "Everything is going to be fine."

Suzanne thought back to that conversation now as she dug a pit to check the snowpack, ignoring Rob's exasperated glance.

"If you're going to stop and do that every five minutes, we're going to be out here for longer than we need to be, and that's more dangerous."

"You know as well as I do that avalanches are most common in the twenty-four hours after a storm." A heavy snowfall increased the risk. The rapid buildup of snow put pressure on the snowpack and, usually with a little help from a human trigger, that pressure was often all it took to release a deadly avalanche.

"Rob's right," Cheryl said. "I know you're a guide, but you're not being paid this time. The forecast is good. And we know as much about the mountain as you do, Suz."

The criticism felt like a slap.

Once, she and Cheryl had agreed on everything. It was the reason they'd made such great climbing partners.

Reminding herself that she was responsible for her own safety as well as that of her companions, Suzanne finished the check she was making and stood up.

This was the last time she would climb with them, and if that decision threatened their friendship, then that was unfortunate.

She'd find other ways to spend time with Cheryl.

Rob had trudged ahead, no doubt to remove himself from the temptation of killing Suzanne, but Cheryl stood watching her, torn between her husband and their friendship. "This trip is supposed to be about having fun. I'm stuck at home with the kids most of the time. You don't know how desperate I've been to get back on the mountain."

Suzanne knew. She also knew that desperation wasn't an emotion compatible with safety.

As a mountain guide, Suzanne was paid to make tough decisions, like turning a client round if the weather changed and she considered the conditions approaching dangerous.

The fact that she was climbing with friends added a layer of complication.

Rob was moving strongly, but Suzanne knew that in a short space of time the mountain would have devoured some of that energy. It would feed on them, test them, push them to their limits.

Usually at this stage in a climb she felt exhilarated. There was a certain sense of well-being and peace that only came from being in the mountains.

Today that feeling was absent.

Suzanne hauled her pack onto her back. "Don't you worry about the kids when you're out in the mountains?"

"Why?" Cheryl frowned. "They're with someone."

"I mean if something happens to you and Rob. I would have thought it would make you more careful."

"Nothing is going to happen to us except that you're going to spoil a brilliant climb with your paranoia. You don't even *have* kids, so what do you know about parenting anyway?" Irritated, Cheryl turned away and Suzanne felt hurt.

"Wait," she called after her. "Cheryl, I'm sorry. Don't be angry."

"You called me a bad mother!"

"I didn't—" Maybe she hadn't said those exact words, but it was true she'd been judgmental. "You're right that I don't know anything about parenting. Can we start this again? This trip was supposed to be a treat. Relaxation."

"You're the one who is tense." Cheryl walked away, leaving Suzanne feeling miserable and frustrated. There was an ache behind her ribs and the pounding of her pulse had nothing to do with the altitude or physical exertion.

She was aware of Lindsey and David trudging toward them. Thankfully they were slower and had missed the exchange.

On the Carbon Glacier, they roped up and navigated the crevasses with care and attention and Suzanne bit her tongue as Rob filmed the avalanches thundering down the Willis Wall.

They climbed through clouds, through deep snow that dragged at their boots and made muscles scream.

Occasionally Rob would slide back and let out a stream of profanities.

By the time they made their final camp at Thumb Rock, Cheryl was smiling again.

They dug out a tent platform, scooped up snow and boiled water as they ate their uninspiring rations. It was bitterly cold and the wind buffeted the tents.

"Sorry about earlier." Cheryl adjusted the flame under the pan. "I guess we have different opinions on it."

Suzanne didn't say that these days they seemed to have different opinions on most everything. "Forget it."

"Rob doesn't believe you should change your life just because you have kids, and neither do I."

Suzanne noticed how tired her friend looked. "How are the kids?"

"Posy is amazing—" A smile crossed Cheryl's face. "Rob is right. She has it, Suz. She's fearless and coordinated. We're taking her hiking next summer. Rob thinks we could pack up and take a couple of months. It's education."

Rob thinks, Rob thinks…

"Won't Hannah hate that?"

Cheryl turned off the flame and made tea. "Rob thinks it will be good for her. He's bought Posy these little hiking boots. You should see them. She looks adorable. I have a picture on my phone. Remind me to show you."

They had three children and the only one they talked about was Posy, Suzanne thought. "Did Hannah like the books I sent?"

"What books?" Cheryl frowned. "Oh yeah. Thanks, but don't send her any more. Rob says it gives her an excuse to avoid exercise and physical stuff."

Suzanne bit back her response. "And Beth?"

"Beth is a girlie girl. All she wants to do is put makeup on people and join the ballet. You can imagine what Rob thinks of that."

Suzanne wondered why Rob thought he had to mold his children in his image.

Cheryl balanced her mug on the floor of the tent. "Can we stop talking about the kids? Today I'm me, and not somebody's mom."

"Sorry. I love your girls, and I don't get to see them so much lately, so I like hearing their stories." She often reflected on how ironic it was that she, who had always wanted a family, was still childless, whereas Cheryl, who had never seemed bothered, now had three.

"I know you love them. Talking of which—" Cheryl's tone was casual as she leaned forward to ease off her boots "—you'd take them, right?"

"Take them where?" In front of them the sun was dipping down, beaming fire across the snow and ice.

"If anything were to happen to us. I'd want you to take the kids."

Suzanne forgot about the sunset. "Me?"

"I don't have family and neither does Rob. You're like a sister to me."

Sisters fell out, didn't they?

Approaching the topic as cautiously as she had the glacier beneath them, she tiptoed over the thorniest issue.

"What does Rob think?" Surely she'd be the *last* person Rob would want caring for his kids.

"Rob thinks we're invincible." Cheryl picked up her tea again. "Look at that view."

Suzanne was looking at her friend. "You'd want me to be their guardian?"

"They love you."

"I love them." *Three kids.* "As you said, I don't know anything about parenting."

"This is all hypothetical. Nothing is going to happen. Especially with you checking the snowpack and every crevasse."

"Right." Climbing with Rob made her jumpy. His lack of caution made her feel the need to be extra cautious.

Cheryl turned to her. "So would you do it?"

"Take the kids? Of course."

Hypothetical.

She repeated the word as she lay that night listening to the wind battering the tent.

At 3:00 a.m. the following morning they made coffee and checked the weather. If they wanted to make the summit, they had to start early because they still had to climb four thousand feet of steep snow and ice up the heavily glaciated north face of Mount Rainier.

"Looking good," Rob said as he heaved his pack onto his shoulders. "Let's nail this thing."

Suzanne led. The ice was hard and her calf muscles shrieked at her.

The mountain was quiet, but that did little to calm her nerves. A sleeping dragon was still dangerous.

As they paused to rest, she looked toward the summit.

"Lenticular clouds."

Rob devoured an energy bar. "Looks like an alien spaceship hovering there. Not a breath of wind."

"They're stationary." Suzanne narrowed her eyes. "A storm is coming."

"Would you listen to yourself? *A storm is coming.*" Rob rolled his eyes. "We're in the mountains, honey. A storm is always coming, it's just a matter of when. In this case we'll be at the summit and back in the valley drinking a beer before it hits."

Suzanne felt her own temper flash. *Don't call me honey.* "Read the weather, Rob."

"Never been much of a reader." He swallowed a mouthful and stowed his water bottle. "If there's a storm coming, we'd better get started."

Lindsey struggled up to them, breathless. "You think we should turn around?"

Rob swore. "This close to the summit? Are you insane?"

Lindsey flushed. "It's not insane to show caution, Rob."

"If you want guarantees, stay at home and knit a sweater."

It was Cheryl who put her hand on Rob's arm and tried to calm him. "I suggest we climb as far as the ridge and then take another look at the weather. If it looks threatening, we can still turn around."

Suzanne wondered if she should point out the obvious. That if Rob wouldn't turn around here, he would be even less likely to turn around when the summit seemed to be within his grasp.

And they still had to traverse the glacier.

"Mind if I lead the next pitch?" Rob adjusted his gloves and settled his pack more comfortably on his back.

Suzanne nodded reluctantly, and they continued the climb.

She just wanted the whole damn day over. She wanted it done so that she could get home to Stewart. He would have made one of his warming soups, a Scottish recipe of his mother's that was so hearty it was a meal in itself.

To take her mind off Rob and the climb, she thought about that.

She thought about the day when maybe she would have three kids, too. She was going to nurture their individuality and treat them equally.

High above them, the snowflakes that had fallen in the night, so soft and delicate, locked together, increasing the weight and pressure. Those small clusters of ice crystals bonded and hardened, bearing down on the snow layered beneath.

Deep in the snowpack, the bond between the layers of snow weakened until the firm tread of Rob's boot was all it took to release three hundred thousand cubic meters of snow.

There was no time even to shout a warning.

15

Posy

Three days after Hannah's arrival, Posy was ready to run away with Luke and not leave a forwarding address. It was turning into the sort of Christmas she'd dreaded, only this time it wasn't Hannah who was driving her insane, it was Beth.

Her sister was obsessed with the job in Manhattan.

Corinna had called three times in the space of an hour the evening before, while they'd been eating dinner.

Each time Beth had said *I have to take this* and stood up to take the call until even Suzanne, with her usually limitless patience, became frustrated.

Hannah had said nothing, which also worried Posy.

It wasn't that Hannah was quiet, because that was often the case. It was more that she seemed vulnerable, and Posy had never seen her sister vulnerable before. She couldn't forget those red eyes and that pregnancy test, but Hannah hadn't mentioned it since and Posy didn't feel comfortable raising the subject.

Was she pregnant or not? Pleased or not?

She knew her parents were worried, too, because she'd seen the looks they'd exchanged. Neither of them knew why Hannah was home early, and when they'd asked Posy, she'd kept her answer suitably neutral. If Hannah was pregnant, then it was up to her to tell people.

She might have suggested she talk to Beth, but Beth didn't seem able to think about anything other than lipstick.

Posy was relieved to be able to retreat to the peace of the hayloft at the end of the day. This morning she'd returned to the lodge first thing hoping to snatch a quiet breakfast with her mother before they drove to the café.

Luke was planning an expedition to climb Denali the following summer and had invited her to join the team. Posy was excited at the prospect of climbing the highest mountain in North America and seeing Alaska. She was determined to find a way to talk to her mother. How could she turn down an opportunity like this one?

She wasn't sure if it was the lure of climbing Denali that excited her, or the prospect of spending more time with Luke. She didn't care. All she knew was that she wanted to do it.

And if she hired someone for the summer to help at the café, maybe she could.

She'd arrived at the lodge determined to have an honest conversation.

Unfortunately, her mother was up late and her sister was up early, which removed any chance of exploiting the quiet time she'd been hoping for.

"What makes you pick up a lipstick?" Beth wandered into the kitchen with a notepad and pen in her hand. In an attempt to try on her new role for size, she'd eschewed Posy's wardrobe in favor of Hannah's. Today she wore a black wool dress with high-heeled boots. Her hair was swept up in an elegant knot and her makeup was flawless. For a meeting in London or New York, she would have been perfectly dressed. For a winter's day in the freezing Highlands, her outfit would have been ridiculous had she been doing anything other than drifting uselessly round the lodge.

Looking at her didn't improve Posy's mood.

Having both her sisters home had more than doubled her workload. She had so much to do she barely had time to take a shower and pull her hair into a ponytail, let alone pick out a lipstick.

She'd been on the go since five thirty and she still had to change the bedding in the barn, feed the chickens and take a bale of hay to Socks before she started her shift at the café.

Realizing that Beth was waiting for her answer, she gave a shrug. "The sheep don't generally care if I wear lipstick. Can you empty the dishwasher?"

"In a minute. My nails are drying, so I can't do anything manual right now. I want to hear your views on this." Despite the threat to her nails, Beth stopped to scribble a note to herself. "I am loving this project, by the way. *Loving it.* I feel like I'm finally doing what I want instead of always being at the bottom of the pile and running round after other people. Do you know what I mean?"

"Not really. I'm still at the bottom of the pile running round after other people." Posy dealt with the dishwasher herself, crashing plates into the cupboard.

Beth missed the irony. "Can you stop for a moment? I want to ask you questions."

"No, I can't stop and I'm not your audience."

"You're *exactly* my audience. This new range I'm working

on is for the woman who doesn't usually wear makeup." Beth walked across the kitchen and poured herself a coffee. "And who *are* those women?"

Posy straightened. "Maybe they're women who have a lot going on in their lives. Possibly a woman who is preparing for a family Christmas single-handed while her sister treats it like a spa break."

Beth raised her eyebrows. "No need to be moody."

"I'm not moody. Just busy. And clear that makeup off the table. I'm trying to make breakfast."

"I'm busy, too. Corinna wants more ideas by start of business, which basically gives me a few hours to do this. I need to understand my audience. What makes a woman reach for makeup in the morning? That's the key question I'm asking myself."

Posy's frustration spilled over like milk that had been left too long on the heat. "Seriously? Beth, you have no idea what's happening with your kids, your marriage is in trouble and *that's* what you're asking yourself?"

Beth put the mug down and coffee sloshed onto the countertop. "You think my marriage is in trouble?"

"I don't know, but you and Jason seem to have had a serious breakdown in communication and the reason I suspect that is because he's there and you're here."

"I know." Beth slumped into the nearest chair. "Why do you think I'm awake at this hour? I can't sleep. I miss the girls. I miss Jason, and I can't see how to fix this. There's not exactly a compromise solution to another baby."

Posy grabbed a cloth and mopped up the spilled coffee, forcing herself to be patient. What was *wrong* with her? She never used to be irritable. "You're not going to fix it by not talking. How many times have you spoken to him since you arrived? Every time the phone goes, it's Corinna." It bothered her that her sister's apparently unshakable marriage had been shaken. It bothered her more than it seemed to bother her sister. Now that the initial *what have I done?* crisis had passed, all Beth seemed to think about was Corinna and the campaign.

"I haven't spoken to Jason." Beth's voice wobbled a little. "I had that one message from him telling me everything was fine. I've been calling every night, but all he says is 'Hi, Beth,' and then immediately passes the phone to the girls. He hasn't even mentioned our fight. I guess he's mad at me for leaving like that, and I'm still mad at him for saying those things. Also, the phone signal isn't reliable. I had to call back three times last night. It's not exactly conducive to deep, honest conversation."

Posy was only half listening. She was wondering who the father of Hannah's child was, always assuming she really was pregnant. Was it a one-night stand? She wanted to talk to Beth about it, but it was obvious that Hannah hadn't told her about the pregnancy test and Posy didn't feel it was her place to do so. "You have to fix this, Beth."

"I don't know how. I may never get another opportunity like this one. For the first time in years, someone wants me for something other than my parenting skills. And not just 'anyone,' but Corinna! Do you have any idea how flattering that is? She is not an easy person to please."

"That's obvious, given the number of times she called during dinner last night."

"Yes, and she wants *me*. I'm going to be the one jetting to the West Coast and sitting in a lunch meeting where I don't have to cut up anyone's food."

Posy didn't understand the appeal, but she did know about wanting something different. "You're sure this is what you want?"

"Yes. For a start, it will make me more interesting."

Posy wondered if she should point out that all this talk of lipstick was boring her to tears.

She watched as Beth stood up and went to top up her coffee.

"Leave some for Mom."

But Beth's head was back in the job she didn't yet have and wasn't being paid for. "The way I see it, my audience is divided broadly into two groups. Those women who have never worn makeup, and those who have worn it in the past but lapsed for some reason. Those lapsed users are going to be a key audience because they have greater potential. I have some great ideas, and I'm almost ready to present them to the team. And for that I need a reliable signal. I can't have it cutting out the way it does when I'm talking to Melly and Ruby."

"It's pretty good from the top of the henhouse." Posy eyed her sister's boots. "Or you could stand on the far wall of the field Socks is in, but you might need to change your footwear."

"You know what? Maybe I'll do that." Beth sipped her coffee. "Whatever it takes to get the job done, right? I'm going to prove to everyone I can do this. Corinna is going to be blown away."

Posy thought to herself that if her sister stood on top of the henhouse to make her call she was likely to be the one blown away. "For what it's worth, I think it's great that you've been at home with the girls. Lucky them, I say. And lucky you, being able to do it."

"I know, but before I had Melly, my career was equal to Jason's. We were earning the same. And now he's pulling ahead."

"Is it a race? I assumed you were a team, rather than competition."

"He's doing better than me."

"That depends on how you define 'better.' You're a good mother."

"Am I? How do you measure good performance in parenting? You don't get a raise or a promotion. My girls aren't exactly saintly."

"But they feel loved and secure." Posy flushed. "Sorry."

"Don't be. Family is the most important thing in the world to you—we all know that. That, and the climbing, is the reason you've never left here and you never will. And I understand that, but I think I need more."

Posy took a deep breath. "Actually, on that subject—"

"You don't need to explain it or excuse it. We all want different things, and that's okay. I understand the importance of family, too. You're there for all those special moments. You're there to catch them when they take their first steps, to listen when they say their first words—"

Posy gave up. Right now it was impossible to get her sister to listen to anything except the sound of her own voice.

"If being there is so important, why are you in such a hurry to go back to work?"

"I'm ready for something more. I'm feeling such an incredible buzz it's almost a physical thing."

"It is a physical thing. It's called caffeine." Posy removed the mug from her sister's hand. "Enough."

"It is *so great* to be working again."

Working?

As far as Posy could see, all her sister had done so far was put on makeup and high heels and stalk around the house with a notepad, muttering to herself.

Were people programmed to want the life they weren't living? Was it natural to question your choices?

Beth tilted her head and studied Posy. "Can I do your makeup?"

"Only if you can do it while I'm moving. I have a ton of things to do."

"No problem. You're on the go and too busy for makeup."
Beth grabbed her bag. "That is the USP of this range."

"USP? What does that mean?" Posy put the milk back in
the fridge. "Unbelievably Stupid and Pointless?"

"Unique selling point." Beth pursed her lips. "You're not
taking this seriously, but I am not going to fight with you.
Nothing can annoy me today."

"It's only seven o'clock. The day is young. If nothing is
going to annoy you, then this is a good time for me to tell
you you're making supper. The ingredients are in the fridge."

"I'm giving myself a break from cooking. I cook for the
girls and Jason every night—"

"Good. That means you've had plenty of practice. And remember, I don't like carrots."

"Unless you let me do your makeup I'll make carrot soup,
followed by carrot casserole, with carrot cake for dessert."

"Fine, do my makeup." Posy slammed the dishwasher shut.
"But remember, I'm a simple country girl, living my simple
country life." The only life she was ever going to live. Maybe
she should run off with Luke. Rent a cabin in Alaska and spend
her days avoiding moose and bears, and her nights having hot
sex. "You have two minutes."

She tried not to fidget while Beth worked. "Don't make
me look like a clown."

"It's going to look as if you're not wearing any."

"If it's going to look as if I'm not wearing any, why bother
wearing any?"

"Stop talking. I can't do this if your face keeps moving.
You were exactly the same when you were little and I tried
to do your makeup."

"It's as bad as I remember it. Also, it isn't going to last five
minutes."

"Ha! This lipstick is *exactly* what you need. According to

the reviews, nothing budges it. You can kiss every man prop-
ping up the bar in the Glensay Inn and you will still be wearing this lipstick."

"I don't want to kiss anyone in the Glensay Inn—"

"Posy!"

Posy clamped her lips closed and tried not to wrinkle her
nose as she felt the stroke and sweep of Beth's fingers, followed
by the flick of various brushes. She followed instructions to
close her eyes, open her eyes, look down, pout—

"If I get teased by the team, I'm coming after you." She
turned her head as her father walked into the kitchen. "Hi,
Dad." She waved Beth and her makeup brushes away. "Where's
Mom?"

"Dad!" Beth sprinted across the kitchen and hugged him.

Stewart hugged her back, staring at Posy over Beth's shoulder. "What happened to your face?"

"My sister happened to my face. Is something wrong with
Mom?"

"She's not feeling well." He let go of Beth. "Her temperature is through the roof. I've persuaded her to stay in bed."

"Oh no. Is it flu?"

Beth put the makeup back on the table. "She shouldn't have
taken that chicken soup to Vicky."

"There is no way Mom would ever ignore a friend in need."
Posy grabbed a tray from the counter. "I'll make her something to eat and take it up."

"I don't think she'll want to eat."

"Drink, then." Posy dumped ice in a jug of water and added
slices of lemon. Her mother was never ill. Maybe anxiety about
Beth and Hannah had weakened her mother's immune system.
Could that happen? "Should we call the doctor?"

"Not yet."

"You look exhausted. Sit down." Posy pushed him gently

into a chair. "Beth will make you breakfast. How about scrambled eggs on toast? Martha laid this morning and I saved the eggs for you. They're in the bowl, Beth."

Beth was scribbling in her notepad. "I just need to—"

"You need to make Dad an omelet. Here's the pan." Posy thrust it at her sister, together with a box of eggs. The way she felt right now, if Beth didn't step up, she'd be cracking those eggs over her head, and not because her sister had once told her it was a perfect treatment for hair.

She stomped up the stairs and met Hannah at the top.

"Hi, Posy. I don't suppose you could—"

"No, I couldn't. My to-do list is already longer than Santa's." Guilt stopped her in her tracks. She'd been wanting Hannah to talk to her, but the timing couldn't have been worse. "Sorry. Bit of a morning. Are you okay? What did you want?"

"Nothing. Forget it." Hannah walked back into her room and Posy stared after her, exasperated with her sister and furious with herself. She shouldn't have snapped. This would have been a perfect time to be caring and concerned and find out the result of that test.

Hearing coughing, she hurried to her parents' bedroom.

Her mother was doubled over.

Posy crossed the room in a flash and set the tray down. Everyone else vanished from her mind as she rubbed her mother's back. "I'm going to make you hot honey and lemon to see if that will help the cough." She put her hand on her mother's forehead and was alarmed by how hot she felt.

"Don't come near me." Suzanne's voice was rasping. "You'll catch it. And you don't need to make me a drink. I'm getting up so I can make it myself."

"You're staying right there. And I won't catch it. I don't stand still long enough for germs to land on me."

"I can't stay in bed. There's too much to do." Suzanne

tried to sit up but immediately fell back on the pillow. "I feel so weak. I can't believe the timing of this, with Christmas so close."

Posy sympathized, but she knew her mother's best chance of recovery was to stay in bed. "You can give me a list of things that need doing." She tried not to think about the list she already had. If she took a few shortcuts, she could handle it.

"All right." Suzanne broke into another fit of coughing. "There's a pen and pad over on the table."

Posy grabbed it. She hadn't expected her mother to literally give her a list. "Okay, go for it." *Please don't let there be too many things.*

"You need to make the cranberry sauce, and freeze it. The cranberries are in the fridge and there are fresh oranges in the bowl. The children love my cinnamon spice biscuits, so you need to make two batches—" The list went on and on until Posy's hand ached almost as much as her head.

How was she supposed to get all this done? Would her mother notice if she used cranberry sauce from a jar?

"No wonder you're ill. Just looking at the length of this list is bringing on flu symptoms and I was healthy five minutes ago."

"I still have ten stockings left to knit for the team fundraiser. You can't do that, I know, so bring me my wool and needles and I'll do it here."

"You need to sleep."

"I can't sleep knowing there is so much to do. You look pretty." Suzanne's voice was raspy. "I don't often see you wearing makeup. Are you going out?"

"Only to the café." Which she was now going to handle alone as both Vicky and her mother had now been felled by flu. "Beth did my makeup."

"I love seeing you girls having fun together. And I'm glad you have help."

Help? So far Beth had been about as much use as a fan in a blizzard.

Nothing was the way it was supposed to be.

Beth, normally her steady, predictable sister, was here without the children and on her phone every two minutes. Hannah, who was the most together person she knew, had been decidedly untogether even when she'd picked her up from the airport. Even the skilled application of makeup couldn't disguise the shadows under her eyes. She wore an air of desperation, as if she was on the verge of running from everything and everyone, including herself.

"I'll send Beth up with lemon and honey."

"No! She shouldn't come near me."

"Why not?"

Suzanne's eyes drifted shut. "If she catches this, it might harm the baby."

"What baby?"

"You don't need to pretend to me. The word is out in the village. Obviously, I would have liked her to tell me first, but I'm thrilled she's pregnant again."

Posy decided she was going to kill Aidan when she saw him. "Mom, she's not pregnant." *But Hannah might be.*

"Then why would people think she was?"

"Misunderstanding. That's what happens in a place where people don't mind their own business. We were talking generally, and someone overheard. Now sleep and don't worry about a thing. I'm going to fix everything."

"I'm officially worried. I'm worried about Beth, worried about Hannah, and now I'm worried about you." She paused to have a coughing fit that almost launched her from the bed.

"You won't be able to cope with all this on your own. There's so much to do before Jason and the girls arrive."

"Beth and Hannah can look after themselves, and we still have a few days until Melly and Ruby arrive. Gives us plenty of time. There is no reason at all to panic."

"I so badly wanted it to be a perfect Christmas for everyone."

"And it *is* going to be a perfect Christmas."

Perfect disaster, more like.

The doorbell went and Posy straightened her mother's sheets. "I need to answer that. It's probably the delivery of yarn you're expecting."

Beth reached the door before her, and Posy heard a gasp of shock followed by a chorus of familiar voices. She peered downstairs.

It was Jason and the girls, together with enough luggage to fill an entire plane.

Posy sat down heavily on the top stair and put her head in her hands.

There was definitely a reason to panic.

16

Beth

The last thing Beth had expected was that Jason and the girls would show up early.

She should have been annoyed that he'd disturbed her private time, but she'd never been more relieved to see anyone in her life.

"We wanted to surprise you." Jason hovered by the front door, as if unsure of his welcome. "Did you need more time on your own? I wanted to be spontaneous."

Melly tugged at his coat. "Now, Daddy."

"You think so?"

"Now."

Jason pulled his hand from behind his back and produced a bunch of white tulips.

Beth gasped. "Where did you find those?"

"We asked the cabdriver to take a detour."

Beth adored flowers, and right now she also adored her husband. "Thank you. They're beautiful."

"I told you she'd like those best," Melly whispered, and Jason winked at her.

"Great advice, Mel."

His hair was messy, his coat was rumpled and he hadn't shaved, but Beth had never loved him more. Even now, after so many years together, seeing him lifted her mood.

The feeling of euphoria lasted until she remembered that they hadn't parted on good terms and that none of their issues had been solved.

She stepped forward and kissed him. His cheek was cold under her lips, his jaw roughened by stubble. "You need to shave."

"I know, but shaving requires time alone in the bathroom."

"Mommy!" Having waited long enough, Ruby pushed him aside to get to Beth and Melly followed, their noisy presence reminding her there was going to be no chance of a serious adult conversation for some time.

Beth closed the front door, put the flowers on the console table her father had made himself from reclaimed wood, and dropped into a crouch so that she could hug the girls properly.

Melly's coat was undone and Beth noticed she was wearing her best dress—clearly Jason wasn't great at saying no, either—and that Ruby's sweater was inside out and her socks didn't match.

It didn't matter, she told herself. They were alive, they were hers and they were here. She was so pleased to see them she could have cried.

She hugged them so tightly Ruby squealed a protest.

"It is so good to see you all!" She kissed first one child and then the other.

"That's a nice dress, Mom." Melly nodded her approval and Beth pulled her close, breathing in her daughter's familiar scent.

She'd missed them so much. "How was your journey?"

Ruby burst into tears. "Daddy left Bugsy on the plane."

Beth looked up at Jason and realized he looked exhausted. "You lost Bugsy?"

She wasn't sure who looked more traumatized, her daughter or her husband.

She expected him to hand the problem over to her along with the kids and the luggage, but instead he crouched down next to Ruby, who was clinging to Beth.

"I called them, honey. They're checking the plane to see if Bugsy is still on the seat."

"What if he isn't?" Ruby was wearing a traumatized expression that only the loss of Bugsy could produce.

"Then we'll work extra hard to remember where you last had him."

"I don't know where I last had him!"

"She had him in that café," Melly said helpfully, "when you gave her that mountain of fries."

Beth raised an eyebrow. "You fed them fries?"

"Thanks, Mel." Jason turned a shade of puce but kept his attention on Ruby. "We'll find him, I promise."

Beth winced. Although she understood what had driven him to say that, she also knew it wasn't wise to make promises you couldn't keep.

So did Ruby. "What if we can't? Melly said Bugsy might be flying somewhere else now. He could even be in Hong Pong."

"Kong," Melly said, and Ruby's face crumpled.

"I can't live without Bugsy." Her voice rose to a shrill wail and Posy appeared at the bottom of the stairs.

"Wait—" She put her hand behind her ear and glanced

around, pretending not to see them, "I thought I heard Ruby's voice, but that can't be right because Ruby isn't arriving for another few days."

Ruby stopped yelling and took a juddering breath. "I'm here, Aunty Posy." She gave a hiccup. "It's me."

Posy continued searching. "That's weird, because I can hear her voice, but I can't see her."

"I'm here!" A gurgle of laughter escaping through the sobs, Ruby let go of Beth and ran to Posy.

"You *are* here." Posy caught Ruby as she ran and swung her high in the air. "Well, hello! And is that Melly I see? No, that's not Melly. It's a beautiful princess. But what would a beautiful princess be doing in my house?" She balanced Ruby on her hip and held out her hand to Melly, who ran across to her with a shy smile.

"What happened to your face, Aunty Posy?"

Posy touched her free hand to her cheek. "Something has happened to my face?"

"You're wearing makeup and you never wear makeup."

"Ah—that. That polished look you're admiring is the work of your clever mommy, who is trying to decide which color lipstick Socks prefers. Perhaps you can come with me and we can ask him together."

Ruby giggled. "That's silly. Socks doesn't care if you wear lipstick."

"No? Try telling that to your mommy."

"You look nice," Melly said shyly. "If you like, I can help you with your makeup every day while we're here. And I can do your nails."

To Posy's credit, she didn't recoil. "That would be great. Thanks, Melly."

Ruby tugged at her. "Where's Grandpa and Grandma?"

"You just missed Grandpa," Beth said. "He was running

late and left a few minutes ago—" she caught her sister's eye "—*after* he ate the delicious omelet I made him."

Posy grinned and shifted Ruby onto her other hip. "And Grandma is ill in bed, so you can't see her right now. Maybe later."

Ruby's face fell. "I wanted to see Grandpa. And I did a special drawing for Grandma."

"You did? That's great. We'll find a way to give it to her later. I am so glad you're here, because Socks has been missing you."

Ruby brightened. "Can we ride him?"

"That's up to your mom." Posy looked at Beth, who felt a rush of anxiety.

Everyone knew horse riding was dangerous.

Jason put his hand on her shoulder. "Let her ride. You know she loves it. She can wear a helmet."

"It isn't just their heads, Jason. It's their spines." Beth bit her lip. "We should have bought chest protectors for them. I should have thought of it. And nowadays they make airbags so that if you fall you pull a cord and you're cushioned. Maybe it's not too late to get them delivered before Christmas."

Why was everyone staring at her?

Posy bounced Ruby on her hip. "I think a helmet is probably enough. I'll be leading Socks. Nothing can happen."

Of course things could happen! No wonder there were so many accidents. People were too cavalier about safety. Which was their business, of course, but she didn't want people being cavalier with her children.

Ruby was holding her breath, her arms clasped round Posy's neck as she gazed hopefully at Beth. *"Please."*

She was in an impossible position. How could she say no?

"All right. But definitely wear a helmet and do everything

Aunty Posy tells you. Don't talk too loudly around Socks, and if you're going to feed him, keep your hand flat or—"

"Beth." Jason put his arm round her shoulders. "They're going to be fine."

"I know, I'm just saying that—"

"You want them to be careful. And they will be. Let them go with Posy. It will give us a chance to catch up."

That was true.

Beth nodded. "Off you go. Have fun."

Ruby whooped and Melly looked excited, too.

Posy took over. "Do you have warm clothes?"

"Yes!" Ruby turned to look at Beth. "Will Mommy go away again?"

"She's not going anywhere. It's Christmas." Posy kissed Ruby on the cheek. "We're all here together. After we've fed Socks, we're going to hang our stockings and you can help me bake Christmas cookies, but first you need to get changed. Then we'll find food for Socks because it's cold out there and he needs extra food."

Beth looked at her gratefully. "Don't you need to be at the café?"

"I'll bonus Duncan heavily to go in early and open up for me."

"Here…" Jason picked out a suitcase. "This is all the girls' outdoor stuff. Gloves, hats, that kind of thing. I'll take it upstairs for you."

"No need, but thanks." Still holding Ruby, Posy picked up the case with her free hand. "Ruby and Melly bring the glamour to this party, and I bring the muscles. Right, girls. Let's take this to your bedroom and find something warm to wear. We'll need to be very quiet so we don't disturb Grandma. She needs her sleep."

"Kiss her better," Ruby said, and Posy nodded.

"Good plan."

"How about Aunty Hannah?" Ruby looked hopeful. "Where's Aunty Hannah?"

"She's working right now, but I know she's going to be *very* excited to see you."

Ruby nodded. "Aunty Hannah works a lot. She has an important job."

"She does."

Ruby patted her shoulder sympathetically. "Your job is to feed Socks."

"That's right. And that's an important job, too, because feeding Socks means the difference between life and death. Not all important jobs come with a six-figure salary." She gave Beth a pointed look before turning her attention back to the girls. "Do you have boots? Because the field is mucky."

Ruby wound her arms round Posy's neck. "How many meals a day does Socks eat? Daddy couldn't believe we had to eat as many times as we did. He said I ate like a horse."

"Well, horses pretty much eat all the time," Posy said, and Melly gave a snort.

"In that case Ruby is definitely like a horse."

Their voices faded as they climbed the stairs together, leaving Beth and Jason staring at each other.

She felt awkward and self-conscious. She knew they had things to deal with, but she didn't know where to start or whether this was the right time. She didn't know why he'd come early. "Child-free time. So rare, we probably don't know what to do with it."

"Yeah." He ran his hand over the back of his neck. "I'm sorry about Bugsy."

"Easily done."

"You never did it."

"I've had more practice than you." She realized how that sounded, and flushed. "I'm sorry. I didn't mean to—"

"It's okay. It's true. You look great, by the way. Melly was right about that." His gaze traveled down her body and lingered on her legs. "Is that dress new? You left without luggage."

"I borrowed it from Hannah. You, on the other hand, don't look great. Did you get any sleep on the plane?"

"Are you kidding? With those two? Fortunately, the woman in the seat near us took pity on me, otherwise I wouldn't have been able to use the bathroom."

Their conversation felt stilted and unnatural.

Neither of them had any idea how to move past the massive boulder that had been dropped into their relationship.

Beth decided that this situation had to be treated like cold water. You just had to jump right in. "Those things I said—"

"Not now." He shook his head. "I know we need to talk, but after two cabs, two flights and nonstop action with the girls, my brain isn't functioning well enough for me to be confident that the words that come out of my mouth are what I really want to say. The conversation is too important to mess up, so let's wait until I've taken a shower, unpacked and caught up on sleep."

She didn't want to wait. She knew couples whose arguments simmered along for weeks, but she and Jason weren't like that. If they disagreed, which happened rarely, they discussed it and fixed it. They'd never had a major problem.

Until now.

"Why don't you take a shower and I'll put the flowers in water and help you unpack?" She looked at the rest of the luggage. "You have more cases than Hannah."

"I didn't know what to pack for the girls, so I packed everything. And I packed some things for you, too, because I knew you didn't bring anything with you. I imagined you ruining those sexy boots of yours walking through a muddy field."

"Take a shower. I'll make coffee and something to eat." She vanished into the kitchen and through the window saw Posy and the girls wrapped up in coats and scarves, tramping through the field toward Socks.

She put the tulips in a vase and stood for a while, watching the children as they clambered over the gate and showered the ever-patient Socks with affection and fresh hay.

Turning away, she poured coffee into a mug and made a stack of buttered toast using the fresh loaf her mother had made the day before.

She piled it onto a tray and carried it upstairs.

The door to her bedroom was wide-open and there, sprawled across the bed, was Jason.

As she set the tray down on the nightstand, he stirred. "Beth?"

"I thought the plan was to take a shower before you had a rest?"

"I need a rest before I take a shower or there's a strong chance I'll drown. It hasn't been officially confirmed, but I think I may already be dead."

"I'm sorry you're exhausted."

"No, you're not. This is exactly what you intended to happen."

He looked so pathetic lying there it was hard not to smile.

"Aren't you at least going to remove your shoes?"

His only response was a grunt, and this time she did smile. "Are you really that tired?"

"Tired?" He cracked open one eye. "Tired is how I feel after a day at work when I've battled commuters, my boss and a bunch of fussy clients. This isn't that. This is so much more. I don't have a word for it, but I know 'tired' sure as hell doesn't cover it."

Beth took pity on him and removed his shoes. "Which part did you find tiring?"

"All of it." His eyes closed again. "There's the eating, of course. That's exhausting, because they eat all the time. Three meals a day, and snacks. No downtime. I might as well have been running a restaurant."

"The downtime is between the meals and the snacks."

"No, that was the time I was preparing meals and snacks, or running out to buy something they wanted that I'd forgotten to buy. *Mommy always has it.*" He opened his eyes again. "Do you know how many times I've heard those words this week? Are you smiling? Is that a smug smile, Bethany Mc-Bride Butler?"

"Maybe a little." It was good to know he finally had more of an idea of her life. "You missed me a bit?"

"No. I missed you a lot. And not just because I have no idea how to make eggy bread the way you do. Melly said it was gloopy, whatever that means, and Ruby said it tasted funny. When they said 'eggy bread,' I assumed the ingredients were eggs and bread, but apparently you put magic in there, too."

"Did you use cinnamon?"

"No, I did not use cinnamon. Where, in the words *eggy bread* does cinnamon appear?"

"I add cinnamon and a touch of sugar, which helps crisp the edges and stops it being 'gloopy.'" She sat down on the bed next to him. "So the eggy bread was an issue. Anything else?"

"I took the wrong color tights to ballet."

"I told you to—"

"You told me to take pink, I know, but I couldn't find pink in the drawer, so I took black, because it was that or be late, and you told me not to be late. I chose what I thought was the lesser of the two sins, but apparently Melly can't dance in black. Something happens to her legs and she can't move unless her legs are pink. It's a medical mystery. And don't even talk to me about getting two kids out of the apartment on time every morning. It's a surprise to me that you don't show up at school in your nightwear."

"Why didn't you tell me you were struggling? When I called, you immediately handed the phone to the girls. I thought you were so mad you didn't want to talk to me."

"The ten minutes when they were on the phone with you was the only time I could get things done. Also, you made it clear you wanted time to yourself and I didn't want to disturb you." He eyed her. "And there may have been pride involved. I didn't want you to know I was incompetent."

She couldn't believe he'd handled it himself. "I expected you to call your mother the moment I walked out."

"I almost did. I even picked up the phone. Then I realized that calling my mother was tantamount to admitting I couldn't handle it. You told me I didn't have a clue what your life was like, and that I didn't spend any real time with my own daughters. That hurt. I wanted to prove that you were wrong, and that I could cope. Sure, I do Sunday mornings in the park, but I knew I could handle the other parts, too. I knew I wasn't as bad a father as you seemed to think and I was ready to produce the evidence."

Tension spread down her spine. "Jason—"

"Except that it turned out you were right."

"I wasn't right. You're a wonderful father."

"Because you make it easy for me to come in and experience the good parts. By the time I get home, you've fed and bathed the kids, and they're in bed with their books and the apartment is tidy. How the hell do you do that by the way? It was a challenge to feed them three times a day, and two nights we gave up on baths. And the apartment looks like we've been robbed. I have never felt so inferior in my life." He reached for her hand. "Which is my way of saying that the evidence proved you right and me wrong. What you do is not easy. I officially admit that it was an incredibly tactless and misinformed state-ment and I hope you'll forgive me."

"As a matter of interest, what was the hardest part?"

"Being without you. Not because you turn our rampaging kids and our chaotic apartment into a family and a home, but because I missed having you to laugh with and talk to." He tightened his grip. "You're my best friend, Beth. I'm sorry for the things I said that night. I'm not surprised you walked out."

"I'm sorry for the things I said, too." She felt so relieved she wanted to cry. She still didn't know what the solution to their problem was, but she felt more confident that they'd find one. They had to. "I'm sorry I walked out like that."

"I'm not." He rolled onto his side and tugged her down beside him. "It was what I needed. And the truth is I loved being with the girls. It was exhausting and terrifying, but I got to know things about them that I never knew before. How about you?" He stroked her hair away from her face. "Have you been having fun being creative again?"

"Yes." She wasn't ready to admit that she was finding Corinna exhausting with her endless demands and emotional blackmail. "It's good to be using my brain again. Are you going to shower and change?"

"Yes, but for five minutes let me savor being able to spread out on the bed without Ruby poking me in the eye. That girl thinks she's a starfish. I used to think our bed was satisfyingly large, but not anymore."

Beth reared back. "Wait—you let Ruby sleep in the bed?"

"Not to begin with. To begin with, I got up every time she called for me, the way you do, but it turns out I'm not made of the same quality material as you, because I was worn down pretty quickly. When I was too tired to get up, she had to come to me, and I didn't have the energy to dislodge her."

"She was messing with you, Jason. Taking advantage."

"Yeah, kids are like predators. They sense weakness and pounce."

She sighed, anticipating the effort it would take her to unravel that particular indulgence. "That is a hard habit to break. You shouldn't have let her stay there."

"I know, but out of the two of us she has the stronger will." He lifted his head and looked her in the eye. "It was survival." His head thumped back again and she straightened.

"Get in that shower, Jason Butler, and then sleep. I'll wake you in an hour."

"Could you wake me in a week?"

"No. It's Christmas and this is family time. Move yourself."

Beth went back downstairs and cleared the kitchen. Through the window she could see the children taking turns to ride Socks round the field, with Posy leading him.

Taking advantage of a few minutes of quiet time, she typed up her ideas and sent them in an email to Corinna. At least the internet was working, that was something to be thankful for.

And she was happy with what she'd done. If nothing else, she'd proved to herself she was still capable of thinking about something other than raising children.

When the girls finally reappeared, they were pink cheeked and smiling.

Ruby bounced through the door, her hair wild from the wind, Bugsy apparently forgotten. "I want a pony, Mommy."

Even Beth wasn't weak willed enough to agree to that. "That's not going to happen while we're living in Manhattan."

"Then I want to come and live here, near Grandma, and Grandpa and Aunty Posy, and then I can ride Socks every day."

Beth took off Ruby's coat and boots and left them in the boot room outside the kitchen. "Your hands are freezing! Come inside and warm up."

Melly was shivering. "Please may we have hot chocolate?"

Melly, ever the princess, and ever well mannered.

"You may. Wash your hands and sit at the kitchen table. Hot chocolate coming up!" Beth looked at Posy, who had just come in through the door, bringing with her a flurry of snowflakes. "Thank you. You're a brilliant aunt."

"It's great to spend time with them. And now I need to get to the café before Duncan resigns. I'm already late. Will you be all right?"

Beth noticed that her sister seemed distracted. "Why wouldn't I be?"

"I know you and Jason have things to catch up on."

"It will be fine."

"You could always ask Hannah to babysit."

"She's not going to want to do that."

Posy knocked the snow off her boots. "Does she seem okay to you?"

"Yes. Why wouldn't she be? What do you mean?"

"Nothing."

Beth glanced toward the door. "I know she's in her room, but that's not abnormal."

"No." Posy eased her feet out of her boots. "I'm sure you're right. Okay, then, girls, take good care of Bonnie for me and I will see you later. Get Mommy to bring you to the café and I will save two of the biggest slabs of chocolate cake you have ever seen."

The girls cheered and Bonnie barked and wagged her tail.

Later, much later, after a day of hot chocolate, stories by the fire and a trip to Café Craft that left both children almost dizzy with excitement, Beth tried to settle the children down.

They were bathed, fed, and she was hopeful of snatching a moment with Jason before dinner.

Force of habit made her clear the bathroom. She swept the bath of ducks and Ruby's favorite squeaky alligator, put the towels on the heated rail to dry and closed the door.

She was about to walk back into the bedroom the girls shared when she heard Ruby's voice.

"I don't want Mommy to *ever* leave us again."

Beth froze. Guilt thudded into her so hard it felt as if someone had kicked her in the chest.

She felt as if she was being torn in two. Who was it that said you couldn't have it all? They'd been right. How did you tell a four-year-old you adored that she wasn't enough? That her mother wanted more. And how was she going to focus on work if she was feeling guilty about the girls all the time?

She put her hand to her mouth. She needed to go into that room, smile like the mommy Ruby knew and reassure her. She couldn't let her feelings show. Ideally she would have taken a minute to pull herself together, but there was no time for that. There was no way Jason would be able to handle a difficult question like that on his own.

And then she heard his voice.

"Sit down, Ruby."

"Want Mommy."

"Mommy is busy right now, and I need you to stop wriggling and listen to me. Remember what you've been learning this week at school? We talked about it. Listening. I need you to do that now." He was calm, but firm, and Beth wasn't the only one surprised by the strength of his tone.

Ruby was, too.

Through the crack in the door Beth saw her daughter sit down heavily on the floor, her mouth closed and her eyes wide as she waited.

"Good girl." Jason joined her on the floor, folding his length into the small space between the bed and the wall. "You want Mommy to be there for you every minute of the day, and I understand that."

Ruby's curls bounced as she nodded, and Beth felt a rush of despair.

No one wanted her to do this. Her kids didn't want it, and her husband didn't want it.

She waited, braced for Jason to say he wanted her to be home, too.

"You know how Daddy goes to work in the morning?"

"You take your coat and your bag. You have important things to do. And you're always talking on your phone."

"Right. And when we get back to New York, Mommy is going to start working, like Daddy does."

Ruby looked confused. "Why?"

"Because Mommy isn't only good at looking after you, she's good at a lot of other things. Mommy loves you very much, but there are things she wants to do, too. Things that are important to her."

"We're important." Ruby's voice was wobbly, but Jason's was steady as a rock.

"You are. But a person can have more than one important thing in their lives. We're a family, which means we don't only think about ourselves, we think about the other people in that family."

"Will she still play with me?"

"Of course she'll play with you. She loves playing with you. She just might not play with you every minute of every day, that's all. And you're going to be spending longer at school with your friends."

Ruby pondered on that. "But who will pick me up from school?"

"We'll have to figure that out as we go along, but someone will, so you don't need to worry about that. If Mommy isn't there, then Nana Butler or I will be there."

"You lost Bugsy." Ruby's tone suggested she considered him the least reliable of the available options.

"That's true. I did lose Bugsy. And if this was a performance review, I'd hold up my hands and admit I made a mistake."

"What's a performance review?"

"It's when someone gets feedback on how good they are at doing things. And when it comes to caring for you and Melly, I know there are things I could have done better."

"Like not losing Bugsy."

"Not losing Bugsy is right at the top of the list. Part of the problem is that your mommy is so good at things, that no matter how well I do it's never going to be as good as her."

Tears pricked Beth's eyes.

"But here's the thing." Jason pulled Ruby onto his lap and wrapped his arms round her. "Whatever you do in life, whether it's being a firefighter or an astronaut or a mommy, if you practice, you can get better at it. And that's what I'm going to do. I'm going to practice so next time you give me a performance review it's a good one."

Ruby thought about it. "You're not as good at things as Mommy, but I still like you."

There was a pause. "That's good—" Jason's voice was rough "—because I like you, too."

Beth leaned her head against the wall and closed her eyes. The lump in her throat was so huge she wasn't sure she'd be able to speak.

At what point was she going to admit that she wasn't enjoying the work as much as she'd thought she would?

She'd wanted this so badly, but now she wasn't sure if it was the right thing for her after all.

17

Suzanne

"Five days! I've been in bed for five days." Suzanne swung her legs out of bed and then paused as the room spun.

"And you need to stay there for another day at least." Stewart put a mug down on the nightstand. The tea was the color of oak, which meant he'd forgotten to take the tea bag out.

She took a cautious sip and tried not to choke. "Delicious, thank you." She put it down again. "I'll leave it to cool down." *And then she'd pour it down the sink when he wasn't looking.*

She hated feeling so helpless. Hated the fact that she didn't have the energy to go downstairs and make her own tea.

It made her anxious to think about how much there was to do.

Stewart had been helping, but he didn't do things the

way she liked them done and doing them was part of the fun for her.

She'd planned on spoiling everyone. Mothering them. She'd been looking forward to family dinners and cozy evenings in front of the fire. Instead her evenings had been spent in isolation. She'd been reduced to waving to her grandchildren from the doorway so that she didn't spread her germs.

The good news was that she'd definitely turned the corner. She no longer had a fever, she was finally sleeping again and she felt at least half-human.

"I'm going to get up today."

"There's no need. Posy and I are on top of everything. We're working through your list." Stewart straightened the bed, somehow managing to leave the bedding more creased and rumpled than before he'd started. "Today is item nine. I'm making cranberry sauce."

"You've never made cranberry sauce in your life."

"Man against cranberry—how hard can it be?"

"Remember to use fresh orange juice."

"Got it."

She knew he wasn't listening. "Oranges, Stewart."

"I know what orange juice is! There's a carton in the fridge. I bought it yesterday."

"I squeeze real oranges."

"You do?" Stewart eyed her. "No wonder you're exhausted."

She sighed. It was impossible to make him understand that the preparations for Christmas weren't a chore to her, they were a pleasure. "How are the girls? Give me an update."

"Everything is under control. I'm holding the fort." Stewart flexed his muscles and winked at her. "I am superman. I can handle anything that comes my way."

Suzanne studied him. "Your sweater is inside out."

He reached behind his neck, felt the label and gave her

a sheepish grin. "I can handle everything except dressing myself."

He always made her laugh. Even when she'd been feeling like death, he'd made her laugh.

She loved him so much it hurt. There wasn't a day when being with him didn't lift her spirits.

"What's happening with Beth? Did you get to the bottom of why she came home early?"

"Beth is fine." He didn't look at her and she studied his face, trying to work out what he was hiding.

"But you're worried about her."

"I'm not the worrying type." He tidied up her knitting and smacked his fist into one of the cushions on the chair.

"Why are you punching the cushion?"

"I'm not punching, I'm plumping. You're always plumping cushions."

"You almost made a hole in it. If that was a living thing, you would have knocked it unconscious." Not to mention the fact that she'd never seen him plump a cushion in all the years they'd been together. Usually he tossed them on the floor. "You're worried, and so am I. I want to know what's happening."

She felt helpless, and she hated feeling helpless.

Stewart removed a feather that had sneaked out from the cushion. "Maybe I am worried, but there's nothing we can do about it. They're not kids, Suzanne, they're adults. It's not our job to fix things for them. It's our job to support them, no matter what."

"Beth and Hannah both came home early. That isn't normal. What if there's something they want to talk through?"

"Then they'd sit down with us and talk. They know they can. They've always known that, honey."

It wasn't enough for Suzanne. "If Beth wanted to talk, she'd talk to you."

"And I've given her the opportunity. We've had breakfast a few times. Took a walk together yesterday. She didn't mention anything."

"She came home without luggage. She never travels without luggage, which means she must have walked out. I don't believe that nonsense about the airline losing her cases. Are she and Jason acting normal? Did they have a fight, do you think?"

Stewart sat down on the chair and shook his head. "I don't know. And even if they did, it doesn't mean it was anything serious. They're both here now and they're sleeping in the same room and laughing together. Beth is constantly fiddling with her hair and makeup, which seems pretty normal to me. That's all I can tell you."

Suzanne reached for her robe. "Why are you making the cranberry sauce? Beth could do that."

"She's a little preoccupied with this job. That damn woman always seems to call in the middle of mealtimes. If you ask me, she's more likely to be the problem than their marriage."

"Corinna? I don't like the idea of Beth working for her again."

"Me neither, but it's not our business." Stewart sounded tired. "It's her decision."

"Maybe, but I'm telling you it's a mistake."

"If it is, then it's her mistake and we have to let her make it."

And that was one of the hardest things about parenting, standing by and watching your child make a mistake. She wanted to jump in and save them from it. She wanted to protect them from every hurt.

"It was easier when they were little." Suzanne slid her arms into her robe and stood up carefully.

Stewart crossed the room in a flash and put his arm round her.

"Steady. I don't want you collapsing."

She smiled up at him. "Because you love me."

"There's that, but also I have no idea how to get blood out of a carpet."

"Oh, you—" She punched his arm and lost her balance in the process. She would have fallen if he hadn't caught her against him.

"You are the most stubborn, infuriating—"

"I think the words you're missing are *beautiful, talented, intelligent*—"

He kissed her. "That, too. Get back into bed. Take another day to rest."

There was a soft knocking on the door and Stewart waited until Suzanne had sat back down on the bed before crossing the room to open it.

Melly and Ruby stood there.

"We made cards for Grandma," Melly said. "To help her get better."

Ruby thrust them into his hand, showering glitter over the carpet.

The girls looked so adorable, Ruby with her riot of curls and Melly with her hair neatly caught in bunches.

"Are you having fun?" Suzanne slid back under the covers. "Have you been riding Socks?"

"Every day. Is there a job that's riding horses? I might want to do that when I'm bigger." Ruby ran across the room to her, evading Stewart's attempt to catch her. "Will you get up soon and play with me?"

"I will. Very soon. Definitely tomorrow."

"Good."

Ruby climbed onto the bed, and Suzanne forced herself to shift away. "I don't want to give this bug to you, honey."

"If you give it to me, then you won't have it anymore." Ruby patted her leg. "I don't mind having it for a while."

The things they said made her laugh constantly, just as they had when Hannah, Beth and Posy were young.

Suzanne resisted the temptation to hug her tightly. "Go back to your sister, honey. And thank you for the cards. They're beautiful, and just looking at them is going to make me feel better."

"I used extra glitter."

Suzanne eyed her sparkling carpet. "I see that. Lucky me."

Beth appeared in the doorway. "Ruby!" She sounded exasperated. "I told you not to bother Grandma. Sorry, Mom. Did she wake you?"

"No. I wasn't asleep, and she's not bothering me. In fact, I'm feeling a lot better." Suzanne watched as Stewart carefully put the cards on display. He might not be good at straightening beds or making tea, but he understood the importance of displaying his grandchildren's artwork.

"If you need anything, call." Beth grabbed Ruby and scooped her up. "Let's go and play."

They closed the door and Stewart looked at the glitter on the floor.

"I like it. I think it should stay."

"You mean you have no idea how to remove glitter from a carpet."

"That, too. You have to admit, it's festive." He glanced at his watch. "Is there anything else you need? I'm due at the Adventure Centre in an hour. I could bring you another cup of tea."

"No! It's fine." She certainly didn't want more tea. She

hadn't figured out how to deal with the one she already had. "Maggie is popping round later to see me. If I need something, she'll fetch it. Thank you for everything. You would have made a wonderful nurse."

"I've always thought my legs would look good in the uniform."

She smiled. "I'm so glad I married you."

"Of course you are. I'm irresistible. You couldn't resist my practiced seduction." Stewart swaggered across the room, ruining the effect by tripping over one of her slippers.

She rolled her eyes. "You have a terrible memory. I was the one who seduced you."

"Not true."

"You were moving too slowly for me, Stewart McBride."

"That's not how I remember it. I was like a rampant stallion."

"A ram—" She laughed until she started to cough.

Stewart handed her a glass of water. "That's your punishment for denigrating my manhood."

"I'm not denigrating your manhood. I'm just saying I was the one who seduced you." She took a sip of water. "Before you go, tell me about Hannah."

Stewart tugged his sweater off and turned it the right way round. "What about her?"

"Does she seem happy?"

"She's spent a lot of time in her room, but that's not unusual. She has a big job, Suzy. We should be proud of her."

"I *am* proud of her, of course I am. But I'm also worried that she shuts people out. That she doesn't trust them." Suzanne adjusted her pillows. "If you get the chance, would you talk to her?"

He found his shoes. "Yes, but you know Hannah doesn't open up easily. I'm not sure what I'm supposed to say to her."

"Nothing. Don't worry. I'll be back on my feet tomorrow and I'll talk to her then."

If she wanted to know what was going on with her family, she was going to have to find out for herself.

18

Hannah

Hannah put the finishing touches to the document and emailed it to the office.

She needed to have a conversation with the team, but the signal had been especially bad for the past couple of days. She hadn't spoken to Angie in almost a week.

Her hand hovered over the keyboard, and then she quickly tapped on the tab saying Our People and brought up Adam's biography and photo.

She knew she needed to talk to him, but she had no idea what to say.

She missed their talks, his smile, his sharp mind and his sense of humor.

She missed *him*.

"Hannah? *Hannah!*"

The door flew open and Hannah flipped her laptop shut. She wasn't used to people bursting into her room, but that was one of the penalties of being at home. Privacy was in short supply.

"What?"

Beth stood there, clutching a towel round her, her hair tumbling loose around her bare shoulders. "Did you use all the hot water?"

Hannah was transported back to childhood when Beth would take up residence in the bathroom and then follow her round the house, trying to do her makeup.

"I took a shower, if that's what you mean."

"Next time, don't spend so long in there. The water is freezing."

"Fine, but while we're on the topic of personal habits, can you not leave your makeup lying around everywhere. It's as if someone has ransacked a beauty department."

Beth walked out and then turned and came back again, this time walking into the center of the room. "Are you okay?"

"Of course. Why wouldn't I be?"

"I don't know. You were quiet at dinner last night and you're spending a lot of time in your room. I hope it's not the kids. Are they too loud?" Beth glanced at Hannah's laptop. "Who is that guy?"

"What guy?"

"The hot guy on your computer screen that you're hiding from me. Actor?"

"A colleague. We work for the same company." She kept her hand on the lid, but of course that didn't stop Beth because this was her family and privacy and respecting personal space wasn't something that happened in the family home.

Beth pushed Hannah's hand away and opened the laptop.

"Wow. Not sure I could concentrate in a meeting if he was in the room. Is he married?"

"No." Hannah closed the laptop again, but instead of leaving, Beth hovered.

"Can I ask you something?"

Hannah hoped this wasn't going to be the usual interrogation about her love life. She really wasn't equipped to handle those questions right now. "What?"

"Would you watch the girls for an hour? I want to spend some time alone with Jason. They're watching TV downstairs in the den, so they shouldn't be any bother."

The last thing she needed right now was to watch the children. Having Melly and Ruby around the house made the whole baby thing a little too real. "I'm pretty busy, Beth."

Her sister's jaw lifted. "They're your nieces. I would have thought you'd be pleased to spend time with them."

"I have work to do. Have you asked Posy?"

"I can't find her. I think she's outside with the sheep or something. Please, Hannah. I need some time with Jason."

It was much easier to say no on the phone than it was in person. "Leave the door open and tell them to call me if they need anything."

"It isn't enough to listen. You need to check on them. With Ruby, silence isn't always good. It often means she's climbing something, and she doesn't usually bother checking whether it's fixed to the ground."

Memories flashed through Hannah's brain like a movie on fast-forward. "I'll check on them."

"Thanks. We'll only be an hour." Beth vanished and Hannah turned back to her laptop, but she couldn't focus on the numbers on the screen.

Another email arrived, this time indicating that Angie needed to speak to her urgently.

With a sigh, she reached for her phone, but there was no signal.

The only way to speak to Angie was to trudge outside in the cold and the snow to make the call.

She grabbed her coat and an extra sweater and left her room.

She paused as she walked past the bedroom Suzanne shared with Stewart. Should she knock on the door and see if there was anything she needed?

If she did that, Suzanne would want to talk and Hannah wasn't ready to have the conversation she knew she needed to have.

Telling herself that she didn't want to risk disturbing Suzanne if she was resting, even though she knew the truth was something different, Hannah walked quietly downstairs and into the den, where the children were snuggled on the sofa watching a movie.

"Aunty Hannah!" Ruby's curls bobbed around her face like question marks. "Come and watch it with us! It's funny. You'll love it."

Hannah glanced at the cartoons on the screen. "In a minute, maybe. Girls, I need to make a phone call."

Ruby's eyes widened. "Are you calling about Bugsy?"

"I— No, not about Bugsy." She saw Ruby's face crumple and instantly her heart started to race. "At least, not only about Bugsy. But while I'm on the phone, I will call the airline, too, and see if there is any news. Can you stay here while I do that?"

Beth's words echoed in her head.

It isn't enough to listen. You need to check on them.

But she was only going to be five minutes. Suzanne was upstairs; both children were occupied with their movie.

"Promise me you'll stay here and that you won't move until I'm back."

"We promise, Aunty Hannah," Melly said, her eyes fixed on the screen. "I'll watch Ruby."

Ruby frowned. "I don't need watching."

"You do need watching." Melly spoke with sisterly superiority. "You left Bugsy on the plane."

"And we're going to fix that." With a final check that they had everything they needed, Hannah pulled her coat on, pushed her feet into an old pair of snow boots Suzanne had left out for her, and walked out into the yard.

Someone had cleared the snow to one side, but the freeze overnight had turned the path slick and icy.

Picking her way to the softer snow to the side, Hannah waved her phone in the air, trying to find a signal.

This was ridiculous. She'd forgotten how patchy communications were. How did anyone function here? It was only when you were without it that you realized how much you relied on technology.

Her toes were freezing and she picked her way carefully across the snow-covered yard and headed toward the field that sloped up from the lodge.

Wondering what had possessed her to think being in Scotland would be any sort of escape, she climbed the gate awkwardly and saw a few precious bars of signal appear on her phone. *Finally.*

Angie answered the call immediately.

"Miss Mc—Hannah! It's good to hear your voice. How is Scotland?"

"Cold." She was relieved her assistant couldn't see her clinging to a muddy gate. "Did you get the report I sent?"

"Yes. The team are meeting now. Adam is going to call you after they're done to—" Her voice vanished and Hannah frowned.

"Hello? Angie? Are you still there?" She checked the connection and stepped up a rung on the gate, trying not to slip. "Angie?"

"Hannah? This line is terrible."

"I know, but it's the only one we have, so let's work with it. First, I'm going to be emailing you something I need you to deal with urgently. It's not an easy brief, but if anyone can do it, you can. Make it a priority." Her fingers were so cold she almost dropped the phone. How long did it take frostbite to set in? "Ask Adam if he can do the coaching session with Michael Barnet that I had scheduled for tomorrow. I was going to do it from here, but that's not going to work." She could hardly coach a general manager on how he was managing the performance of his team while she was shivering in a field and playing hide-and-seek with an elusive phone signal. "Any problems from the rest of the clients?" She listened while Angie talked and made the occasional interjection, "Mmm, well, that is a key element of introducing organizational change…" She shifted her position on the gate as one of her hands grew numb. "We need to review the project plan and discuss priorities for January. Is that everything?"

"Yes. We have a team meeting in the morning, so if anything comes out of that, I'll call you. Unless you want to call in to the meeting?"

"I don't think that's going to— Agh—" Hannah screamed as something wet and warm touched her frozen fingers. She snatched her hand away and in doing so let go of the gate. She lost both her phone and her balance, felt her stomach swoop and landed in an ungainly heap in the churned-up frozen mud and snow by the gate.

Winded, she lay there for a moment, and then a big, shaggy head lowered toward her.

Hannah screamed.

The pony threw up his head, startled.

"Socks." Posy's voice came from a distance. "Socks!"

The pony turned in the direction of her voice. With a delighted snort, Socks ceased his exploration of the strange human lying in his field and turned back to the gate.

By the time Posy had swung herself over the gate, Hannah had managed to sit up.

"Are you all right? Are you bruised? You have a bloodcurdling scream, by the way." Posy dropped the bale of hay she was carrying and dropped to her knees beside her sister. "Did you hurt yourself? Say something! You're making me panic."

"You're in the mountain rescue team. You're not supposed to panic."

"It's different when it's your sister. Especially when you said you might be pregnant." Posy flushed. "I know it's none of my business. You don't have to talk about it if you don't want to. I'm worried, that's all."

"I am pregnant." Oh God, had she hurt the baby? It hadn't even been born yet, and already she'd harmed it. Instinctively she lowered her hand to her abdomen, even though she knew it would make no difference. "Do you think I'm going to lose it?" And it was only now, when that possibility presented itself, that she realized how much she didn't want it to happen.

"Of course not. You didn't fall far and it was a soft landing, but I don't think lying on your back in snow and mud is good for you, so let's fix that at least." Posy held out her hand and helped her up. "What are you doing out here? Beth and Jason walked past me ten minutes ago and said you were watching the girls."

"I had to make a short phone call." It had been a while since Hannah had felt so useless and humiliated. The previous time had been in the mountains, too. "I didn't know I was going to be attacked."

"Socks is more scared than you."

"*I* scared *him*? I didn't push my face in his and almost savage him."

"He wasn't savaging you."

"What was he doing there?"

"This is where he lives. You were the one in the wrong place. He was being friendly." Posy wrapped her arms round the pony's neck and gave him a reassuring hug. "Do you need therapy? Poor Socks."

"Poor Socks? What about me?" Hannah could barely talk through her chattering teeth. She didn't dare look at the state of her coat. And then she remembered Angie and felt a flutter of panic. She didn't want her team to see anything other than her most professional self, but this time her camouflage had well and truly disappeared. "I don't know what happened to my phone. I was in the middle of a conversation."

Posy glanced around. "I see it." She jerked her head. "Over there. That gives a whole new meaning to talking a load of horseshi—"

"Do *not* say it!" Hannah picked her way across uneven, frozen ground and retrieved her phone, which, by some improvement in her luck, was still working. Angie, however, was long gone and Hannah had no way of knowing what she'd heard. She pushed it into her pocket and noticed her sister's shoulders were shaking. "Could you at least try not to laugh?"

"I'm laughing with relief. I was worried you'd hurt yourself. Oh, Hannah, Hannah—" Posy doubled over, almost choking, and Hannah felt a rush of exasperation and also envy that her sister could find the amusing side to almost any situation. She wanted to steal some of that lightness and wrap it around her serious self.

"I'm glad I provided entertainment." She knew she was being stiff, but she couldn't help it. "Please don't worry that my call was important and that my career might well be over."

"I won't." Posy wiped her eyes on her sleeve. "Just kidding. Don't the people you work with have a sense of humor?"

"I have a serious job. I'd rather people didn't laugh at me." Especially at the one thing in her life she considered herself to be good at. "Do you think we can go back to the house now?"

"Yes, but I should warn you that you're going to be scrubbing red streaks off the kitchen wall."

"Excuse me?"

"Beth left all that easy-to-use makeup lying over the kitchen table, despite my constant pleas for her to clear it up. You left Ruby alone. Those two actions have collided with cataclysmic consequences. What did Beth call that color? Everyday Red? It's not looking so hot on the wall, I can tell you, but I can confirm that Ruby did find it incredibly easy to use."

Hannah felt a rush of horror. "I only left them for five minutes." She stumbled back across the frozen field with her sister, anxious about the children. "And I checked on them. They were both safe and comfortable. Five minutes."

"Five minutes and a lipstick is all it takes for Ruby to decide she is Michelangelo and the kitchen wall is the ceiling of the Sistine Chapel. Calm down. It will be fine."

How could her sister be so relaxed? "She was watching TV!"

"Ruby isn't a child who sits for long. She's always on the move."

Guilt pricked. It had been years since she'd had responsibility for a child. Still, she should have remembered. "You were the same. I had to watch you constantly."

Posy frowned. "You watched me?"

"Yes."

"When? How old was I?"

"Forget it. Forget I said anything." Why had she? She was

feeling things she didn't usually feel, and saying things she didn't usually say.

"I don't want to forget it." Posy stopped walking. "You babysat me? Where were our parents?"

"Climbing. They usually left us at home."

"They didn't get a sitter?"

"Sometimes, and sometimes Suzanne came, but there were usually a few hours when it was just the three of us."

Posy turned the collar of her jacket up. "So—you are pregnant. Are you—"

"Keeping it? Yes." She was surprised by how defensive she felt. How fierce. Not for a moment would her child think it wasn't wanted.

And she knew now it was very much wanted.

"I was going to ask if you were pleased." Posy's voice was soft. "Do you want to talk?"

The wind was icy and Hannah's fingers were frozen. It was hardly the place for a heart-to-heart and yet her sister's words made her feel warmer than she'd felt in a long time. "No, but I appreciate the offer."

Posy took off her scarf and wound it around Hannah's neck. "Have you told the guy who—I mean, the father?"

Hannah snuggled inside the scarf, touched by the gesture. "No. I suppose I should be glad there's no signal, given I don't know what I'd say to him. It's not exactly your everyday conversation."

She didn't have a clue what his reaction would be.

Hannah liked to plan, and she'd had no plan for this nor had she had time to formulate one.

And she was tired, so tired. Was that normal? She had no idea.

"For what it's worth, I'm a very engaged aunt. Always available for babysitting duties."

"Good. I'm going to need the help because I'd like not to be a terrible mother." Somehow it seemed easier to admit how she felt to Posy, who didn't seem to have a particularly high opinion of her anyway.

"Why would you be a terrible mother?" Posy pulled her hat down over her ears. "I think you'll be a great mother."

"Based on what? The fact that I fell off the gate, potentially damaging a child that hasn't even been born yet? Or that I left my nieces unattended because I thought they'd be fine?"

"They are fine." Posy shrugged. "Let's keep things in perspective. So the house might need redecorating, but no one *died*."

"Somehow I don't think Beth is going to be as calm about it. She'll be angry, and I don't blame her. It was careless of me."

"You don't have kids. I'm sure Beth didn't know any of these things until she had kids. We learn through experience. There are going to be plenty of ways in which you are brilliant."

"You think?" Was it pathetic of her that she needed that reassurance?

"I know. For a start, look how efficient you are. You will probably keep a spreadsheet, tracking Bugsy's whereabouts at all times. And it's not as if you haven't had experience. As you said, you looked after me and I'm still here. Was I hard work?"

Hannah remembered the challenge of looking after Posy. "It was like herding cats. You were a ball of energy, impossible to occupy and determined to climb everything. Sadly, I wasn't such a great climber, which meant that retrieving you from the top of cupboards was a challenge."

"How old was I? When did I walk?"

The wind was bitter and they were standing in a field reminiscing?

Hannah shivered. "I don't remember you walking. I only

remember you climbing. Dad talked about it all the time. He was so proud of you. In the summers when we traveled around and virtually lived in the van, he'd come and grab you and take you to wherever he was hanging out with climbing friends, so he could show you off. I used to hear him boasting, *Have you seen my Posy? She's a dynamo. She can climb anything. Oh yeah, she's my daughter, all right.*"

Posy stared at her. "That's the first time I've ever heard you talk about our father." She looked as surprised as Hannah felt.

It wasn't a subject she usually touched. She wasn't sure what had made her touch it now except that lately she seemed to be doing all sorts of things she didn't normally do. Being pregnant seemed to have affected her internal wiring. "We should get back—Ruby and Melly might be—"

"In a minute. Mom's there, and she's feeling better, so I'm sure that if there's screaming she'll investigate." Posy put her hand on her arm. "He took all three of us climbing?"

"No. Only you."

"You and Beth never came?"

Hannah felt tension rise. "Only one time. After that he left us in the van and took you."

"What happened that one time? Why didn't he take you, too?"

"I wasn't much of a climber. And climbing was the only thing Dad really cared about."

Hannah? No, she hasn't got it. There are days when I wonder where the hell she came from!

Hannah hadn't even known what "it" was. All she'd understood was that she lacked something, and that the deficiency in her makeup made her a source of deep embarrassment to her father.

She did her best to please, but to her he was a daunting figure, a lion of a man with a loud laugh and a restless energy. He rarely shaved and swore a lot. *Fuck this* and *fuck that.*

Hannah felt tense and awkward in his presence, and the conversation was like a foreign language. In the evening, her father would gather round the campfire with friends and numerous beer bottles, and Hannah would lie in her bunk and listen as words and phrases wafted toward her. The talk was of overhangs, the Yosemite Decimal System, free soloing; of harnesses, bolt hangers and anchor chains.

She always waited for the conversation to move on to other things she could understand, but it never did. Climbers, she discovered, talked about climbing and nothing else. Whenever conversation turned to some climbing legend who had achieved an incredible first ascent, her father would start planning a trip, too. She'd heard people call him a badass and a thrill seeker. She'd also heard him called a pothead, but had no idea what that was. All she knew was that his whole life was dedicated to doing something she didn't understand at all. She was scared of heights and didn't see the point of climbing.

Beth didn't particularly enjoy climbing, either, but her love of makeup and all things girlie amused their mother.

It was obvious to Hannah that she had nothing to redeem her in the eyes of either parent.

"But you were good at other things," Posy said. "You're smart. That must have made them proud. I bet they boasted about you, too."

There was no way she was going to admit how badly her parents had destroyed her confidence, or how she'd twisted herself into a million different shapes to make them proud, before eventually giving up and accepting the truth—

That not all parents loved their children equally.

"We need to get back to the kids." She went to step forward, but Posy blocked her path.

"You didn't feel they were proud of you?"

"I know they weren't." If she said *I got an A in Math, Daddy,* her father would scratch his jaw and try to find something to say, *That's great, I guess.* "People value different things. Our parents valued athletic ability, and as you know from my recent attempt to balance on a gate, I'm sadly lacking in that. That last summer before the accident, I taught you to read."

"Yeah?" Posy slid her arm into Hannah's and the two of them walked toward the lodge, their boots crunching on the new snow. "You were eight years old and you taught me to read? That must have made our parents proud, surely?"

Don't waste your time. She'll learn to read soon enough. We don't need her turning into you!

"Dad thought there was plenty of time for that when you started school. He was worried that an interest in books might stop you climbing."

They reached the back door and walked into the boot room. Hannah tugged off her boots, wondering how it was that a person's voice could stay in your head for twenty-five years.

Because she knew her love of books irritated her father, Hannah had read under the covers with a flashlight. The worst time for her was summer, when the whole family left their small rented home in the mountains, squashed into the van and drove between the Rockies and the Cascades, tackling different climbs.

Space was limited, and each child was allowed one small bag.

Hannah had crammed hers full of books.

Posy levered off her boots. "Tell me about that one time."

"What time?"

"You said they only took you climbing one time."

One summer, instead of staying in the van and losing herself in fictional worlds that all seemed more appealing than her own, she'd forced herself to try climbing.

She'd been determined to prove herself and bring the same expression of pride to their father's face that he wore when he looked at Posy.

In the end all she'd proved was that she didn't have the aptitude or attitude.

"It wasn't a resounding success."

She'd frozen on the rock, terrified by the drop, her teeth chattering, each moment of her agony intensified by her father's impatience.

For God's sake, climb! How are you even my child?

Weird how different kids can be, he'd said to a climber friend without even bothering to lower his voice.

His obvious embarrassment and the sympathetic expression on the face of his friend had unglued her frozen hands. Determined to climb and be like her sister, she'd thrown caution to the wind and tried to find a handhold on the smooth rock.

Posy closed the back door, shutting out the cold. "What happened?"

"I fell." And she still remembered the gut-swooping rush as she'd lost her grip and fallen through the air.

"And Dad caught you?"

"No. He was too busy excusing my lack of athletic ability to his friends."

She'd hit the ground so hard she'd thought she'd broken every bone in her body. As it turned out, she'd broken only one.

Her arm had been twisted at a funny angle, bone protruding through her skin.

Something flickered in Posy's eyes. "You were hurt?"

"Yes, but it turned out to be a good thing. I was allowed to spend the rest of the summer in the van." Hot and itchy from the plaster, resentful and humiliated, but safe with her books.

"You must have hated me."

"What? No! I adored you." The words flew from her lips before she could stop them. "Everyone adored you. You were bold and engaging and you never stopped smiling. Dad told everyone you were his favorite."

It was a moment before Posy answered, and when she did, her voice was quiet. "That must have hurt your feelings horribly."

"It was a long time ago." But not so long ago she couldn't remember the misery. "We should go and find the girls."

"I want to talk. Why do we never talk like this?"

Because it was like having her insides scooped out with a sharp object?

"I don't know, but I need to clean the walls before Beth and Jason come home, or I'll never hear the last of it." She'd already said more than she'd ever intended to. "I'm not in the mood to go ten rounds with Beth. Or you, for that matter. I know you're stressed and busy. Tell me what needs doing for Christmas. We'll handle it together."

"Can you pluck a turkey?"

"No. And I know you're winding me up. There has to be something on that list I can do."

Posy unzipped her jacket. "The day they died—were we on our own that day?"

"The list—"

"Were you on your own?"

Hannah sighed. Her sister showed the same stubbornness she had as a child when she'd been determined to climb on top of the fridge. "We had a sitter, but when they were late arriving back, she left and told me they wouldn't be long. She was annoyed because they hadn't left her enough money. And

they never did show up. You were sick. You had a temperature. I didn't know what to do. I tried calling, but they didn't
answer the phone."

"That must have been scary."

At the time she hadn't been scared, or even anxious—that
part had come later. At the time she'd been angry. Angry that
climbing always came before family. Angry that they'd abandoned their responsibilities to go up another mountain. Angry
that they couldn't even be bothered to pick up the phone when
she called. She'd even left a message saying *This is about Posy,
not me*, in case that increased the inducement to respond.

I'm in the wrong family, she'd thought over and over again,
and when she'd closed her eyes, she'd imagined herself waking up and finding herself with different parents.

And that, of course, had been exactly what had happened.

19

Beth

"You think wanting to work makes me a bad parent." Beth slid her arm into Jason's as they strolled to the edge of the loch. There was a short, circular walk that meandered around the edge of the water. In summer, there were nesting birds and brown trout. Now, in winter, the loch had a glassy stillness and an icy calm. Beyond them, the forest stretched like Narnia, the trees weighted by snow, merging with the snowy peaks behind.

"That's not true. It is true that I couldn't understand why you wanted to go back to work, but that was because I thought I knew what your day involved. I've discovered how wrong I was."

"But you want another baby. And that's not something that's easy to compromise on."

Jason stopped walking. His breath made clouds in the freezing air and he tugged her against him. "I'm not going to deny that I'd love another child, but it's an emotional reaction, not a logical one. Your relationship with your sisters has its ups and downs, but I also know you love having them in your life. It's as if the three of you are in an exclusive club."

"Sometimes they drive me insane."

"I know, but even in your lowest moments, have you ever wished you didn't have sisters?"

"No." She didn't even need to think about that one. "They understand me. We've shared the same experiences, and that binds you together in a way that nothing else does."

"Even though none of you talk about it."

"We don't *want* to talk about it, and each of us understands that. It doesn't need explaining or excusing. And it isn't just the accident that binds us. It's a hundred other small things that seem like nothing on their own, but together make up a history."

Jason nodded. "I envy you. I envy that the three of you share that history. It's only at Christmas that we all come together, but I always see it. Even when you fight, there's an intimacy to it. It isn't a fight any other three people could have. You have this whole secret life and connection that no one else is part of. And yes, friends can be like family, but they're not family and with family you try that little bit harder. Look at you and Hannah—she drives you crazy, but have you ever been tempted to give up on her?"

Beth swallowed. "No. I'm incredibly proud of her. She is so smart. And even if she wasn't smart, I'd still be proud of her. She's my sister."

He stroked her hair back from her face and tucked it under her hat. "And that's what I want for our girls. When we're old and wrinkled and causing problems, I want them to be able to call each other and say *Do you know what our parents said today?* I want them to support each other."

"I want that, too. And I think they will. Although they're different and they sometimes fight, the girls are close."

"You've encouraged them to be kind to each other, to care about each other. You've knitted our family together like glue." He took a deep breath. "And that glue isn't going to fail if you go back to work. So if that's what you want, then you should definitely do it."

"What about another baby?"

"After caring for the two I already have, I've been rethinking that. As you gathered from our daughter's frank revelations, when it comes to parenting, I'm a failure. You should fire me."

"I don't think you're a failure."

"I lost Bugsy."

"That was a misdemeanor, not a fireable offense. Oh, Jason—" She stood on tiptoe and locked her arms round his neck.

"I've been thinking about what it was like when you were in the delivery room." He wrapped his arms round her tightly. "All that panic. I'm not sure I want to go through that again. I think I was having my own little midlife crisis. I guess once you acknowledge that you've had your last child, you know your life is going to enter a different phase and I wasn't ready to accept that."

"And now?"

"I love the way our family is. I love you. I don't want anything different."

Beth felt nothing but relief. "I love you, too." She eased away. "I'm never going to be wrinkled by the way. That's not going to happen. Nor is gray hair."

"I think I saw one." Jason tugged off her hat and she shrieked and made a grab for it.

"My ears will freeze. And if you point out my gray hairs, I'm divorcing you."

"Don't ever divorce me." He pulled her into his arms and kissed her, his mouth warm and skilled on hers. "I love you, Beth McBride."

"I'm Butler."

"You are." He smiled against her lips. "And you're staying that way." He took her hand and they carried on walking round the lake, content in each other's company.

"We don't spend enough time just the two of us."

"Agreed." His hand tightened on hers. "We'll do more of it."

It felt like a fresh start, standing here surrounded by such breathtaking beauty, planning for the future.

"It's lovely being able to leave the girls with family, knowing they're safe. And that's what we need to put in place back home. Reliable childcare. If your mother will help, then when I'm at work I can focus on what I'm doing without worrying about the children."

She wouldn't be one of those mothers who constantly felt torn in all directions. All it required was organization. Juggling. She'd have clear work time and family time. She pictured herself giving interviews to some of the glossy magazines on how she balanced career and family. In her head she staged the photos. The children would be sitting at the kitchen table writing stories or filling in their scrapbooks, a plate of healthy snacks within reach. Sliced apple and carrot. Maybe celery sticks. Beth's laptop would be closed on the counter, proving that when she was in family mode, it was all about her children. If her phone rang, she'd let it go to voice mail because listening to her children meant giving them her full attention.

She thought about the details as they walked back to the house.

Basking in the glow of the perfect imaginary life she'd created for herself, Beth pushed open the kitchen door. She gave an anguished scream, stopped without warning, and Jason slammed into her.

"Sorry! What the——" He saw what had made her stop.

It was like a scene from a horror movie.

"Is that...*blood*?" Beth was shaking so badly she almost collapsed on the spot. Panic weakened her limbs. There had been an accident. A bad accident. "Ruby? Where's Ruby?" Only later would she reflect that she'd called only her younger daughter's name, as if knowing instinctively that she was the only one likely to be connected to this carnage. "Is she injured? Dead?" There was no sign of the children, and both her sisters were on their hands and knees scrubbing at the wall. "What happened? Did you take her to the hospital? Is she alive?"

"Will you calm down?" Posy blew her hair out of her eyes. "If this whole PR thing doesn't work out, you might want to consider a career as an actress. Not Shakespeare. One of those cheap horror movies where the girls walk into dark buildings going *Is anyone there?* and scream all the time. No one is in the hospital. And it's not blood. It's lipstick, although I admit it's a good color match. I think they should rename it Vampire, not Everyday Red. And, by the way, I can confirm the accuracy of their claim that no kiss is going to shift this lipstick. We've tried soap and water and pretty soon we're moving on to neat bleach. Nothing is budging it from the paintwork."

Beth's legs were so shaky she leaned against the wall for support.

She'd been sure it was blood.

Jason stepped past Beth and scanned the extent of the damage. "Shit."

Ruby bounded into the kitchen at that precise moment and gasped with delight. "Daddy said shit."

Why was it that children never listened when you wanted them to, but listened perfectly well when it was something you'd rather they didn't hear? "Daddy said shut," Beth said. "Shut. He wanted me to shut the door. It's cold out there."

Ruby looked unconvinced. "But—"

"Go and find your sister, Ruby. Daddy will be there in a minute. We'll talk about this later." She waited until Ruby had slunk away, then turned back to the room.

Jason was staring at the wall with something close to wonder. "Ruby did that? She has talent. It's magnificent. It reminds me of an early Picasso—"

"Jason!" Beth felt a rush of exasperation. "The door, before we all freeze."

He roused himself. "Sure. Can I put myself on the other side of it?"

"No. You can follow Ruby and don't take your eyes off her. I'll be along in a minute."

Bonnie padded into the room and Beth gave another gasp as she saw the red streaks on the dog's golden fur. "She— Oh no—"

"Yup." Posy glanced at the dog. "Bonnie is modeling Sexy Scarlet. And it looks good on her, don't you think? I am going to have to lock her up or we'll have puppies by New Year." She kissed Bonnie and Jason slid quietly from the room.

All Beth's frustration and anxiety exploded. "How could you let this happen? You were supposed to be watching them. When I think what could have happened…" She could barely breathe. "Ruby could have wandered into the mountains and got lost! She could have been buried in a snowdrift and frozen to death. She could have run into the lane and been hit by a car. Cut herself with a knife in the kitchen…"

"I'm sorry. I had to make an urgent call." Hannah looked stricken, while Posy dipped the cloth into the sudsy water and rubbed at the wall.

"It couldn't have waited? It was an hour—that's all! One hour." Beth forgot that only ten minutes earlier she'd been telling Jason she wouldn't not have her sisters for anything in the world. Now she could cheerfully have throttled both of them. "Work should *not* come before family."

"Yeah?" Posy threw her a cloth. "Says the work-obsessed woman who left the table at least eight times last night to take calls from her psycho boss. Wipe the self-righteous look off your face, Bethany Alice McBride, and start cleaning. Or you can wash my dog. Whichever you prefer, but do something. Don't just stand there lecturing us."

Beth stood in shocked silence. When had she last heard Posy stand up for Hannah? She couldn't remember. And while it was true that she was juggling family and her new role, she wasn't *obsessed.* And how could they be so unsympathetic when they were the ones to blame? "You shouldn't have left them."

"You shouldn't have left your makeup all over the table," Posy snapped. "If you'd cleared up as I asked you to, this wouldn't have happened, so at least admit you share the blame."

Beth didn't want to share the blame. "They could have had an accident."

"But they didn't, so we're all good." Posy exchanged looks with Hannah. "I can't budge the red. You?"

"No. I'm doing better with the plum color. It isn't quite as resistant."

"What is in this stuff?" Posy scowled at Beth. "You should check the ingredients, because if this is what it does to the wall, you're not putting any more of it on my face."

Hannah examined the stubborn streak. "We should search the internet for solutions. Maybe lemon juice or something?"

Beth felt overwhelmed. "I need to check on the girls."

Posy's cheeks were flushed from the effort of rubbing. "I checked on them just before you arrived. They were in the den, writing their lists for Santa. And before you panic again, I confiscated the glitter."

"They've already written lists for Santa. We did it weeks ago."

"Well, they're doing another one." Posy rubbed hard at a red streak. "You left us in charge, we get to choose the activity and you don't get to criticize."

Beth dumped her coat over the back of a chair. "What if they ask Santa for something different? The gifts are bought and wrapped." She couldn't bear the idea that they'd be upset on Christmas Day. "They can't change their minds."

"Well, tell them—" Posy floundered. "I don't know. Tell them Santa likes surprises."

"Do they still believe all that?" Hannah rocked back on her heels. "You could just tell them Santa won't be coming because he doesn't actually—"

"Santa won't be coming?" Ruby's voice came from the doorway. "Why won't he be coming? Because I drew on the walls? Does he know I was bad?" Her voice cracked. Her bottom lip wobbled.

Beth scooped her up. *Could this day get any worse?* "What Aunt Hannah means is that she doesn't believe Santa will be coming to *her.*"

"Why? Has Aunty Hannah been naughty?"

Beth tried to carry Ruby out of the room, but she twisted and wriggled until Beth had to put her down.

"Aunty Hannah—" Ruby ran across to Hannah, ignoring the dripping cloth and the marks on the wall. "Why won't Santa be coming to you? What did you do?"

Beth was so tense she felt as if her spine might snap.

If her sister rejected her little girl this time, that would be the final straw.

She was not going to bite her tongue.

She watched, her heart in her mouth, as Ruby crawled carefully onto Hannah's lap and wrapped her arms round her.

So trusting, Beth thought, terrified for her daughter, who was blissfully unaware of the rejection that might follow such an unrestrained display of affection.

She stepped forward, determined to intervene so that little Ruby could keep her belief in people intact for a little longer, but then she saw Hannah's arm come around her.

She froze, watching as Ruby kissed Hannah on the cheek.

"Have you written him a letter, Aunty Hannah?"

"I— No," Hannah said. "I haven't written him a letter."

"Then he can't know what you want. You should write. It's not too late. I could help you write it." Ruby slid off Hannah's lap and tugged at her sleeve. "You can use my sparkly pens if you like."

"Sparkly pens," Posy muttered. "I removed the glitter, but I forgot about the sparkly pens. Danger is everywhere."

"Sparkly pens." Hannah stood up slowly and took Ruby's outstretched hand. "That sounds like fun."

Fun? Had Hannah actually said it sounded like fun?

Beth couldn't remember a time when her sister had voluntarily played with the girls.

"Wait!" Posy levered herself to her feet and dropped the cloth in the bucket. "I am not cleaning this wall by myself while you lot get to write to Santa with sparkly pens."

"It's important, Aunty Posy. All my pens are in the den." Ruby dragged Hannah out of the room, the conversation floating back to them. "What would you like for Christmas, Aunty Hannah?"

"I don't know."

"You must know. Think really hard. Everyone has *something* they want. If you had one wish and you could have anything in the world, what would you have?"

The voices faded, so Beth missed Hannah's answer.

She looked at Posy. "What's happened to Hannah?"

Posy was staring into space.

"Posy?"

The glazed look in Posy's eyes faded. "What?"

"What are you thinking?"

"Did you know Hannah broke her arm?"

Beth glanced toward the door. "She looked fine to me."

"When we were kids. Dad took her climbing. She fell off a rock. Do you remember that?"

Beth looked at her sister, and then the red streaks of the wall. "What is the relevance of that question?"

"Do you remember it?"

"No." Beth rubbed her forehead with her fingers. "Maybe. Vaguely. I drew on her plaster. And it was her right arm, so she couldn't use it for weeks. You don't remember?"

"I don't have any memories of that time, apart from Suzanne hugging me."

"Why are you bringing this up now? I'm dealing with a crisis, and you're reminiscing about the past?"

"The crisis is in your imagination, but you're right, forget it," Posy said, and Beth felt a rush of frustration.

"Hannah doesn't believe in happy endings. If she tells Ruby that Santa doesn't exist, I will kill her."

"She's not going to say that, but just in case she lets something slip by accident, we'll go and check on her. We can scrub the lipstick off the wall later. Come on. Time for sisterly teamwork. Let's have fun."

It sounded surprisingly appealing. Beth relaxed a little. "All of us?"

"It's Christmas. If we can't all go wild with sparkly pens at Christmas, when can we?"

Beth had taken one step toward the door when her phone rang. She pulled it out of her pocket and her relaxed mood evaporated. "It's Corinna. I should—"

"You shouldn't. Please tell me you are not going to take that call. We're about to have sister time! God knows, that doesn't happen often. Corinna can wait." Posy paused with her hand on the door and Beth was caught in a storm of indecision.

She didn't particularly want to take the call, but she felt as if she should.

She knew it was expected of her.

Hating herself, she answered her phone. "Hi, Corinna—"

Posy's smile faded. "Because nothing comes before family, right?" Shaking her head, she walked out of the room.

20

Posy

"This isn't easy to say, so I'm just going to come right out with it. And if it's all the same to you, I'd rather you didn't interrupt until I'm done." Posy settled herself comfortably. After so many attempts to tell someone how she was feeling, she was determined to say it this time. "Luke has asked me to climb with him next summer. That's right, you heard me. He's putting together an expedition to climb Denali, in Alaska. Don't be alarmed. It's going to be safe, I promise, and I'll train and everything. He seems to think I might even be able to get sponsorship from one of the big companies that make all the outdoor gear, which would be cool because what's hard about being paid to wear clothes you're wearing anyway?" She drew breath. "I can see you're surprised, and I don't blame you. After all, I'm the girl who has never lived away from home apart from when I went to college. But the thing is, I want to do this badly. I guess we know where I inherited those climbing genes from. But I don't want you to take it personally. It's not about you. It's about me. You do understand that?" She closed her eyes, struggling with her feelings. "Why do I feel guilty? Because I love it here. And I love you. I'm not leaving because I don't love you. I hope you know that."

"You're in love with a chicken?"

Posy opened her eyes.

Luke was leaning against the door of the henhouse, his eyes bright with amusement.

She felt her face heat. "What are you doing here? You're supposed to be writing."

"The first thing you need to know about writers is that they will do just about anything to avoid having to actually write."

"That makes no sense."

"To a writer, it would make perfect sense. Not all writing involves tapping keys on a laptop. I call this thinking time. I walk and pretend it's work. In this case, I came looking for you. And I hate to ask the obvious question, but why are you talking to a chicken?"

"This isn't any chicken. It's Martha." She scrambled to her feet, self-conscious. Being this intimate with someone was new to her. She didn't know what their relationship was, or how she felt. She didn't know how *he* felt. Was she a way of passing the time until he left? Or was there something more going on? She was so unsophisticated it was embarrassing. Maybe she should talk to Hannah and get some advice on how to handle casual relationships. "I've been thinking through what I'm going to do about that thing we talked about."

"You mean my trip to Denali?"

"Yes. I thought if I talked it through out loud, it might help me make a decision. Martha is an excellent audience because she doesn't interrupt, nor does she assume she already knows everything there is to know about me. Also, it's useful to rehearse what I'm going to say to my mother later."

He probably thought she was crazy. He was sleeping with someone who talked to chickens.

"Why do you need to rehearse?"

"The fact that you have to ask me that tells me you don't know my family well. Several times over the past few weeks I've tried to drop hints to people that I may be interested in a life beyond this valley, but no one listens. They assume they already know what I want, so yes, I need to rehearse. I need to be firm, so that people don't dismiss what I'm saying. I need people to see me as I really am, not the way they think I am. Although I think I'm guilty of doing that, too…" She frowned as she thought about Hannah. "When you know someone well, it's hard to see them differently."

Luke dug his hands into his pockets. "Did Martha have any advice for you? Or did she think the situation was a question of chicken and egg?"

"Are you mocking me?"

"No. I'm laughing at you in a kind and gentle fashion."

"Yeah? Because it sounded a lot like mocking."

His smile faded. "Why didn't you talk to me about it?"

She felt her heart thud. "You're part of the problem."

"How so?"

"Until I met you, I'd only ever vaguely thought about leaving. I wasn't serious about it. It was a niggle that I was easily able to ignore. And then you appeared and…and…you gave me a reason to leave. You dangled this glittering diamond in front of me—"

His eyes narrowed. "Diamond?"

She flushed. *Stupid, Posy. Stupid, stupid, stupid.* "Not the sort of diamond you wear. The sort you dream about. The sort you covet. I'm talking about the trip. Denali…"

"You don't covet a real diamond?"

Was he teasing her? She didn't even know. "Can we change the subject before I make a total idiot of myself?"

"You're not making an idiot of yourself. Why would you think that?"

"Because I'm no good at this!" She raised her voice and Martha gave a startled squawk. "When it comes to relationships, I'm pretty much a beginner."

He gave her a slow, sexy smile. "Really? I wouldn't have said that."

She met his gaze. "That's physical. I'm good at physical stuff—I'm naturally athletic—"

"I'd noticed."

"I'm talking about the other stuff. The emotional side of things. I haven't got what you might call a ton of experience. Sex is the easy part. That's not complicated. It's like climbing an ice wall. You do what you do, but the rest of it—" she breathed "—that's complicated. I don't know where this is going, or how you feel about leaving, or how I feel about you leaving, or how I feel about me leaving or what this means, or—" She broke off with a gasp as he tugged her against him and kissed her.

He kissed her until her nerve endings sizzled, her heart was pumping and her thoughts were more tangled than they'd been at the beginning.

When he finally released her, she looked at him dizzily. "I don't know why you did that, and I'm not sure it helped."

"I did it because I knew it would feel good."

"I suppose you think you're cute."

"I'm a man. That kiss reduced my abilities to think about anything that didn't involve being naked with you." He cupped her face in his hands. "You seem to have a lot going on in your head. Instead of talking to Martha, you really should talk to me."

She wasn't sure she was ready to do that.

"I'll think about it." Posy bent and stroked Martha's thick feathers. "Thanks for listening, my little feathered friend."

She checked the other chickens and walked to the door, her feet rustling though the thick layer of straw.

Luke closed his hands over her shoulders. "Posy—"

"What?" She found his gaze unsettling and she was already unsettled enough for one lifetime.

"Nothing. Never mind." He released her. "There are a million things I want to say, but a henhouse isn't the place to say them and I'm worried about the impact on Martha."

Posy secured the door and followed Luke out to the path that ran between the barn and the lodge.

"I should go." She felt awkward suddenly. "I have a million things to do in the house, and I want to check on Mom. I want to make sure she's eating properly. She wants you to join us for dinner tomorrow, by the way. It will be the first family dinner we've had since everyone came home, because Mom was in bed to start with and then didn't want to infect anyone, so she mostly stayed in her room. Will you come?"

"If it's a family dinner, are you sure I'll be welcome?"

"She specifically asked me to invite you. She likes you." She saw his hesitation and wondered if she'd put him in an awkward position. "You can relax. It's not 'meet the parents' or anything."

"I've already met your parents."

"I know, but I saw you hesitate. You definitely hesitated."

"The reason I hesitated has nothing to do with you and me." He paused again. "Is your mother better?"

That was why he'd hesitated? Because he was concerned

for her mother? "She's better, thanks. And she won't have to do anything. My sisters and I will cook, although I haven't broken that news to them yet."

"In that case I'll be there. Thank you." He glanced back at the barn. "Much as I'd rather procrastinate, I need to finish my draft. I'll see you later."

He walked away, leaving her none the wiser about her feelings or his.

In a few months his book would be finished and he'd leave. She could watch him go, or she could leave with him.

She thought about it as she walked back to the lodge and carried on thinking about it as she heated soup and took it up to her mother.

As she walked past the bathroom, she could hear the shower running and sounds of someone being sick. Hannah's bedroom door was open, so presumably she was the one using the bathroom.

Posy felt a flash of anxiety and paused outside the door. She wanted to offer support but wasn't sure if her sister would want it. She remembered Hannah holding Beth's hair back after her first experience of alcohol, but that wasn't the same thing, was it?

Balancing the tray of food on one hand, she tapped on the door with the other, but there was no answer.

Singing Christmas carols to cover the sound of Hannah being sick, she elbowed her way into her parents' bedroom. "How are you feeling?"

"Better, thank you, although if you're going to carry on singing, that might not last long." Suzanne was sitting up, her knitting on her lap. "Is someone being sick?"

"No. It's the shower." Posy nudged the door closed with her hip. If Hannah wanted to tell Suzanne, then that was up to her, but she wasn't going to hear it from Posy. "You're not as pale. That's good."

"You, on the other hand, look exhausted. Have you been running around after your sisters?"

"No. They're helping out."

"Even Hannah?"

"Especially Hannah, and here's the proof." Posy settled the tray on her mother's lap. "Roasted tomato and red pepper soup. Hannah made it for you."

"I didn't know she could cook."

"It came as a shock to her, too." Posy wondered what her mother was going to say when she found out Hannah was pregnant. To the best of her knowledge, she was the only one who knew, which increased her feeling of responsibility. She wasn't sure she was being much help. "Can I borrow your water jug? While Hannah's in the shower, I'm going to nip into her room and water Eric. Back in a minute."

She pulled the bedroom door closed behind her and pressed her ear to the bathroom door again.

The shower was still running.

"Hannah?" She tapped gently on the door. "Are you all right?"

There was no answer, and short of breaking the door down, there didn't seem much she could do, so she carried the water jug into Hannah's room.

The first thing that struck her was how tidy the place was. Posy's loft occasionally looked as if it had been raided, but everything in Hannah's room was neat and in its place. There were no clothes strewn on chairs, no shoes scattered on the floor. Even the books on the nightstand were stacked with their edges aligned.

A laptop was open on the desk, showing a spreadsheet so complicated it made Posy's eyes cross to look at it. She stared at it for a moment, remembering what Hannah had said about their parents valuing only athletic ability.

Then she turned her attention to the Christmas tree. "Hello, Eric." She checked the moisture in the soil with the backs of her fingers and then slowly added water. "Who's a thirsty boy, then?"

She was clearing up a few fallen needles when Hannah's phone rang.

Posy almost dropped the jug. It was rare to get a signal in this part of the house. Typical that the call should come in when Hannah was in the bathroom.

Should she ignore it? No, Hannah was always saying how important her work was. Posy might not be able to rub her sister's back while she threw up in the toilet, but at least she could take a message.

Deciding that she was quite enjoying this new role of supportive sibling, she grabbed the phone and answered it. "Hello?"

"Hi there, is that dancing pizza girl?"

Posy opened her mouth to say *wrong number*, but the man kept talking, and because he had a velvet smooth, deep voice that made you feel as if you were being stroked with a fur glove, she kept listening.

"Angie told me she'd spoken to you, and that before you were cut off, you screamed. So naturally, we're all wondering what happened. Have you been kidnapped by Highland warriors? Carried away by a man wearing a kilt?"

"Er—"

"You're not answering my emails and I'm worried. I love you, remember? How is Posy? Is she still sick? It must have been something serious to make you drop everything and sprint back to Scotland."

Sick?

Posy sat down hard on the bed. "Who is this?" *And who,* she thought, *is dancing pizza girl?*

"Who is *this*?"

"Hannah doesn't eat pizza. She doesn't touch carbs."

There was a long silence. "Which one of her sisters are you? Beth or Posy?"

"Posy."

"Are you better? Hannah was worried about you. She jumped straight on a flight."

Posy knew she couldn't possibly have been the reason Hannah had jumped on a flight. "I'm feeling a lot better, thanks for asking."

"That's good."

Posy leaned back on the bed, wondering what illness or accident she was supposed to have suffered. Should she try to sound croaky? Weak? "You seem to know more about me than I do about you." Evidently Hannah's pregnancy hadn't been the result of a one-night stand, as she'd assumed. She eyed the bathroom door, trying to hear if the shower was still running. "You've been seeing each other for a while?"

"Six months. I'm Adam."

Adam, who her sister had been dating for six months. Adam, who loved her sister.

She'd assumed Hannah's relationships were all casual. She'd had no idea her sister was so deeply involved with a man.

Dancing pizza girl?

Posy wanted to meet that version of her sister. And she wanted to meet the man who brought out a side to Hannah that the rest of them didn't see.

"Good to meet you, Adam."

"How is she doing? She was pretty stressed before she left."

Posy stared across the room to the closed bathroom door.

Presumably he didn't know Hannah was pregnant. "She's still pretty stressed."

"It's frustrating not to be able to talk to her."

"Yes, the phone signal at Glensay Lodge is more unpredictable than the weather, and that's saying something. It would probably be easier to get on a flight and have the conversation in person. In fact, why don't you do that? It's a great big old family Christmas here, the more the merrier. But either way, you don't need to worry about her. She seems okay, and she has Eric to keep her company—"

"Eric? Is he the outdoor type?"

Posy eyed the Christmas tree. "You could say that. He's tall, reasonably broad and likes a drink." She heard the bathroom door open. "She's coming, so if you hold on, I'll— Hello?" But the signal had gone.

Posy put the phone down and stood up as Hannah walked into the room.

With wet hair and no makeup, she looked younger than usual.

"Who were you talking to?"

"Your phone rang—I answered it." How much should she say? She and her sister were getting along well for the first time in ages. Posy didn't want to do anything to shatter their fragile truce.

Hannah was rubbing her hair with a towel. "My phone? But there's no signal in this room."

"Sometimes there is. Annoying, I know. The suspense kills."

"Who was it?"

"It was Adam." Posy noticed the change in her sister. There was a slight stiffening in her shoulders, and a blankness to her expression. It was as if she'd drawn the blinds, ensuring that no one could peep through the cracks and see her thoughts.

Hannah stopped drying her hair. "Did he leave a message?"

"No, but we were cut off before we finished talking."

"Why didn't you call me?"

Because I was in shock. "You were in the shower. I was about to hand you the phone when the signal died. He sounded nice." She tiptoed carefully. "I assume he's the father."

Hannah looked alarmed. "You didn't tell him?"

"Of course not. I'm your sister. I am a barrier between you and the world."

Hannah relaxed. "That's good."

"You're feeling sick?"

"All of a sudden. Probably psychological."

And that, Posy thought, was all she was going to get.

Not wanting to push her luck, she changed the subject. "I've been planning Mom's dinner tomorrow night. You know how desperately she wants Christmas to be perfect, and so far it hasn't been because she's been ill. I feel so bad for her."

"Yeah, me, too." Looking distracted, Hannah grabbed the hair dryer.

"I thought you, Beth and I should make a massive effort to make Christmas extra special for her, starting with the dinner tomorrow."

"What would that involve? I'm not plucking a turkey, and I have no idea how to knit."

"I was thinking more about us working hard to get along well. No bickering. We agree with each other. We're kind to each other. We listen and pay attention. Be perfect sisters." It sounded hard even to her and she was the one suggesting it. It didn't surprise her that Hannah looked amused.

"Sounds like the most stressful dinner we will have had in a long time, but sure. I'm on board. You'll need to tell Beth to leave her phone upstairs, because if that woman calls her, you can bet your life she'll be answering. She can't help herself. And if she answers, you'll yell and that will be the end of sisterly harmony."

"You yell, too."

"Because that woman is a monster and I can't bear to hear her bullying Beth."

Posy stared at her. "You think that, too?"

"Of course. It's a fact."

Posy sighed. "She's going to be a tough boss."

"I'm a tough boss," Hannah said, "although I'd also argue that I'm fair, clear and consistent in my expectations. Corinna isn't a tough boss. She's a bully. It's different. Part of the reason Beth wants to go back to work is for a confidence boost, and working for a difficult boss usually has the opposite effect."

Posy knew nothing about the corporate world, but what Hannah was saying made sense to her. "Beth thinks it's a huge compliment that this woman wants her as part of the team."

Hannah frowned. "I don't think that's what is going on."

"What do you mean?"

"Nothing. Forget it."

Posy didn't want to forget it. "You help corporations sort themselves out. You have the brain the size of a planet. Can't you help Beth?"

"What makes you think she wants my help?"

"Well, she certainly needs it. You're her sister. That gives you the right to interfere without permission. And think about the alternative—if you don't help her, she'll go and work for that woman again and it will be awful."

"I'm not sure that's what will happen."

"You think Beth is going to turn her down?"

"No. I think—" Hannah shook her head and selected a hairbrush. "Never mind. Let's talk about tomorrow. What are we going to cook? What's Suzanne's favorite food?"

Posy had to admit she occasionally found her sister exasperating. "I haven't finished talking about Beth. You make these vague statements, and then you don't finish them."

"Because I don't have all the facts necessary to reach an informed conclusion."

"You can't just gossip and speculate like normal people?"

"No." Hannah plugged in the hair dryer.

"The way your brain works is scary. I used to be so intimidated by you."

Hannah looked startled. "I intimidated *you*?"

"You used to look at a set of numbers that made no sense at all to me and make perfect sense of it. I hated that I couldn't do it, too. I felt inadequate. Why are you laughing? And why use that tone?"

"Because you intimidate me, too."

That was ridiculous. "How could I possibly intimidate you?"

"Do you want a list?"

Posy discovered that, yes, she did. "Tell me."

"Well, there's your athletic ability, to begin with." Hannah fiddled with the brush. "You're coordinated and physically strong. You would never fall off a gate."

"You wouldn't fall, either, if you wore the right thing on your feet."

"You climb mountains."

"Anyone can climb a mountain. The people we rescue come from all walks of life and have different skill sets."

Hannah gave a half smile. "Exactly. You're the one rescuing them. You're brave and capable. You make me feel—" she paused "—cowardly."

Posy sat back down on the bed. "That's crazy."

"You can do any number of practical things, from fixing roofs to delivering lambs."

"Lambs mostly deliver themselves."

"You know what I mean."

Posy didn't really. She'd never imagined she might intimidate anyone, let alone her sister. "I suppose we have different skills."

"That's true. I'm a facts person." Hannah faced the mirror
and turned on the dryer.

"Do you rely on facts to help you figure out relationships?"

Hannah turned the hair dryer off and met her gaze in the
mirror. "Excuse me?"

"Relationships." Posy felt herself turn pink. "I'm not good
at them." Maybe if she opened up, her sister would, too.

Hannah gave a faint smile. "You're asking me for advice?
Is this some sort of joke?"

"No. But you're smart and logical, and I thought you
might—"

"Relationships defy logic. It's the reason I'm no good at
them, either."

Posy gave a grunt and launched herself off the bed. "Some
help you are. In answer to your question about tomorrow,
Maggie has made us a venison casserole. She brought it round
yesterday when she came to see Mom. We'll do it with potatoes. Can you do mash? I'll roast some parsnips in maple syrup.
I'll make a soup. Beth is great at dessert, so I'll ask her to do
something. Whatever happens, we're not letting stress into the
room." Posy paused, wondering how far she dare push this
new relationship. "On that note, I thought we might make
something easy tonight."

"Suits me. What did you have in mind?"

Posy decided to test the water. "How would you feel about
pizza?"

"I don't eat pizza, but the girls will love it, so go ahead and I'll make myself a salad."

"You don't eat pizza? Never?"

Hannah frowned. "You know I don't. Can I dry my hair now?"

Dancing pizza girl.

"Sure. Dry your hair."

It had never bothered her before that she and Hannah weren't particularly close, but suddenly it bothered her a lot.

What did she have to do to get her sister to talk to her?

21

Suzanne

Never before had she seen her family trying so hard to be on their best behavior.

Suzanne sat at the kitchen table, feeling weaker than she was willing to admit. The doctor seemed to think she was past being infectious, but she knew she had a way to go before she was back to her normal self. She should probably have stayed in bed, but there were so few occasions when the whole family was together that she wanted to make the most of it. And anyway, they were the ones doing all the work, trying to coordinate their movements like a synchronized swimming team who had never met before and couldn't find their rhythm. She found it endearing that they seemed to think she wouldn't notice how hard they were trying and wondered how long it would be before one of them burst a blood vessel.

For once, no one was sniping. There was no tension in the atmosphere.

At least, not much.

Posy peered into the pan as Hannah worked. "You're using olive oil in the mash, not butter? Why?"

"I like olive oil."

"But you don't even eat carbs." Posy opened her mouth and closed it again. "Lovely. Delicious. Great choice. If you wanted to—"

"I don't."

They moved around the kitchen awkwardly, clattering plates and pans, laying the table, adding ice to jugs of water and occasionally bumping into each other.

If Suzanne hadn't had such a headache, she would have laughed.

She'd always known how different they were. Their personalities hadn't changed much from when they were children. There was Hannah, the organized one; Beth, dreaming away as she whipped the cream; and Posy, who bounced through life as if she was on a trampoline.

Why had she ever thought she could control their relationship with each other? The best she could ever have hoped for was to provide the opportunity for them to bond and she'd done that.

Beth opened the fridge. "Posy, did you use the cream?"

"I added some to the soup."

"That was my cream. For my dessert. I'm about to whip it."

"You'll have to whip a little less." Posy added fresh parsley to the soup and Beth drew a deep breath.

Suzanne waited for the explosion, but instead Beth smiled.

"The cream will be perfect in the soup."

Suzanne caught Stewart's eye and he shrugged, indicating that whatever was going on he had nothing to do with it.

He stood up and fetched her a glass of water. "Are you sure you shouldn't be in bed? We could bring your food up on a tray."

"I'm tired of being in bed. I'm fine right here."

She could tell he wanted to argue, but he also knew how much it meant to her having everyone home.

He settled for sitting next to her. "If you're going to faint, let me know and I'll catch you."

"Have I ever fainted?"

He helped himself to bread. "The first time you saw me, you came close. But no one is blaming you for that."

Normally she would have thought of the perfect comeback, but today her brain refused to cooperate.

Into the pressure cooker of family time walked Luke.

Posy immediately dropped the spoon she was holding.

"It's snowing again." Luke stamped the snow off his boots and hung up his coat. "There's a storm coming in. Perfect writing weather."

Posy retrieved the spoon and Suzanne noticed that her cheeks were flushed.

She also noticed that her youngest daughter was the only one who didn't immediately greet Luke. Given that Posy was usually chatty and comfortable with her lodger, Suzanne thought it reasonable to assume that something had changed between them.

Attraction? Affection? Love?

Whatever it was, it pleased her to see it.

That fiasco with Callum had upset Posy badly. It wasn't easy having a relationship in a small community, and Callum had been clumsy in his handling of the breakup.

To the best of Suzanne's knowledge, Posy hadn't been in-volved with anyone seriously since.

"Come on in, Luke." She gestured to an empty chair. "I've

barely seen you lately. I hope you're warm enough over there. Plenty of logs? Is your fridge full?"

In some ways, he reminded her of Stewart at the same age. He had the same athletic build and strength. The same quiet focus and passion for what he did. But it was a passion, she noted, that didn't tip into obsession.

She liked him.

"The barn is very comfortable. Posy has been looking after me. Something smells good. Can I do anything to help?"

The fact that he offered was enough for Suzanne. "You brought wine. That's all the help we need."

"Take a seat, Luke." Stewart half rose to his feet and gestured to an empty chair. "Welcome to the madhouse. How is the writing going?"

"Ah, the question every writer dreads." Luke sat down, glancing at Posy as he did so. "It's coming together slowly. I'm at that stage when I can't believe the book will ever be finished. I have to look at the books I've written before to convince myself it's possible."

Beth glanced up from her bowl of whipped cream. "How many books have you written?"

"This is the third."

"It's a book about survival?"

"That was book two." Luke shook his head. "This is *Top Climbs in North America*."

Posy served the soup, giving Luke an extra-large portion.

The conversation turned to food, and Christmas, and then Hannah cleared the plates and they moved on to the casserole.

Suzanne wondered if Stewart had been right and she should have stayed in bed. She was starting to feel light-headed.

"The mash tastes funny," Ruby said, poking at the food on her plate.

"It's delicious," Beth said. "Eat."

"But—"

"How's Vicky, Mom?" Beth passed the bowl of parsnips across the table. "Is she better?"

Posy dug into her food. "She's working a half day at the café tomorrow."

"The mash tastes funny," Ruby said.

"Eat what you can and leave the rest on your plate." Jason was clearly embarrassed by his younger daughter. He leaned closer and spoke to her quietly and Suzanne saw Ruby's cheeks flush and her eyes grow shiny.

Watching her granddaughter took Suzanne's mind off her aching head and tired limbs.

Posy had been a fussy eater, too. Cheryl and Rob had let her eat whatever she wanted, but Suzanne had been so appalled by the child's diet it was the first thing she'd changed, and she'd done it without hesitation or guilt.

The only thing she'd never been able to persuade Posy to eat was carrots.

"I can't figure out why your name is familiar—" Beth was still talking to Luke "—but in the spirit of honesty I must tell you I've never read your work, so I know it isn't that."

"His books are everywhere." Posy reached for a jug of water and filled her glass. "Even if you haven't read them, you will have seen them. That's probably how you know his name."

Beth was frowning. "Maybe."

Suzanne noticed that Hannah was quiet.

Her hair had been blown into a smooth sheet, her skilled application of makeup giving her an air of sophistication.

She remembered Hannah the night of Cheryl and Rob's death, waiting quietly in the house, cooling Posy's fevered skin with wet cloths.

The police had offered to talk to the girls, but Suzanne insisted she should be the one.

Drowning in her own grief, she'd forced herself back to the surface so that she could be a life belt for her best friend's children.

Hannah had stared into space, until Suzanne had begun to wonder if she'd understood what she'd heard. The therapist she'd talked to briefly had emphasized the importance of using the word *dead* in the conversation, so she'd done that and winced as she'd said it, feeling as if she was hitting these already-bruised children with a rock.

She hadn't known which child to deal with first. Each had different needs, and she had her own needs, but those had taken fourth place.

Without Stewart, she would have crumbled. Or would she? She'd been all those children had left, and she never would have let them down. They were her focus. Her reason to drag herself out of bed every morning, to battle the guilt and the depression, to haul herself into each day with a sense of purpose.

They'd been her life belt, too, she realized. Caring for them had forced her to care for herself.

"Wait!" Beth dropped her fork with a clatter and the conversation faded away. "Luke."

Luke sat still. There was a watchfulness about him that hadn't been there before. "Yes?"

"Luke Whittaker."

Posy looked annoyed. "Beth, I don't know what's wrong with you, but—"

"I know why your name is familiar. You left a message on my phone a couple of months ago. You wanted to talk to me about—" Beth stopped in midflow and her gaze snaked to Suzanne and away again.

Suzanne knew that look. It was the particular one her family used when they were trying not to mention the accident. She didn't like talking about it, and they respected that.

But why would Beth think Luke had called her? And why was she using that tone? She'd never heard Beth speak so sharply.

She waited for Luke to deny that he'd left a message and laugh at the mistake.

He put his fork down, too. "You didn't return my call."

"You didn't mention it," Beth said. "When I met you in the café that day, you didn't say who you were."

"I introduced myself."

"But you knew I hadn't linked your name with that phone call." Beth stood up quickly, her chair scraping the kitchen floor. Her voice was thickened, but whether from fury or hurt, Suzanne couldn't tell.

Her brain felt slow, as if she was running behind everyone else struggling to catch up. She had a bad feeling about all this. A very bad feeling.

"He called me, too." Hannah put her napkin on the table, even though her plate was still half-full. She was calmer than Beth, but her voice was steely. "What are you doing here, Luke?"

"Now wait just a minute." Posy put her glass down so hard that the water sloshed over the side. "Is this how we speak to guests now? And why would Luke have called you? He doesn't know you." She sprang to Luke's defense, facing her sisters like a little tigress.

That was something Suzanne rarely saw, either. Normally Posy was so easygoing and even tempered, but tonight no one seemed to be their best self.

She'd never seen the three of them so upset.

The harmonious atmosphere was cracking. Her dreams of a perfect Christmas were splintering in front of her.

Whatever Luke's reason for contacting the girls, she needed to get to the bottom of it. She needed to protect them.

"You're writing about the accident!" Beth slapped her hand on the table. "That's what you do, isn't it? You write about everything to do with mountains. You're a journalist."

"I'm not a journalist. I'm a mountaineer and a writer."

"Journalists are writers. Or do you find it easier to wiggle your way into people's lives if you hide that fact?" Beth turned to Hannah. "He called you, too? I wish I'd known. We could have compared notes."

"Beth!" Posy glared at her sister, but Beth ignored her.

"And when neither of us took your call, you headed straight here and targeted Posy. You have some nerve. We've had plenty of calls from people like you over the years, but no one has actually gone as far as sleeping with my sister to get the information."

"Oh thanks." Posy sounded close to tears. "Always nice when your sister reveals the details of your personal life at a family dinner. Remind me *never* to share anything with you ever again."

"Beth!" Jason's voice was a sharp reminder that the family included children.

For a moment it seemed as if Beth hadn't heard him.

He said her name a second time and she turned her head, blinking like someone emerging from a deep sleep.

She saw Ruby's anxious face and Jason's taut expression.

"Sorry." Beth looked conflicted. Apologetic. "Jason—"

"I'd like to sleep with Aunty Posy." Ruby spoke in a small voice. "Since I lost Bugsy, I don't like the dark."

Melly hushed her, sensing adult disharmony. "You can sleep in my bed tonight."

"Do you promise?" Ruby was the only one round the table who looked happy.

Holding Beth's gaze, Jason stood up. "I'll take the girls into the den. We'll turn the volume on the TV up." He gave Beth a brief nod and lowered his voice. "Keep it down."

"I can leave my mash?" Ruby clearly thought Christmas had come early and she danced out of the room without protest.

Suzanne wished she felt half as relaxed. Her heart was pounding. She felt a little sick, and she didn't think that had anything to do with the remnants of her illness. When she reached for her glass, her hand shook a little. Luke had wanted to talk about the accident? Why? "You had other calls from journalists? Why didn't you tell me?"

"Because you don't like talking about what happened, and we respect that."

They'd been protecting her?

She looked at Luke, but his face was expressionless.

"I can assure you I'm nothing like any other person who might have contacted you in the past."

Beth's eyes narrowed. "I suppose you consider your brand of journalism to be vastly superior." Now that the children were out of the room, the bite was back.

"That's not the reason."

Suzanne wondered why her daughter didn't just ask the reason instead of making assumptions, but Beth seemed to think she already had all the facts. "Did you get the information you needed? Good quotes? When's the story running?"

Was he really writing a story? The thought of it terrified her. She didn't want to relive it the way she'd relived it again and again over the years.

She'd thought the nightmares were the only reminder of that day, but it seemed she was wrong. It was never going to go away. The questions. The speculation. The blame.

Her palms felt clammy and her pulse was pounding.

Then she felt Stewart's hand close over hers, strong and

steady. He could have shut down this whole conversation, but he clearly thought it was something they needed to hear. And he was right, of course.

Whatever this was, she'd get through it. *They'd* get through it—

Posy half rose to her feet, ready for a fight. "Beth—"

"Who are you writing for?" Hannah took over the interrogation. "Newspaper? Online blog? And what's your angle? Twenty-five-year anniversary? Or are you going to pretend that being here is a coincidence? We're not going to let you hurt Suzanne—please be clear about that."

Hannah was defending her? Despite the tension, Suzanne wasn't oblivious to the irony. Her girls were joining together to protect her. She hadn't seen such a display of teamwork or sisterhood for years. It was more authentic than the robotic interactions that had started the evening. If it hadn't been for the subject matter, she would have considered it a breakthrough.

But did it have to be this issue that brought them together?

Did they really have to dig it up again?

Luke put his fork down. "It's not a coincidence."

Posy sat down hard on her chair, the fight draining out of her. "It's not?" She was clearly as confused and shocked as Suzanne. "I don't get it. You're here because— What is going on?"

Suzanne wanted to echo that question.

Why did Luke want to talk to her about the accident? If he wasn't a journalist, then what was his interest?

"I'm not here to write up the story and I'm not here to interview anyone. And it certainly isn't the reason you and I got together." He held Posy's gaze. "You know that."

"Do I?" Posy's voice wavered. Evidently she was fighting a battle between what she believed and what she wanted to believe. "Did you call my sisters?"

Suzanne was fighting a battle, too. She liked Luke, but now she was worried that her daughter was with a man who didn't deal honestly with her.

"He did," Beth said. "His message said, 'I'd like to talk to you about the accident and your parents.'"

"And what I'd like to know," Hannah said, "is that if you're not a journalist, if you're nothing like the other people who have contacted us over the years, then why are you interested?"

There was a long silence, broken only by the almost-audible throb of suspense.

"Because your parents weren't the only ones to die in that accident," Luke said finally. "Mine died, too."

Suzanne felt disconnected from what was going on around her.

His parents died, too?

But that would mean—

There was a commotion, with everyone talking at once, and then a sudden silence when everyone turned to her to assess the extent of the damage caused by that unexpected revelation.

Her mouth was dry. "Lindsey and David, the other couple who were climbing with us that day, had a son."

"That's me." Luke held her gaze. "I'm their son."

She felt Stewart's hand tighten on hers, but she didn't look at him. She was forcing herself to think back to that time. "Their surname was Palmer. Yours is Whittaker."

"I was adopted by my mother's sister, Trudy. Her married name was Whittaker. There was a lot of interest in that accident. They wanted me to be able to have a normal childhood, leave it behind. They raised me as their own. Gave me their name and a home. They lived in Manhattan and that couldn't have been further from my early life. I vanished off the scene. I wasn't really the person the world was interested in."

"That was me." Suzanne forced the words past dry lips. She

knew the increase in her pulse rate had nothing to do with her illness. "I was the only survivor. I was the one they were interested in. I knew about you, but I didn't know your name. I asked about you. I asked Trudy, but—"

She was suddenly drenched in sweat and she knew it had nothing to do with the flu.

She could still hear Trudy Whittaker's voice as she'd hurled grief-laden accusations at Suzanne.

How were you the only one left alive? How did you manage to save yourself and not my sister?

She'd asked the same questions of herself, but that didn't make them easier to hear.

It was clear from the look in Luke's eyes that he knew the details. "Trudy died a couple of years ago."

Suzanne took a breath. "She blamed me. She thought it was my fault."

"Which it wasn't." Stewart shifted closer and put his arm round her. "You know it wasn't."

"My aunt knew that, too." Luke was calm. "For years afterward, she'd talk about it. How she'd been so torn apart with grief that she'd taken it all out on you. She'd wanted someone to blame, and you were the only one left alive."

"If there was blame," Stewart said, "it should have been laid squarely at Rob's door."

Luke nodded. "I know."

That wasn't the reaction Suzanne had been expecting. "How can you know?"

"Because over the years I've talked to people. Done some research. There are people out there that knew him. Climbed with him. Rob had a reputation for pushing it further than was safe. He wasn't just daring, he was reckless. He took risks. There were plenty who wouldn't climb with him."

Stewart pushed his plate away. "Suzanne wouldn't have climbed with him, either, if it hadn't been for Cheryl."

"So basically you're saying that our dad killed your dad," Beth said in a small voice. The fierceness had been replaced by uncertainty.

"Enough." Suzanne pulled away from Stewart. She had to deal with this. She had to handle it. "Rob was their father. We shouldn't be talking about this."

"I'd like to talk about it." Posy's cheeks were as white as the snow that lay beyond the window. "Is it true?"

"It's true." This time it was Hannah who spoke and they all turned to look at her. "I used to hear them talking. Mom used to say, *I want you to promise me you'll turn back, Rob, if the weather turns*, and he'd shrug her off and refuse to promise anything of the sort. She'd say, *You're a father now*, and he'd say, *I'm the man you married*."

And that, Suzanne thought, sounded exactly like Rob.

"So Beth is right. He killed them all," Posy said flatly, and Suzanne leaned forward.

"No, honey. The truth is sometimes these things just happen. There weren't any red flags that day. If there had been, I would have turned back. There were niggles, that's all. Things that didn't feel right, but to be honest that was probably more about the way we were all feeling. There were tensions in the group, but I don't believe those tensions played a part in the accident. In the end we were in the wrong place at the wrong time."

"But you wouldn't have been in the wrong place at the wrong time if it hadn't been for my father."

Hannah straightened her shoulders. "Ninety percent of avalanches are a result of human triggers."

The fact that Hannah knew that statistic even though she

had no interest in mountains said a lot about the trauma she'd suffered.

Beth turned to Luke. "I'm sorry you lost your parents. But why would you come here and not say who you were? Why not just be straight from the beginning?"

"I wasn't sure how to approach it. It's the reason I contacted you first, and not Suzanne. I wanted to talk to you about the right way to do it. That accident traumatized a lot of people, my aunt included. She behaved badly. She hurt you, and I didn't want to waltz in here and add to that hurt." He looked at Suzanne. "I know this apology comes decades too late, but she was ashamed of the way she spoke to you that day. She wanted to reach out herself and apologize, but she didn't know how. She knew she'd caused you a great deal of anguish and she thought by getting in touch she might reopen the wound and make it worse. And that's the reason I didn't want to show up here without warning. I wanted to take my time and work out how much damage I'd do by suddenly appearing after all these years. I arrived here, expecting to stay a week at the most, but I fell in love with the barn, the place and—" he paused "—the life you have here."

Suzanne had a feeling he'd been about to say *I fell in love with Posy.*

It seemed like hours ago that she'd been wondering about their relationship, not minutes.

She glanced down at the food congealing on her plate.

You did what you could to bury the past, and then something happened and you realized it was right there under the surface just waiting to be exposed. "I'm sorry to hear about Trudy, and sorry that we didn't have a chance to talk. I didn't get in touch with her, either, because I knew she blamed me and at the time I felt that blame was justified."

Stewart started to speak, but she reached out and touched his arm, silencing him.

"After the accident, I asked myself time and time again what I could have done differently. Could we have taken a different route? Could I have tried harder to get Rob to turn round? I examined every option. I asked myself constantly whether I could somehow have avoided what happened. If I'd done something different, would four people now be alive?"

Hannah stood up. "The facts seem to support the theory that they wouldn't, and it's the facts that we should believe. And here's another fact. My father was a bully." Her voice shook, as if it was taking all her courage to voice those words. "He wanted things his way, and when people didn't fall in line, he got angry with them. Do not blame yourself, Suzanne. I don't know if it was Dad's fault, but I know for sure that it wouldn't have been yours."

"I know that, too." Posy walked round the table and hugged Suzanne. "We don't have to talk about this. I know how much you hate it. Luke, I think you should leave now."

Luke hesitated. "Posy—"

"I understand that this is personal for you, too, but it's upsetting for Suzanne and I think you should go."

"I agree with Posy," Hannah said. "I understand that you also had a trauma in your early life, but whatever you thought might be achieved by coming here now after all these years, it was selfish of you not to consider what stirring it all up might do to my mother. I won't have you upsetting her."

My mother.

Suzanne stirred. Had she heard correctly? It was the first time Hannah had ever referred to her as *my mother.*

Her heart felt as if it was swelling. It pressed against her chest, pushed at her ribs and trapped the air in her lungs.

And then she saw Luke's expression and realized that this moment of joy was going to have to be postponed.

"Luke—"

"They're right, I shouldn't have come. It felt like the right thing to do, but I can see now it wasn't." He pushed away from the table and stood up. "I'll pay the rent up until the end of February as we agreed, but I'll leave tomorrow."

"Sit down, Luke. I'd like to talk to you." She really did, although it was clear she was going to have to deal with her family before that was possible.

Already Beth looked ready to pounce. "Mom, you don't have to talk to him. This time of year is difficult enough for you without having to think about this."

"I agree with Beth," Posy said, and Suzanne sighed. For years she'd been desperate for them to bond, and they chose this moment.

"Girls—" Extracting herself from Posy's hug, she stood up, too. Her legs felt shaky, and she wasn't sure if that was the remnants of flu or a reaction to everything that had happened. "It's my turn to say a few things. First, it's true that I don't generally like talking about the avalanche. It's been my way of not letting it dominate my life. But somewhere along the way I've led you to believe that I'm fragile, and that's not true."

Beth frowned. "Mom—"

"I appreciate you trying to protect me, but next time you get a call from a journalist that concerns me, you're to give me their number so I can speak to them direct. Are we clear?"

"But—"

"Are we clear?"

Beth and Hannah exchanged glances. "Yes."

"Good. And now I'd like all of you to leave so that Luke and I can talk without interruption."

Posy dug her hands into the pockets of her jeans. "No way. I'm not leaving here. You're going to have to drag me."

Suzanne looked at Stewart. He was quiet, thoughtful, absorbing it all.

He was worried about her—she knew that. But he was also the one person who would understand why she needed to do this.

He stood up. "I think we should leave your mother to talk to Luke."

Apparently his voice held more weight than hers, because the three girls looked at each other and reluctantly moved to the door.

Beth hovered. "We'll be right outside."

"You will not." In other circumstances Suzanne might have smiled. "You will take your coats and go for a walk."

Hannah looked bemused. "It's snowing."

"Then go to the Glensay Inn and have a drink by the fire. You're only together once a year. I'm sure you'll find plenty to talk about."

The three of them filed out of the room, leaving her with Luke and Stewart.

She looked at her husband, who had supported her through all the difficult times that had followed the accident. "Stay," she said, and Stewart closed the door and walked back into the room.

"Wasn't thinking of leaving." He grabbed a bottle of single malt and set it down in the middle of the table along with three glasses.

Luke pushed his plate away and settled back in his chair.

He could have walked out, Suzanne thought. He'd been subjected to hostility, accusations and multiple questions, but he was still sitting here.

He had strength, both physical and moral.

His parents would have been proud.

Luke pushed the sleeves of his sweater up to his elbows and leaned forward. "You have questions, I'm sure. There are things you want to know."

"I want to know about *you*." Suzanne couldn't believe he was sitting at her kitchen table, right across from her. "I've thought about you often over the years. I wondered how you were doing, and whether your life had been destroyed by what happened." She'd worried and worried, and mixed in with the worry was the guilt. Always the guilt. It had gnawed at her gut like acid.

Stewart sloshed whiskey into the glasses. "He doesn't look destroyed from where I'm sitting. Drink, Luke?"

"You think I'd say no to a single malt? Particularly that particular single malt."

It was all so normal. So relaxed.

Suzanne watched as Luke lifted the glass and drank. She saw the movement of his throat and the glint of fire in his eyes.

She realized she'd continued to think of him as a little boy. Orphaned. Vulnerable. Broken.

But there was nothing broken about the man sitting across from her. He hadn't hidden from life, he'd embraced every second. He radiated strength and energy. He was vital and alive, and seeing him so whole and healthy healed a few more of the cracks in her heart.

"Posy says you climbed Rainier." She couldn't imagine it. She'd never wanted to set foot on the mountain again after what happened.

"Oh yeah." His smile was a bright light in a dark tunnel. "I laid that ghost to rest when I was eighteen."

Not scared, or even scarred. Not damaged.

"Tell me about yourself," she said. "I want to know how

you grew up in Manhattan but ended up a climber just like your parents. I want to know all of it."

It was time to stop letting her mind and her conscience paint a picture of his life. Time for reality.

Time for the truth.

22

Posy

"Well," Beth said, plonking herself down at the usual table near to the fire.

"Well," Hannah said, lowering herself more carefully.

"We were trying to protect her and she threw us out." Posy gestured across the bar to Aidan. "Can you believe that?"

"What I can't believe," Beth said, "is that Luke Palmer slept with you. That is a low thing to do."

"Whittaker," Posy snapped. "And you're assuming that his interest in me was part of some devious scheme." She hadn't had time to digest the revelations of the past couple of hours herself, and she certainly wasn't ready to talk about Luke with anyone. She felt confused, angry, betrayed, affronted and, yes, maybe a little foolish. It was the first time in a while she'd been intimate with anyone, and with Luke she'd shared more than she ever had before. And now, thanks to Beth, she was won-dering if anything they'd shared had been genuine. "Frankly I wish I'd never told you. Sisters are not supposed to betray a confidence. Nor are they supposed to make you feel like crap."

"These were exceptional circumstances," Beth muttered. "I didn't mean to hurt you. I was protecting you. I'm not going to sit around and watch some guy take advantage of my baby sister."

"First, I'm not a baby. Second, I don't see how something consensual and enjoyable can come under the heading of 'tak-ing advantage,' and third, I do not need you or Hannah to protect me, although I have to say that the two of you work-ing together is scarier than any rock face I've ever climbed."

Aidan approached, his usual friendly smile on his face. "Beer for Posy, white wine for Beth—" He put the drinks on the table. "What can I get you, Hannah?"

"Sparkling water," Hannah said. "Thanks, Aidan."

Posy stared moodily into the fire.

When exactly would Luke have told her the truth? Would he have told her before the expedition? Maybe they would have been sharing a tent one night and he would have turned to her and said, *By the way—*

She'd thought they were close.

She'd thought they had a special connection.

She was an idiot.

"We should talk about this," Beth said, "instead of drown-ing our sorrows."

"The sorrows are mine." Posy slumped in her chair. "And right now the only thing I want to drown is Luke."

Had the whole thing just been about sex? And if that was what it was, how did she feel about that?

It wasn't as if either of them had made promises.

"I'm sorry. I shouldn't have said anything at the table, but do you think it's possible you're transferring your anger with Luke onto me?"

"No. You're getting the anger you deserve."

Beth looked chastened. "In that case I'll drown my sorrows, too." She glanced at Hannah. "Why are you drinking water? Do you have to be a killjoy? Can you stop being perfect for five minutes?"

"I'm not perfect. And I'm not telling you what to drink, so I don't see how I'm a killjoy." Hannah unwrapped her scarf from her neck, sending snowflakes fluttering.

Posy wondered when she intended to tell Beth she was pregnant. At this rate the baby would be born before Hannah told anyone. On the other hand, given Beth's tendency to blurt out secrets whenever she felt like it, she couldn't exactly blame Hannah for keeping her news to herself.

Aidan arrived back at their table with a bottle of water and a glass filled with lemon and ice. "Do you ladies want to eat?"

"Thanks, but we've had dinner."

"If you had any of that yummy sticky toffee pudding, I could probably choke it down." Beth tucked her bag by her chair and gave her sister a defensive look. "Thanks to our little family crisis, I didn't finish my meal. Of course, that could have been because of the olive oil mash, which, as my daughter pointed out, tasted funny."

Hannah crossed one slender leg over the other. "Do you know what butter does to your arteries?"

"It sets them up ready for sticky toffee pudding. Bring it on, Aidan. Better bring three spoons."

"Two spoons," Hannah said. "I don't eat carbs."

Posy thought about her conversation with Adam. "You eat pizza." She reached for her beer and took several large swallows. "You dance around pizza."

Hannah stared at her. "Excuse me?"

"Nothing. Forget it." She couldn't focus on Hannah right now; she was too busy feeling sorry for herself.

Hannah leaned forward and removed the bottle from her hand.

"For once in our lives we need to have a serious, sensible conversation, and if you drink too fast, you won't be able to walk."

"In case you hadn't noticed, I'm experiencing a crisis in my love life. I'm allowed whatever comfort I need, particularly as I'm not getting it from my sisters."

Beth was frowning. "What did you mean about dancing round pizza?"

Posy shook her head. "Nothing. And can I just say that I'm not finding either of you particularly sympathetic to my plight."

"I don't see your plight." Beth took a sip of her wine. "You've been having sex with a steaming-hot guy. And you said you didn't want me to protect you." But she leaned across and gave Posy a hug.

"Oh." That hug threw Posy. "I thought you were mad."

"Not with *you*. You weren't to know he was a rat. There were no outward signs of ratlike behavior."

"We don't know he's a rat." Hannah twisted the top of her water and poured half of it into her glass. "He may genuinely care for Posy."

"So why didn't he tell her the truth?"

"Because life is never as simple as you seem to think it is." Hannah put her gloves on the table, stacking one on top of the other so that the fingers matched up exactly and from the top it looked like a single glove. "I suppose we should brace ourselves for the fact that Suzanne will be upset when we go home. That conversation is going to have brought it all back. She didn't look that great when we left."

Posy hated the idea that Suzanne might be upset. She hated even more the thought that Luke might be the reason for it.

Aidan put a plate of sticky toffee pudding in front of Beth. "Can I get you ladies anything else?"

Posy took the spoons from him. "No, this is great. Thanks, Aidan." She waited until he was out of earshot before speaking again. "I admit I'm pretty mad with Luke for not saying something right away. It's a weird feeling knowing you've been intimate with a man who wasn't who you thought he was. It feels as if I've been sleeping with two different people. Does that make me unfaithful?"

"How could you not *know*? Didn't you do an internet search?" Beth removed the clip from her hair and then bent and pulled a lipstick out of her bag. She swiped it onto her lips.

Posy was momentarily distracted. "How can you do that without a mirror? And why isn't it all over your face?"

"Because I know where my mouth is. Surely the first thing you do when you date a new man is an internet search. He could have been a serial killer."

"Because serial killers generally post all their details on the internet so their victims are warned in advance. And I did a search. I searched for Luke Whittaker and it gave me information on Luke Whittaker. Oddly enough, there was no message there saying, *Hey, Posy, Luke Whittaker is actually Luke Palmer and his parents were killed at the same time as yours.* I guess the internet isn't as reliable as people think. And, by the way, your job as my sister is to offer support, not make me feel like an idiot. I'm hurt, too, you know?"

Beth slid her lipstick back into her bag. Her cheeks were flushed. She looked awkward and guilty. "We didn't mean to hurt you, but you needed to know the truth. You were the one who said that sisters are supposed to tell each other the truth."

"If the truth is so important to you, why didn't you talk to me about the phone calls?"

"We didn't talk to each other, either." Hannah, ever logical, tried to defuse the situation. "We never talk about the accident."

Posy knew she was probably overreacting, but she felt attacked and, yes, a little stupid.

She dug her spoon into Beth's pudding. Talking like this with her sisters was new to her. She wasn't sure what she thought of it. Right now, she didn't feel so great. On the other hand, it was good to know her sisters were in her corner even if they had gone about it the wrong way.

"We didn't know he was going to show up here," Beth said. "We thought by ignoring his call, the whole thing would go away. This time of year makes me tense."

Hannah sipped her water. "It makes us all tense. Why do you think I skipped it last year?"

"You said it was because you had a pressing need to be somewhere else on business."

"I lied." Hannah put the glass back down. "I was going to come. Right up until check-in opened for the flight, and then I chickened out."

Posy wondered why a trip home would require courage. "What happened?"

Hannah dipped her head and her silver earrings gleamed in the firelight. "I couldn't face everyone working so hard to pretend they love Christmas."

"I love Christmas," Posy said. "I genuinely love Christmas. I love the smell of fir trees, and cinnamon cookies, kids being excited—"

"If you love Christmas so much, why are you always so stressed about everything?"

"I'm not always stressed. I know how difficult this time of

year is for Mom, and she always tries so hard to make Christmas special, so I always want Christmas to be perfect, too. But it's harder than all the magazines and TV ads make it look, and I end up feeling like a failure. No one on TV has a five-mile-long to-do list. My turkey is never as glossy looking as the ones in the adverts, and no one in our house sits around with dopey smiles on their face, watching indulgently while perfectly behaved children poke Christmas gifts. And while we're talking about it, why is it that on TV the needles never fall off the Christmas tree?"

Hannah topped up her water. "Because those images are fake. The turkey has probably been sprayed with something, and the needles have been glued on the damn tree. Those ads are the result of overpaid advertising executives sitting in a room trying to work out how to persuade gullible people like you that a perfect Christmas can be bought for the right amount of money."

"Excuse me," Posy said, "but I am not gullible."

"Excuse me," Beth said. "Are you saying my advertising executive husband is overpaid? And before you answer, you should probably think about your own salary."

"I'm not paid to dupe someone into thinking a certain lifestyle is possible if particular products are purchased. It's a particular type of dishonesty."

"Oh *please.*" Beth turned to Posy. "*Stop* eating my pudding! There's only a mouthful left."

"I'm saving you from yourself. And how did we get onto the subject of Jason's salary? We were talking about Christmas."

"Mom wants it to be perfect because she's overcompensating," Beth said, "but I don't know what your excuse is."

"I don't need an excuse. I'm naturally a very Christmassy sort of person."

"Prickly you mean? Like holly?"

"I do not mean that. For me, Christmas is about warmth, coziness and family time." Posy reflected on what Beth had said. It was true that their mother tried too hard to make Christmas perfect. Also true that overcompensating played a significant part.

"For me, Christmas is about the kids." Beth put her spoon down. "I want to make perfect memories for them. I want them to associate it with sleigh bells and sparkly lights and all those extra trappings that unscrupulous ad people like my husband flash in our direction."

Hannah stared into the fire. "For me, Christmas is all about the accident. Suzanne overcompensates, but given the choice, I'd avoid it altogether. Every year I just want it to be over."

Posy saw the agony in her eyes and suddenly she forgot all about Luke and her worry about what would happen next.

Hannah had been older. Of the three of them, she'd been the most affected by their parents' death.

She'd never thought of Hannah as vulnerable, and yet over the past few days she'd discovered how wrong she was. She thought of Hannah with red eyes, Hannah anxious that she'd be a terrible mother, Hannah with wet hair, wondering why Adam had called.

And now Hannah admitting how difficult she found this time of year.

Posy had never heard her sister talk like this before. She knew it was a huge thing for her and wanted to acknowledge that somehow, but she was afraid of saying the wrong thing.

For once, Beth was silent, too.

Remembering how it had felt when Beth had hugged her, Posy reached across and rubbed Hannah's hand. "How can we help?"

Hannah seemed to pull herself together. "You can't. I'll deal with it. I always do."

"But you deal with it alone," Posy said, "and I don't like the thought of that."

Beth nodded. "I don't like it, either. We're a team. A unit. And right now it feels good. We should do this more often." She glanced round the pub, soaking up the atmosphere. "I'm almost glad Mom threw us out. A roaring log fire, a big, warm Scottish welcome and family. We don't often get to talk like this. Why don't we?"

"Because we're only ever together at Christmas."

"But we don't usually do it even then. This should be a new tradition. Every Christmas the three McBride sisters will go to the pub and speak the truth about their lives. I'm loving the honesty. We are the Christmas Sisters. Forget Santa sweaters, I'm ordering matching T-shirts for us to wear on Christmas Day."

"As long as you don't expect me to wear it." Hannah stroked her hand over her soft cashmere sweater, as if she was afraid Beth might be about to rip it off.

Posy wondered how far this new honesty stretched. Did she dare ask about Adam? From what he'd said to her on the phone, Hannah was a different woman with him and she wanted to know that person.

She decided to risk it. "Tell us about Adam with the sexy voice."

"Adam is a colleague." Hannah glanced at them and must have seen something in their faces, because she sighed. "All right, I admit he's a little more than a colleague. We've been seeing each other."

Beth fiddled with her spoon. "He was the guy in the photo?"

"Yes."

"Why does he call you 'dancing pizza girl'?" Posy ignored Beth's look of surprise.

"Sometimes we work late and he orders pizza and, yes, there may have been the odd occasion when I may have eaten a slice. And once, we were messing around and he taught me to tango."

Her sister messed around? She knew how to dance a tango?

Beth blinked. "Are you in love?"

"I'm not in love." Hannah stared into the fire. "I don't have those feelings."

"If he got you dancing round a pizza box, you're definitely feeling something." Posy looked at Beth. "By the way, I blame you. Why didn't you tell us she was seeing someone?"

"Because I didn't know. She makes excuses rather than meet up, presumably because I'm boring."

Hannah frowned. "You're not boring."

"I am boring. All I talk about is the kids."

"Because you love them, and you're proud of them. And why wouldn't you be? You're a great mom, Beth. I don't see the problem."

"The problem is that you don't like them."

Posy froze. *Oops.* Beth had said the same thing that night in the car on their way from the airport, but Posy had assumed it was because she'd overindulged on the champagne.

Hannah looked astonished. "That is ridiculous."

"You never come to the apartment. You make excuses so that you don't have to meet up, and when we do, you insist on meeting in restaurants. I try not to be hurt because I know kids aren't your thing, but they're your nieces and the truth is you find them difficult to be around."

Posy had an uneasy feeling their sisterly bonding moment might have tipped over the edge into something infinitely more dangerous.

"Maybe we should—"

"That isn't true." Hannah was pale.

"You don't avoid coming to my apartment?"

"That part might be true, but it isn't because I don't love the girls. I can't believe you'd think that."

"You left them alone this afternoon."

"That's because I'm inept, not because I don't love them."

There was something about Hannah's unflinching honesty that made Posy's heart ache, but she also felt for Beth because she knew this was a sensitive issue for her.

"Do you think we could go back to—"

"No," Beth said. "If we're having a sister night where we're all honest, then we're going to be honest."

"We weren't really having a sister night," Posy said. "Mom threw us out, and—"

"It's turned into a sister night. And this has been on my mind for a while, so I'd like to talk about it if that's all right with you. Tell me the truth, Hannah."

Posy wondered whether she should try to shut this down. Seeing her sisters hurting was harder to handle than the situation with Luke.

Hannah sat very still. "The truth is that I find it hard being with the kids because Ruby reminds me of Posy."

Posy stared at her. "This is *my* fault?"

"It takes me right back to the night they were killed. When they died, you were devastated. You kept saying *Mommy, want Mommy, where's Mommy?* and I didn't know how to comfort you." There was a sheen in Hannah's eyes and Posy could actually feel her distress.

It was uncomfortable to witness.

She shifted in her seat.

The surrounding pub noise faded to an indistinct blur. "I don't remember it."

"But I do remember it, and it was awful. I felt inadequate and hopeless. Your pain was so huge it swallowed me up.

Watching you howling for our parents, and knowing I could do nothing to ease your pain was like having my insides removed with a blunt object. From that night onward, every night you cried, I almost had an anxiety attack." Hannah drew in a steadying breath, as if reminding herself it was in the past. "Then somehow it became any child crying. I saw a therapist a couple of times, but that didn't work for me. So instead I avoided children."

"Including Ruby." Beth spoke quietly, all traces of defensiveness gone.

Hannah rubbed her fingers across her forehead. "Yes. Anyway, you asked the question and I answered."

Posy swallowed. "You're saying I put you off love?" She felt responsible, even though she knew it was ridiculous to feel that way.

"I don't know. I'm not a psychiatrist."

"What about me?" Beth leaned forward. "Where was I in all this?"

"You clung to Stewart. You were always a daddy's girl."

"I clung to Suzanne," Posy said. "That's my earliest memory. I was in bed all warm and safe and being cuddled. She was amazing."

"That wasn't Suzanne." Hannah fiddled with her glass. "That was me."

"No, it was Suzanne. I remember her reading to me in bed. That's my earliest memory."

"I was the one who read to you in bed. You slept with me every night after they died. You and your rabbit, whose name I have forgotten but whose lumpy form has stayed with me."

Posy was stunned. She felt as if she'd been blown over by a strong wind.

The warmth, the security, the kindness, the cuddles—

"It was you?"

"Yes. Thanks for remembering by the way. Makes all the trauma worth it." On the surface, Hannah seemed to be back in control again. Posy might even have thought she'd imagined the stress if it hadn't been for the rhythmic tapping of her sister's foot under the table.

She was still struggling to get her head around this new information. "But—"

"You clung to me for six months. Until we moved here, in fact. Then you seemed to settle down and just get on with your new life. It was as if your old life had never existed."

"If we used to be so close, what happened?"

"I guess I pulled away," Hannah said. "It seemed an easier, less painful way to live."

There was a silence. It was Beth who broke it. "I didn't know. It didn't occur to me that was your reason for staying away from the girls. I…I'm sorry I said those things."

"Don't be. I'm glad we cleared it up." Hannah gave a wan smile. "I have some issues. I'm the first to admit it. You do, too."

Beth looked puzzled. "I don't have issues."

Posy took another big swallow of her drink. "You have issues."

"Is this a conspiracy?"

"No. It's the truth. You have issues." Maybe it wasn't the right time to say it, but it seemed as good as any. "You are super protective of your children."

"Every mother is protective of her children."

Hannah finished her drink. "You're not protective in the way other mothers are. You are overprotective. You see disaster everywhere. You catastrophize."

Beth stiffened defensively. "Not true."

Posy glanced at Hannah. "Let's forget it. It's understandable."

"Understandable," Hannah echoed.

Beth sat up straighter. "I don't want to forget it. And if you're implying that an accident that happened twenty-five years ago has impacted on the way I raise my children, I can tell you that's not the case. Give me an example of when I've been overprotective."

Posy hesitated. "You virtually hyperventilate whenever the girls want to ride Socks."

"Everyone knows you should wear a helmet when riding. It's common sense."

"Yes." How could she say this as gently as possible? "But given the chance you'd special order chest protectors and airbags."

"Plenty of riders protect themselves from falling."

"Maybe for competition-level eventing, but to ride my ancient pony around a field? I don't think so."

Beth clasped her hands in her lap. Her knuckles were white. "Socks is a large animal. Any horse can stampede."

"I think it takes more than one horse to stampede, and Socks has arthritis. It hurts him to trot. Stampeding would be way beyond his capabilities."

Beth flushed. "All I'm saying is that it could happen."

"And that," Posy said, "is my point. You react to all the things that could happen. Not what has actually happened. Catastrophizing."

"I anticipate accidents, that's all. That's how I prevent them happening."

"I think you live every possible accident," Hannah said slowly. "You see it in your head and it freaks you out."

Beth looked as if she was about to deny it, then slumped. "You're right, I do. I'm always imagining something terrible is going to happen, like it did with us. I'm scared, and I manage that by doing everything I can to stop bad things happening.

I try to control every little thing. It's exhausting." She stared into the fire. "I have issues."

"Maybe it's time we dealt with our issues," Hannah said.

"Yes. I need to try harder to relax. I don't want to raise nervous children." Beth's phone rang and she dug frantically in her bag, sending them a look of guilt and apology. "It might be an emergency. I *will* try being more relaxed, but I'm going to start tomorrow. Right now I have to answer this in case Ruby has drowned in the bath, or escaped through the back door, or—" She checked the number. "It's Corinna—"

"That really is a catastrophe." Hannah reached across, snatched the phone from her hand and switched it off.

"What are you doing? I need to answer that!" Beth launched herself from her chair and snatched it back. "You'll get me fired!"

"She can't fire you. She hasn't employed you yet." Hannah put the phone on the table. "If it had been Jason or one of the girls, I can understand why you'd take the call, but as this is an evening of truths, then I will point out that Corinna is using you. She's using you as free labor and you're letting her."

"It's a goodwill gesture. I need to impress her."

Posy was thinking about what Hannah had said. How could her memory have failed her so badly? How could she have remembered the love, but not the person giving it? She stared at her sister's slim shoulders and elegant form and tried to remember snuggling in bed with her. When, and why, had her memory decided it was Suzanne?

Hannah was focused on Beth. "Do you really want to work for that woman?"

"Yes. She's smart, she's creative, she's driven." Beth paused. "And she thinks I have the exact set of skills she needs for this account."

"And what are those skills?" Hannah held her gaze. "Why do you think she wants you in particular?"

"Are you implying I don't have skills? I am the one who has profiled the target audience. I understand the woman who used to wear makeup but whose life is now just too busy, and perhaps she's lost a little confidence and— Oh…" Beth's voice trailed off. "She didn't want me to identify the target audience. She wants me because I *am* the target audience."

Hannah said nothing, but there was sympathy in her eyes.

"This is the part where you tell me I'm wrong," Beth said in a small voice.

"You're not wrong."

Posy tried to soften it. "She could be wrong. She doesn't know for sure."

"I know for sure," Hannah said, and Posy felt an ache in her chest.

This night was turning out to be worse than any of her most grueling rescues out on the mountains. She felt battered and bruised.

Beth had been so excited about the job. She didn't want to see her hurt. "Look on the bright side—you got all those free samples. Although not Everyday Red, because that is mostly on the kitchen wall." Deciding that humor might not be the way to go, she gave Beth's arm a squeeze. "There are other jobs. Better jobs." Were there? She didn't know, but she thought it best to sound encouraging.

Beth stared at her phone without touching it. "She invited me in because I've been at home with kids for seven years. I'm not her top pick for her new team, I'm her market research project. I'm a lab rat."

"I don't see you as a rat." Posy gave Hannah a desperate look. She'd started this, and now she needed to shut it down in a way that didn't leave Beth feeling awful.

Beth put her phone back in her bag. "Goodbye, dream job."

"Working for Corinna is no one's idea of a dream job." Hannah was brisk. "She has no idea how to manage people. Never work for a bully, especially when they own the company."

This time Beth didn't argue. "You're right. She is a bully. I knew that, but I tried to forget it because it seemed like an easy way back into work and hearing that she wanted me for her new company boosted my confidence when I was feeling low. But she doesn't really boost your confidence—she destroys it because you never quite measure up." Her voice faltered. "She has this way of making you feel that if you're not bringing your A game to every conversation you're a failure. When I worked for her before, I spent my whole time waiting to get fired. She makes you feel so useless you become convinced no one else will ever want you. And when anyone did find the courage to leave, she gave them a lousy reference."

"So I ask you again," Hannah said. "Do you really want to work for her?"

"No, but no one else will take someone with my profile. I've been at home for seven years. My confidence is rock-bottom because I haven't been working." She glanced at Hannah. "Why are you looking at me like that?"

"Your confidence is at rock bottom because the last person you worked for was Corinna and she left you feeling as if you didn't measure up. The worst thing you could do is work for her again. You want an energetic, positive work environment where your skills will be valued."

"Do I have skills?"

A smile spread across Hannah's face. "You do. All the qualities that made you good at your job before you had kids are still there. You've been focusing on different things, that's all. So you need to shift the focus back."

"I've lost my contacts."

"Which you built up from nothing in the first place and can undoubtedly do again. You need some coaching to work out what you want and how to best use the skills you have."

Beth stared miserably at the fire. "And who is going to do that for me?"

"I am."

"You'd coach me?"

"Yes."

"Are you going to bill me?"

Hannah rolled her eyes. "I'm not even going to dignify that with an answer."

"I know how busy you are," Beth muttered. "I'd owe you, big-time."

"There is no owing between sisters. And I'm sure there will be a time in the future when I'm going to need your help, too."

Posy wondered if Hannah was thinking about the baby, and what lay ahead for her.

"You're going to make me cry, and my mascara isn't water-proof." Beth rummaged for a tissue. "You really think someone else will want me?"

"I know they will."

Posy felt a rush of warmth that had nothing to do with her proximity to the log fire. Hannah was going to help Beth. Up until tonight she'd felt as if the three of them had mostly lived their lives swimming along in separate lanes, but now they were all in the same lane, looking out for each other. "This is good." She raised her almost-empty bottle. "To the Christmas Sisters."

She promised herself that she was going to do her bit, too. She was going to be more understanding. If Hannah wanted egg whites, Posy would whisk her egg whites. She could always make custard with the yolks.

Wrapped up by this warm blanket of sisterly togetherness, they left the pub arm in arm.

"It's freezing," Hannah said. "Why did we walk?"

"Because we'd had a drink. Also, it's only ten minutes away."

"Ten minutes seems like ten hours when your toes are frozen. And I don't like walking down country roads in the dark."

Posy steered her round a patch of ice. "You're such a townie."

"I am. We should call a cab."

"This isn't Manhattan. There's only Pete, and he was at the bar, so we don't want him driving us."

"If he's the only cab in town, why was he at the bar?"

"Because the whole village is in the pub, so he knows no one is going to need him."

Clutching each other for warmth and stability, they stumbled along the lane toward the lodge, using the light from Posy's phone to see where they were going.

Beth started singing carols and Posy joined in until Hannah threatened to drop her in the ditch.

As they turned the corner, they saw a car outside the front door, the engine still running.

"That's a cab," Hannah said. "You said there were no cabs."

Posy peered at the logo on the side.

"Not local. It's an airport car."

As they watched, a man stepped out from the back and handed over a couple of notes.

He wore a long, dark coat with the collar turned up against the cold.

Posy guessed he was a couple of inches above six foot, and there was an edge of sophistication to his looks that should

have made him look uncomfortably out of place in these surroundings, but somehow didn't.

He looked expensive, she thought. And if she'd wondered
for a moment who he was, she didn't have to wonder for long
because beside her Hannah made a strangled sound.

"Adam?"

Adam? The expensive guy was Adam?

Posy's first thought was that he looked as good as he
sounded, and her second thought was that Hannah didn't
generally like surprises.

Was she going to be pleased to see him?

She could feel Hannah's fingers digging into her arm.

"What is he doing here? There is absolutely no reason for
him to be here, except—" Hannah paused for a moment, her
breath clouding the freezing air, and then she turned to Posy,
all the warmth frozen out by the ice in her eyes. "Did you
tell him to come?"

"No! I mean—" Posy thought back, her heart plummeting
"—not exactly. I might have mentioned it when we were joking about the terrible signal. I said it would be easier to come
here in person to have a conversation, but I didn't think…
New York is a long way… Why would he… He said he loved
you."

Hannah looked stricken and she snatched her hand away
from Posy's arm as if she couldn't bear to touch her. "What
have you *done*?"

The fragile shoots of their new relationship froze and
snapped.

If Posy had hoped that the evening had signaled a fresh start
and a new closeness with her sister, that hope was dead now.

"Hannah—I was just trying to—"

"To what? To interfere, like you all do? *Is Hannah seeing
anyone? When is Hannah going to settle down?* What business is

it of yours? So much for being the barrier between me and the rest of the world. Or were you trying to ruin my life?"

"No."

I love you. You're my sister. I've messed up and I'm so sorry.

Posy didn't know what to say. And she had a feeling that nothing she said was going to make a difference.

23

Hannah

The front door opened and her whole family was crowded there. Suzanne and Stewart, with Melly and Ruby peeping around their legs. No doubt Jason was hovering in the background, too.

Flanked by her sisters, Hannah felt as if everyone was looking at her, waiting for her reaction.

Her reaction was one of panic.

She hadn't had time to get used to the idea of being pregnant. She hadn't worked out how she was going to handle it. She didn't know what part Adam would play, or if he wanted to play any part at all, and she didn't know how to handle that, either.

She certainly wasn't good with men showing up on her doorstep unannounced.

She'd planned on taking the few weeks over Christmas to think hard about what she wanted and how much of a risk she was prepared to take. Her intention had been to come up with a plan and then execute it carefully, step by step. Instead she felt as if she was being swept along by a tidal wave, gasping and drowning, unable to save herself.

How could Posy have done such a thing?

And what had possessed Adam to show up here without speaking to her first? Why wasn't he in the Caribbean as planned?

Like it or not, he *was* here, and she had no choice but to invite him in and accept the overenthusiastic scrutiny of her family. She could almost feel their minds working. They'd be asking themselves questions. They'd be asking *her* questions.

She felt as if his arrival had somehow exposed her.

Digging deep to find the part of her that used to feel in control of her life, she walked toward Adam, trying hard not to slip on the icy surface.

Posy reached out to her. "Do you want to take my—"

"No, I don't." She wasn't holding on to anyone. The only person you could really trust in the world was yourself. And fortunately, this time, she didn't let herself down. Her feet planted firmly and she didn't slip. "This is a surprise." She could see from the wary look in his eyes that he could tell it wasn't necessarily a good one.

"I took a chance."

And that, she thought, was the difference between them.

Hannah didn't take chances. She never leaped unless she knew her landing was secure. She never started a journey without knowing her destination.

The cab drove off and she noticed the small suitcase by Adam's feet.

"Come inside!" Suzanne opened the door wider. "You must all be freezing."

Hannah didn't want to step inside. She wanted to run. She didn't care if she slipped on the ice and fell flat on her face.

It was only as she stepped through the door that she remembered Luke and the reason they'd gone to the pub in the first place. It seemed like a lifetime ago that she'd been talking with her sisters. She'd felt lighter than she could ever remember being. That part of her that had been closed for a long time had begun to open up. After Beth had revealed her own insecurities, Hannah had been on the verge of telling her about the baby and admitting her own feelings of vulnerability and inadequacy. She'd considered asking Beth's advice.

Now she felt herself shutting down again, ready to protect herself.

Suzanne offered her hand to Adam. "I'm Suzanne. Good to meet you. I apologize for this rather crazy household."

Hannah could imagine how this seemed to Suzanne. *Hannah has a love life! Finally.*

She felt the same suffocating pressure she always felt when she was back home.

Adam shook her hand, all charm and confidence. "I'm the one who should be apologizing for descending unannounced. I've booked a room at the pub—"

Oh great, Hannah thought. So now the whole village would know Hannah McBride finally had a man. He might as well have taken out an ad in the local paper.

"You don't need to stay there. We have plenty of room. I'll call the pub and cancel your reservation." Suzanne enveloped him with the same warmth and welcome that ensured that Café Craft was always bursting at the seams with people.

It hurt Hannah that it might not occur to Suzanne that this wasn't what she wanted.

No one paid attention to what she wanted or needed. No one seemed to care. All they cared about was that she fitted into the way they saw the world. That her life was the way *they* wanted it to be.

Melly's eyes were round with admiration. "Are you a prince?"

Adam laughed. "Now, why would you think that?"

"You're very tall, and you have dark hair, and you look a bit like Prince Charming."

"I hate to disappoint you, but I'm not a prince."

"Are you Aunty Hannah's boyfriend?"

Adam paused. "I'm her friend."

Ruby stepped forward. "Did you fly in an airplane?"

"I did."

"Did you see Bugsy?"

"Okay, I've got this—" Beth stepped forward and scooped Ruby up. "You girls should be in bed! Why are you up so late?"

"Because Daddy let us for a treat. He didn't think you'd find out."

"Traitor," Jason muttered. "Come on, girls. Upstairs."

"Will you read us another story?"

Hannah was feeling trapped and on the verge of panic. She was going through possible scenarios in her head—Tell Adam right away? Postpone telling him?—when Beth spoke.

"As a special treat, would you like Aunty Hannah to read you a story?"

Melly looked as if Christmas had come early. "Tonight? Yes!"

"Yes!" Ruby echoed. "As long as she does it with voices."

Jason's gaze flickered from Hannah to Adam. "But Hannah probably wants to—"

"It would be such a treat for the girls," Beth said quickly.

"I'm sure Adam won't mind. There's a fire in the living room and Dad has an exceptional bottle of single malt. We'll entertain Adam while she reads to the children. Thank you, Hannah." She made it sound as if Hannah would be doing her a huge favor and Hannah felt her throat thicken.

Beth wasn't pushing her toward Adam. She was giving her the opportunity to gather her thoughts.

She turned to Adam. "Do you mind? Make yourself at home and I'll be down as soon as I've settled the children." She said it as if "settling the children" was something she did often, and the faint lift of his eyebrow was the only indication that he recognized an avoidance tactic when he saw one.

Adam was many things, but slow wasn't one of them.

"Sure." His voice was neutral. "I'm not a man to refuse the offer of a good single malt."

Hannah followed the girls upstairs, only half listening to Ruby's excited chatter.

Anticipating the conversation with Adam, and the interrogation from her family, didn't encourage her to rush the story.

She slid off her shoes and lay on the bed next to Ruby while Melly snuggled into the other bed.

"What are we reading?"

She read long after Ruby had stopped reaching out to turn pages and point to the illustrations, and long after Melly's eyes had drifted shut.

When she knew she couldn't hide in the girls' room any longer, she turned the light out and walked quietly to her own room. From downstairs she could hear the occasional rumble of conversation interspersed with laughter.

She was standing by the window trying to work out what to do, when there was a tap on the door.

Braced for a difficult conversation with Adam, she was surprised to see Stewart standing there.

"Can I come in?"

"Of course." Hannah's tension rose. She'd been rude, she knew that. She'd flouted all the house rules about hospitality and probably embarrassed them. It wasn't the first time Christmas had been stressful, and it probably wouldn't be the last, but that didn't stop her feeling guilty at the part she'd played. "I was about to come downstairs."

Stewart pulled out the chair by her desk and sat down. "You don't have to do that."

She felt a spasm of guilt. "I shouldn't have come home. Suzanne always wants Christmas to be a happy time and I've ruined it. Is she very upset? Are you worried about her?" Why was it she could never be what people wanted her to be?

And now she'd even disappointed Stewart. Kind, rocksolid, unflappable Stewart.

"You haven't ruined anything. And it's not Suzanne I'm worried about, it's you."

"Me?"

"You've never brought a guy home before, and it's pretty obvious to me that you didn't invite Adam. And then there's the fact that you arrived home early, and looking pretty miserable."

The fact that she'd been so transparent was embarrassing, not just for herself but also for Adam.

"I didn't expect him to show up here. I'm sure you have questions—" The situation was so awkward and uncomfortable.

"Only one question." Stewart leaned forward. "What would you like me to do?"

"Do?"

"About Adam. It doesn't matter to me why he is here, or who thought what. The only thing that matters to me is what you want." He sat quietly for a moment, staring at his hands as if he didn't quite know what he should be doing with them. "Whatever you'd like me to do, I'll do it. I'll fix it in whatever way you'd like it fixed. If you want him to leave, then say the word and I'll deal with it. You don't have to see him if you don't want to. He can stay in the pub tonight and I'll take him back to the airport tomorrow."

"You don't think I'm capable of handling this myself?"

"You're more than capable of handling it, but I'm your dad and I'm offering to handle it for you. Everyone needs a little help once in a while. I'm offering mine, if you'd like it. Sometimes in life it's okay to take the easy path. I can see this is tough for you, so let me protect you from it."

Hannah was so touched that for a moment she couldn't breathe.

There was an ache in her chest that grew and grew.

He'd come to her room not to lecture her on her manners, but to offer his protection.

She turned away quickly so he wouldn't see the tears in her eyes. They scalded, welled up, threatened to spill.

I'm your dad.

"It's complicated. I've been seeing him and—well, I'm pregnant." She had no idea what possessed her to blurt it out like that, but if Stewart was surprised by that revelation, it didn't show.

"How do you feel about that?"

She rubbed her arms, trying to warm herself. "Adam is the father, but I haven't told him."

"Is that why you came home early?"

"Yes. I guess you could say I panicked. I always have a plan, as you know, and this wasn't part of my plan." She leaned against the window, wishing she was braver. She should tell Adam straight out and ask him what he wanted to do, but their relationship was a new and fragile thing and she didn't fully understand it. He said he loved her, but love, as she well knew, was unreliable. Like Christmas, it came with expectations.

What if she couldn't be what he wanted her to be? She liked things to be logical, and there was nothing logical about love.

"Do you love him, sweetheart?" The kindness in Stewart's voice was a balm to her raw, exposed feelings.

"I don't know. I think so, but I always thought it would be a happy feeling and in fact it's just scary. I'm sure that sounds crazy to you."

"Doesn't sound crazy. Feelings are scary things."

Hannah managed a smile. "You don't find anything scary."

"I find plenty of things scary."

She turned her head. "You climb vertical rock faces for a living."

"Rocks you can see and touch and learn about. They're tangible things, but feelings—" he shook his head "—they're like the weather. They're the part you can't control. If you don't care about anything, then you're invulnerable, but once you care—well, you can be hurt. And people can disappoint and let you down."

"I know. I've disappointed more people than I can count." And she'd damaged her relationship with Posy again, just when it had felt they'd reached a new understanding. The thought depressed her more than she would have imagined possible. She'd actually enjoyed their brief moment of companionship. For a moment she'd seen a future where she and her sisters were closer. She'd started to think maybe she could handle it.

Stewart stood up and walked across to her. "You've never disappointed anyone, Hannah."

She knew that wasn't true.

"I'm never quite what people want me to be." And she knew that most people didn't see what lay beneath the surface. Except for Adam. *Dancing pizza girl.* "I like things I can be sure of. Numbers, facts, company growth—those are all things that seem logical to me. Those are things that behave in a way I can predict. Love, I don't understand. It seems so random. You can't measure it, and you can't control it. You can love someone with all your heart, but that doesn't mean they're going to love you back. And that isn't something you can work on, or try harder at—I know because I tried." She felt Stewart's hand on her shoulder, warm and comforting.

"I'm guessing it's not Adam you're talking about here, but your father."

It didn't surprise her that he understood. She knew there hadn't been much love between Stewart and her biological dad. "I don't think about it much. I don't want you to think that. It's just—"

"This time of year." He rubbed her shoulder gently. "I know. It hits us all in one way or another. Wounds heal, but they still leave scars. And that conversation with Luke stirred it all up again."

"I always regret that they died without giving me a chance to make them proud. Dad wanted me to be a certain way, and I wasn't."

"That's not true. Your dad was proud of you, but he was a complicated character." Stewart let his hand drop. "I'm no psychologist, but I suspect it was more that he didn't know how to relate to you. All Rob knew was climbing. I doubt he ever read a book in his life. And you were so smart. Scarily smart. I remember Suzanne used to come home after she'd babysat you and she'd be full of stories of what you'd done. *Hannah said this, Hannah is reading this.*"

"I tried so hard to make him love me."

"You wanted his love and approval. That's a natural thing. This probably doesn't help, but I'm sure he did love you even though he didn't do a good job of showing it." Stewart put his arm round her shoulders. "When you came to us, you were so wary. You never really let us get close."

"I didn't know how to behave. I didn't know what to do. If my own parents didn't love me, why would anyone else? Why would you? What was I to you but a burden?" She brushed the tears away from her cheeks with the palm of her hand and the next moment she was being folded against Stewart's chest. She felt the softness of his sweater against her cheek and the security of his arms.

"You were never a burden. You were the best thing that happened to us."

"How can you say that?" Her voice was muffled against his shoulder. "You and Suzanne never even got to have kids of your own because of us."

"We had three beautiful girls." He eased her away from him so that he could look at her. "You are my daughter. You've been my daughter from that first day Suzanne brought you to our apartment with your suitcase of books and a terrified look on your face."

"This is embarrassing." Hannah sniffed. "I'm too old to be crying on your shoulder."

"You're never too old to cry on your dad's shoulder, although I have to admit I hate to see you cry." He wiped her cheek with his thumb. "We probably should have had this conversation twenty years ago, but I think we've both spent enough time thinking about the past, so let's just make sure we get it right from here. I've never had to beat up one of your boyfriends before. Not sure I know how, but I'm willing to give it a go if you'd like me to."

She gave him a watery smile. "He's stronger than he looks."

"He looks pretty strong, but I have muscles. Your mother married me for my muscles. And my good looks and charm." Stewart gave her a squeeze and then let her go. "What do you want to do, sweetheart?"

"I don't know. I wanted time to think about this and work out how to handle it. I wanted to plan."

"Maybe the two of you could work it out together. For what it's worth, I like the fact that he came here in person."

She found a tissue and blew her nose. "You don't think that makes him a stalker?"

"I think it makes him a man who doesn't give up easily, and who cares enough to make an effort. And maybe also a man who knows you better than you think."

"He knows me pretty well." She scrunched the tissue into a ball. "He says he loves me."

"I suspect a man like Adam says what he means. Doesn't strike me as the type to play games."

"I believe he thinks he does, but love isn't reliable. Love breaks down all the time, doesn't it? People are happy one minute and divorced the next. It's the most unpredictable, unreliable emotion."

"Sometimes things go wrong, that's true, but often they go right. Suzanne and I have been together for a long time."

"That's different. You're perfect together."

"We're not perfect and we've had our difficult moments, like any couple, but I don't think a relationship has to be all roses and kisses to be love. At least I hope it doesn't." He scratched his jaw. "Good job Suzanne can't hear me say this, because she'd roll her eyes. Come to think of it I don't think I've ever bought her roses, although I've done all right with the kisses."

It made her smile. "You stood by her side when she became guardian to three kids. You were right there for her, even though you didn't have to be. You weren't even married. You could have walked away." It still amazed her that he hadn't.

"I wanted to be with Suzanne. Getting you was a bonus, but if she'd inherited a zoo, I would still have been there."

Hannah had a lump in her throat. "I'm no expert, but I'm guessing that means more than roses."

"I'm no expert, either, but it seems to me that a man doesn't travel that far to see a woman unless his feelings are strong. Of course, you'd be better off talking to Suzanne or one of your sisters about this. Or you could talk to Adam. That seems to make the most sense. If you'd like to do that, I'll send him up. If not, I'll send him away."

"Don't send him away." He'd come all this way, the least she owed him was a conversation.

"If you change your mind, I'll be downstairs."

She stopped him when he reached the door. "Stewart? Is Suzanne okay after that conversation with Luke?"

"Better than okay. It was unexpected, but life is full of the unexpected and it did her good to finally talk about it. I've never been sure that her determination never to discuss it was a good thing." He paused, his hand on the door. "We're pleased you came home. It's the best Christmas gift you could have given us. I'm going to send Adam up now."

Hannah wondered if she had time to rush to the bathroom and wash her face, but already she could hear male voices at the bottom of the stairs and the sound of Adam's firm tread.

Aware that he didn't know which room was hers, she walked to the door.

Their eyes met.

She felt that little shock of electricity that she always felt when Adam was near. It was a reminder that she wasn't quite in control of everything, and it unsettled her.

She couldn't believe he was actually here, in the wilds of Scotland.

He walked into the room and closed the door behind him, firmly, as if he wanted to make sure that whatever they said to each other remained private.

"I owe you an apology."

It was the last thing she expected him to say.

Surely, she was the one who owed *him* an apology. "I didn't expect to see you. I didn't expect you to come."

He gave a half smile. "We were in the middle of a chess game, and it was your move. I'm a completer finisher."

Despite everything, it made her smile. "You came all this way for me to beat you?"

"What can I say? I'm also a masochist."

Her smile faded. "I was rude."

"No." He walked across to her but kept his hands in his pockets. He didn't hug her or touch her. "I don't know what possessed me to fly here without calling first. I'm not normally so impulsive. Or insensitive."

"Posy possessed you. She suggested it."

He shook his head. "Don't blame her. I was the one who acted on the suggestion."

"You told her about the pizza and the dancing."

He rubbed his fingers across his forehead. "She answered the phone. I assumed it was you because I've never known you to be separated from your phone. I was halfway through the conversation before I realized it wasn't you on the other end. It's my fault, not hers. And I should have asked you before I flew over here, but I was afraid that if I called you, you'd stop me and I badly wanted to see you."

"Why?"

"Because I missed you." This time he did touch her, but gently. Tentatively. He smoothed her hair back from her face and studied her. "Have you been crying? Dammit, Hannah!" He let his hands drop and stepped back. "I've never seen you cry. I don't ever want to make you cry."

"I'm not crying."

"Don't lie to me. I'll leave, right now. Just promise me you'll stop crying."

She'd never seen him so unsure of himself. "I don't want that."

What did she want? She had no idea.

This was the perfect time to tell him she was pregnant.

But how should she say it?

She'd planned on doing some research on how best to tell a man he was going to be a father. In her head was a complicated playbook full of different alternatives. What she'd do if he freaked out, if he wanted nothing more to do with her, if he happened to think it was the best news ever—

She hadn't planned on him showing up here unannounced before she'd firmed up her strategy.

"Don't leave." She'd take it a stage at a time. If he wasn't leaving right away, then there was no hurry.

"Are you sure?" He stood still, not taking a step toward her. "I don't want you to feel pressured."

"I want you to stay."

This time he did step forward and he pulled her into his arms. He kissed her, hugged her tightly and then glanced around the room, his gaze settling on the Christmas tree. "This is a great room. I like the tree."

"That's Eric," Hannah said. "Posy named it. My sister names everything, from pigs to chickens to Christmas trees."

Adam tensed. "Eric? The tree is called Eric?"

She nodded and he swore under his breath.

"She told me you were doing fine because you had Eric. I thought— I assumed Eric was a man."

Hannah gaped at him. "That's why you flew all the way here?"

"It played a part." There was a livid flush across his cheekbones. "Embarrassed though I am to admit it, I may have been a teeny bit jealous. Of a fir tree. If it's all right with you, I'd rather that didn't leave this room."

She couldn't help it. She started to laugh. "Oh, Adam—"

"Are you laughing at me? Because I can tell you I've had the most stressful flight of my life imagining you with this Eric. Your sister said he was the outdoor type, and I was imagining big shoulders and—" He broke off. "Is it going to damage our relationship if I kill your sister?"

"Not at all. I was going to kill her myself. It's the reason I came upstairs."

"I thought the reason you came upstairs was to escape from me." He kissed her again. "Your sister was being protective, which I like, but I don't much like the idea that I was the one she was protecting you from."

Hannah swallowed. "It's complicated."

"Not from where I'm standing." He pulled her against him. "Eric needs to know that I'll fight him for you."

"As a matter of interest, what would you have done if he'd been a person?"

"I don't know. You're assuming there was some logical thought behind my actions, but the truth is I went all Neanderthal and jumped on a plane."

"They didn't have planes two hundred thousand years ago."

"I don't think Neanderthals were called Eric, either. You have no idea how relieved I am not to find you sharing your room with a kilt-wearing, muscle-bound Highlander." He brought his mouth down on hers and she felt the familiar kick of heat that only ever happened with him. Her body melted, pleasure sliding through her with delicious sweetness. Before she'd met Adam, she'd never known a kiss could be so intimate and yet the way he kissed her was so personal, so knowing, that it was almost as if he had a blueprint that showed him the location of all her nerve endings. He held her head, stoking sensation with the slow slide of his tongue and the gentle pressure of his fingers. She felt dizzy and disorientated, as if she'd drunk a glass of whiskey too fast or spun like one of the ballet dancers Melly loved to watch.

Without lifting his mouth from hers, he backed her to the bed and tumbled her onto the mattress.

Hannah gasped. When she was with him, she didn't just lose her balance, she lost a part of herself. The part she relied on to keep herself safe. "We shouldn't—I'm not sure—" When he was kissing her, she couldn't hold the thought for long enough to finish the sentence. "It's complicated."

"This part isn't complicated." His hands were in her hair, his mouth trailing over her jaw, her throat, her shoulder. With a smooth sense of purpose, he slid off her sweater and unbuttoned her shirt, giving himself access to bare skin. "This part isn't complicated at all."

She tried to respond, but all she could manage was a faint murmur and he lifted his head, slowly, reluctantly, as if someone was dragging him away from her.

He fixed her with his gaze, the thoroughly male assessment leaving her breathless. "Do you want me to stop?"

Given what he was now doing with his hands, she didn't consider that a fair question.

He gave a slow smile and, as he stroked his way down her body, Hannah discovered that she definitely didn't want him to stop. Nor did she want him to fly home or sleep in the pub.

She wanted him to stay right here with her. She wanted it enough that she was prepared to expose their fragile relationship to the scrutiny of her family. She wanted it enough that she was prepared to deal with Suzanne's expectations.

In a tiny corner of her mind, buried under an excess of sensation and endorphins, was the knowledge that she still had to tell him she was pregnant.

But not tonight.
It had been a long day. An even longer evening.
Hopefully it would also be a long night.
There was plenty of time for that conversation.

24

Posy

Refusing her mother's offer of a nightcap, Posy stomped her way across to the barn, her feet crunching through fresh snow. It coated the trees, bending branches and muffling sound. It reflected the moonlight, removing all need for a torch.

Normally the landscape soothed her, but tonight not even the crisp cold air or the soft smell of wood smoke drifting from the lodge could lift her spirits.

She was still angry with Luke and humiliated, but her overwhelming emotion was one of misery. Not misery because of Luke. Misery because she'd upset Hannah. For the first time in ages, they'd shared confidences and laughter. She'd learned new things tonight. Things about their past relationship. Things about her sister. There had been a shift in the atmosphere and for a fleeting moment she'd felt a closeness that she couldn't remember feeling before.

But she'd killed it.

Why had she opened her big mouth and suggested Adam come?

On the other hand, she'd intended it as a joke. How was she to know he'd actually do it? She didn't know many men that committed.

Callum hadn't bothered showing up for half their dates and he lived down the road. He never would have flown across the Atlantic.

And as for Luke—

Luke hadn't told her the truth.

What else was he hiding from her?

Snow fell in spiraling lazy swirls, adding layer upon layer to the already-dense carpet on the ground. It was piled in fresh heaps around the barn and stretched up into the mountains. Above the peaks the moon hovered, beaming light down onto the slopes below.

Posy might have admired it, but her vision was blurred.

Tears scalded her eyes and she stopped walking for the simple reason that she couldn't see where she was going.

She blinked, scrubbed at her face with her gloved hand and breathed in the smell of home.

Leaving this place didn't feel like such a great idea anymore.

Was that really what she wanted? Maybe not, and certainly not with someone who had lied to her. Her mind, which had been so sure, was now filled with nothing but doubt. Worse, she no longer trusted her own judgment.

Was Beth right? Should she have checked him out in more detail? Was she ridiculously trusting to assume that people were who they said they were?

Light glowed through the windows of the barn and she

felt a flash of anger as she thought of Luke dropping a bomb into her family, and then guilt that she hadn't even paused long enough to ask her mother what they'd talked about together and how she felt about it. Her own feelings were too big to leave room for anyone else's. She'd wanted to run after Hannah and explain that it wasn't her fault, but she knew her sister well enough to recognize when talk would be useless.

Instead she'd stood in frozen politeness as Suzanne had invited Adam in, the warmth of her welcome a direct contrast to the chill emanating from her eldest daughter. Whiskey had been pressed into his hand and fresh logs added to the fire. Far from being upset, Suzanne had seemed unusually happy. Of course, that might have been because a tall, dark, handsome man had turned up on the doorstep looking for Hannah. Suzanne probably thought Christmas had come early.

Posy stamped her way up the steps that led to the hayloft.

It was going to be another one of those family Christmases that was filled with tension.

What have you done?

Her sister's accusation still rang in her head. Not in a good way like the church bells on Christmas Day, more like a death knell.

Posy hadn't hung around to see what was going to happen next.

For all she knew, Adam might already be on his way back to the airport.

Was Hannah even going to tell him she was pregnant?

Telling herself that it was none of her business, she reached her door and fumbled for her keys. She was never, ever, interfering with anyone else's relationship again. It wasn't even as if she was an expert.

"Posy?" Luke's voice came from the bottom of the stairs. "Can we talk?"

"No. I've had enough human interaction for one day." She stabbed her key into the lock so hard that if the door had been a living thing she would have killed it.

Bonnie sprang to her feet and welcomed her with the riotous unbounded joy that was one of the many reasons Posy knew she would never, ever, choose to live her life without a dog.

She dropped to her knees and hugged her, smiling as Bonnie's whole body wagged along with her tail. "I want to move into your doggy world and never meet a human again."

"I'm assuming I'm the reason for this new life choice." Luke stood in the doorway and Bonnie bounded across to him and offered an ecstatic welcome.

Posy reflected on that traitorous instinct as Luke closed the door, sealing out the cold.

The hayloft was her personal space, designed to offer maximum comfort on cold winter nights. Lamps sent soft light spilling across the wooden floors, and thick rugs and warm throws turned the place into a cozy cocoon. The original rustic oak beams were still in place and the vaulted ceiling gave an illusion of space, although in reality the loft wasn't big. In the summer the views across the trees and the loch were stunning, but in winter it had its own special magic.

Luke stayed by the door, as if expecting her to thrust him back through it. "Five minutes of your time. That's all I'm asking for."

"That's five minutes more than I'm prepared to give."

"You're angry."

"You think? What gave me away? Is it the fact that my expression generally matches my mood so what you're seeing here—" she drew circles in the air around her face "—is angry face, not happy face, puzzled face or concerned face. If I had a lied-to face, I'd be wearing that one, but I don't have that face. You, on the other hand, give nothing away. When we were naked in that bed, I had no idea you weren't who you said you were."

"I am who I said I was."

"You have a whole history that you forgot to mention."

"I didn't mention it to begin with because I wasn't sure how to handle it. It's a sensitive topic and I didn't want to upset you all. I'm not here to write about the accident. I never was."

"Maybe not, but you're here *because* of the accident. You didn't just pick us randomly from a map. What I don't understand is why you didn't just call and say, *Hi, remember my parents? I'd like to talk to you all.*"

"It wasn't that simple. You were too young to remember it, but immediately after the accident, tensions were high."

"You mean that your aunt behaved like a crazy woman, although how she could possibly have been in a position to form an opinion on what happened when she spent her days working in a Manhattan high-rise is beyond me." She knew she was being unfair, but her sense of betrayal blocked her ability to be calm and rational. Instead all she could think was what it must have been like for Suzanne, physically and emotionally bruised by her own close brush with death, tormented by her own questions as to whether she could somehow have avoided what happened.

Posy had the insight to know her reaction was about more than Luke. It was about Hannah. It was about the complexity of relationships.

"Trudy was close to her sister—" he hesitated "—to my mother. She was distraught."

"I saw the news footage. Your aunt was like a wild animal, yelling and hysterical."

There was one photo in particular that she remembered where Luke's aunt had cornered Suzanne and was clearly shouting. Suzanne had the look of an animal being hunted. It had made Posy feel sick to see that photograph.

Luke took his boots off and walked over to her. "I'm not defending her. And you're right, part of her reaction stemmed from the fact that my aunt didn't understand climbing at all. She lived in a city and worked in an office. She loved art and opera. She didn't understand why her sister chose to climb, she didn't understand the appeal or why anyone would take a risk. We both know there are two types of people in this world—those who understand climbers, and those who don't. Answer a question for me—when you go out on a rescue, are you angry with the people for exposing themselves to the elements?"

Posy stared at him, wrong-footed by the question. "No."

"You go into those mountains, in sometimes lethal weather conditions, to find someone who put themselves in that position through choice. No one forced them to go. It was voluntary. And there you are, having to take Bonnie out into the snow and bad weather. Both of you could be killed. That doesn't make you angry and frustrated?"

Posy stared at him. "Of course not."

"Right. But someone from the outside, who doesn't have that love for the mountains, passion for climbing or understanding of the pull of the outdoors, doesn't get it. You've seen it as often as I have—people being blamed for being 'selfish.' For putting other people's lives at risk. And yet the rescuers themselves don't feel that way. They understand what draws people to the mountains."

"So you're basically saying your aunt's behavior should be forgiven because she didn't understand the whole mountain climbing thing."

"I'm giving you the context for her reaction. And the need to blame someone is a common aspect of grief."

"And she chose to blame Suzanne, who was already traumatized. Did you know that she gave up guiding after that? She never climbed again. She felt responsible."

He took the hit without flinching. "And my aunt contributed to that."

"Yes. And also to the nightmares and the continuing feelings of survivor guilt that never go away. You have no idea." Posy scrambled to her feet and took off her coat, shaking snow over the floor. She wasn't going to be sweet-talked. She wasn't that easy.

"I went through it, too, Posy." For once, he wasn't smiling. "I lost my parents that day."

All the fight went out of her.

She dropped onto the sofa, exhausted and confused.

She felt something wet on her hand and glanced down to see Bonnie licking her.

"Your dog is worried about you." He paused. "And so am I."

"It's a bit late to be worried about me."

"This thing between us—I didn't expect it to happen."

Neither had she, and she didn't know what she was supposed to do about it. "You should leave. I'm taking a group from Edinburgh climbing tomorrow, and I should get some sleep." She levered herself off the sofa. "Close the door behind you."

He hesitated and then walked to the door.

It was only when it was obvious he really *was* leaving that she discovered she didn't want him to.

As he bent to pick up his boots, she stopped him. "I have one question. If Beth hadn't outed you tonight, when would you have told me? Would you have told me?"

"Of course. As for when…" He shrugged. "I was enjoying what we had, and I was afraid to ruin it. I intended to say something as soon as I felt the time was right, but the longer I left it the harder it was to find that time."

"Well, at least that's honest."

He'd lost his parents, too.

And he hadn't uttered a word against Suzanne, even though he wouldn't have been old enough to make his own judgments when they'd died. There must have been times when he'd asked himself if Suzanne was to blame.

He'd also lost his aunt, who had presumably been like a mother to him.

She discovered that she wasn't angry anymore. Life, she knew, was complicated. Also unpredictable and, for some, far too short, which made it all the more important to make the most of every moment of time.

Her sisters wouldn't understand, but that was their problem.

Making a decision, she stood up. "I'm sorry you lost your parents. I'm sorry you've lived with that, too, and I'm sorry I yelled. I'm sure your aunt was a good person." She stood in front of him, the pools of melted snow by the door oozing through her socks and chilling her feet.

"She was a good person. Good people sometimes behave badly."

She had a feeling she'd done just that.

Presumably he was as protective of his family as she was of hers.

Posy put her arms round his neck and rose up on her toes. "Kiss me."

His mouth hovered close to hers. "Does this mean I'm forgiven?"

"I'll let you know." She drew his head down and felt a flash of desire so strong it made her gasp against his lips.

"Are you making your decision on that based on what happens next?" He fumbled with the zip of her jeans. "Because you might give me performance anxiety."

She ripped at his jacket, tugged at the hem of his sweater

and almost stumbled stepping out of her jeans. "I have a feeling you'll cope." She'd never been in such a hurry for anything before, but Luke, for once, didn't share her haste.

There was a flush across his cheekbones, and his breathing was unsteady, but he held her shoulders, keeping her at arm's length.

"There's something else I need to say."

She could barely focus. "Can it wait?"

"No, because I don't want you to accuse me of keeping things from you."

Now what? "Whatever it is, tell me. I should warn you that unless you are about to confess to a series of major crimes likely to earn you a lengthy jail sentence, nothing is likely to make a difference to what happens next."

"In the spirit of honesty and having everything out there, I should confess that I think I may have feelings for you."

Relief mingled with giddy delight. "You only think?"

"It's all new to me."

She had feelings, too, and she wasn't sure if those feelings were a good thing or a complication, and right now she didn't care.

She tugged his shirt out of his jeans. "Let me know when you have it figured out, but in the meantime I think the best thing is if I distract you." She grabbed him and pulled him across her living room toward the bedroom.

They stripped off the rest of their clothes, clumsy in their haste, and he tumbled her down onto the bed, trapping her beneath him.

His mouth was hot and urgent and she responded in kind, slaking her hunger. Even though the relationship was still relatively new, she already knew the feel of his tongue and the touch of his fingers. There was a greed to the way they took from each other, and a generosity in the way they gave.

They rolled so that she was on top and she pushed her fingers into his hair while she drank from the heat of his mouth. The kiss was incredible, electrically charged, desperate, and when she was dizzy with it, drowning, he flipped her onto her back again so that she was underneath him.

He cupped her face with his hand, his gaze locked on hers.

His eyes were a shade somewhere between blue and gray. They made her think of mountains and mist, and of still winter mornings. She'd seen his eyes bright with laughter and gleaming with determination, but right now they were fierce with need.

He'd said he had feelings for her, although he hadn't said what those feeling were, but she saw it in the way he looked at her and felt it in the way he touched her.

Later, they might put words to those feelings, but for now this moment was all that mattered.

She heard the wind rattle the windows, but inside the hayloft it was cozy and warm and here in her bed the temperature was close to scorching.

He lowered his head again, and this time he kissed his way down to her shoulder and then lower, exploring the tips of her breasts with his tongue until she arched under him. She felt the slow slide of his hand over her thigh and the intimate pressure of his fingers as he stroked her with erotic precision.

Her body felt heavy, her brain slow and her thoughts disorientated. She wondered how it was he knew exactly how to touch her. "Don't stop."

"I'm not stopping." Instead he shifted his position and she felt the weight of him, the power of him, and then he sank into her, driving deep, silencing her choked cry of pleasure with his mouth.

For a moment they stayed like that, locked together, all thought suspended by pleasure.

Then he started to move, slowly at first, and she wrapped her limbs around him and arched her hips, matching the rhythm he set, digging her fingers into the hard muscles of his shoulders. She held on to him, needing to feel something solid and safe to counteract the dizzying lightness she felt from being with him.

He kissed her mouth, her jaw, the curve of her neck, all the time keeping up the same relentless rhythm, driving her closer and closer with each measured thrust.

She let go, gave in to it, whispering that she wanted him, needed him. Her heart was hammering, her muscles clenched, and when she tipped over the edge with gut-swooping pleasure, she cried out his name and took him with her, the spasms of her body dragging him to the same point.

Afterward she lay with her head on his chest, feeling the unsteady rise and fall of his chest. She felt weak and achy and totally incapable of moving, but he didn't seem inclined to move, either.

He held her tightly as if he had no intention of letting her go.

He was the first to speak. "I have a question."

She smiled against his skin. "You have to ask?"

"My question isn't performance related." He kissed the top of her head and smoothed her hair back. "When I leave, will you come with me?"

She lifted her head, wishing he hadn't chosen this moment to raise the topic of leaving. "You've booked the barn until March."

"That's the first thought that comes into your head? That you'll have a vacancy?"

Her heart bumped against her chest. "You've become use-ful for mountain rescue training sessions. It's not easy finding volunteers willing to hide in a freezing snow hole while they wait to be found."

"I wonder why." He lifted his hand and wound a wayward strand of her hair around his finger. "So you'll miss your lodger, and your dogsbody. Nothing else? Because it seems to me that although I've laid everything on the line here, you haven't done the same."

"I know." She rolled away from him and lay on her back, staring up at the wooden beams that stretched across her bedroom.

"Is this because you think I wasn't honest with you? For what it's worth, I had a good conversation with Suzanne after you left. It made me wish I'd contacted her sooner."

"That's not the problem."

"Then what is?"

She felt a flash of frustration and something that was close to despair. "I can't just leave, Luke. I can't just walk away from my life."

"I thought you wanted adventures."

"I do."

But the whole thing had become more complicated because now she wanted him, too.

So where did that leave her?

25

Beth

"I didn't even know Hannah was seeing anyone." Beth sat on the floor of the bedroom the following morning wrapping the last of the parcels while Jason kept watch at the door for inquisitive children. She'd packed the children's gifts into separate bags so that she didn't mix them up. "Why do you think she didn't mention it?"

"Presumably because she didn't want to talk about it."

"But she talked about other things." And Beth was still stunned by how unusually open her sister had been about their past and her feelings about the children. On the other hand, judging from the look on her face when Adam had stepped out of the car, there was plenty she hadn't told them about her love life. "We talked about the accident."

"You're kidding." Jason leaned against the door. "You never talk about the accident. Is this because of Luke?"

"I think he was probably the trigger."

"Did it upset you, honey?"

She looked up at him, warmed by his concern. "No. It felt more like relief, because I got to understand how Hannah was thinking and feeling. Also, I realized the accident is part of the reason I'm so anxious about the children."

"I know."

"If you knew, why haven't we ever talked about it?"

"Because you hate talking about the accident. It stresses you." He picked up a roll of tape that had somehow landed at his feet. "But you do worry a lot, and I hate to see it."

"Do you think I've made the children cautious?" That was the last thing she wanted.

"If you'd seen Ruby climbing on the table this morning, you wouldn't be worried. I'm more worried about you. If you want to see someone—talk to someone—"

Beth took the tape from him and cut another length. "I was wondering that myself. I'll think about it."

"I'm pleased you had a good talk with your sisters. Is that why you rescued Hannah downstairs?"

"She looked as if she needed rescuing. I was worried about her." And she was worried about Posy, too, but she'd stomped off before Beth had found a chance to talk to her.

Presumably she'd wanted some space after Hannah's explosion. It must have upset her.

Contemplating the complexity of families, Beth stuck tape on the last parcel. "Done. All ready to stuff into stockings. I can't wait to see the kids' faces on Christmas morning."

"All Ruby wants is Bugsy. I've been on the internet whenever I can get a signal, and I can't find anything that looks remotely like Bugsy. There's a rabbit on eBay, but it looks psychotic and it's the wrong color."

"She's had Bugsy since she was a baby. They've probably discontinued it."

Jason was appalled. "They discontinue popular toys? Where is their sense of responsibility? I feel terrible. Melly says Ruby isn't sleeping well. I'm the worst father in the world. Dammit, we should have bought five spares."

"Spares?" Beth stuffed the bag under the bed. "I'm impressed. That's advanced parenting stuff. A few weeks ago, you wouldn't have thought of that."

"I was a different person a few weeks ago. Or maybe I was the same person but with different priorities. From now on, when we buy something that important to the girls, we buy spares. We should have done it with Bugsy."

"I did."

"You—" Jason stared at her. "What?"

"I bought spares, although not five. I bought three."

"Three?" He breathed an audible sigh of relief. "Then you have two spares back home? That's the best news. You're an incredible mother, Beth."

It was time for a confession.

Beth stretched out her legs and winced. "I'm not incredible."

"But if you have two spares back home—"

"I didn't say I had spares back home."

"But—"

"This isn't the first time Bugsy has taken an unscheduled, unaccompanied trip without leaving a forwarding address."

There was a long silence. "You mean you lost Bugsy, too? When?"

"The first time I lost him was—"

"Wait—there was more than one time?"

Beth squirmed. "I left him in that diner near the park. We

went in for milkshakes one day, and Ruby started having a tantrum—I can't remember why. Everyone was looking at me in that way they do when your kids misbehave. They're all thinking about the way they'd handle it and how you're not doing it right."

"I know that look." He caught her eye. "I didn't use to know that look, it's true, but then I spent time with them. Now I know that look."

"All I wanted was to get out of there as fast as possible, so I threw some notes on the table and—" she dragged in a breath "—I left Bugsy. Right there on the seat. I called them later, but it had gone. So I used a spare Bugsy."

"She didn't notice?"

"I might have roughed him up a little to add to the authenticity."

Jason looked stunned. "And the second time?"

"I left him on the subway."

He rubbed his hand over his jaw. "You're telling me you lost Bugsy twice, and you never said anything? I thought you were perfect."

"No one is perfect, Jason. We're human. We do our best, and that's all anyone can do. You put me on this pedestal, and it was flattering, but it also always made me feel like a failure because I knew I wasn't that woman." She swallowed. "It wasn't only that I felt you didn't know the kids, I felt that you didn't know me, either." It was the most honest she'd been with him.

"I love you. I don't care if you make mistakes. You have no idea how much better it makes me feel to know you lost Bugsy, too." Jason pulled her to her feet. "And, by the way, I still think you're an incredible mother in every way."

"I don't have a spare Bugsy."

He wrapped her in his arms and she felt a rush of desire. "I love you."

"I love you, too."

"Mommy? Can I ride Socks?" Ruby wandered in and they broke apart.

Jason nudged the bag of presents farther under the bed with his foot. "No, honey. It's snowing out there."

"But I like the snow."

"Maybe later if the weather improves, but right now Aunty Posy is busy and there's a storm forecast."

Beth saw Ruby's lip wobble and picked her up. "The best thing to do in this weather is to bake a cake with Grandma. What do you think? We'll do it together, the three of us."

Ruby pondered. "Okay. But I want to ride Socks later."

Beth carried her downstairs to the kitchen and pushed open the door.

The place smelled of cinnamon and cloves and Suzanne was sifting flour into a bowl.

Beth was relieved to see her mother looking relaxed and content.

Ruby wriggled out of Beth's arms and clambered onto a chair. "Can I help?"

"Of course, but what's our first rule when we cook?"

"We wash our hands." Ruby slid off the chair again, hastily washed her hands and then dripped her way back to the table.

Suzanne handed her the spoon and pulled the bowl closer. "Do it gently, so that the flour doesn't fly over the table."

Beth's phone rang. It was Corinna. Her heart started to pound. Tension knotted in her stomach. Last night she'd ignored the call, but she didn't feel she could do it again. Why did she feel such a compulsion to answer it, knowing that Corinna was just using her? Her pulse started to race at the thought of what might happen if she ignored the call again. "I need to take this."

Ruby's face crumpled. "You said you'd cook. You promised."

Guilt was an ache under her ribs. "Start with Grandma, and I'll join you in a minute." Beth caught her mother's eye. "It will only be for a minute. It's important."

Suzanne said nothing. Instead she distracted Ruby, making her giggle by drawing shapes in the cake mix.

Beth stepped out of the room and then stopped.

What was she doing? This was insane.

Hannah was right about Corinna. She was a bully. Beth didn't want to work for a bully.

And there was no obligation on her whatsoever to take this call. She'd call back at a time that suited her, and that wasn't going to be when she was enjoying time with her family at Christmas.

Instead of answering the call, she rejected it and let it go to voice mail.

Maybe she wouldn't bother calling at all.

If she could get a signal, she'd send an email later telling Corinna she was no longer interested in the job.

In the meantime, she was going to bake Christmas cookies with her child.

Her hands were shaking as she pushed the phone into the pocket of her jeans and returned to the kitchen.

Her mother looked at her. "Did you lose the signal?"

"No. I decided to call her back another time." Her hands were actually shaking a little. "Probably a crazy decision."

Her mother smiled. "Sounds like a good decision to me."

Beth was about to join Ruby at the table, when the back door opened and Posy walked in.

She stamped the snow off her boots and unzipped her coat. "It's like the Arctic out there."

Beth searched for evidence that her sister had spent the night crying. Had she and Luke had a confrontation?

Ruby abandoned the cooking and ran across to her. "Can we ride Socks?"

"Not right now." Posy scooped her up and swung her round. "He's in the farthest field and it's freezing. Also, it's snowing again."

"I don't want him to die."

"Die?" Posy stroked Ruby's hair. "Why would you think he'd die?"

Is that my fault? Beth wondered. *Have I taught her to think the worst?*

"Because it's so, so cold," Ruby said, and Posy shook her head.

"He's not going to die. He has a very thick coat, tons of hay, and there's a shelter he can hide in if he needs to." Posy turned as Luke walked in behind her. He was carrying logs and had a backpack slung over his shoulder.

"What are you doing here?" Beth glanced from him to her mother, feeling a rush of protectiveness. Did she want Luke in her kitchen?

Suzanne looked up from the dough she was rolling out. "Bethany Butler, this is my house and everyone is welcome here." She smiled at Luke. "Thank you for the logs. Posy will put them in the basket in the living room. Why don't you sit down and warm up? I'll make some coffee and you can have one of these cookies Ruby and I are baking. Did you bring those photos you promised to show me?"

"I have them here." He pulled a laptop out of the backpack and placed it on the table a safe distance from Ruby's cooking.

Posy left the room to take the logs next door and Beth followed her.

Hannah was curled up on the sofa with a book and Beth wondered why she was alone.

"Where's Adam?"

Hannah didn't look up from her book. "He had to finish a piece of work."

Posy dumped the logs in the basket next to the fire. "I know you didn't want him here and I'm sorry, but the guy flew all the way here from New York, so don't you think you should at least talk to him, Hannah?"

Beth saw Hannah flush and intervened. "You're not exactly in a position to make observations on relationships. You're sleeping with the enemy."

Now it was Posy's turn to flush. "He's not my enemy. Can we all agree that our choices are our own?"

"You are having sex with a man who lied to you. And to Mom."

"In case you missed it, Mom welcomed him into her home."

"That's Mom. She's the most generous person on the planet. This stuff upsets her, Posy!"

"That's true in general, but this isn't upsetting her. And you don't have the monopoly on protecting her. I care about her, too. We all do." Posy straightened. "You think Dad would let Luke through the door if seeing him made Mom feel worse?"

They both knew how protective Stewart was.

"I guess not. But that doesn't mean you have to have a relationship with him. I'm worried about you, too."

"She has a point," Hannah said. "Luke hurt you."

"And last week when I was climbing, I scraped a lump of skin off my hand. Hasn't made me give up climbing." Posy looked annoyed. "You can't live your life too afraid to do things in case you get hurt. If you get hurt, you heal. And while you're lying there healing, you can think about how much fun you had."

Hannah frowned slightly and then went back to her book.

Beth stared into space. *If you get hurt, you heal.*

Her sister was so casual about it. Unlike Hannah and Beth, she didn't spend her life trying never to be hurt. She'd freely entered into a relationship with Luke, apparently relaxed about how that might turn out. Posy did what she wanted to do and had confidence that she could handle what came her way.

Beth wanted to be more like that.

She was about to say something else when Ruby ran into the room.

"Mommy, did you call them about Bugsy again?"

Beth's heart sank. "I did, but so far they haven't found him."

She needed to tell her daughter that she had to learn to live without Bugsy.

This new version of herself needed to start right now by tackling a difficult subject.

"Ruby—"

"I had an idea!" Ruby could barely contain herself. "I could write to Santa!"

"Honey, that isn't—"

"I think it's a great idea." Hannah put her book down. "I'll help you write the letter and you can sign your name. We can use your pretty glitter pens."

As Ruby sprinted from the room to find her sparkly pens, Beth felt a rush of frustration.

"I was about to tell her the truth."

"She believes in Santa." Hannah stood up. "You said you didn't want to spoil that."

"But now you've postponed the misery until Christmas morning. If I have to handle her being upset, I'd rather do it now, but you've made sure I can't."

Hannah paused by the door. "Beth—"

"If you're about to tell me to calm down, then don't. I

know you mean well, but the truth is you don't know anything about children."

There was a hideous silence, and then Hannah turned and
followed Ruby out of the room without saying anything else.

Beth bit her lip. "Now I've upset her."

"What you've done is knock her confidence." Posy sounded
weary. "She doesn't think she's good with kids, and you've
made her feel she's right in that assumption. You should cut
her some slack."

"I'm the one who will have to figure out how to explain
to Ruby on Christmas morning that Santa doesn't always give
us what we ask for, even when we're good."

"Is that such a bad lesson? We don't always get everything
we want—that's a truth of life." Posy watched as the fire flickered to life. "I understand that you want to keep the Santa
thing alive, and that's natural. Christmas is a magical time
when small children are around. But you can't raise kids to believe life is always going to be smooth. Sometimes life throws
rocks at you, and when that happens, they need to learn to
dodge when they can and get back up if they're hit. You need
to teach them to handle the rocks."

"You're saying I'm not a good mom."

"I'm not saying that. I'm saying that being a good mom isn't
just about protecting your kids from hurt, it's about showing
them how to cope with hurt. It's about teaching them resilience
and giving them the tools to handle whatever comes their way."
She walked out of the room and Beth stared after her.

Deep down she was uncomfortably aware that Posy was
right.

She needed to stop protecting her children from every little hurt.

Could she do that?

26

Hannah

The storm hit later that morning, the wind whipping at the windows and roaring through the trees. Some snapped at the roots and came crashing down, others bent and groaned under the pressure.

It sounded as if someone was wailing outside the window.

Hannah wondered if she was the only one who thought it sounded like a baby crying. Or maybe it was a reflection of the fact that all she could think about was the pregnancy.

Beth's words had hurt her.

You don't know anything about children.

And yet here she was, pregnant. She had seven and a half months to figure it out.

Bad parenting could really screw a child up. No one knew

that better than she did, and she didn't want to be the one to ruin a child's life.

She knew she should tell Adam about the pregnancy, but she hadn't got used to the idea herself yet. She hadn't had time to process it herself, let alone work out what she wanted to say to him.

And how could they possibly have a conversation like that under the microscopic gaze of her family? It was excruciating.

She felt as if everyone was watching her and making judgments.

They gathered round the table for lunch, and she was relieved that Luke also joined them.

It reduced the chances of her being asked anything personal.

Adam was seated to her right and Ruby had insisted on sitting to her left.

Hannah was grateful for the excuse to avoid the awkward conversation for a little longer.

"Santa will come, won't he, Aunty Hannah? What if the reindeer can't make it through the snowstorm?"

Hannah caught her sister's eye. "I—well…" She honestly couldn't do this. "He's going to make it."

"But how?"

Hannah was conscious that anything she said was probably going to be the wrong thing. "He's had a lot of practice—I guess he knows what he's doing." Which was more than she did. She didn't have a clue.

"I hope so, because he's bringing Bugsy."

Beth stabbed a spoon into a bowl of roasted parsnips but said nothing.

Suzanne was carving the meat when Posy's phone beeped.

Stewart's beeped at the same time.

Posy dug her phone out of her pocket and seconds later was

on her feet. "Sorry, we need to go. We've got walkers stranded three thousand feet up in blizzard conditions."

Suzanne paused, the knife in her hand. "But you haven't eaten—"

"We'll be fine."

"Can't they send the helicopter?"

"Can't fly in this." Posy grabbed a hunk of bread and spread it thickly with butter. "Too much clag and snow."

Adam reached for his wine. "For the urban uninitiated— what's clag?"

"Thick fog." Posy stole a slice of chicken from the plate. "Zero visibility. Basically no helicopter is flying to help them, which means we'll have to do it on foot." She ate as she walked to the door. "Don't wait up for us."

Suzanne put the knife down. "You think it's going to take that long?"

"Maybe." Stewart grabbed his coat and reached for his boots. "We'll take the tracked vehicle and get as close as possible. Also comes in handy as a storm shelter if we happen to need one."

Hannah felt her stomach lurch. She caught Suzanne's eye. Both of them remembered that night.

Posy whistled to Bonnie, who left her position by Ruby's chair and bounded to the door, tail wagging. "At least someone likes searching in a blizzard."

Luke stood up, too. "Could the team use some help?"

Posy glanced over her shoulder. "Skilled help such as you, definitely. You've already trained with us three times. Are you sure you want to spend your afternoon on an exposed mountaintop where winds are gusting at ninety miles an hour and the wind chill is minus twenty-five?"

"Can't think of a better date."

Hannah was baffled. She didn't understand her sister at all, but Luke seemed to. Maybe they were well suited after all.

There was a flurry of activity. Stewart kissed Suzanne, and then they were gone, the door torn out of their hands by the wind, and then slamming shut behind them.

A moment later they all heard an engine roar to life.

"I apologize, Adam." Suzanne finished carving the chicken. "Family lunches aren't normally as crazy as this one."

Adam stood up and passed her the plates. "I don't find it crazy."

He looked comfortable, which somehow made Hannah feel worse.

Beth looked at Suzanne. "How can you let him go if it worries you so much?"

"Because he's doing something he loves. And so is Posy. I wouldn't want to stop them doing something they love. Does it worry me? Of course. Do I relax for a moment when I know they're out there in the mountains and the weather is bad? No. But I tell myself that they know what they're doing. And neither of them is a risk taker. They don't go looking for danger."

They ate lunch, and then Ruby grabbed Hannah's hand.

"Will you play with me?"

Worried that she'd do something else that would upset her sister, Hannah forced a smile. "I'm not that great at playing, Ruby."

"I'll show you how," Ruby said kindly. "You can learn. All you need is practice. We'll play libraries. I'll bet you're good at libraries because you like books."

Hannah stood up. Why would such a simple statement feel like a thump in the chest? "I'll come and play with you. We can play anything you like." She knew she should be talking to Adam, but the weather was too wild to go for a walk and she didn't fancy hiding away in her room, where anyone walking past could be listening.

Adam stood up. "I have a proposal to finish, so I'll go and do that. Thank you for a delicious lunch."

Hannah played with Ruby for a few hours. It was just the two of them in the downstairs den, and she found herself relaxing.

First they made Christmas decorations, using copious amounts of glue and glitter, much of which landed on Hannah's jeans.

After an hour, Melly joined them. "Can I do your makeup, Aunty Hannah?"

Hannah dutifully sat on the floor while Melly carefully made up her face. She was already covered in glitter. How much worse could she look?

"You're very pretty, Aunty Hannah." Melly turned her attention to Hannah's hair. "You'd look good with ribbons."

Hannah, who had never considered herself a ribbon type of person, sat still while Melly brushed her hair and tied it in a pink ribbon.

She didn't dare look in a mirror.

"It's my turn to play with Aunty Hannah." Ruby grabbed her hand and tugged her across the room. "You need to lie on the floor. I'm going to bury you and then rescue you. You're allowed to scream if you like, because you're very scared. I'll reassure you."

Hannah was hiding under a pile of sofa cushions for the fourth time, when Adam walked into the room.

Ruby was delighted by the arrival of more potential victims. "Would you like to play my rescue game? I'm a firefighter and you're buried."

"That is one of the most appealing offers I've had in a

while," Adam said soberly, "but I was hoping to steal Hannah away. I need her help with numbers."

Ruby was understanding. "She's very smart."

"She is."

Hannah crawled out from under the cushions. She had glitter on her trousers and a ribbon in her hair and she didn't need a mirror to imagine how she looked. In fact, now would probably be a good time to scream.

The corner of Adam's mouth flickered and she stood up, embarrassed. She felt uncomfortable playing with children in front of an audience because she knew she wasn't good at it, although it had to be said that Ruby had been adorably forgiving of her lack of talent.

It's okay, Aunty Hannah. I know you didn't mean to do it wrong—

Still, having Adam witness her inadequacy in the childcare department right before she told him she was pregnant wasn't great timing.

Or maybe it was. At least it should be patently obvious to him why she was nervous.

She followed him to the bedroom and closed the door behind them. "You've been working on the proposal?"

"It's done. I thought you'd like to check it." He glanced at her. "I bet if we were to switch the lights off, you'd glow in the dark. I particularly like the pink ribbon. I hope that's a look you're going to bring back to New York with you."

"My face is itching from all the makeup, but I don't want to take it off."

"Why not?"

"Because I don't want to offend Melly. She's very proud of her work."

He studied her for a moment. "I'm telling myself that you're playing with your nieces because that's what you want to do, and not because you're trying to avoid me. You still haven't told me why you came home early, or why you lied about Posy being ill." He put his hands on her shoulders. "Is this because I pushed our relationship too hard? Does me telling you I love you make you uncomfortable?"

It was so much more complicated than that.

He let go of her. "I shouldn't have come. It wasn't fair on you. I should have called first, but whenever I call, there's either no signal or you don't pick up. I'm a person who, if their route is blocked, takes a different route. You know that about me. It was driving me crazy not being able to see you and talk to you, so after I spoke to Posy, it seemed like the right thing to do." He walked to the window and stared at the sunless sky and the swirl of threatening gray. "It's wild out there. Will your sister be all right?"

Right now she wasn't thinking about Posy, she was thinking about him.

Was it really fair to tell him she was pregnant while he was here, surrounded by her family? There was no neutrality here. No comfortable way of him extracting himself from what could be a hideously awkward situation.

"Posy is good at what she does. She's careful. So is Stewart." Still, she felt a lurch of worry. Suzanne had been good at what she did, too. She'd been careful. "I'd better check on Suzanne. She's going to be worried."

He shifted his gaze from the view to her face. "Why do you call her Suzanne? I noticed that your sisters call her Mom."

"It was my way of keeping some distance."

"Why did you feel you needed to do that?"

She sat down on the bed. This part, at least, she could be honest about. While the wind battered the windows and shook the house, she told him all of it. How her father had always been impatient with her. How she'd felt they hadn't wanted her. How she'd known she wasn't the favorite.

"I didn't have skills they admired."

"I didn't feel that they loved me, and if they didn't love me, why would Suzanne?"

The words flowed surprisingly easily and he listened without interrupting, his gaze fixed on hers, while outside the wind lashed at the windows like a wild animal.

It was only when she finished talking that he spoke.

"You call her Suzanne because you were afraid of getting close to her?"

"It felt safer. Loving someone who doesn't love you back hurts. And you can't make someone love you."

"You don't think Suzanne loves you?"

"I know she does. But at the beginning I felt like a burden. When you've spent a lifetime guarding yourself, it's hard to change."

"You guard yourself with me, too. And I've put extra pressure on you by being here. Go and talk to Suzanne, Hannah. She's going to be worried sick about Posy and Stewart. Your dad."

There was so much more to say, but she had no idea how to say it, so she left the room.

If the weather improved, they could go for a walk tomorrow. It would be easier to talk outdoors.

The kitchen smelled of Christmas and Suzanne was bustling around, an apron tied around her middle.

She smiled as Hannah walked into the room. "I see you've been spending time with Melly."

Hannah touched the pink ribbon ruefully. "What gave me away—the glitter or the ribbon?"

Suzanne pulled a loaf of bread out of the oven. "I think

you've made your niece very happy. I've made two different soups and frozen them, and I'm on my second batch of bread."

"What can I do to help?"

"Nothing. This is how I stay sane when your father and sister are out on the hills. If I'm busy, I don't think." Suzanne eased the loaf out of the tin. "I shouldn't worry, but it's blowing a gale out there, so it's impossible not to. I try not to smother them. Mostly I succeed. I've done a better job with them than I have with you."

"What do you mean?" Hannah picked up a cloth and took the empty loaf tin from Suzanne.

"I worry about you."

"What happened that night damaged all of us in different ways."

"Yes, but we both know that for you much of the damage happened before that night." Suzanne sifted flour into a bowl. "We've never talked about your relationship with your father."

Hannah wasn't sure she wanted to talk about it now. "What is there to talk about?"

Suzanne reached for a bottle of olive oil. "He wasn't an easy man. I hated that you felt you had to try so hard to win his love. You had so many special gifts, and because of him you never valued them. It upset me. Cheryl and I had more than one fight about it."

That was news to Hannah. "I didn't know that."

"I hoped it would change. Maybe it would have done, who knows. But when they died in that horribly sudden, tragic way, I was worried that you'd somehow be left with this feeling that you weren't enough. Seeing you wary about people, believing it was safer to keep your distance, almost broke my heart. I wanted to wrap you up and keep you safe, but the damage was done and you wouldn't let me close."

Hannah felt something stir inside her. "Mom and Dad

dumped us with you. You and Stewart were young—you had your whole lives ahead of you and then out of nowhere you suddenly had three children. All your own plans, dreams, adventures went out of the window." She'd never voiced any of this before. "There must have been so many things you wanted to do that you were never able to do because of us. You had to move because you needed help from Stewart's family, and you never had kids of your own because of us. You gave us so much and I gave you nothing back." And the guilt was always there.

"Having you was a gift. Don't ever doubt that." Suzanne wiped her hands and sat down on the chair next to Hannah. "The truth is, I envied Cheryl her three girls. The three of you were everything I would have wanted in my life. When she died, a part of me felt guilty because I got to have you and she didn't. I was determined to be the best mother possible. Not because I felt I owed it to her, but because that's what I wanted. I wanted to protect you, and see you with the confidence to hand out your love again, knowing it would be valued and accepted. I wanted you to trust someone and feel close to them."

"I trust you, Suzanne." Emotion built inside her, pushing past the barriers she used to keep it inside. "I've always trusted you."

The back door rattled and they both glanced up hopefully, but it was just the wind.

Suzanne glanced at Hannah. "You said that I felt a responsibility and I did, of course. Anyone would in those circumstances. You suffered a shocking bereavement and I was terrified of doing something that would make things worse for you. I couldn't give you your mother back, so I tried to do the next best thing, which was to do things the way I thought she would have done them. At the beginning I was always asking myself, *What would Cheryl do?* I felt as if she was hanging over my shoulder, watching me. I could hear her voice saying, *Relax, Suz, you're too uptight.* That voice drove me crazy, and I drove Stewart crazy. He used to tell me that we had to do it our way, that if you were going to be our kids, then we had to raise you as our kids. We had to decide what was right and how we wanted to do that. I felt out of my depth. Most parents have a chance to prepare, but we became parents overnight. It was less a steep learning curve and more a vertical cliff face."

Hannah thought about how terrified she was about her ability to be a good parent. How much harder would it be to inherit three traumatized children?

"You could have put us up for adoption. You didn't have to put yourself through that."

"It never occurred to me not to take you in. You needed security. I never had security growing up, and it was a horrible feeling. I was never sure that the ground I was standing on wasn't going to give way. I was never sure of anything until I met Cheryl. And then Stewart. I wanted you to know that no matter what, Stewart and I would always be here for you."

"I've always known that." But this was the first time she'd acknowledged it.

She knew there had been times when she'd been difficult to handle. When she'd given nothing back. Last year she hadn't turned up for Christmas at all. And had Suzanne and Stewart made her feel guilty about that? No. They'd been loving and accepting in the same way they always had.

"It became easier over the years," Suzanne said. "I decided that there was more than one way of being a good mother. Maybe I wasn't doing it the way Cheryl would have done it, but I was doing it the way I thought was right. You were my girls. And occasionally I would feel guilty, because I got to have this wonderful family that Cheryl couldn't enjoy."

"Was it hard moving to Scotland?" It was something else she'd often wondered.

"No. It was the best thing we could have done. Back home, everyone knew about Cheryl and Rob. You were 'those poor children.' If we'd stayed, you never would have had a chance to move away from that. The accident would have hung round your necks, and mine. I could see people wondering if I was the reason they died. I asked myself that same question a million times. I didn't need other people asking it, too. Stewart said we were moving so that he could be close to his parents and they could get involved, but he also did it so that we could have a fresh start."

Hannah had always known they'd made a sacrifice. What she hadn't thought about was how brave they'd been. Suzanne's honesty about the problems they'd faced was humbling.

"I don't think I've ever thanked you properly for everything you've done. I'm grateful, I really am."

She should have said it before. She should have told them every single day how wonderful they were.

"Oh, honey, I know. You're a smart, strong, wonderful woman and I'm so proud of you." She squeezed Hannah's hand. "I'm always here, if you need me. I hope you know that."

Hannah realized that her mother—and she did think of her as her mother—always put her family before herself. "Has it upset you, talking to Luke?"

"Quite the opposite. He's living a good life. It does me good to know that. It does me good to know he still goes into the mountains, that he doesn't blame me for his parents' death. He carries the past, of course, but it hasn't shaped him."

It had shaped her, Hannah thought. She'd let it shape her.

She'd let it dominate her choices. Not just the accident, but her relationship with her father.

That was going to change. She didn't know anything about raising a child, but she knew she didn't want it to be afraid of the world. Protecting yourself locked out hurt some of the time, but it locked out the good stuff, too.

"It's good to be home, Mom." She felt relaxed and comfortable in a way that she never had before.

There was a sheen in Suzanne's eyes. "It's good having you home." She cleared her throat and stood up. "Why don't I make us some tea? It's going to be a long night. I thought I'd do homemade pizza for the children. They can help with the toppings. That will occupy them for a while."

"I'll sort out toppings." Hannah went to the fridge and pulled out cheese, olives, mushrooms and ham.

"If you chop them up and put them in bowls, that would be great. Ruby loves putting them on the pizza herself."

Hannah found a knife and a chopping board. She'd never done this before, worked side by side in the kitchen with her mother.

"You're probably wondering about Adam." Hannah sliced ham and dropped it into one of the bowls. "I haven't mentioned him because I—well, my relationships don't usually work out, and then I feel bad that I've disappointed you."

"Disappointed me?" Suzanne abandoned the dough. "You could never disappoint me. I hope I've made that clear tonight."

"I know it's what you want for me."

"All I want is for you to be happy. That's all I've ever wanted." Suzanne brushed the flour from her hands. "I want you to have the best life possible."

Hannah smiled. "You want me to be married with ten kids."

"That's not true." Suzanne smiled, too. "Well, maybe it's

a little true. Ten kids might be a few too many. For what it's worth, I like Adam. He was prepared to take a chance. I like a man who isn't afraid to take a risk for love. It suggests a certain boldness, and I admire that."

She admired it, too. Maybe she'd even find inspiration in it.

"I'm pregnant, Mom." She looked for surprise in Suzanne's face and didn't see it. "You knew? I told Dad, I assumed he'd—"

"Your dad would never discuss anything the two of you talked about in private."

"Then how—"

"I heard you being sick. Posy closed the door and started hollering Christmas carols. Lord knows I love your sister, but I don't love her singing, and given that I'm pretty sure she wasn't doing it for my entertainment, I'm assuming she knows, too."

"She took me to buy a test when I arrived. I should have told you first." And now she wished she had. She wished she'd asked advice instead of keeping everything to herself. "I haven't told Adam. I'm still figuring out how best to do that."

Suzanne nodded. "You're the smartest person I know. You'll work it out. And if you need to talk, I'm here. I'm pleased you felt able to talk to your sister and your dad."

Thinking about her dad made her check the time. "Is it worth calling them?"

Beth clearly had the same thought, because she walked into the kitchen looking anxious. "Should we call Dad and Posy?"

Suzanne shook her head. "Dad will call when he can. I don't want to take his mind off the job."

Beth sat down on the nearest chair. "I hate thinking of them out in this storm. I don't know how you stand it. I'm trying not to catastrophize, but it's not easy." She picked a piece of ham out of the bowl and nibbled on it. "You two are looking serious. Were you talking about Dad?"

Suzanne said nothing and Hannah knew she was leaving the decision on how much to say up to her.

She sat down, too. She didn't know how she was going to do this, but she knew she didn't want to do it alone. "I'm pregnant."

Beth gasped. "You are? That's wonderful. When did you find out? Why didn't you tell me?"

Hannah flushed. "Because you think I'm terrible with children, and right now I don't need another blow to my confidence."

"I do not think that." Beth looked horrified and then contrite. "This is because I overreacted about Ruby and the Santa thing? That is nothing to do with you, and everything to do with my neurotic nature. I'm sorry for being so irritable. Forgive me. How are you feeling?"

"I feel fine." It felt strange to finally talk about it. "A little sick, but that might be psychological. A little tired, but that's probably because I don't sleep well."

"Is Adam pleased?"

"He doesn't know. I haven't told him yet." She waited for Beth to tell her all the reasons why she should do so immediately, but Beth didn't.

Instead she nodded. "The tiredness could be because of the pregnancy. I remember when I was expecting Melly, I was exhausted from about seven weeks. And I was working then, of course, as you are. That makes it tougher. I used to fall asleep on the sofa every day when I got in from work. Jason used to have to wake me up to eat dinner. It was grim. Then it passed and I was really energetic for a few months, until right at the end."

"I remember that." Suzanne put mugs of tea in front of them. "You used to call me and talk about it."

Hannah cupped her hands around the mug. "You think it will pass?"

"I'm sure it will. For me it was around thirteen weeks, I think." Beth frowned. "Or maybe it was twelve. It's hard to remember. I'm going to email you the details of my doctor, because she was brilliant. You don't want them to do a ton of tests you don't need."

She hadn't even got as far as thinking about doctors or tests.

She felt a little overwhelmed by how much she didn't know, then realized that Beth seemed to know all of it.

"I'll swap you career coaching for baby advice."

Beth grinned. "Done."

"Do you have books you can lend me?"

"Yes, but I've read them all and had two kids, so you can just ask me. The only thing I can't help you with is how not to worry. You're on your own with that. You're going to be a brilliant mother, Hannah. There's never been anything you're not good at."

"Climbing." Hannah gave a faint smile. "I'm terrible at climbing."

"Me, too." Beth stole an olive from the bowl. "And it's hell on the nails."

Suzanne laughed. "It was the helmet you used to hate most. Made a mess of your hair."

Beth stroked her smooth, silky hair. "It's all about priorities. I like to look my best, and I don't look my best when I'm hanging from a rock screaming with fear." She leaned forward. "If you need company for your first appointment, call me. I'll come with you."

That offer melted the last of Hannah's reserve.

Whatever had made her think she had to handle this alone?

Whatever happened with Adam, she had her sister. Both her sisters. She had her family.

"Thank you."

"I should be the one thanking you! I can't believe Ruby and Melly are going to have a cousin. And Jason will be a very engaged uncle, which should satisfy his need for another baby in the family. Hold that thought." She glanced toward the door. "I hear the patter of not so tiny feet."

Seconds later, Melly came into the room clutching Betsy, Beth's ancient doll.

"I don't like the wind, Grandma. Will the roof blow off? Will it be like the *Wizard of Oz*?"

"No, honey. Stay in the kitchen. It's not as loud in here. Do you want to make pizza with us?"

Ruby trailed into the kitchen after her sister. "I want a cuddle." But instead of going to Beth, she went to Hannah.

Hannah hesitated and then bent and scooped her up.

She rubbed Ruby's back and talked to her, remembering all the times she'd done the same thing with Posy.

Suzanne was right. There was more than one way of being a good mother.

She just had to find the way that worked for her.

She wasn't going to let the past shape her future.

In the morning, she was going to talk to Adam.

She'd waited long enough.

27

Posy

Posy arrived back at 3:00 a.m., cold and tired.

She stripped off her outdoor gear, crawled on top of her bed and fell asleep with the rest of her clothes on. She slept like the dead, unmoving, and then woke again at eight, freezing cold and aching all over. Bonnie was still curled up asleep, snuggled in the remains of the heat from the log burner.

Dragging herself to the shower, Posy stepped under the scalding jets and tried to warm herself. She had a massive bruise on her thigh where she'd slipped and fallen, and a graze on her cheek from a rock that had been dislodged by someone's foot and made contact with her face.

She stepped out of the shower and examined herself in the mirror.

She looked a mess. If she borrowed some of Beth's makeup, she might be able to hide it from her mother.

Bonnie padded over to her and gave her a worried tail wag.

"Don't you start. And you don't look so great yourself, by the way," Posy told her. "Definitely a bad hair day."

It had been a long and difficult rescue, with the weather some of the worst she'd experienced.

She pulled on a warm, dry sweater and was drying her hair when there was a knock on the door.

"You can come in. You don't usually wait to be invited." She'd expected Luke, but it was Hannah.

Her heart plummeted.

They hadn't spoken properly since Hannah had yelled at her.

Did they have to do this now?

Yes, she felt guilty, but she didn't have the energy to take a pummeling from her sister. She was physically and mentally exhausted.

On the other hand, she'd done the wrong thing. Hannah was having a rough time, and she'd inadvertently made things harder.

She rubbed the sleep from her eyes and took a closer look at her sister. "You look tired. Late night?"

"I went to bed at the same time you did."

"What?" Posy pulled her damp hair into a ponytail. "Why?"

"I kept Mom company until you both came home."

Mom.

Posy wondered if her sister realized what she'd said. "That was nice of you."

Hannah was shivering. "Posy—"

"Is this about Luke? Are you and Beth staging an intervention?"

"No, I—"

"If it's not Luke, then that means you've come because you still blame me for the fact Adam is here."

"That isn't—" Hannah glanced at Posy's bare legs and gasped. "Your leg is purple. What happened?"

"I fell. It happens. Don't tell Mom or she'll worry, and don't tell the rest of the team or they'll laugh."

"Shouldn't you go to the emergency department?"

"It's a bruise." Posy opened the door wider. "Come in, before it turns into a bruise and frostbite."

"Have you put ice on it?" Horror on her face, Hannah hurried to the freezer and pulled out a bag of frozen peas and wrapped it in a towel. "Press this against it."

"Like I'm not cold enough already. And since when have you been a first aid expert?" But she was touched and more than a little relieved that her sister no longer seemed to be angry with her. She pressed the peas to her leg. "I owe you an apology. I was going to talk to you yesterday, but we were called out before I could get you alone. Did you seriously stay up with Mom?"

"Yes. Neither of us could sleep, so we sat by the fire and talked for ages, about everything. It was cozy." She rubbed her arms and Posy put the peas down.

"I'll light the log burner. You're cold because you have no fat on you."

"If you're going to make a joke about pizza—"

"I'm not. After the night I had, my sense of humor has fused. I need coffee." Posy lit the fire and walked to the kitchen. Something was obviously wrong with her sister and she fished around for the right question to ask.

She made coffee and handed her sister a mug. "Look, about what I did—"

"It doesn't matter."

"It does. I shouldn't have said what I said on the phone to

him even as a joke. I shouldn't have talked to him for so long without hammering on the bathroom door, but he sounded nice and he said he was in love with you and—" she shook her head "—and now I'm sounding like Mom. Sorry. From now on, I'm not interfering in anyone's love life ever again. I'm here for sympathy, and nothing else. But for what it's worth, I'm sorry I made things harder for you. It must be really awkward."

"It's not awkward." Hannah closed her hands round the mug to warm herself. "He's gone." She walked to the windows, keeping her back to Posy. "You can see for miles from up here. It's like living in the treetops."

"Wait—did you say *gone*? You sent him away? Are you *insane*?"

"What happened to not interfering or even passing an opinion?"

"It sounded good in theory, but in practice I find I can't sit here while you tell me that perfect piece of manhood has gone. What exactly are you looking for? I mean, he's gorgeous, he was sweet with the kids and he *obviously* loved you. Why would you send him away?"

"I didn't." Hannah turned. "When I woke up this morning, he'd left. He got a car to the airport."

"How? Have the roads been cleared?"

"I don't know how, but Adam would have found a way. He always finds a way. He's a fixer. If there's a way of doing something, Adam will find it. He's that type of person."

Posy thumped her mug down on the countertop. "You didn't know he was leaving? This is how he responds to you telling him you're pregnant? Because I swear I'll—"

"I haven't told him."

"He didn't leave because of the baby?"

"No. He left a note saying that he shouldn't have come.

That it hadn't been fair of him to put that pressure on me. He thought a conversation about it would put even more pressure on me, so he made a unilateral decision."

"Why didn't you tell me this right away?"

"I tried to, but you seemed to think I'd come here to black your eye."

"So he left because he was being thoughtful." *Stupid man.* Posy had never felt more out of her depth in her life. She had nothing wise or sensible to say on the subject of relationships. Give her a vertical ice face any day. "And you're relieved he's gone."

"I'm not relieved." Hannah's eyes filled. "I spent half the night working out what I was going to say to him, and when I was finally ready to say it, I wake up and he's not there."

"You were going to tell him about the baby?"

"All of it. That I love him. That I'm pregnant—" She choked on the words. "Mom and I talked for ages last night. We talked about Luke—"

"Luke?"

"About how he hasn't let the accident influence the choices he has made. And I realized I've let the accident, and my relationship with our father, influence almost every decision I've made. Beth is overprotective of her kids, Mom is overprotective of me and I'm overprotective of myself! I use avoidance to protect myself from hurt and it has to stop."

Posy found it hard to believe she was looking at her strong, secure, sorted sister. "I see that, but you're assuming he'll hurt you. Maybe he won't." She wished she wasn't handling this conversation on less than five hours of sleep. "I don't have anything wise and expert to say. I wish I did. But I do know Adam is a decent guy. A good guy. And I think you already love him, so how is it going to hurt less if you send him away?"

Hannah sniffed. "Since when did you get so good at logic and reasoning?"

"Since I've been spending time with my exceptionally smart older sister," Posy said.

"I don't think I'm brave enough for love. You throw yourself into it. Look how you are with Luke—*we'll see how it goes*—you don't try and protect yourself. You don't worry about what happens if it goes wrong. You treat love the same way you treat the mountains—you just get out there and savor every moment."

"Because I've been lucky. I've never doubted I was loved, Hannah. I've never felt I had to change, or that I wasn't good enough."

Posy put her arms round her sister and felt her tense.

"What are you doing?"

"I'm hugging you. I'm reminding you that whatever happens, you're not on your own. If you're asking me how to love without being hurt, I don't know the answer, but if you're asking me if it's worth risking hurt to have love in your life, then my answer is yes." She hoped she wasn't being too glib about it. If Luke ended up breaking her heart, would she feel it was worth it?

She stood for a moment wondering if she'd said the wrong thing, and then Hannah hugged her back.

"I missed you."

Posy's throat thickened. "Missed you, too. You couldn't handle me being hurt, but look at me now." She squeezed her sister tightly. "I don't remember the pain, Hannah. I only remember the love. And that's because of you. You surrounded me with love. That's my earliest memory. If I'm confident and secure, it's because of you."

Hannah pulled away so sharply Posy almost lost her balance. "I need you to do something for me, before I change my mind."

"Name it."

"I need you to tell me which cab company might be able to cope with the weather conditions. I could do it myself, but it will take too long. I want to go to the airport. I'm going after Adam, and I want to do it right now before I change my mind."

Posy grabbed her jeans from the back of the chair and pulled them on. "I'm your cab. And I don't charge. You're going to tell him you're pregnant? Let's do this." She gulped down the remains of her coffee and grabbed her coat. "Call him right now and stop him getting on that plane. We need reinforcements. Where's my phone?" She found it in her coat pocket and for once had a good signal. She called Beth, who answered in a sleepy voice. "Wake up! We'll meet you by the car in five minutes… I know you normally need more than five minutes to get ready, but just this once please rise to the occasion. It's a weather emergency." She used their childhood code. "Are you listening? You can do your makeup in the car."

Hannah shook her head. "Why did you wake Beth up?"

"Because this mission may require two of us. One to drive, and one to stop you changing your mind and jumping out of the car. Also, Beth will want to be part of this. You should probably tell her you're pregnant. She might be able to help you."

"I told her last night. And I told Mom."

Posy felt a rush of relief that she no longer had to watch what she said, but also a warmth that Hannah had felt able to tell them. "I'm glad."

"The only person I haven't told is Adam. Maybe this is a stupid idea. The airport isn't the best place to have a conversation like this."

"Call him." Posy felt almost as desperate as her sister because she knew this situation was partly her fault. "Please call him."

Hannah fumbled for her phone. "The signal has gone."

"Then we'd better hope the planes are iced up and delayed. Move!" Posy grabbed her keys and sprinted down the lane toward the car.

Beth was standing there, her hair tangled and her face free of makeup.

"What's wrong?" She stifled a yawn. "For the first time ever, the kids sleep late and I get woken by my sister."

"Stop whining. This is a crisis."

"And I'm here. I answered your SOS. I just wish you'd chosen to have your crisis at a more civilized time."

"It's not my crisis. Get in the car." Posy sprang behind the wheel and Hannah slid in behind her. Beth climbed in next to her and had hardly closed the door before Posy pressed her foot to the floor.

The car screeched out of the drive, bumping over potholes and skidding.

"We're going to die," Beth said, "and I can't die without saying sorry to Hannah." She twisted in her seat. "I really didn't mean to yell at you about the whole Santa thing. I feel terrible about it."

"It's okay," Hannah said, and Beth shook her head.

"It's not okay. I've been thinking about it all night. I really am sorry. You are sweet with the girls, and they're loving spending time with you. And Posy is right that they need to learn they can't have everything they want and I need to relax more and learn to handle them not being happy the whole time. I'm trying—I really am, but I'm a work in progress. If we survive this car ride, I swear I'm going to try harder."

"*If* we survive?" Posy shifted gears and Beth groaned.

"I'm doing it again, aren't I? Catastrophizing?"

"You're doing it again."

"I'm not that brave, that's all. I'm the sister who liked to play with dolls, not knives. And on that subject, I'd rather not arrive at the airport with blood smeared on my face. It's not a good look. Could someone at least tell me why I'm risking my life? And it had better be good."

A moment before, Posy had been exhausted, but now she felt energized. "We are chasing love. More specifically, we are going to catch Adam before he gets on that plane."

"Why didn't you say so right away?" Beth brightened. "That's so romantic. I love it." She reached back and squeezed Hannah's leg. "It's like the movies. We all need makeup. Good thing I carry an emergency supply kit, just in case."

Posy grinned. "Because a makeup catastrophe is the worst catastrophe of all." She glanced at the tubes and bottles that appeared on her sister's lap. "My emergency supply kit includes dressings, sutures, a tourniquet—"

"We encounter different types of emergencies." Beth applied her makeup with the speed of a pro. "Try to hold the car steady."

Posy contemplated swerving to be annoying but decided it wasn't worth having to deal with the fallout. "I don't know why you're bothering. You're not the one declaring your love to a man."

"I'm an extra. Extras get hair and makeup, too." She clutched the door as Posy sped along the road. "And when the paramedics come to cut me out of the car, I want to look my best. Do you want to borrow my lipstick, Hannah? A little blush? You look as if you've been sucked dry by a vampire."

"Unlike you, I can't do my makeup in a moving car."

"Give me a time check. How long do we have?" Posy glanced in her mirror at Hannah, who was pale and tense. Beth was right; she needed color in her cheeks.

"I've checked the departures and there's a flight leaving in an hour. I'm guessing he'll be on that one. I'm not even sure I want to do this. I don't even know what to say."

"You're going to tell him the truth. You're going to tell him you love him. You're going to tell him you're pregnant." Posy swung round a corner and Beth grabbed the door to steady herself.

"I'm excited about this, by the way. I like the idea of being an aunty. I get to have all the very best bits of having a baby without the exhausting stuff."

"Shut up," Posy said, "or the next time I swing round a corner I'm opening the car door."

"All I'm saying is that it's going to be wonderful. This is thrilling news."

Hannah closed her eyes. "*Terrifying* is my word of choice."

"We all need to be braver." Posy gripped the wheel as the tires slewed from under her. "Okay, hold on there, I've got this—no one panic."

"It's a bit late for that." Beth reached back and handed Hannah her makeup. "You're the bravest person I know. I couldn't walk into a room with all those scary CEOs and tell them what to do, and yet you do it all the time. You open a spreadsheet and those numbers mean something to you. They'd give me a panic attack. And you can talk to anyone because you are so well-read you are never stuck for conversation. I know it's not the same thing and you'll probably laugh at me, but I was terrified going to meet Corinna that day. I felt like a fraud. So I have a trick I use whenever I'm scared."

Hannah poked around in the makeup bag and pulled out a lipstick. "Which is?"

Beth flushed. "I pretend I'm in a movie."

"A movie?" Posy peered through the snow and wondered

how fast she dared drive. "Which movie? Something scary and terrifying, I hope. Preferably with dinosaurs."

"Whatever movie fits the scenario. It's easier to pretend I'm playing a character than it is to be me. For that interview with Corinna I felt like a fraud. But I dressed the part, and the boots nearly killed me by the way, and before I got in the elevator I told myself I was in a movie, and I was playing a bright young thing who was going to turn the company around."

Hannah eyed the road ahead, then took a chance and swept the lipstick over her lips. "So I need to think of a movie where a woman chases through an airport to tell a man she loves him?"

"You can write your own movie," Beth said. "But the part you're playing is a beautiful, confident woman with great legs and incredible hair—"

"Shallow as a rock pool," Posy muttered. "I would have gone with big heart."

"For example," Beth said, "on the outside you look sleek and together. No one would guess that you're plotting how to do away with your younger sister."

"I'm the one driving her to the airport."

Hannah handed the makeup back. "So I'm a character who is chasing through an airport to tell a man she loves him. Why didn't I tell him before now? Why leave it until the last minute? Maybe my character is a wimp, like me."

"Your character is a spy." Beth found a blusher and handed it back to Hannah. "Use this. You're a beautiful spy and he's a spy, too, for the opposite side, so you've both been fighting what you're feeling. Your name is Hannahskya, or Hannahova."

"Hannah Over sounds like a call sign." Posy snorted with laughter. "Hannah, Over and Out. There is no way I'd go and see this movie, by the way. It's going to be a flop at the box office."

Beth ignored her. "You are both about to embark on dangerous missions, but you have this one last chance to tell him how you feel before you are dropped from an airplane over the mountains of Kazakhstan."

"There are some great mountains in Kazakhstan," Posy said. "You could drop me there any day."

No one was listening to her.

But Hannah did appear to be listening to Beth.

"What if he rejects me?"

Posy heard the vulnerability in her voice.

"He's not going to."

Hannah was silent. "I wish I had your confidence. We're assuming we can even catch him before he flies. He's not responding to my call. Maybe he doesn't want to talk to me."

"He's probably already on a call. You're always on the phone and the two of you seem well matched. If you ever get married, you can include that in your vows—'Do you take this woman and her phone…'"

Posy beeped as a driver pulled out in front of her. "What does he think he's doing?"

"It's you I'm worried about." Beth covered her eyes with her hands. "I've been on fairground rides less scary than this. And that's a statement of fact, not catastrophizing."

"I'm pretending I'm in a movie. I'm playing the part of a getaway driver in a heist." Posy noticed Beth fiddling with her phone. "Who are you texting?"

"Jason. I want him to know that I love him and the girls, in case anything happens to me."

"Look on the bright side. Thanks to you at least he now knows how to take care of the kids."

"If it's all the same to you, I'd rather he didn't have to. And, by the way, it is not going to make Mom's Christmas if all three of us die in the same accident."

"Catastrophizing!" they all yelled and then started to laugh.

"We're here!" Posy saw the lights of the airport in the distance. "I'm going to pull up outside and you are going to race into the airport. Try calling him again."

"I tried a moment ago. His phone is going to voice mail."

"Then leave a message. Try again because the tension is killing me. I know this is partly my fault."

"It's not your fault." Hannah was trying to smooth her hair with her fingers. "It's my fault. If I wasn't so messed up about relationships, I would have told him the truth back in Manhattan instead of running home."

"Leave the damn message!" Posy swerved out a lane to overtake two more cars and then swerved back again.

Hannah left a message. "Adam, it's me. If you get this in time, I was thinking— I just wanted to say—"

"Don't get on that plane! She loves you," Posy and Beth yelled together, and Hannah hung up.

"That was embarrassing. You do realize he is actually going to listen to that at some point, don't you?"

"Yes, and we are hoping that point is going to be sooner rather than later. Now get out of the car and run. This is not the time to worry about rejection." Posy screeched to a halt outside departures and Hannah stumbled from the car.

"Where will you be? How will I find you?"

"We'll find you." Posy watched Hannah fly into the airport terminal and wondered if she might be even more nervous than her sister. Adam had probably already left. Or maybe he'd had enough of trying to get Hannah to open up.

What if this had been another of her terrible ideas? The last one hadn't exactly turned out well.

"Follow her, Beth." She pushed her sister out of the car. "I'll park and meet you in there."

"I don't want to get in the way! You can't have three people in a love scene."

"Then pretend you're an extra! Play the part of an interested bystander or something, but keep an eye on her. If this goes badly, she is going to be in pieces. We're the ones who are going to pick those pieces up."

Maybe she hadn't always been the best sister—in fact, she knew she hadn't—but it wasn't too late to make up for it.

28

Hannah

"Excuse me, so sorry—" Hannah sprinted, weaving through people and luggage as she ran.

The airport was packed with people setting off on their Christmas getaway, making forward motion harder. She bumped into people and sent parcels swinging into legs. She dodged trolleys and jumped over bags. Her usual dignity and restraint had abandoned her, which was bad news for anyone in her path.

She collided with a man loaded down with luggage and gasped out an apology, before surging forward and catching another person with her elbow. "So sorry, it's an emergency—"

Parents grabbed children and pulled them out of her way, sending her looks that would have singed the ends of her hair if she hadn't been moving so fast.

She felt desperate, wild, determined to reach Adam before he left. Determined to speak before she lost her nerve.

She had to tell him that she loved him. She had to explain everything, even if he rejected her afterward. She had to *know*.

She raced toward security, scanning the line of people waiting to go through to the departure lounge. She saw harassed parents, a few tired-looking businesswomen, impatient men, but no Adam.

And then she heard the final call for the flight and realized he must already be in the departure lounge.

The disappointment was like a physical blow. She stopped running and bent double, her breath coming in tearing pants.

She was too late.

She waited for the stitch in her side to ease and for her breathing to slow to something close to normal, and then she lifted her head.

Tears burned her eyes and she turned away, intending to walk back to the car, when she spotted a tall, dark-haired man striding toward her carrying an overnight bag.

"Adam!"

Her legs shook suddenly, and then his smile wrapped itself around her heart and joy exploded inside her.

She raced to meet him and he caught her to him with his free arm, hugging her tightly.

"I thought you'd left." She clung to him, her face buried in his shoulder. "I thought I was too late."

"I was about to board when I picked up your message." He dropped his suitcase and took her face in his hands. "That thing you said—could you say it again?"

What had she said? The whole car journey had been a blur. "I told you not to board—"

"Not that part."

"My sisters told you that I'm in love with you."

"That part." His eyes darkened. "I don't suppose you'd like to say it yourself, would you? I prefer to go direct to the source for my information."

"I love you."

He hauled her close, kissing her hair and her face. "Do you know how long I've waited to hear you say that?"

"Awhile, I guess. You're a patient man."

"*Desperate* would be a better word." He crushed his mouth to hers. "I almost didn't switch my phone on. Can you imagine how I would have felt if I hadn't picked up that message until New York? You know how to keep a man in suspense. Why did you wait for me to leave to say it?"

"Because I'm stupid and cowardly. People think I'm reserved and unapproachable. They think I don't feel emotion."

"Oh, honey—" he lowered his forehead to hers "—you're not cold. And you feel plenty of emotion. You're just not that great at expressing it."

The fact that he understood brought tears to her eyes. "I'll try harder."

"Don't. Our relationship isn't an exam you have to pass." He brushed away her tears with the pad of his thumb. "I don't want you to change. When have I ever indicated that I want you to change?"

He hadn't, she thought. Not once. "I've never felt particularly lovable."

"Then I need to work harder at showing you that you are."

She clung to him, feeling the hard swell of his biceps through the soft wool of his coat. "There's something else I have to say."

"You can say it as many times as you like. I'm not going to stop you, but we could consider going somewhere more private."

"In a minute." She had to do it now, all of it, before she

changed her mind. She was vaguely aware of people glancing in her direction on their way to passport control. "You asked me why I came home early—"

"You panicked. You were scared of my feelings, and scared of your own." He pushed her hair back from her face, his hand gentle.

She felt her heart ache. "That's not the reason." She spoke before she could think of all the reasons why she probably shouldn't. "I'm pregnant, Adam. I'm going to have a baby. And I know that's a shock. I mean we used— I've thought about it, and I think there was one time—"

He stilled. His hand dropped to his side. "Pregnant?"

"Yes." She waited, hoping for the best even while her fragile heart expected the worst. "It doesn't have to make a difference. I don't want you to feel pressure. I can handle it. There's any number of ways we can— And if you don't, I can…" *Why was she so bad at this?*

"Pressure?" He looked stunned. "This is why you ran that day? The reason you came home early?"

"I didn't know for sure then. I hadn't done the test. I did that when I arrived here. I imagine you're feeling—"

"Why don't you stop imagining how I'm feeling and ask me?"

Her heart was thudding. "How do you feel about it?"

"I'm shocked, obviously, but not in a bad way. I wish you'd told me right away. That's a hell of a lot for you to be handling on your own. No wonder you were so stressed."

"I'm not as evolved as you are. I needed time to figure out how I felt." She was barely aware of her surroundings, of the echo of announcements and the people flowing around them.

"I hate to think of you panicking by yourself."

"I'm used to handling things by myself. And I wasn't really by myself. I panicked with Posy, and then with Beth and my mom."

Adam's eyes narrowed. "You called her mom."

Hannah felt herself flush. "Yes."

"I didn't think you were close to your family."

"We weren't, but—" she shrugged "—we've talked quite a bit lately, and it turns out we're a lot closer than I thought."

He smiled. "That's good."

"Yes. Yes, it is, but—"

"But?"

"The relationship I really need to fix is the one I have with you. And I have no idea what happens now. You've never been interested in anything long-term."

"That was before I met you. Before I fell in love with you. Does that sound like a cliché? If so, I'm sorry. You want me to prove I love you?" He raked his fingers through his hair, his breathing unsteady. "I'd never played chess before I met you."

She stared at him. "You said you played."

"Because you challenged me to a game, and I was so crazy about you I would have said yes to anything. Alligator wrestling, snake charming, ballet dancing—actually, maybe not ballet dancing, but pretty much anything else—I would have had a go."

She thought back. "But we played together. You won twice."

"I'll pretend not to notice that you've memorized how many times I won." He moved her to one side as a family of five thundered past with suitcases. "I taught myself from YouTube. And from some insanely frustrating program that lets you play against a computer, which, by the way, I don't recommend. You're as good as the computer and a hell of a lot sexier."

"You learned chess so you could play with me?"

"Yes. And I also had myself switched to the Carlton Myers

Account so that I would have an excuse to work with you and stay late in the office."

"You said you had a keen interest in their business model."

"I lied. The only thing I had a keen interest in was you."

She was staring. She knew she was staring. "I had no idea."

"I know. I took hideous advantage of your trusting nature." He lowered his mouth to hers and kissed her briefly. "And I flew all the way here without calling first because I didn't want to give you a chance to turn me away. And I left, even though it killed me to do it, because I thought that was what you wanted. Are you crying? God, I've made you cry and that is the *last* thing I wanted to do." Appalled, he brushed away her tears with his fingers.

"They're happy tears." She leaned her head against his chest, her heart full. He'd learned chess so he could play with her. Switched accounts. Crossed an ocean. "I wish I'd talked to you sooner."

"So do I, then you might have saved me a terrifying car ride with a cabdriver who didn't seem to notice the ice on the roads."

She felt his arms come around her, locking her against him. It felt good, she realized. Leaning on him felt good.

She lifted her head and met his gaze. "It's quite a leap from man about town to daddy."

"I've always been pretty athletic." His smile had gone and this time his expression was serious. "I can make that leap, Hannah. We'll make it together."

She smiled through her tears. "I don't know much about babies."

"Then it's a good thing there are two of us to figure it out."

She put her arms round his neck. "So what do we do now?"

He tilted his head and listened to the announcement. "I just officially missed my flight, so I guess I'm going to need somewhere to stay tonight. And tomorrow is Christmas Eve, so I doubt I'll be able to get a flight then, either. I don't suppose you have any suggestions?"

"I might have some ideas." She kept hold of him, too afraid of letting him go. "Can you handle my family, or would you rather stay at the inn?"

"That depends," he said. "Do you think your father will punch me for making you pregnant?"

"I think he's more likely to pour you a whiskey and shake your hand."

"In that case what are we waiting for?" He took her hand and picked up his suitcase. "How did you get here? Did you drive on those lethal roads?"

"Posy drove. She's the adrenaline junkie of the family. She could definitely have a career as a racing driver. I was so afraid I might have missed you. I don't know what I would have done if you'd already left."

He lifted his head and smiled. "I have a suspicion you would have been all right."

She followed his gaze and saw Posy and Beth standing a discreet distance away. Their arms were linked and they both looked anxious.

When Hannah smiled, they both whooped and ran across to them.

"There is no way Posy is driving us home," Beth said. "I've been given a second chance at life, and I'd like to take it. And that is *not* catastrophizing."

29

Suzanne

On Christmas morning Suzanne was up early to make pan-cakes for breakfast with her grandchildren.

The storm had passed. Fresh snow layered the paths and loaded the trees, the surface glistening in the sunlight. Until Stewart had time to clear it, they were snowed in. Which was, she thought, a perfect way to spend Christmas.

She rinsed fresh berries and took a moment to enjoy the view from her window. It was a picture-book day, the tops of the mountains sharp and clear in the early-morning sunshine. The sky was a rich Mediterranean blue, although she knew the temperatures would be Arctic.

It was a day for wearing thick socks and soft sweaters, for gathering round the Christmas tree and sipping hot drinks in front of the flickering fire.

This morning she'd woken feeling better. Her headache had gone, her limbs no longer ached and she finally felt energetic again.

Better still, the tension that was so often a part of Christmas was absent.

She'd finished knitting the Christmas stockings, but there were things on her list she hadn't done. Normally that would have stressed her, but this year it didn't seem to matter. It didn't matter that she hadn't made the extra puddings as planned, or that she hadn't had time to roast chestnuts.

"Grandma?" Ruby's voice came from behind her. "The mixture is lumpy."

She turned her attention back to her grandchildren.

Ruby wore a sweater and socks over her pajamas, and her hair was caught up in bunches that Melly had carefully secured with tartan ribbon.

She looked so much like Posy at the same age that Suzanne caught her breath.

"Keep whisking. These pancakes are going to be delicious."

They'd come a long way. Such a long way.

She heated the pan and Melly climbed onto a chair to help with the cooking.

Suzanne stood close enough to intervene at the first sign of danger, but Melly was careful, her tongue caught between her teeth as she concentrated and flipped each one carefully.

The pile of soft, fluffy pancakes on the plate grew. When the mixture was finished, they put the plate on the table, along with the berries and a jar of the Scottish heather honey that Suzanne sold in the café, and Melly ran out of the room to call everyone to the table.

The wind had stopped howling the day before and there was a stillness and calm.

"Granny, do you think I can ride Socks today?"

"We'll ask Aunty Posy when she wakes up."

"Will she wake up soon? I woke up at five o'clock, but Melly was asleep, so I lay there and didn't move."

"You're a thoughtful girl."

Stewart emerged, his hair spiky from the shower. "I need to clear the paths. Posy and Luke will struggle to get from the barn."

"She's in the mountain rescue team. If she can't find a way to get through the snow, there's no hope for the rest of us. Sit down for a minute." Suzanne rummaged in the cupboard for a jar of her whiskey marmalade, which she knew was Jason's favorite. She'd given away so many as gifts she had only one left. "The pancakes are warm and the coffee is brewing. Merry Christmas."

Stewart kissed her, taking his time over it. "Merry Christmas. You're looking unusually relaxed. Usually by now you're running round slamming turkeys into ovens."

"I feel unusually relaxed."

"It's because I've been helping her." Ruby climbed onto a chair. "Merry Christmas, Grandpa. Santa came."

"That's good news. Glad his sleigh didn't get stuck in all that snow."

Ruby looked at him pityingly. "The reindeer fly."

"Of course they do. There are days when I wish I could fly, too."

"Will you have to go and rescue people today, Grandpa?"

"I hope not." He sat down next to her. "I plan on playing with my grandchildren and eating my Christmas lunch. Let's hope everyone else does the same and that no one gets into trouble today."

"Why did those people get in trouble? Were they naughty?"

"The people the other night? No, they weren't naughty.

But they didn't have all the skills they needed for the walk they planned. Do you know what a compass is?"

"I know." Melly sat on the other side of him. She was wearing a new princess costume that Suzanne assumed had been a gift from Santa. "It's something that tells you which direction to go."

"That's right. But these people—" Stewart served the girls pancakes and then added two to his own plate "—they put their compass in the same pocket as their mobile phone."

"Was that bad?" Ruby stuck her spoon in the honey, dribbling most of it over the table instead of her pancakes.

"Turns out it was bad, because the case for the mobile phone had a metal closure and that reversed the polarity."

Suzanne poured herself coffee. "Grandpa means that the compass gave them the wrong information and they went in the wrong direction."

Jason walked through the door, yawning. "That happens? Seriously?"

"Yes. North became south, and that's the way they walked. Unfortunately, south wasn't where the road was, so they became lost."

"And you rescued them," Ruby said, jumping off her seat to run to her father. "Merry Christmas! Santa came."

"Well, of course he came." Jason scooped her up and sat down with her on his lap. He picked up the jar near him. "Mmm. Whiskey marmalade. My favorite. This whole room smells like Christmas."

"We put cinnamon on the pancakes," Melly said.

"Better eat them fast before everyone else wakes up and wants some." Stewart helped himself to another one, but at that moment everyone else piled into the room.

Beth was wearing a bright blue sweater and a pair of large silver earrings.

"You look pretty." Melly smiled her approval. "Grandma knitted that sweater."

"She did, and I love it." Beth kissed her mother. "You've come a long way from the days of scratchy, itchy sweaters."

Suzanne gave her a push. "I've had some practice. Sit down and eat."

Hannah and Adam appeared amid a chorus of "Merry Christmas." Suzanne noticed that Hannah looked different. Her hair was loose around her face and she was smiling and relaxed as she talked to Adam.

"I've told him he has to taste your honey, Mom."

"Help yourself to pancakes, Adam, or if you prefer, I made a delicious warming porridge—"

"Oatmeal," Hannah translated, and Adam raised an eyebrow.

"You think I don't know what porridge is? I did my research before I came here. I know everything there is to know about Bonnie Prince Charlie and distilling a fine Scottish malt."

"The Highlands is the biggest whiskey-producing area in Scotland," Stewart said. "It's a centuries-old tradition. The springwater here runs over volcanic mountain rock. If you're sticking around for a while, I'll take you to the distillery for a tour. I went to school with Tom Mackay, so we'll be treated well."

Adam put his hand on Hannah's knee. "That sounds like a good enough reason to stay."

The two men were soon deep in conversation, comparing bourbon to whiskey, and Suzanne rolled her eyes as they started planning a trip to Kentucky, where there were, according to Adam, more barrels of bourbon than there were people.

"We're going to need more pancakes, Grandma," Melly said, and Suzanne reached for the flour and the milk.

"We are. Are you going to help me?"

Ruby paused with her fork halfway to her mouth. "I hear bells. What are those bells?"

"I hear bells, too." Jason picked her up and carried her to the window. "Well, look at that."

"It's Socks! And he's pulling a sled."

Suzanne smiled. That was one way of navigating the snowy path from the barn to the lodge.

The room descended into chaos as people left the table and Ruby begged to go for a ride in the "sleigh."

Suzanne abandoned the pancake mixture as Posy walked through the door, trailing snow.

Her cheeks were pink and she looked frozen.

"Cold out there. Merry Christmas."

Stewart half rose to his feet. "I wondered if I'd have to clear the snow before you could walk over here."

"It's soft." Posy hung up her coat and dragged Luke into the room.

Ruby had forgotten about pancakes. "Can I go on the sled?"

"You certainly can." Posy kissed her. "Has Santa been?"

"We opened our stockings," Ruby said, "and he didn't bring Bugsy." Her lip wobbled. "But you can't have every single thing you want."

Suzanne felt a pressure under her ribs. That was the hardest lesson of all to learn.

You couldn't have everything you wanted, but if you were lucky, you had the things that mattered.

Beth gave a determined smile. "But you have lots of other lovely presents."

"I do. And I made pancakes with Grandma." Ruby finished eating and the moment breakfast was over she shot into the living room to get ready for present opening.

"This is for Mommy." She handed a present to Beth. "From Daddy."

Everyone found somewhere to sit, squeezing onto the sofas, finding a space on the floor. The children sat by the tree, close together.

Sisters.

Suzanne watched as Beth sent Jason a curious glance and unwrapped her present. It was a laptop bag in soft leather.

"If you're going back to work, then you need to look the part," he said, and Suzanne saw Beth's eyes grow shiny.

"I told Corinna I didn't want the job."

Posy rocked back on her heels. "Well, hallelujah."

"I'm glad," Jason said. "That was a good decision. But there will be other jobs."

"There will definitely be other jobs. Hopefully ones that don't require you to work for a psycho nutcase." Hannah moved closer to Adam. "We'll help you. As soon as we're back in Manhattan, we'll come over to the apartment and make a plan."

Melly scrambled to her feet with another gift. "This one is for Adam, from Hannah."

Adam raised his eyebrows. "You got me a gift, even though you didn't know I was going to be here?" He opened the small box and grinned. "Is this what I think it is?"

"It's the key to my apartment." Hannah went from confident to unsure, and even a little shy. "I thought, maybe, you could move in. Because my place is a little bigger than yours, but—"

"No buts. I'm moving in." Adam caught her face in his hands and kissed her.

Suzanne held her breath. She could feel the emotion flowing between them. No movie or book she'd ever read had affected her the way watching the two of them did. It wasn't just the fact that Adam was kissing Hannah, it was the *way* he was kissing her, and the way she was kissing him back. In that moment, she'd lost her reserve.

This was what she'd wanted for Hannah. Love. A love she could trust. A love she believed in and felt she deserved.

She turned her head and looked at Stewart and he gave her a brief smile, reading her mind.

Melly put her hands over Ruby's eyes.

"I'm okay with kissing," Ruby said. "I don't mind kissing. Kissing is a happy thing. Is it my turn to open a present now?"

"I think it is." Hannah extracted herself from Adam so that she could search under the tree. "Here's one with your name on it. It says it's from Santa."

"But I already opened my presents from Santa."

"Maybe he dropped this one on his way to fill your stockings. Or maybe he forgot and came back a second time."

"It's wrapped differently from the others," Ruby said. "Different paper."

Smart girl, Suzanne thought, but Hannah was one step ahead of her niece.

"Maybe a different elf wrapped it."

Beth and Posy exchanged glances. Suzanne could see them wondering what had happened to their sister, but she knew that the only thing that had happened to Hannah was that some of her confidence had returned.

Hopefully over time, she'd find more of it.

Ruby tugged at the ribbon and tore at the paper. "It's a box."

Hannah sat on the floor next to her. "The gift is probably inside the box. You need to open it."

Bonnie loped over to her to nose at the gift and Posy half rose to pull the dog back, but Hannah slid her arm round her and stroked her absently, watching as Ruby pulled the lid off the box.

The little girl gasped. "Oh!" And then she burst into tears.

Beth looked alarmed and Melly leaned closer, investigating the source of all that emotion. "It's Bugsy!"

"What?" Jason levered himself off the sofa and reached down into the box, but Ruby grabbed Bugsy and clutched it against her chest.

"He's home. He's mine."

"He *is* yours." Jason looked at the familiar rabbit in disbelief. "Where did he—"

"I wrote to Santa." Ruby squeezed Bugsy hard, tears pouring down her cheeks. "Actually, Aunty Hannah wrote to Santa for me, but I told her what to say and I signed my name."

There were tears in Beth's eyes, too, as she looked at her sister.

"How... I don't know..."

"It's Christmas," Hannah said softly. "Lots of good things happen at Christmas."

That was true, Suzanne thought, looking at Adam and then at her three daughters.

She'd never thought she would see them this relaxed and happy together.

The next hour passed in a whirl of gifts and laughter.

Luke gave Posy a beautiful photographic book of the mountains of North America and Alaska.

Suzanne flicked through it quietly, pausing as she looked at the photographs of Mount Rainier. There was sunset and sunrise, sunshine and storm.

"You don't have to look at that, Mom." Posy tried to take it from her, but Suzanne shook her head.

"It's a beautiful mountain."

Her life had changed that day, and for years she'd associated it with bad things. She'd punished herself with thoughts that were often irrational.

She'd imagined Cheryl watching from some dim and distant place, judging her.

I entrusted you with my girls.

She'd always thought that the responsibility for everyone's emotional well-being was hers. That any discord between the girls was somehow a reflection on her.

Now she saw how absurd that was.

This wasn't Cheryl's family, it was hers.

And they were doing just fine.

Feeling ridiculously emotional, she went through to the kitchen to check on the turkey.

Posy followed her.

"Can I talk to you, Mom?"

"Of course." Suzanne kept her back to her, and by the time she'd lifted the turkey out of the oven, she was back in control. "I need to start using the gym. This thing weighs a ton."

"It smells amazing." Posy leaned forward and sniffed. "You're a fabulous cook."

"You're good, too. You're doing a great job in the café. Your brownies are as good as mine." Suzanne basted the turkey and then realized Posy hadn't responded. "What did you want to talk to me about?"

Posy flashed her a smile. "Nothing. Forget it. Are you done? I'll lift the turkey. Hauling yourself up a rock face builds muscles in the right places." She lifted the turkey easily and slid it back into the oven. "If it's all right with you, I'm going to take Ruby for a quick ride on my improvised sleigh. It's pretty cold out there, so we won't be long. And I'm going to make sure we don't lose Bugsy."

Suzanne leaned against the counter. "You followed me in here to say something. I want to know what it was."

Posy shook her head. "It's Christmas Day—it's the wrong time to talk about this."

"Does 'this' have anything to do with Luke?"

"Not really. Well, sort of, I suppose—" Posy paced to the window. "It's pretty out there today."

"Do you love him?"

"I don't know. Maybe. Probably." She swallowed. "He's asked me to climb Denali with him next summer."

Suzanne felt her heart pound a little harder. It was a reflex reaction. She ignored it. "That sounds like a wonderful adventure. I've never climbed it, but Stewart has. You should talk to him."

Posy turned, cautious. "It wouldn't upset you if I went?"

It would scare her senseless, but she'd control it.

Hiding her response from her daughter, Suzanne walked across to her. "Is this what you wanted to talk to me about? You've been worried about telling me? How long have you been thinking about it?"

"Awhile. I didn't know how to raise it. I didn't want to worry you. And you need my help here, and summer is a crazily busy time and—" she spread her hands "—well, you've always assumed I was going to take over the café one day, and—"

"And you don't want that."

There was a long pause.

"I don't think I do." Posy looked so miserable it made Suzanne's heart hurt.

"You've obviously felt this way for a while. Why didn't you say something sooner?"

"Because you need me here."

"Oh, honey." Suzanne pulled her in for a hug. "Do I love having you here? Of course. You're my daughter and you also happen to be great company. But if you weren't here, I'd find someone else to do the work. As it happens, Vicky wants to increase her hours, so that's perfect timing."

Posy sniffed. "She does?"

"Yes. And although this might come as a surprise to you, Stewart and I are capable of feeding Martha. We'll even water Eric, although I can't promise to talk to him the way you do."

Posy gave a choked laugh. "I don't want to make you unhappy. I never want that."

"What I want is to see you happy and doing something you love. If there are things you want to do, you should do them." Suzanne realized she should have said this long before. "Climb Denali. Travel with Luke. Take risks. Have adventures. Look forward and leave regrets behind. I don't ever want you to wonder if you should have done something, or could have done something. Go and do it. Live a full life."

"I've never gone far from home before. I've never left you." There were tears on Posy's cheeks and Suzanne brushed them away.

"Home will always be here. We'll be right here whenever you want to come back. And the world is a small place now. We can talk on the phone, and Skype, and who knows— maybe it's time Stewart and I became more adventurous in our traveling. We should take a few risks of our own. We can all meet up somewhere." As she said it, she realized that it sounded good.

She and Stewart needed to look forward, too.

Posy kissed her on the cheek. "You're amazing—do you know that?"

"She *is* amazing." Stewart walked into the kitchen. "I hate to interrupt your heart-to-heart, but Ruby and Melly are desperate to ride on the sleigh if you're ready. Beth has dressed them in so many layers I doubt they'll be able to bend in the middle."

"That sounds like my sister. No doubt they are also equipped with avalanche transceivers." Posy blew her nose and went to fetch her coat. "Girls? Your carriage awaits."

There was a flurry of activity—squeals, giggling, chatter, Bonnie barking.

One minute the kitchen was crowded with people and the next moment they'd gone in a flurry of cold air and laughter.

Beth and Hannah were the last to leave and Suzanne heard the two of them talking.

"Where did you find Bugsy?"

"I don't know what you're talking about. I gave Ruby a firefighter outfit." Hannah slid her feet into boots. "Santa found Bugsy."

"Be serious."

"I am serious." Hannah batted her eyelashes at her sister. "Are you telling me you don't believe in Santa? Bethany Mc-Bride Butler, I'm shocked."

"Was it eBay? Because Jason and I searched everywhere. And how did you get him here in time?"

"I still don't know what you're talking about, but I'm sure Santa has access to an excellent courier company when he needs one. Also, an excellent personal assistant who always manages to arrange the impossible and will most certainly receive a handsome bonus as a reward for her skills."

"It must have cost you a fortune."

"Still don't know what you're talking about."

The two of them went outside, closing the door behind them.

She'd spent too much time worrying, Suzanne thought. Too much time trying to fix things that in time would fix themselves. Too much time trying to mold her family into the shape she thought it should be, rather than letting it find its own shape.

She didn't know what would happen with Posy and Luke,

but if what they shared was strong enough, then it would work. If it didn't, they'd handle it.

Any one of the girls could have problems in the future and, knowing life, they probably would, but she believed they had the strength to weather those problems.

And they had each other.

They weren't just the Christmas sisters. They were the McBride sisters.

Stewart put his arm round her. "What did Posy want to talk to you about?"

"She wants to climb Denali in the summer." There was more, of course, but she'd tell him about that later.

Stewart thought about it. "She has good Alpine experience and she did that crevasse training last year. She's qualified to do it. Which route? The West Buttress?"

"I don't know. Haven't talked details."

"And you're okay with it?"

"I'm going to find a way to be okay with it. I'm going to learn to be as brave as our girls." She leaned her head on his shoulder. "And on that subject, I thought, maybe, you could take me climbing with you one day."

"Seriously? You'd like that?"

She'd been thinking about it since her conversation with Luke.

The accident hadn't just killed her friends, it had killed her sense of adventure.

And she'd let that happen.

"I'd like it. Nothing too challenging, at least not to begin with. But I'd like to get back out there again." If Hannah could face her fears, then so could she. "I used to feel guilty that these kids were mine. That this life was mine."

"And now?"

"I don't feel guilty. This has always been a tough time of

year. I've always felt that I had to compensate, to make up for what was missing. But the things that make it perfect aren't the turkey, or the decorations, or homemade cookies."

"You're telling me this *after* I hung a million sets of fairy lights?"

She smiled. "I haven't done half the preparation I usually do, and yet I feel happier than I ever have. Merry Christmas. I love you, Stewart McBride."

"I love you, too. Merry Christmas." He pulled her against him, his arms strong and sheltering.

It occurred to her that the only thing that really mattered was having people you loved in your life. Even when those people were shrieking and stuffing snowballs down each other's necks as Posy, Beth and Hannah were doing right now, family was what mattered.

She was grateful for hers.

★ ★ ★ ★ ★

ACKNOWLEDGMENTS

The idea for this book came to me during a holiday in Greece, although I'm not sure what it says about my brain that I dream about a snowy Christmas while basking in sunshine.

Right from the start the story flowed for me. The characters seemed real and I felt part of the McBride family, but, as is always the way, the book in my head doesn't make it onto the page without help. Fortunately, my editor Flo performed her usual magic, asking probing questions, untangling my thoughts and making suggestions that vastly improved the story. I think she knows how much I appreciate her, but I'm putting it in writing to make sure.

I'm grateful to my literary agent, Susan Ginsburg, for her insightful thoughts on the early version of this manuscript, and for being so generous with her time and advice.

I'd like to thank Lisa Milton and Manpreet Grewal from the UK team for providing a fresh look when the book was in its final stages. Their comments were hugely helpful and I'm grateful for their enthusiasm and commitment to my books and my writing.

Special thanks to Dianne Moggy and Susan Swinwood for

encouraging and supporting each new step of my career. I know how lucky I am to be working with you.

It takes a village to put a book into the hands of readers, and I'm sincerely grateful to each and every member of the publishing teams at HQN in the US and HQ Stories in the UK. Without the wonderful work of sales, marketing and PR, no one would be reading my books. Particular thanks go to Sophie Calder in the UK and Lisa Wray in the US, who work so hard and who sensitively fit publicity requests around my deadline panics. I'd also like to thank Anne Sharpe, who turned around the all-important copy edit of this book quickly so that we could meet tight production deadlines.

Writing this book was an intense, all-consuming process, and without my family putting food and drinks in front of me, I might have starved or died of thirst. Living with an author takes a special kind of patience. Fortunately for me, they have it.

My biggest thanks go to my readers, who continue to buy my books, email me kind words, message me on Instagram and Facebook, and generally encourage me. I'm fortunate to have such a fantastic, enthusiastic and kind bunch of readers. I hope this book makes you smile and gives you the sense of comfort you deserve.